ORDINEM LEGACY

Part 1: Becoming

By Maddie Caser

Acknowledgement

Writing the first part of Ordinem Legacy was such a great experience! Certainly one of the best and most fulfilling, especially in term of personal development. I have learnt so much and it has been an incredible adventure so far. I cannot wait to continue writing Ordinem Legacy story!

This experience would simply not have been the same (or maybe even possible) without the help, support or expertise of certain people:

Gil, I thank you for being a supportive partner and reading my manuscript with a keen eye. I cannot thank you enough for encouraging me to pursue my passion. Thanks for being so patient and reassuring me in my terrible moments of doubts. You are the best!

Hélène, I am so glad you accepted to work on the design and illustration of Ordinem Legacy first cover. You have done an amazing work and I couldn't be happier with the result. You completely succeeded in understanding the atmosphere I imagined for the cover. Thanks for your patience, professionalism and true creative skills.

Karen, you did a great work at correcting my first manuscript, proofreading it and suggesting edits. Thanks for your time and putting your heart into it. It was very nice working with you.

Sivan, you have been incredibly helpful! The second stage of the editing phase felt infinite! Thanks for patiently working with me on the final edits! You are a gem!

Liva, thank you so much for reading my first draft and telling me how much you loved it. This made me realise maybe I could do this. Thanks for accompanying me through my writing process and reading the rough ideas coming out of my brain. I am forever thankful, you gave me the confidence I needed to write Louise's story.

Oriane, you have a keen eye for details and you always give good advice! On top of that, you always know how to motivate me and give me a little push when I need. In any circumstances, you believe in me and for that, I am so grateful! In addition, thank you for being so committed to the beta reading despite the constraints!

Angela, thanks for sharing your contact and putting me in touch with Karen. You saved me so much time and headache finding the right fit for me. Also, thanks for helping me out with my last-minute grammar doubts!

Héloïse, I thank you for encouraging me through the whole process of writing and producing Ordinem Legacy. Thanks for listening to my fears and doubts and most importantly for rationalising them!

Lola, thanks for taking some tasks off my shoulders, you saved me so much time and enabled me to keep my focus on my editing work.

Manue, thanks for sharing your reliable thoughts on the book cover drafts!

Cécile, you are simply the best cheerleader in *da* place! 'To your book!'

And of course, John, our cherished dog, the best writing companion and armrest in the world!

Last but not least, thanks Moma, for always believing in me.

Chapter I

I woke up late, struggling to open my eyes and my head feeling very heavy. I have never been an early bird, but when I glanced at the clock, I was surprised to see it was 2pm. Lazily, I got up and was surprised to see I was still wearing my going-out outfit – I must have passed out on my bed when I got home. My mouth was very dry, obviously due to the amount of alcohol I drank last night. I wasn't keen to see my face in the mirror, so I went to the kitchen and got myself a large glass of cold water. Two seconds later, it was already empty and I poured another one. I finished it as fast as the first one, but still my thirst did not seem to lessen. Another glass went down. With each gulp, the echoing, banging sound in my head seemed to be more bearable. My stomach reacted to the sudden large quantity of hydrating liquid – it growled and I felt hungry. Even though it was afternoon, I started my breakfast ritual with a non-negotiable cup of Earl Grey tea and two pieces of buttered toast. While the bread was going golden in the toaster, I began to recall last night's events; however, today, it seemed to be particularly harder than usual. Slowly, flashes of last night came back to me, but I couldn't remember how I got home, although this was standard for me. For some reason, it often appeared to be the same missing part after a drunken evening out.

As I was finishing my last piece of toast, I heard the landline ringing. I considered ignoring the awful ringtone, but it annoyed me so much that I picked up to put an end to the noisy torture. A familiar voice spoke:

"There you are! Finally, I get you on the phone!"

"Hi Naomi!" She is my best friend.

"Louise, I have been trying to call you since noon, which I judge a reasonable hour, but your mobile seems to be off."

"Yes, sorry, I just got up and didn't have a chance to switch my phone on yet."

"Did you get home OK?"

"I guess so."

"Ah! The usual blackout! Actually, I meant to talk to you about that."

"Oh, please Naomi, spare me, it's just alcohol, it happens to the best of us!"

"Sure, but I feel you have been having more of these episodes recently."

"Well, you feel wrong then!"

"No, I am not, you should get checked out by your Doctor."

"Would that shut you up?"

"Yes! And I do hope I won't have to lecture you with an '*I told you so*'."

"Anyway, I am going to ignore you and move on to something more of interest to me, did you get that hot guy's phone number last night?"

"Change the subject if you like but you won't get rid of me so easily my lovely! And, of course I got his number!" Naomi didn't like giving men her phone number, she would rather take theirs and be the first to get in touch. According to her, she was proceeding like this so that first, she could change her mind; second, to be the mistress of her own life and not to wait for things to happen and finally, so that she could show off her confidence. But this last interpretation was one of my own and also one of the many reasons I loved her so much.

"How do you feel about debriefing over late afternoon coffees?" she added.

"Sure, definitely, I just hope this hangover is going to disappear at some point!"

"Don't tell me! OK hun, it's already 2.30, so shall we say 4.30 at the usual café?"

"That's a date!"

"You wish!" she joked.

We hung up and I headed to the bathroom, still not looking forward to seeing my face! I was so pale and looked exhausted – that was not a good look! Not liking my reflection, I jumped in the shower and started a thorough cleaning mission: body and face scrubs, shampoo and conditioner. I always felt filthy after a good night out and I usually took a shower before going to bed, but that part was a failure last night! The thirst hit me again, until it got so unbearable that I drank hot water straight from the shower head. It was just a flavourless tea after all! I reluctantly switched off the tap – I have always found hot showers to be such a treat, especially since I came back from my wild traveling days, where I had to use buckets of cold water to wash.

I got out of the bathroom and went straight to my laptop to turn the music on – not too loud though, as the pounding in my head was finally quieter and I did not want to jeopardise this moment of peace. Then, it was time to initiate what I called the 'Back to Life process', which was going to be hardwork considering the state I was in. First, I took care of my long brown hair, neither straight nor curly but somewhere half way. I liked my hair, mostly because it did not need much maintenance! After combing it, I plugged in the hair dryer for a few minutes to help it dry faster. The next task consisted on finding myself a decent outfit. I loved clothes but not in a fanatical way, and it definitely did not amuse me to try them on for hours. I found pleasure in finding the right thing to wear in the minimum time. Today, was going to be a simple pair of tight khaki jeans, my favourite Batman hoodie and a pair of a limited-edition Air Force trainers. I was not a big fan of handbags, I found them annoying to carry around, so whenever I could avoid them, I did. Make up was going to be as minimal as always: a bit of blusher and mascara. In addition, I fancied some red lipstick and also found some powder to cover my pale face.

All ready, I tidied up my flat a little as I was a bit of a messy person. I grabbed my phone and turned it on while plugging in the charger. As soon as it connected to the network, a storm of messages arrived. Naomi had indeed been on my case since midday. A few more texts found their ways to my screen. I received a funny message from a guy I remembered meeting last night. He was quite handsome and had a fantastic sense of humour. We got on very well and spoke for a while. He was now asking me out for a drink, but at the thought of alcohol I felt dizzy and decided to postpone my reply. My attention went to the clock – it was 3.30 – I had forty-five minutes left to do whatever I fancied. Naomi lived only twenty minutes walk away and the café was halfway between our respective places.

The thirst came back. Bloody hell! That was annoying and really intense. I was used to drinking more water than usual after nights out, but this was different. I was so thirsty that I imagined even a fountain of water would not be sufficient to counteract the dehydration. After two glasses of water, I gave up and tried to forget the discomfort: I went through a few bits and bobs; changed my week-old bed sheets; turned on the washing machine and wandered online. Time flew by, nevertheless I managed to leave my flat on time.

The weather was not so good for the beginning of October: the sky was cloudy and a bit dark, but at least it was not raining. The temperature was decent, which allowed me not to wear a jacket on top of my hoodie. I plugged my headphones into my phone and turning on the music, I started walking to the café, determined to ignore the terrible thirst that was still drying my tongue and throat. Not surprisingly, I reached our haunt before Naomi, she was always five to ten minutes late, her signature if you ask me! I greeted the staff who recognised me as we were regulars and sat at a free, clean table. I ordered a large glass of water right away. As soon as Charlie, one of the waiters, brought it over and put it on the table, I took it to my mouth and drained it. He looked amused:

"Rough night?" he asked with a cheeky grin.

"Rougher than I thought!" I smiled.

I was busy checking my phone when Naomi entered the place with her distinctive natural elegance. She spotted me right away and steered herself towards me.

"Hey Louise! Pardon my bluntness, but you look tired! I didn't realise you drank that much last night!" she said, surprised. So much for my make up efforts!

"Nice to see you too!"

"Don't be so touchy!"

"No seriously, I am fully aware of how bad I look and I don't really understand it, I don't recall drinking that much either!"

"Don't worry, you're just paler than usual, that's all, only I can tell, but you are still fine to the rest of the world!"

Charlie came back and took our order. We came here at least once a week, so we tried different drinks not to feel like two old biddies stuck in their habits! It was probably due to our summer jobs as waitresses, when we used to mock the rude ladies who came to the place every day, sitting at the same tables and drinking the same things! I ordered a vanilla latte and Naomi a cappuccino. We did not fancy anything else, so there would be no sweet treats today.

"So, tell me, have you texted this boy yet?" I started.

"Nope, I haven't thought of it actually, I have been busy all day but I expect I will at some point!" She sipped some of her cappuccino.

Naomi and I were best friends – we did have disagreements sometimes, but we never argued. We had the same principles and ideas about life which made us really close. We have known each other for sixteen years, having met at school and remained inseparable friends since then. Our first encounter was very genuine and spontaneous, we were fifteen at the time: she arrived in our class as a new student and asked if she could sit next to me. There was something in the way she spoke, her tone was very confident and kind at the same time – she seemed cool. From this moment, we never parted and soon after we met, we knew each other perfectly. Some people were a bit confused by our 'fusional' friendship, including several of our friends who liked to joke about us and said a few times that we should get married. Originally from Brighton, her family had moved to London because of her parents work. Although the Brighton-London commute was a piece of cake, her parents fancied moving to the city and raising their daughter there. Whenever Naomi was home sick and missed the pebbles and the sound of the waves and seagulls, we would just hop on a train and travel there. However, these days, we had to find some other ways to deal with her feelings, as adulthood came with responsibilities you cannot run away from or forget about, like work for example! We still spent occasional weekends in Brighton, but much less than we used to. It was not so bad – the adult Naomi was not the sad or emotional type, but had grown into a pro-active moving forward kind of person. Plus, we both loved living in London.

Naomi was also intrigued by my story I supposed. My parents died when I was eight, so my grandparents took me in and raised me. I cannot complain, I had a good childhood considering my parents weren't there. I remembered how happy I was whenever we went to our old family holiday home in the country. We knew everyone there and I am sure that my love for nature and animals comes from those visits. As soon as Naomi entered my life, she joined us there every time we went.

"Oh, by the way," I said, "I got a text from the guy I was chatting with for a while last night and he's asked me out for a drink!"

"Of course he has, Louise! Have you replied yet?"

"No, I haven't, unlike you I have been busy for real!" We laughed as we both very well knew that we had not been up to much so far, except for recovering! "But anyway, how did you get back home last night or should I say when and with whom?" I continued.

"Well, after I met that cute guy, I ran into Ian who was with a couple of mates, you were still there by the way."

"Oh yes! I remember, we were about to leave."

"Well, we were but Ian and I got to talk and dance and—"

"Shag!"

"Louise!"

"I'm joking, you know I like Ian. I just don't get it with you two, there is obviously some serious chemistry there – he is smart and good looking, you like him and you have already tested the goods!"

"No, I don't like him!" she lied childishly.

"Yes, you do!"

"OK maybe a little. But it's not that easy, we are both super busy and I believe we get on so well because we keep it fun and casual!"

"To be honest, whatever rocks your boat, but he might be after something more serious, and if so, you would be a fool to push him away. You shouldn't fear your feelings or his."

"What makes you say that? Do you know something?"

"Why? Would you like that?"

"No ... I mean ... maybe ... whatever! What do you know?" She could not resist.

"I know he likes you! Come on, the way he looks at you all the time, it is pretty obvious! But anyway, I totally understand if you guys are good with what you have."

"Yes, we are. I don't want to have relationship headaches you know, my job is going super well, I enjoy my life as it is and I am free!"

"Fair enough! As long as these are the real reasons."

Ian has been around for quite a while. We have known him for a few years now, we had some friends in common who introduced us at one of our house parties. He was a very nice guy – a real one, not one of those toxic imposters. Recently, he had just opened his own veterinary clinic and was quite successful. He and Naomi hit it off almost instantly. They were both crazy about animals. I cannot count how many animals she rescued or made her parents adopt when she was younger. I could really relate to that as I also went gooey whenever I saw a puppy in the street! Their relationship heated quite quickly, but they always kept it casual. Ian was working loads at his previous vet job to save enough money to open his own place and Naomi, well, she was doing crazy hours at the office. I was very fond of Ian, so naturally I was hoping she would give them a chance.

We carried on chatting and commenting on last night events until something strange got my attention: I felt a subtle chill on my spine that steered my eyes towards the window we were seated by. At first, I thought it might not be properly closed, but it was. Then, I saw a man standing outside, leaning on a lamppost in the shade. Although I did not recognise him, he looked oddly familiar. He was staring at us so intently that it felt as if he was close to us. It gave me goosebumps all over my body. Naomi realised something was up and looked through the window not quite as discreetly. The man kept staring, then smiled and walked away. I felt really weird and the searing thirst came back. I must have looked distressed because Naomi took my hand and asked me what was wrong.

"Nothing, I mean, I don't know. I just feel weird and I am so bloody thirsty!" She looked hard at me and ordered a glass of water. Charlie came back with it in less than a minute.

"Definitely rough then!" he said, laughing. Naomi did not get it since she had missed the first part of the joke and ignored his funny comment, while I smiled at his humour.

"There is your water." She handed the glass over and as she saw me draining it, she checked my eyes again. "Have you spent the afternoon smoking weed?"

"Nope, but maybe I should have!" I replied with a smile.

"Do you know that guy? I think I saw him briefly last night outside the club. I remember because I noticed he was checking you out when we got in and then we met the others and I forgot to tell you!"

"I am not sure to be honest! I feel like I do, but I can't put a name to his face or even tell you where we would have met! Maybe I was already drunk when we had a chat, therefore cannot remember it!"

"I wouldn't forget him, he is fit! Seriously that's strange! Either you are really hungover, or your drinks were spiked last night!"

"Frankly, I don't know what to think, and please before you even get started, don't try to freak me out!"

"I am only underlining the fact that in addition to recent occasional blackouts, not remembering people you just met is not reassuring."

"They aren't blackouts Naomi! Only unimportant little confusions!" Naomi was a bit of a hypochondriac, however I must admit she had been working hard on it and made a lot of efforts to be more reasonable. I changed the subject and we moved on.

Later that afternoon, we ended up in the middle of a car boot sale. I have always loved antiques and vintage stuff. One of my favourite activities was to find an old piece of furniture and give it new life. I love wood, the way it smells, working it and the satisfying feeling of achievement when I am done with it. I made most of my furniture at home and sometimes I did special orders for friends or even occasional clients. A few years back, my dream was to open my own shop with unique pieces of furniture. However, I got another good job instead, so I kept it as a hobby.

We were strolling around, chatting about random stories and gossiping when I started to feel very hot and uncomfortable, which did not go unnoticed by Naomi.

"What's up Louise? You are all red all of a sudden!"

"Yes! I feel like I am having a hot flush! Is it time for the menopause already?" I laughed.

"Louise! You're crazy you know! Are you still thirsty? Maybe we should get you a bottle of water or something to hydrate you!"

"I suppose," I said, kind of giving up.

Conveniently, we happened to walk past a man who was selling chilled bottles of water, so we bought two of them considering the amount of water I had been drinking since I woke up! After finishing the first bottle, I started to feel a little bit better. However, something else was also going on: it was like someone was persistently staring at me – I could feel a presence. I looked around, probably looking a bit puzzled, but saw nothing. This was going to be the strangest hangover in my whole life. Maybe that was what older people meant when they said hangovers were harder to bear with age. I decided to ignore the feeling and carried on browsing with my friend.

"By the way Louise, you never told me, how was your visit in France? We didn't even have a chance to talk about your meeting last night!"

"It was great, my colleague Joshua was with me, you've met him before. The winemaker gave us a tour of his vineyard in the Loire Valley. We also had a wine tasting later in the afternoon. His white wine is a lovely Chenin Blanc, crisp and chalky but also rounded by slight quince and pear flavours, just as I like it!"

"That's great! Sounds lovely! Are you going to make him an offer?"

"Well, we discussed prices and I think we can find some common ground. Joshua and I drew up an offer on the trip back to London, but we didn't get a chance to have it approved by Eleanor, our boss, as you know! Anyway, the client does not expect us to get back to him before Tuesday."

"Great! So, you landed a new client! Smooth as usual!"

"This one is for Joshua, I just accompanied him as his manager. We struggled to find a convenient time for this meeting for quite a while, so I wanted to show the client our appreciation."

"Yes, I see what you mean! That's good news! I would say '*let's celebrate*' but I don't feel like having a drink at all!"

"Don't worry! Me neither!"

"What about you, how is work treating you?" Naomi was a public relations manager for an ethical fashion brand.

"It's fine, nothing new. I don't mind a bit of quiet considering how hectic it was during fashion week!"

After a while, we decided to head back home. I arrived around 7.30 and started to feel hungry. Naomi had gone home and I was by myself now. I went to the fridge but nothing seemed appealing, although there was plenty of choice. I decided to go for a pizza; I knew it was not the healthiest option, but it was definitely what one needed after a rough night out. I switched the oven on and put the junk food in. While it was cooking, I took my laptop, put some music on, checked some stuff online and wrote a few emails. My hunger pangs grew and by the time the pizza was ready, I was starving. I ate it so fast I could not believe it. My stomach hurt due to the large amount of food absorbed in such a little time, but strangely the feeling of hunger was still there. It was exactly like when I smoked weed and had the uncontrollable munchies, except this time no drugs were involved. I drank some more water, but the mixture of hunger and thirst quickly became unbearable and I started to feel dizzy. I lay down on my sofa and the room slowly stopped whirling around me, however I still felt uneasy. I closed my eyes and all of a sudden, I was somewhere else...

Chapter II

All was blurry, I felt like I was floating over the floor, as if my mind was out of my body. The scenery was familiar though – it was the club we went to last night. I could see Naomi dancing like there was no tomorrow and the guy who had chatted me up, talking with his mates. Everything was happening very fast, as if it were playing in fast forward. The whole night went by, but I could not stop it: I was just a spectator. Despite the speed of the images, I could distinguish every moment: when we danced altogether, or with different partners; ordering at the bar; drinking and chatting; meeting new people and so on.

The images slowed down a bit when we were about to depart. We were talking about leaving, but then Ian turned up. Naomi's face lit up and her smile was so inviting that he came over as soon as he spotted her. I was used to this – I knew it meant I was going home by myself and she was probably going back with him. I did not mind at all. After I picked up my belongings that I had left in the club cloakroom, I walked towards the exit. Some of our friends were smoking outside, so we said our goodbyes and I looked for a taxi to drive me home.

The images paused when I got in the taxi, as if I was meant to acknowledge where I was, as if something was about to happen. The driver informed me that his credit card reader was out of order so it was cash only, which I accepted. I could see myself looking at the cab meter increasing at a rapid rate and then checking my purse for cash. I thought I had enough, but I only had a twenty pound note in my wallet and nothing more. Although it appeared to be a replay of what happened last night, it was as if it was happening for the first time, since I previously had no memory of anything at all after coming out of the club.

Unfortunately, the meter was showing £19.80 and I was not quite home yet. I decided I could walk the remaining distance, I mean, I was only five minutes away. I told the taxi driver to stop and paid him. He seemed like a nice guy and I am pretty sure he would have given me a ride all the way home if I had explained my situation. However, at the time it did not seem to matter and I simply did not think about it. I was a bit drunk and not at my best! Although I was under the influence of alcohol, I could still walk straight and balance on my high heels – I was not swaying awkwardly.

I was only a few hundred metres away from taking the last left turn to my house, when I heard loud male voices. They sounded rowdy. I realised they were after my attention and I could hear them whistling and calling me, like I was a dog. I wondered how these morons could expect any friendly inter-action after that. But let's face it, these sorts of men were not after a meeting, but rather to scare their prey and convince themselves their little testicles were bigger than grapefruits. I am quite a strong character and scaring me off is not easily done, but at that moment, I just wanted to go home. I thought it would be better to ignore them for now, so I just sped up a little thinking they would simply give up.

***

I was suddenly back on the sofa – I was all sweaty and very hot. I had dozed off and had the weirdest dream ever. The clock showed 10pm. I could now remember everything, which was a good thing; at least I now knew how I got home last night and Naomi would most definitely be happy to hear that.

My stomach was rumbling and my throat was dry. I had some more water and went to the fridge to find something filling. I could not understand what was going on with me. Usually, I struggled to finish a whole pizza, but today it was just not enough. I made myself some cheese toasties, hoping that would do the trick. While they were getting nicely hot and crusty under the grill, I walked to the window as I was in desperate need of fresh air. I saw someone sitting on a bench outside my flat, looking up at me. I stared back at him, but it did not stop him; he smiled and kept looking right at me. It startled me a little, but I held his stare. He kept smiling and for some reason it felt soothing but at the same time intriguing. The grill timer went off and I jumped with surprise. I quickly glanced at it and when my eyes went back to the man outside, he was gone. "*Weirdo!*" I thought to myself.

The extra food didn't do the trick and I was still craving more, which frustrated me and sparked a rush of anger. Rage went through my veins, I felt like kicking everything and screaming my despair.

Suddenly, in the midst of all the confusion, I understood. The man below my window was the same who had been standing outside the coffee place this afternoon. I was so wrapped up in my unusual state, that I did not even realise and relate these two moments. Was this man stalking me? Why? I remembered feeling odd when I first saw him this afternoon, but he seemed strangely familiar and safe. Who was he? I had a strong urge to know him and find out what he wanted from me.

Quickly, I took a jacket and rushed outside. I must have looked like a crazy woman; I felt completely disorientated and did not know where to start looking. I turned left and went down the road almost running. The hot flush hit me again while the thirst and hunger were destroying my insides. My heart was pounding so hard, I thought it was going to come out of my chest. There was no sign of anyone, except for one or two people walking their dogs. I was extremely irritated, which led to a feeling of fury invading my whole being. I needed to let the adrenalin out and sought for an escape, so I ran as fast as my legs could go for as long as I could breathe.

Sometime later, I stopped – my legs were aching and my face was burning from the physical effort. I had no idea where I was and I felt as though I had lost the control of time and space, as well as my mind. I was exhausted and disorientated. Of course, I had taken nothing with me – no phone, money or even a travel card. I had left my house in such a rush and did not think I would end up doing my own mini-marathon. I had no idea what time it was. My heart beat gradually steadied and my body temperature slowly came back to normal. But the anger and thirst persisted, although they seemed to be slightly more controllable for now.

Alone in the darkness of the night, I walked back in the opposite direction so I would return home. After a while, I recognised the area and it was very far. It would take me two hours or so to walk back to my house. I searched my pockets and found a few coins, but that wouldn't get me anywhere. However, perhaps I could ask in a corner shop if I could call someone and pay them with the little change I had. Luckily, a few minutes later I found a 24/7. As I walked in, the lady behind the counter looked at me warily, which was completely understandable considering the state I was in. There was a clock hanging on the wall and I was shocked to see the time! I must have been running for at least a good hour – I had no idea I was capable of such an achievement. Despite my surprise, I approached the lady.

"Hi, I am really sorry to bother you but I am lost and I left my money and phone at home. Would you mind letting me use your phone? I've got about one pound with me to pay for the call."

She looked at me and seemed to judge I was trustworthy, as she handed the handset over to me with a quick smile. I thanked her and called Naomi right away. It was late and I would not be surprised if she didn't pick up at this time of night. We knew each other's phone number by heart, so if there was an emergency we could call one another quickly. I tried twice, but she did not answer. Anxiety overtook me and I had no idea what to do next. The woman was watching me and I detected pity in her eyes.

"Has nobody picked up the phone for you dear?" she asked gently.

"I'm afraid not," I replied, upset that I would have to walk back home.

"What are you going to do now, can I help you in some way?" she continued.

I had no answer to her question and felt so helpless. My legs started shaking and I felt light-headed. I collapsed on the floor and everything went black. Sometime later, a very strong smell of mint brought me back to consciousness. I opened my eyes with difficulty. Slowly, the fuzzy shapes became defined. I recognised the woman from the shop with another young man next to her.

"She is coming back to us. Bring her a sweet drink like an apple juice – she needs the sugar – she is exhausted," ordered the woman to the man.

"Dear, are you alright? Are you hurt?" she asked kindly.

"I ... I ... I'm fine, I guess, I don't know. What happened?"

"You fainted, you look like you've been through a lot dear, take this." She handed me the bottle of apple juice that the young man had just brought over. I drank it very quickly and it did help. The motherly behaviour of the shop lady made me feel safe and I wanted to snuggle up against her, like a child would do with her mum, but I was aware it wasn't appropriate to do that, so instead I focused on getting my head together.

"Thank you so much for your help, I am terribly sorry for troubling you."

"Shh now! Don't you worry, are you sure you are alright? Did someone hurt you?" she asked seriously.

"Oh no, nothing that bad! I just got lost while going on an impromptu night run. I was so absorbed in my thoughts, I lost track of time."

"You look very tired and that's probably why you fainted! Now, what matters the most is to get you home so you can get some much-needed sleep. My son will drive you back." Her firm tone indicated that it was not negotiable. I looked at her with relief.

"What's your name?"

"I am Karuna and this is my son Rasul," she said with a gesture to introduce him.

"Well, it is lovely to meet you Karuna and Rasul. I am Louise but I would have preferred meeting you in a more pleasant situation. I am very lucky you were here and I must apologise for the drama I caused and thank you for your kindness."

"You are welcome Louise. We were bored anyway! A bit of action is quite exciting!" she said with a broad smile, winking at the same time. "Now, please – let's sort you out. Can you stand up yet?"

"Let's see," I said, feeling more motivated.

Her voice was warm and full of compassion. Rasul was looking at me encouragingly. I nodded and started to rise slowly to my feet with Karuna's and Rasul's assistance. Thankfully they helped me, otherwise it would have taken me some time to succeed by myself. She sat me down on a chair while Rasul was getting the car. By the time he parked in front of the shop, I was feeling much better and I could stand and walk. Karuna gave me another bottle of juice and accompanied me to the car. As soon as I was properly seated and belted up, I gave her a long look and smiled with all my heart. She nodded to me and Rasul drove off.

Although Rasul seemed a little uneasy to have a stranger in the passenger seat, I could see he was regularly checking on me in case I passed out again. Except for me giving him directions, we didn't speak – he seemed to know I was too exhausted for polite conversation. He had the same kindness in his eyes as his mother.

When we finally arrived at my flat, I thanked him many more times. He laughed shyly at my persistence and waved goodbye from the car. He patiently waited until I went in and only then did I hear the engine switch on. Once inside my flat, I could not comprehend what had just happened to me, but had a strong feeling of exhaustion and I just wanted to go to bed. As I was undressing, my mobile phone rang: I ignored it but it rang again; I looked at the screen – it was Naomi. I knew I had to pick up.

"Thank god you are safe! What happened? I got two calls from an unknown number, which frightened me at this time of the night, so I called back and got this lady on the phone. She told me that I must be the person you tried to call and then she told me you fainted in her shop, that you were lost and—"

"And I am fine, honestly Naomi. I am really sorry for scaring you, but I was lost and I am now safe and sound at home. I am extremely tired, so would you please let me explain this to you tomorrow, when I'll be more rested?"

"But, Louise, how the hell did you end up there at almost midnight?"

"Please Naomi, I promise I will tell you everything tomorrow."

"Fine, but you better not forget! I was seriously freaked out! Sleep tight then, I will be waiting for your call!"

"Oh, I don't doubt you will, sorry girl, you know I love you but I am dying to go to bed now, goodnight." As soon as my head touched the pillow, I fell into a deep sleep.

Chapter III

I woke up covered in sweat. I must have had a restless night as my bed sheets were all over the place and I was topsy-turvy – my head was where my feet normally were and vice versa. Opening my eyes was not an easy task, but still I felt more rested, or at least slightly more alive than yesterday. As my brain woke up, it struck me that today was Monday, as in first day of the week, as in first working day! Usually, it was absolutely impossible for me to wake up naturally without the help of an alarm, which meant that I had overslept! Shit! My boss was going to kill me! I looked for the alarm-clock and was shocked at the time written on the digital screen! It was impossible! I took my phone to double-check and got the same result: it was 5pm, I swore.

I had numerous missed calls and texts. Many were from Naomi obviously, others from colleagues and of course from my horrible boss. I remained in shock for another five minutes, sitting on my bed and trying to think of an excuse. I could not tell Eleanor I had overslept almost ten hours; she would think I was taking the mick!

I needed a cup of tea; this was too much to handle for a sleepy brain. As I turned the kettle on and brewed the loose-leaf tea, I read the texts and listened to the different voice-mails. The first voice message came from my colleague Charlotte, at 10am: *"Hey Louise, where are you? Eleanor is looking for you, she looks pissed. Hurry up and get ready to tell her your* best *'why I was late' story ever! See you in a bit!"* I was supposed to start at 9.30am, and my boss despised tardiness, big time. The second message left at 10.13am hit my ears: *"Miss Bailey, Eleanor speaking, your boss should you forget. I hope you have an excellent excuse to be late and an even better one to explain why you did not care to call in this morning and inform us,"* and that was it. Her voice was icy and her tone completely indifferent to the fact that something could have actually happened to me. She was going to give me such a hard time! The third message was another one from Charlotte, at 11am: *"Seriously hun, what on earth are you doing? It's not like you to be so late and unreachable, please get in touch ASAP!"* Oh dear! I had two more texts from my colleagues Tom and Joshua, also letting me know Eleanor was very angry and asking me to call them back. The last one was from Naomi, at 1pm: *"Louise, Charlotte called me very worried as she has no idea where you are, although you should be at the office. I tried to call you tons of times, even on your land-line but no answers. I texted you too, but nothing. Can you please call me back when you get this? It would be nice to know you are safe and well!"* She sounded so annoyed. I felt bad that everyone was worried because of me.

I took my cup of tea and sat down on the sofa. I had no idea what to do or what to say. Obviously, the first person I ought to call was Naomi; she must have been checking hospitals and police stations by now. I rang her number and she picked up after the first ring tone; I didn't have time to say anything, she simply said "Open your door now!". I did not understand at first, but when I heard three knocks on the door, I did. As soon as I opened it, she stormed in. She had many expressions passing over her face, but I could mostly identify relief, worry and anger. I kept silent and so did she, which did not happen often. She looked at me from head to toe and realised I had just got out of bed. She took my hand and led me towards the sofa. We sat quietly. She was obviously waiting for me to say something, but I didn't know where to start.

"OK Louise, first you need to tell me what happened today and what happened last night, because I have a very strong feeling – and you don't need to be a genius to know it – that both are related. But first of all, are you alright?"

"I don't know to be honest Naomi, I woke up twenty minutes ago, I didn't realise I had overslept that much. When I came back last night, I must have forgotten to set my alarm. I was so tired – actually no, that is not the right word, I was knackered, drained like I have never been before!" She saw sparks of panic in my eyes and took my hand.

"Calm down, it's OK. We are going to figure out what is up with you. The lady from the shop told me you looked in a very bad state when you came in, that you fainted and then you struggled to get back on your feet. She was very worried about you."

"Yes, Karuna was brilliant, I am lucky she was there, I was so out of my mind with panic. I need to visit her and thank her."

"What happened last night after I left you?"

I told her the story: the hunger, the thirst, the hot flush and the need to escape that caused the massive freak out. She listened patiently. Then, she asked the question I was hoping she wouldn't.

"Why did you go outside in the first place? I thought the hot flushes started when you were outside. What made you go out?" I didn't know what to say. I could not lie to her, but at the same time she would definitely dislike the truth if I told her.

"I was looking through the window and thought I saw someone I knew so I wanted to check." She looked at me dubiously. "I don't know what else to say, it didn't seem that much of a big deal to come out and see. I walked around the block and then everything started."

"OK, that's strange. I think we need to get you to your GP and get you all checked out!"

"I think that might be a good idea."

"Have you called work yet?"

"Nope, you were the first person I rang. To be honest, I have no idea how I am going to get out of this situation. I got so many voice-mails from colleagues and from Eleanor. I don't know what to say."

"I see, well, you can't tell her the truth. Let's try to get your GP on the phone and ask if she could see you as an emergency. I'll do the talking though."

With that, she did not give me a chance to reply and took my phone. Nothing about Naomi's behaviour was surprising as I would have done the exact same thing for her. We had spent too many years together and if we were a couple, we would probably get bored with each other due to the lack of surprises! Naomi was very persuasive and I have always admired her eloquence. After talking to the receptionist, she got through my GP, which was a miracle!

"Hello Doctor Madison, I am so sorry to bother you and I do understand you are very busy, but I wouldn't insist if this wasn't an emergency. I am calling on behalf of Louise Bailey, she is one of your patients and she is very weak, so I told her I would call. She has been feeling really strange these past couple of days. Last night, she had intense hot flushes that drove her outside to get some fresh air but she fainted and collapsed on the floor. Some people helped her back to her house and she went to bed. But then today, she woke up at 5pm – who gets seventeen hours sleep straight except an exhausted or ill person? Please Doctor Madison, would you see her today?"

She didn't stop talking until she finished her story. I have had the same GP for years, so she knew me quite well and after that dramatic story there was little chance she would say no to Naomi's request. She told her we could come anytime and that she would squeeze us in at the first opportunity. After thanking her and hanging up, my friend handed the phone over to me and gave me the 'call work' look. I reluctantly took the mobile and dialled Eleanor's direct line.

"Hmm ... Hello Eleanor, I am so—"

"Let me guess, you are so sorry, OK, have you got anything better than that?" she asked rudely.

"Actually yes, I have been really ill, I am going to the GP now—"

"And what kind of illness is that – hay fever, the flue, or maybe a brutal hangover?" This woman was a nightmare; she would not let me speak. Her favourite thing to do was to terrorise everyone at work. She knew my temper and I had had a few arguments with her already. She didn't like the fact that she couldn't intimidate me and so wouldn't miss the chance to humiliate me.

"Well, Eleanor, in case you hadn't noticed yet, I am not a teenager getting trashed at weekends and skipping school on Mondays. I am ill, I will be more than happy to bring you a note from the GP." She was so insulting that words came out faster than diplomacy would allow, although I have never been notorious for being diplomatic!

"Fine, you are ill, but this does not explain why you haven't had the decency to call us and let us know you were going to be missing today!"

"I just woke up—"

"You are right Louise, waking up at 5.30pm is definitely adult behaviour!" she said sarcastically, "Well, on that note, let us know when you will be back, as we have tons of work here, goodbye."

She gave me no chance to explain and hung up. I was livid – her lack of concern was so rude. She didn't believe me and was clearly reproaching me for not having a legitimate reason to miss work. It was even more infuriating since I had never missed a day of work before, even if I was sick. Plus, reacting like that after Joshua and I landed her a new supplier was so ungrateful.

Naomi looked at me with concern when she saw my red cheeks and my hands shaking from exasperation. It took me a minute to calm down and I told Naomi I would be ready to go shortly. I only needed a quick shower and to brush my teeth – minimum hygiene was always a must. During the process, I noticed something different in the mirror and looked closer: my pupils were more dilated than normal and some tiny nerves had exploded, which gave me a few red spots in the white of my eyes. I didn't look good! My gums were painful too; I have always had a little sensitivity – hence the constant use of soft toothbrushes – however it was really hurting much more than normal. I got dressed and put some sunglasses on to hide my alien eyes. I didn't bother with make up or anything that would enhance my appearance. I needed to look as bad as I really felt, so the GP examination could be as accurate as possible. Meanwhile, Naomi was booking a cab to pick us up and drive us to the medical centre. It was not very far, but she didn't want to take any risks and I didn't mind to be honest. We went downstairs and the taxi arrived at the same time. I used the ride to text my colleagues who had contacted me today and let them know I was alive, but in a bad state.

Fifteen minutes later, we had arrived and introduced ourselves to the person at the desk who invited us to sit in the waiting room. Soon after, the doctor called us into her office.

"Thank you so much Dr Madison for finding me some time, I am so grateful," I started.

"That's OK, but we don't have much time, so let's go straight to the point of your visit. Tell me, what happened?"

"Pretty much everything Naomi told you over the phone. I have been feeling exhausted and weak: I am dehydrated, hungry and I keep having hot flushes – I even fainted once."

"Also, she has been having some memory loss lately, like certain recent events that she doesn't fully remember!" Naomi added.

"Is that true Louise?" asked the doctor.

"Well, they are not exactly memory losses, but rather confusion regarding some events. And to be fair, they could totally be due to alcohol consumption or maybe other substances at party time."

"OK. Well, I am going to proceed with a quick check-up and if necessary, organise a blood test." As she talked, she was putting her pad and pen away, indicating the physical examination was about to start. First, she took my blood pressure, a little bit low but nothing too worrying. Then, she checked my ears and eyes, again all was fine; I even had the feeling that my sight was better than usual. She carried on with my reflexes, my heart rate and pressed on specific areas including my stomach.

"Despite a few little things to keep an eye on, there is nothing to worry about for now. You seem a bit weak as your blood pressure and pulse checks have shown. I think you've been feeling overwhelmed. Have you suffered any traumatic events recently?"

"Nothing at all."

"Have you been under pressure at work or elsewhere?"

"No, at least not more than usual."

"Have you been doing a lot of sport lately?"

"No, but I did run for an hour last night at fast speed, which is what drained me."

"Hmm, and have you been feeling depressed?"

"No." She was silent for a bit while she entered the information on her computer.

"OK Louise, it certainly looks to me like you are suffering from overwork or something is troubling you. I don't mean to be blunt but you do look exhausted. I know you Louise, I know what you are like and it is not the person I have in front of me now. You need to rest, and I would like you to get a blood test just in case. It would be wise to check your thyroid gland among the usual tests. I would also recommend that you stop work for the rest of the week. If you feel better, of course you can go back, but I would rather have the results of your blood sample before you do so."

"That's fine by me," I said while she was checking her computer screen.

"You can come back on Wednesday at 4pm for the blood check, I am afraid we don't have any earlier time slot. I am writing you a sick note for work."

"OK. Thank you so much, I really appreciate it." We all stood up, she handed me my papers and we said our goodbyes.

"Do you feel OK to walk home?" Naomi asked as we were coming out of the medical centre.

"I think so." We started on our way to my flat, with Naomi holding my arm.

"So, I guess the Doctor was quite reassuring. It's nice to know you are not going to die, at least not today!" she said laughing. Naomi and I were used to having fun and not so much accustomed to drama, or at least when we were confronted by it, we tried to keep smiling. I laughed and carried on:

"Who knows, I could still die in my sleep tonight! Aha!"

"You are not allowed! How are you feeling anyway?"

"Alright but not at my best, I am really thirsty again."

"Well, to be fair you only woke up a little while ago and you didn't drink anything except a cup of tea. Let's stop at a corner shop and get some drinks, but no beer for you!"

We carried on talking and walking, reaching my house twenty-five minutes later and by then I felt revived. We talked about dinner and Naomi decided I needed something to regain energy, so she decided to make me fresh Bolognese. It made me really happy; her pasta dishes were always great! I had nothing in my fridge for it, so she went to the shop to buy the food we needed and got the meat from the local butcher. This woman was amazing! The doctor had urged me to rest properly and mellow out, so I began rolling a joint. There was nothing like pot to chill me out. Before I smoked it, I sent an email to Eleanor, explaining my GP had put me on sick leave and that she would find the documents she needed attached to the email. I did not want to have to think about her or work.

Chapter IV

I woke up in the middle of the night, lying on my sofa, covered with a blanket. I must have fallen asleep while Naomi was still here, but she made sure I was comfortable before she left. My gums were hurting me quite badly, so I drank a glass of water but it didn't help. There was half of my joint in the ashtray, I took it and went to the window to get some fresh air while smoking the rest of it. I started to think about the stranger: he was a gorgeous dark-haired man, tall, the features of his face were well balanced, his lips were very sensual and his skin was smooth and light coloured. His parents probably came from different places and their union resulted in a beautiful being. The thought of him gave me goosebumps, and I wondered again who he was. After yawning quite a few times, I resolved to go to bed and fell asleep instantly.

***

I was dreaming. I found myself on a little green wooden dory boat, attached to a very basic pier, on a shady pond just after sunset. The colours in the sky were amazing and it seemed I was waiting for someone. Suddenly, two cold hands settled on my shoulders and chills ran from the bottom of my spine to my neck. A delicate, soft kiss was planted on the side of my neck. Before I had the chance to turn around, a man appeared right in front of me. Thanks to the swiftness of his movement, he only slightly rocked the boat. My eyes were wide open and happiness was flowing through my veins. The man had a broad and charming smile, he was stunning. He was tall, had brown hair, perfect skin and piercing hazelnut eyes that sometimes appeared green depending on the light. He came closer to me and kissed me with intensity; it felt so good and right. His hands ran over my arms, his touch was electrifying and I could feel desire emanating from both of us.

***

Suddenly, I woke up. I was in shock as the man I had just dreamt of, was none other than the man who was stalking me. I still had no idea who he was though. Why would my brain take me there? The scene felt so real, not like one of these intense dreams that can happen sometimes, but as if the same scene had occurred before, like it was a memory deeply buried inside me. It felt as though my mind was disclosing safely guarded information in a timely manner and it was time for me to know it. I was seriously considering that the dream was reality, especially since I had a similar occurrence yesterday, taking me though the lost parts of my memory and allowing me to understand how I got home early Sunday morning. Although, I had no clue when and where the pond scene had taken place, I somehow knew it was real; I remembered the moment itself but nothing else around it.

I sat on my bed, unable to think further. The last couple of days had been incredibly odd and I wasn't sure if I was in a middle of a never-ending dream or if I was losing my mind. I stared at the whiteness of my duvet, trying to remain calm even though my gums were painful as hell. With my hand, I felt for a glass of water on my bed-side table, my eyes held on the duvet as if they were stuck. When I got it in hand, I brought it to my mouth and drank it straight down, but unsurprisingly it didn't help the pain nor the thirst. Again, a wild feeling of fury ran through my body – my heart was racing and my cheeks were burning. My fingers closed up on my palms and I clenched my fists so hard that my nails pierced through my skin. Immediately, drops of blood started trickling down my wrists. Its smell was strong and metallic and the dark liquid was tickling my skin. Slowly, my eyes followed the thin stream of blood; it was now dripping onto my duvet and had formed a little puddle. Everything was in slow motion, and the smell of the blood felt weirdly comforting, which was quite frightening. I could not stop looking at it – I was hypnotised. My whole being was compelling me to lick my wrists and hands. I could not feel the pain caused by the fresh wounds on my palms, all I could feel and smell was the blood. As I was getting more and more distressed by the unnatural situation, I was trying to fight this morbid desire to drink my own blood.

Suddenly, an unusual noise brought me out of this scary episode. I snapped out of it and shook my head. I heard the same noise again. It was coming from the lounge window. I wiped my hands and arms on the duvet already tainted by my blood and then quietly walked into the living room, guided by the moonlight. Nothing was there, the window was closed and the door was locked – nobody was in here. I walked to the window and looked outside. I could not believe my eyes: the stalker was here again! It seemed as though he had been waiting for me to see him. I couldn't move, unsure whether I should be scared or trying to find out who he was. I kept staring, right into his eyes. He held my stare and smiled. He didn't flinch. I decided I would not move until he left or gave me a sign of something, whichever, but something to explain all of this. As if he read my thoughts, he broadened his smile and showed his perfect teeth. His gaze was powerful and in a sort of bizarre way, it made me feel safe. Our eyes were locked for a moment, but it felt like an eternity. And for this short time, all anger, thirst, nervousness and pain went away, although my heart was still racing. Finally, he started to move, as if he was leaving.

Only then, I realised he held a lily in his hand which was, as a matter of fact, my favourite flower. It could not be a co-incidence! After tonight's dream, I could not possibly believe that. It deepened my desire to talk to him, but I blinked and he was gone. I knew I wouldn't find him unless he wanted me to. I had learnt my lesson last night, so going after him was definitely not a smart move. I decided to let him go and went to the bathroom to clean myself up. My mind was calm again, which pleased me. I returned to the window in case my mysterious stalker had decided to come back, but he had not. However, something white on the outer windowsill got my attention ... the lily ... the same one that was few minutes ago in the hand of my new admirer. What was he trying to say? I opened the window and took the flower. Its fragrance was exquisite! I was confused and torn between two opposite feelings: the first of happiness, as many people would be after someone offers them the perfect flower; the second of anxiety – who could this man be? How did he know my taste in flowers and how had he managed to get it up on my window ledge so fast?

With thousands of questions whirling around my head and absolutely zero answers to any of them, I decided to stop thinking. Clearly, if the man wanted to hurt me, he would already have done so, unless he was a real psychopath, who was enjoying playing with his prey before killing. In either case, he was gone and I was safe, at least for tonight. I was going to give some serious thought to tonight's events tomorrow, when I would be more able to function. This episode had mellowed me out and I was finally calm. It was an ideal time to go back to sleep, plus I was exhausted. Back to my bed, I fell into a deep sleep right away.

***

This time, my dream took me to a beautiful botanical garden. It was winter, but the greenhouses were filled with lush vegetation and amazing flowers. The floral scent was delightful and the moist, warm air felt like I was on holiday on a tropical island. I was wandering along the path, taking in all the diverse beauty of this place. I must have been there for a while already, as it was the end of the day and they were probably going to close soon. I saw a stunning flower that I did not know, I came close to it and could not resist touching the velvety petal. Then, I heard somebody talking:

"You shouldn't be doing that Miss." I turned and saw a man. Thinking it must be one of the garden employees, I apologised.

"I am so sorry Sir, I couldn't resist. You are doing such a great job, all of the greenhouses and gardens are magnificent. Sorry, I just could not resist!"

"You do not need to use flattery, I don't work here!" he said amused while broadening his smile. I felt a bit silly and laughed.

"Oops!" I looked at him and could not help noticing how attractive he was.

"I am the one who should apologise in fact, I didn't mean to startle you! It is nice to see someone truly moved by the wonders of Mother Nature – you intrigued me! Sorry for intruding."

"Oh! I see, well I found the flower so beautiful..." I stopped, his gaze was so intense, it mentally threw me off balance and I was instantly infatuated with him.

"May I walk with you? The garden doesn't close for another hour."

"You may, but first tell me, what's your name?"

"Oh! Of course! Where are my manners! I am Aiden, what about you?"

"Louise!"

"Well, very pleased to meet you Louise!"

"You too Aiden!"

We walked in silence and stopping here and then, observing the beautiful flora surrounding us. The silence was not awkward at all, quite the opposite actually; it was simply good to share this moment together, although we were both complete strangers. It was exactly like being friends with someone since forever and spending quality time not talking, just being with each other. I stopped in front of some beautiful lilies – my favourite flowers – and breathed in their heady scent for a little while. Aiden noticed it and smiled, but did not say anything. When it was time for the garden to close to the public, I looked at my watch and it was time for me to leave.

"Is it time for you to go already?" Aiden asked softly.

"Yes, it is."

"Alright then, would you like to meet again? There is a wonderful place I would love to show you!"

"Sure!" I did not even think and my answer came out straight away. "I mean, why not, I am curious!"

"Great, shall we say tomorrow at 7pm? Can you meet me in front of the British Museum?"

"I will do." We looked at each other warmly and waved our goodbyes.

***

Again, I jumped out of bed and this time it took me a while to find my composure. I recalled the dream perfectly. It felt as real as the previous one. I focused and mentally reconstructed the face of the man in my dream. Once I could visualise his features, it hit me hard! Aiden was not just a beautiful dream figure, no, in fact, it was Aiden who I had dreamt about earlier on and had been stalking me. What the hell was going on?

I could not go back to sleep after such a huge revelation! I was starting to put the pieces together. Since the first time I had seen him outside the café with Naomi, leaning on the lamppost, I had a feeling I knew him and he inexplicably felt safe. Plus, Naomi had said she had seen him before we entered the club on Saturday night. How curious! Then, he turned up in front of my flat, clearly looking to get my attention, staring and smiling at me. How could he know where I lived? The coffee place could have been an odd coincidence, but not my home! After that, he found his way into my dream and showed me an intimate romantic interlude on a pond where we were obviously in love. Was that a fantasy? Later that same night, he got my attention at the window and left me a lily on the ledge.

It didn't make any sense until that last dream. Did he use this lily as a trigger to revive part of my memory? And if so, why had these memories disappeared in the first place? When did the events occur? And why the heck I could not remember any of them! I freaked out – was my sanity in danger? Sleepless, I went over and over the same events.

After an hour of torturing myself, I decided the truth may be hidden in the dreams. They had revealed interesting moments so far. I did not doubt Aiden would be back. I needed to talk to him and hear his story to find out what was happening to me. I unsuccessfully tried to go back to sleep and gave up. It was the middle of the night, so I started going through my unsorted paperwork and bills to occupy my brain.

Chapter V

Around 6.45am, the dark blue sky of the night lightened, forecasting the fast-approaching sunrise, which somehow cheered me up. I was still going through my papers, nearly at the end of it though. It did a great job of taking my mind off everything: the puzzling drama with Aiden, the physical struggles such as my terrible thirst and painful gums or the freaky blood episode.

I went to make my morning cup of tea and came back to the sofa. I always find the first sip so soothing! Then, my eyes caught sight of part of a photograph peeking out from under the remaining pile of papers. I pulled it out and did not understand what I was looking at. It was a photo of me in an unknown setting, at an unknown time. I froze. Despite the mysterious content of the picture, something was certain: I was happy – super happy, like 'best day of my life' kind of happy. I looked so fulfilled, as if I didn't need anything else.

I was at the top of a hill and the landscape was beautiful. It looked like an ocean of emeralds. The mix of colours in the sky was stunning: purple dominated the scene, while disappearing orange and pink beams indicated the sun had recently set. My hair was floating in the air and my cheeks were a little red. I inspected my hair style to determine when this picture had been taken. Considering I don't change my hair often, it only showed that it had been taken some time in the last year or so. Dammit! Why didn't I remember where or when? I was deep in thought when my phone rang. I saw Naomi's face on the screen and I picked up right away:

"Good morning sunshine! I didn't expect you to be up already!" she started.

"Morning! Yes, I have been awake since 4am!"

"That's weird, you are usually such a good sleeper!"

"I know, right?! I must be getting old! Anyway, how are you?"

"I'm fine. Actually I am glad you are already up, would you like to have breakfast with me before I go to work? I can bring everything and be with you in 15 minutes if I can hop on the bus straight away."

"OK sure, that would be nice!"

"Fine, I'll bring the usual?"

"Yep! See you in a bit!"

I looked around and tidied up the table where I had been sorting out my papers and hid the mysterious photo. I jumped in the shower and got ready before Naomi arrived. Twenty minutes later, she knocked on the door and I let her in.

"So, how is my Louise doing today?"

"Fine I guess, still a bit strange but it's still too early to feel an actual improvement, isn't it?"

"Let's see if there is any change tomorrow! So, how did Eleanor react to your week off?"

"Not well I'm guessing!" I shrugged.

"What do you mean, didn't you talk to her?"

"I forgot to tell you, I emailed her when we got back from the medical centre while you were shopping for dinner. I let her know that Dr Madison had advised a week of sick leave and attached the letter and form. She didn't reply and probably won't. I sent the email on high importance setting and requested a notification of delivery report, which I got by the way."

"She is terrible, isn't she?"

"Yep, anyway that's her problem. She does not give a shit about her employees so I am not going to feel bad for being ill!"

"Damn right!"

We carried on chatting about random stuff, like work, friends, couples we knew and upcoming events. An hour later, she left for work. Naomi had been with her company for almost three years now and was really good at her job. Everybody praised her work and her colleagues respected her. She had been putting so much effort and devotion into her work, so I was glad she got the appreciation she deserved.

A few minutes later, I got a text from her: "*Completely forgot to tell you. An after-work party has been put together for Friday eve at my office. You are so my +1! Love you!*" Typical Naomi! I replied with an enthusiastic "*yes!*" and entered the event in my phone.

These past few hours and days had been crazily intense and I needed to release the pressure to be able to think straight again and make sense of what I was experiencing! Whenever I feel overwhelmed, I like to go to the gym, do a bit of cardio and then hit the boxing class. It always works! Even if the doctor had recommended rest and to avoid any physical effort, I decided to choose my sanity over my exhaustion, but I would be careful not to push myself too far though. On the way there, I started to feel really guilty for not telling Naomi what was going on with me – she could handle it for sure, but the real question was: could I? I needed to know more before we could have this talk.

At the gym, it felt good to see the regular staff and customers. After a quick cardio session, I took a break to rehydrate and then went to the boxing class. My usual trainer was working afternoon shifts, so I introduced myself to his colleague who I had met a couple of times before.

"Oh yeah, I've seen you a few times – you train with George usually, right? I don't mean to be rude but you do look a bit tired and pale, are you sure you are up to taking this class today?"

"Yes! I'm not going to lie, I'm not at my best but I need it! I feel so stressed I need to unleash it!"

"Fair enough! But if I see it's getting too much for you, I will ask you to leave the class on the spot."

"Sounds fair to me!"

He gave me an encouraging look and went to start his class. After an hour of punching and kicking, I started to feel tired. We had thirty more minutes to go, but I knew I could do it, so I powered through.

After showering, I left the gym feeling much better. On the way back, I grabbed some take away lunch and stopped in a square nearby to eat it. I wasn't used to being free during weekdays, it was great! It was a lovely day, sunny and warm for the time of year. I have always enjoyed the little break offered by the green spaces in the city. I could not live in the countryside full-time as I would become bored so quickly, but I needed to go there sometimes to rest up and enjoy the natural environment.

Looking around, I felt a bit odd: I had this sensation of 'déjà vu' but could not tell from when or where. This place was familiar, but I was unable to tell why. Perhaps the green scenery reminded me of some kind of childhood memory from our house in the country.

When I arrived home, it was early afternoon, but I was tired and fancied a nap. I had had very little sleep last night and then burnt all my spare energy at the gym. As I got into bed, I saw the blood stains on the duvet cover and it sickened me a little. I looked at my palms to see the wounds that had caused the crimson blemishes; I had completely forgotten about them. To my surprise, there were no wounds to be seen, nothing, not even small scars! I shivered. That's probably why I did not pay attention to them, I did not feel a thing and had forgotten about them. I kept looking at my palms trying to make sense of this new puzzle. After a few minutes, I reasoned that maybe the bleeding episode was also a dream. I had to admit that these days, it was hard to know what was real or imagination! I was too tired to figure out what happened, so after changing the bed sheets, I decided to let it go and went to bed. My sleeping cycle had been completely messed up, therefore I would take whatever I could get. Plus, a new dream could lead to more clues. I started to sink into the mattress and my mind travelled through time.

***

I was waiting in front of the British Museum at 6.59pm. It was already dark, so it must have been one of the autumn or winter months. I was excited and had butterflies in my stomach. At 7pm sharp, a car approached and I recognised the driver – it was Aiden.

"Good evening Louise, would you like to get in?"

"Hello Aiden! That's what I call perfect timing!" I opened the car door and got in. "I did not expect you to turn up behind the wheel of a car. Don't you use public transport?"

"Ah! I don't mind it, although I would rather walk, if I can spare the time. However, public transport won't take us to the place I'd like to show you."

"Is this your way of telling me we are going outside London?"

"Yes, if you don't mind of course."

"I didn't see that coming. You do realise we just met."

"Is this your way of telling me I look suspicious?"

"Ah! Well, you don't, but if it was so easily spotted, we would all be safe!"

"Fair point. I didn't think it through, but I can guarantee I will behave!" He smiled.

"If you guarantee it, then it makes it OK, right?" I responded sarcastically.

"I promise!" he said charmingly as he drove off.

I was fully aware it was irresponsible for me to get into a stranger's car, but I was completely infatuated with him. Also, I swore to myself I would run away at the first sign of danger, providing I could see it coming. It reminded me of the adventures I had when I travelled in my twenties: sometimes, certain situations or people seemed dodgy because of our western upbringing, but turned out to be interesting encounters and usually greatest stories to tell came out of them. I wasn't really a suspicious person; however, I have always followed my common sense and instincts. In this instance, I sensed that Aiden had good intentions.

We chatted all the way and I found out that Aiden was a Londoner, born and raised, and that he was working for a consulting company in the sustainable development sector. He travelled often, sometimes last minute. He was an only child and had lost his parents long time ago, just like me. He also loved music and played the piano. He asked me questions about myself, which I happily answered and by the time we reached our destination, Aiden no longer felt like a stranger.

We had been driving for an hour or so before we passed through a small town. Aiden drove a little further, and soon after we arrived at a small cottage. He parked just in front of the entrance and turned off the engine. Once he switched off the car headlights, it was dark outside and I could barely see. Luckily, we were only a few steps away from the door. I looked at him a little surprised, having no idea where we were. He gave me a reassuring smile and got out of the car. He walked round to my side and opened the door for me. I thought it was a bit old school of him, but I was charmed. As he led me towards the cottage, he looked at me and said, "You are going love it!". I smiled and followed him through the darkness. It was very bizarre, Aiden was so new in my life, but I trusted him and my mind was at peace.

We entered the cottage quite easily; a key was hidden under a plant pot near three small steps leading to the main door. Aiden knew exactly where he was taking us. Inside, it was even darker and I could smell the thick layers of dust everywhere. Nobody had lived in this house or at least not on a full-time basis for years. Aiden switched on the light but nothing happened. After a few minutes, our eyes became accustomed to the dark and we could find our way around the furniture. Then, I realised I could use the flash-light on my phone. As I drew the phone out of my pocket, Aiden gently put his hand on mine and I shivered as our skin touched.

"No, no, no, don't use a flash-light, the neighbours might think we are thieves."

"I did not see any houses around!"

"There are! Anyway, it is not a problem, I know the way by heart, so follow me – I'm taking you to another room."

"You mean the special room where you leave the people you abduct?" I teased.

"I really didn't think this through, did I? I can see why all of this seems a bit odd, but trust me, you will love it!"

"Well, I guess it is too late to back out now!"

I knew I was not being cautious and I hoped nothing bad would happen. I mean, if I was watching this scene on TV, I would be screaming at the character not to follow the cute guy! But somehow, I could not resist and I really believed Aiden had something to show me.

We walked along a corridor until we stopped in front of a door. I could feel Aiden's excitement and I could not help to smile. Plus, I was dying to find out what the mystery was all about! The door was locked with a coded padlock, but Aiden knew the code and opened it easily. Inside it was pitch black. We waited a few seconds. A staircase started to emerge from the dark. Aiden gently took my hand and led me down the stairs. My heart was pounding from fear, excitement and adrenalin. He must have noticed because he squeezed my hand and whispered, "Trust me". We reached the bottom of the stairs only to find another closed door, with three padlocks. Aiden took three little keys out of his pocket and opened them all. What was this secret place? Finally, he opened the door and hundreds of different scents filled the air. Then, Aiden lit an old oil lamp – it was dim, but just enough for us to see. We walked in to find a stunning greenhouse full of lush plants. I was in awe! I could not believe what was in front of me, it was gorgeous! Aiden walked me through it very slowly, so I could take my time to enjoy the precious flowers and plants.

"Aiden, this is marvellous! What is this place?"

"I knew you would like it! I cannot tell you too much otherwise I will have to kill you!" I laughed. "This place belongs to a friend of mine. He doesn't use the house much and he is kind of agoraphobic. He has a very soft spot for rare flowers and plants, so he likes to stay in his 'floral cell' as he calls it!"

"Impressive! This is truly amazing! How could you be so sure I would love it?"

"Something in the way you behaved at the garden yesterday, I could see you liked to be connected to nature."

"Just like that?"

"Your body language gave you away and you seemed so peaceful."

"I didn't know you had studied me that much!"

"Let's just say I have been around a lot of people and learnt to read them and anticipate their next move. It is like people working in the service industry, after a while they learn how to read people!"

"I guess!"

"My friend isn't here at the moment, so we can take our time."

"Great! Let's have a look at those orchids." We strolled through the greenhouse and Aiden told me about the different species on display – he knew a great deal and was fascinating. After a while, he looked at me and said:

"I have a final surprise for you, I believe our escapade would not be complete without taking a peek at your favourite flower."

"What do you mean? How do you know my favourite flower?" He did not answer and walked me to another side of the greenhouse instead. At the sight of them, I gasped! How did he guess?

"At the garden, something in the way you looked at the lilies gave you away."

"I cannot believe it!"

So many emotions went through me: it was a mix of surprise, excitement, happiness, amazement and a tiny bit of fear. Aiden seemed to have sharp observational skills, such as the way he read me and reassured me with perfect timing. We stayed there for a few minutes contemplating the beauty of it all. When I was ready, he took my hand again and led me back up the stairs. He carefully took the time to lock the doors and we went the same way back to the main entrance. After locking the final door, he put the key back under the plant pot and we made our way to the car. Before he got the chance to switch the ignition on, I put my hand on his and thanked him for the wonderful evening. Our eyes locked for a while and we shared so much chemistry. I was even more attracted to him; I had never experienced such strong feelings in such a short time for anyone else.

***

I woke up at 8pm and realised I had been dreaming again, but I received a text from Naomi that distracted me. She was asking how I was doing, so I replied telling her what I had been up to today. She gave me a hard time for going to the gym, but eventually she understood how it helped me feel better.

I was well rested which was great, but also very hungry. I knew just what to do. There was a fabulous Indian restaurant close by, and I often dropped by and ordered their delicious chicken curry to take away when I was too lazy to cook like tonight. On my way back to my flat after picking up the dinner, I felt good. I always loved walking in the night and finally my mind was empty.

Chapter VI

Back home, I got comfy on my vintage armchair and ate my curry while watching a documentary about wine. I worked for a company that supplied unusual or exceptional wines to restaurants and fancy hotels. My great-grandfather was the last of a long line of a winegrowing family in France. When he passed away, his children were still young and my great-grandmother did not have the resources to continue the family business. She sold her inheritance and moved to England.

I loved wine and perhaps I unconsciously followed my family legacy. I studied at business school and travelled for a couple of years to different vineyards around the world.

During a trip to South Africa, I met a brilliant man, Alastair, who ran his own wine dealership in London. We hit it off right away and after a few wine tasting sessions, he offered me a job, which I accepted. All was going well until he retired and sold his company to someone he thought was a good person. Turned out she wasn't! Part of the deal was that Eleanor had to keep the employees on in order to protect our jobs and ensure a smooth takeover. It started out fine for a few months, then Eleanor's true colours came out.

Since Alastair left, work never had the same ambiance. We used to have fun and close super deals, following the 'Work hard, play hard' motto. We would go on awesome seminars and Alastair was always pushing us to learn and develop our skills. Our company used to be one of the top in Britain. Currently, business was good, but not as successful as before. Eleanor changed our product line and target market: we became more of a mainstream wine distributor with occasional high level deals. A few of my colleagues left to work with competitors, but most of us have stayed here, although we are not as motivated. We still felt we owed it to Alastair to hold the fort and Eleanor knew it. We have been working for her for almost two years now and I cannot recall any kind words from her to anyone. Sometimes, we organised dinners with Alastair and his husband, which brought back happy memories of time before Eleanor.

After finishing my dinner and the documentary, I tidied up my take away box and other rubbish. I looked at the time and it was already 10pm. Having slept the whole afternoon, I was not tired, not even one bit. My thoughts started to race – I was wondering if Aiden would come back tonight and if he did, what would be the best way to approach him. So far, he was always ahead of me. Of course, he had the considerable advantage of knowing what he was doing, whereas I had no clue. I was sure of only one thing: he was not willing to talk to me yet and if I spotted him outside, he would be gone by the time I reached him. I needed to take him by surprise. I could hide outside and catch him when he arrived. That sounded like a good plan! Or did it? Oh well, what was the worst that could happen? I would be in front of my house. Plus, more than fifteen years of experience in martial arts did make me feel like I could handle a confrontation!

I put on some warm dark clothes and tied my hair up, which made me look like a professional thief. Hopefully there wouldn't be any robberies nearby! I took a small bottle of water and some bananas considering my recent issues with hunger. I left the light on in the living-room, so it would look like I was home from outside. On my way down the stairs, I realised I was maybe putting myself in danger, but I didn't stop.

Outside, the air was cool and the sky was free of clouds. It was a beautiful night. I went to Aiden's stalking spot and looked around for the ideal hideout. There were a few trees on the side of the road, which seemed perfect. I put my drink and food on the ground and waited behind the trees.

At first, I was so convinced I would catch him that my motivation kept me going for two hours. After that, I started to get bored and read a biology article on my phone. I was very fond of science although I didn't have a brilliant scientific mind. I had specific interests mostly in biology, medicine and technology.

This article concerned what is commonly referred to as "zombie animals": it occurs when some parasites or animals infect another one, as a host body, and control their minds to achieve a specific goal, generally related to reproduction. One example, is a spider from Costa Rica which gets infected by a parasitic wasp – the latter injects its larvae inside the former, along with new directions to follow. Instead of carrying on with its spider life and working on its web, it will start making a silk cocoon to host the larvae. When it is done, the future wasps kill their host from the inside and move to their new home. Freaky but fascinating!

Then, I went through my messages – I was really bad at replying! Whenever I had a few minutes to spare, like on the bus or the tube, I would take a look at my texts and reply. I found the text that the Saturday night guy sent. I apologised for my delayed reply and told him I was ill at the moment but would be in touch soon. It was a bit late to send the reply right now, but thanks to technology I could set an option to send the message later, so I picked 10am.

I looked at the time: it was 2am and still no signs of Aiden. I had already eaten all my bananas and was almost out of water. I decided to power through for a little longer and sat down leaning on one of the trees. My eyelids were really heavy and in seconds I was gone.

I woke up at 4am still sitting on the ground. I panicked at first and then realised all was OK – all my belongings were still here ... and there was a lily next to the banana peels! Unbelievable! Aiden must have come when I was asleep and have nothing better to do than tease me. This man was playing with my nerves. I was so annoyed. Upset and disappointed, I picked up my phone and keys and went home. I thought it would make a statement to throw the flower in the bin along with my other rubbish. Then, I quickly showered, as I could feel my gums starting to hurt and wanted to go to sleep before the pain made it impossible.

Around 11am, I jumped out of bed breathing heavily. I just had the worst nightmare ever! There was blood everywhere and I was swimming in a pool of blood and I could not get out. The image remained the same, but I felt a mix of very intense emotions such as anger, despair, pain, frustration, loneliness and fear.

It took me a while to come back to reality, but eventually I did. I hadn't had a nightmare for a while, and this one was particularly gruesome. I used to have a lot of them when I was a child. For a few years after the death of my parents, my nights were haunted by horrible images. They finally stopped when I was about twelve years old.

I was physically drained. I had very little energy and I supposed the physical work out yesterday was hard on my body, but I did not want to go back to sleep and risk another nightmare.

I settled on the sofa with my laptop and decided to catch on the TV shows I had been missing. At lunch time, Naomi called, telling me she would come pick me up at 3.45pm to go to the blood test appointment. It completely slipped my mind. Good thing that she called, otherwise I would have had to explain why I had forgotten it, and obviously I was not going to tell her about my Aiden drama, not yet.

When I went downstairs, the temperature outside was decent. I waited a few minutes before Naomi arrived in a cab, and we headed to the medical centre. We arrived on time, I checked in at the desk and the receptionist told me to wait for a nurse to come and take me to the blood test room. As we were about to sit in the waiting room, Dr Madison walked past with a patient. She saw us and made her way over.

"Ah! Louise, how are you feeling today?"

"Hello, I'm fine, still a bit weak, but fine, thanks."

"Yes, your body is slowly recovering, so please rest in the meantime. I know you are very active, but it is not the right time for it." I thought of my workout session and felt a bit guilty.

"Yes sure, no physical exertion for me!" Naomi's glance showed she was not too happy about my little white lie.

"That's what I like to hear! All done with your test?"

"Not yet, the nurse should be coming any minute now—"

"Louise Bailey?" I heard a voice from behind the doctor.

"Yes!"

"Hello, I am Lacey and I will be taking care of your blood test. Would you like to follow me?"

"Sure! Naomi, are you OK staying here?"

"Yes! You know I hate needles!"

"Louise, let them know at the desk that you would like to see me when you get the results, so I can translate them for you," she offered.

"I will, thanks and I will see you soon then!" I looked at the doctor and waved her goodbye. She smiled as I walked away and she turned to Naomi.-

Lacey took me to a room full of medical equipment and told me to sit down. She first checked my blood pressure and then prepared my arm. She put plastic gloves on, applied a tourniquet around my arm and disinfected the area where she wanted to put the needle. Her movements were very neat and professional. She was also very kind, which helped me relax. She asked me to make a fist, and it reminded me of the blood incident in my bed. As she started to insert the needle, she was surprised by the toughness of my skin.

"OK Louise, I am afraid it might hurt a bit, your skin is very thick, so I will have to push the needle in slightly harder, alright? Once the needle is in, you will be able to release your fist."

"Whatever you need!" I said uneasily. She tried again and managed to successfully penetrate the skin. I could see a look of concern on her face, although she was doing her best to hide it.

"Well, your blood is quite thick, it will take a bit longer to fill up the tubes. Sorry for the inconvenience."

"Don't worry!" We both smiled politely.

When she had the quantity of blood she needed, she removed everything and put a plaster on the wound left by the needle. She warned me to rest as much as I could, as my blood pressure was very low. She added that I would be informed by text when my results would be ready to pick up, probably by the end of the week. I left the room after thanking her and went back to Naomi in the waiting room. I found her reading a fashion magazine.

"Hey, I am all done, let's go!"

"How did it go?"

"Fine, like a blood test!"

"Did it hurt?" Naomi was very sensitive when it came to needles and blood!

"Yes, a bit."

"What do you want to do now?"

"I would quite like to go home, I am knackered!"

"Fair enough. By the way, the doctor had a chat with me and wanted me to make sure you understood that you needed to rest and eat properly if you wanted to get better. So, no more gym sessions, even if you think you can handle it!"

"First, I have never eaten as much as in these past days and I do sleep as much as I can."

"Just passing on the message!"

"Naomi, would you like to stay and have dinner with me tonight at my place?" I asked anxious to change the topic.

"If it's an early one, yes – I have a date tonight."

"Do you now? Why haven't you said anything?"

"It pretty much got planned on the way to your flat and after that, well, we were kind of busy, but I'm telling you now."

"That's cool! Are you excited?"

"Let's say I am looking forward to going out! So, to your place now?"

"Yep, shall we just order some food, what do you fancy?"

"Something fatty! How about burgers?"

"You read my mind! What time are you meeting ... what's his name?"

"I am meeting Arthur at 9pm for drinks in some place he chose in the city centre."

"Cool! OK, let's get ourselves home so we can talk about it!"

We took the bus; I was too tired to walk and took Dr Madison's advice seriously. After fifteen minutes, we reached home. Everything was exactly the same as I left it.

"I can see you've been catching up on TV shows!" said Naomi.

"Isn't that what you do when you are stuck at home?"

Naomi and I had been living in the area for quite a while, therefore we knew exactly where to order from and what restaurants were the best around. I looked for some take away menus and found the home-made burger place we liked. We are proper foodies: we eat well and love food. We usually go to restaurants about three or four times a week – together or with other friends or dates. Being a wine professional, food is very important to me and I always enjoy finding the perfect match.

At 6.30pm, our burgers arrived. Early dinner was good for me too, as I really wanted to catch up on my sleep. My burger came with bacon, mature Cheddar cheese and pepper sauce – I couldn't deal with ketchup or mayonnaise or any kind of industrial sauce, I found them disgusting! Naomi had one with

Portobello mushroom, Brie cheese and bacon. We shared a large portion of curly fries. Half way through my burger, I was parched and drank a few glasses of water. An hour later, we were done and completely full. I noticed Naomi looking at the clock.

"Hun, do you want to get ready here?"

"Oh, that would be great, I can't be bothered to go back home, also I don't think I can move for the next half hour!" she said as she showed me her swollen stomach.

"No problem at all, you know where everything is, let me just sort you out a towel and you are good to go!"

I brought her the towel and she disappeared into the bathroom. We often stayed at each other's places, so we knew our way around. We even had clothes and toiletries in both flats, so we didn't have to plan in advance. When she came out of the bathroom, she did her make up and started examining the outfits she had here. She found something she liked, except for the top, so she borrowed one from me that she loved. She was ready by 8.20pm and left for her date. I gave her only one instruction: to text me after the date. My home felt empty without her, but I got over it and resumed binging TV shows. However, after twenty minutes, I paused the media player, as I could not focus on the screen. My mind was busy thinking about Aiden. We had some kind of connection, I could feel it, but wasn't able to explain it. I was secretly hoping he would come back tonight and that he would give me a chance to talk to him this time. But after last night, it was clear he was avoiding a meeting. I wondered about it a bit longer and eventually fell asleep on the sofa.

Chapter VII

All was dark around me. I could only hear some kind of beat – it sounded like the clack of high heels hitting the ground. Slowly, the black disappeared and colours developed. The image was gradually forming and I could begin to distinguish the scenery. It was me, walking down the street – a bit faster than usual – going home. It seemed my dream was taking me back to Saturday night again. Two guys were trying to get my attention by whistling or other kind of moronic noises that would never in a million years get me to look at them. They began to follow me. Were they trying to scare me off or worse? I was ready, I knew they were behind me and I was very much aware it would be them or me. I could more or less get an idea of the distance between us – they were getting closer. I wasn't scared; I have been practising martial arts since I was a kid, so I was more concerned about controlling my reaction. Any good fighter could be a lethal weapon, so we aren't usually allowed to fight outside training or competition, but should it happen it has to be controlled. As they were about two metres from me, I turned around swiftly:

"Can I help you with something?"

"Yes sure, how about you show us what is under that dress?" said one of the scum. They both were revolting.

"How about no! Why don't you go fuck yourself instead?" I wasn't going for jokes.

"Oh! Did you hear that Dave? You know how much I like them feisty!" He looked at his mate and back at me with leering eyes and carried on, "And I know how much you like to watch me play with the feisty ones!"

He moved aggressively towards me. I had already analysed my surroundings and had stopped in a specific place on purpose. Just next to us, was one of those post boxes made of steel, which would be an excellent landing spot for one of these two predators. As soon as his hand touched my arm, I pulled him down and kneed his face and as his head moved upwards, I threw in a few hard punches and knocked him out. His friend froze and did not believe what was happening. I did not give him a chance – punched him in the face and then kicked him in the leg. He fell and smashed his head on the mail box, which was exactly what I had intended. I called the police without leaving my name and left.

A few metres away, there was the left turn leading to my street. Before I reached it, I heard a curious moaning noise in-between two cars. It sounded like somebody had been hurt or was crying, so I went to look for the source. Maybe the two vermin had already hurt someone before they saw me. A young woman was lying there sobbing. I gently reached down to her. Out of the blue, she grabbed my arm and pulled me with such strength that I could not fight her off. I felt much pain on my wrist, like an open wound. I wanted to run off, but I could not move as her strength was extraordinary and I began to feel dizzy. Suddenly, a man jumped between us. I heard a horrifying crack, as in one fast motion he broke her neck. Then, my arm was released. I had suffered a huge wound to my arm which was gashing blood and I felt very weak. The man looked at me with horror and sorrow – it was Aiden.

"No! Louise, I am so sorry! Please stay with me, I am going to help you, don't close your eyes!" I could hear him, but could not process the information or control my body: my eyelids were so heavy, I could not keep them open. I felt myself drifting off to deep sleep.

"Louise! Don't! Please don't! Stay awake! Don't make me do this, I cannot be here if you are not. Louise?" I could not respond and looked like a dead body lying on the floor in a puddle of blood.

"Damn, it's too late! Louise, forgive me!"

As I lay there, I could hear the sound of a police siren in the distance; I was lifted up and felt myself being carried away rapidly up the stairs; a key opened a door and then a metallic taste invaded my mouth while I felt a gentle suction on my wounded wrist. Then, my body switched off and I lost consciousness. There was nothing but complete darkness: I couldn't feel, hear, smell, taste or see. I was gone.

***

I awoke, very slowly, from what felt like the deepest sleep ever. As I struggled to open my eyes, the horror came over me. I remembered the dream perfectly. Once again, my stalker had found his way into my head. It took me a few minutes to calm myself down. For the first time since I became ill, I was scared. My mouth was dry, my gums painful and my stomach was growling. I got up, still in shock and made my way to the kitchen, where I drank a litre of water and fixed some food. I kept seeing the horrible images of the new nightmare. There was no doubt it showed the second part of my first dream, one that I hadn't suspected was missing. Could it be that I never really made it home? It was impossible, I was here now. All of this made no sense, maybe the dreams weren't true and I was just stuck in some kind of fantasy world.

The clock showed 3am. I still hadn't calmed down, so I rolled a joint to relax and went to smoke at the window. A few minutes later, Aiden appeared. He stood right in front of my flat and looked at me sadly. He said something, but he was too far away. He said it again and this time I heard, "I am sorry". I must have lip-read him, as I could not possibly hear him from that far away and he was not shouting at all – the complete opposite actually. Still looking at me, he sat on the bench close by. It felt like an invitation to go and meet him, so I went for it. A part of me thought that he would be gone by the time I got outside, whereas another part of me was hoping to finally get answers. When I opened the outside door, he was there and he had not moved. I went closer and sat down next to him. I started:

"Who are you?"

"Don't you know?"

"I think I do, but why are you sorry?"

"Don't you know?" he repeated.

"I hope not." We stayed quiet for a long minute, both of us feeling sad. I could not get my head around that last dream and strangely enough, he seemed like he could not either. I carried on, "Why are you here?"

"For you."

"Meaning?"

"I am always there for you."

"Are the dreams true? And why are you in them?"

"They are. I used to be part of your life," he said with so much sorrow in his voice that it was almost heart-breaking.

"Are we together or something?"

"We were ... until we had to end it."

"We had to?"

"You will remember soon enough."

"Is this why you have been playing hide and seek with me? I have to remember by myself?"

"Yes, at least I think it is best. Our story is ... peculiar. You would not believe me if I told you now and I can't blame you! I can help you put the pieces together, but the rest has to come from you. Once you accept the truth, we will move on, but until then, you will be stuck in this state and you won't survive it. I need you to embrace the dreams and open your mind, so you can see the past."

"You sound like a lunatic! What am I supposed to do with this information?"

"That's my point, open your mind to the impossible."

"I don't think I can do it ... not after ..." I paused.

"After the last dream?"

"How do you know about it?" I looked at him with surprise

"I know a lot of things about you Louise, we are special – we are connected."

"What did you do to me?" I asked angrily, beginning to understand Aiden's involvement. He was speechless, his head down. "What – did – you – do?" I started to shout and my blood was boiling.

"I had no choice, you were dying ... and ..." he said, keeping his head down.

"What – did – you – do – to – me?"

"I ... I intervened."

"How? When the dream finished, I was ... I was ... dead. But now, I am not."

"I promise everything will make sense."

"Aiden, you don't understand, I cannot take this any longer. I feel like I am going mad, it is way too much to take in."

"Like I said, I am always there for you. Do you trust me?"

"As a matter of fact, I do, but I don't even know why!" I said, still frustrated.

"The inner you, or your subconscious, knows you can. I can help you, however we need to get away from here. Can you get away without anyone like Naomi asking questions?"

"What! How do you know about Naomi?"

"You have told me so much about her!"

"What the hell are you talking about? When?"

"Louise, we have known each other for almost a year, I know who you are. And I know exactly what you are going through.

Right now, you don't see it, but later you will understand why I am helping you this way."

I remembered the romantic dreams and his good intentions. "OK. I think I can get away, but I will have to lie, which is never good as Naomi has a nose for it!"

"I trust you will do fine, just be as much persuasive as you can be."

"OK, I can try."

"I will pick you up tomorrow evening at 7."

"I will be ready."

"Until then, please rest and don't forget your subconscious retains the truth."

He walked me back to the entrance of the building and said goodnight. I went upstairs back to my flat and collapsed on the sofa. I was tired, but I was scared to fall asleep. It was not natural to dream of one's own death. After that, I wasn't sure I could take more of these horrific scenes. I knew I was going against Aiden's advice, but right now I just could not deal with the pain and fear. Instead, I focused on a believable story to tell Naomi. What could I possibly make up? The woman knew me by heart! Sometimes, I would go away on business trips to meet current or new suppliers, but since I wasn't working this week, this one would be hard to pull off.

I kept thinking; my excuse could not be work related ... however – inspiration arrived – my hobby could be one! I would tell Naomi I had received an inquiry from a couple somewhere outside the city, who had seen some of the furniture I had made and wanted me to refurbish an old family chests of drawers. Therefore, I needed to pay them a visit to agree on a deal and see the antique. Naomi would totally buy that; she was always encouraging me to develop my network of contacts and clients, so I could one day be my own boss and an official designer. I made peace with myself about lying to her as it was for her own good. I was hoping this trip with Aiden would answer all my questions and solve the mystery. I decided I would counterbalance my lie by telling her the truth as soon as possible. Thinking about Naomi, I remembered the party she had invited me to on Friday night and it was now early morning Thursday. There was no way to get out of it, so my trip with Aiden would have to be short. He would have to understand.

I leaned back and calmly breathed in and out really deeply, with the aim of emptying my mind. Images quickly forced their way in so I let them – that must be what Aiden called the "inner me". First, vivid flashes appeared of many different places at different times: I could see some kind of citadel looking over a medieval city; the same botanical garden I had dreamed of; a forest; countryside; roads and mountains. Those images kept flashing in my head for a while, allowing me to understand that Aiden and I had been to many places together.

Soon, the first light of day streamed through the window blinds. Once again it made me feel better, safer. I needed to come up with a plan to explain to Naomi that I was going away for a day. I checked the time on my phone, it was 6.30am, a bit early to text her. I saw a message from her, which she had sent around midnight. I was so taken in by my own drama that I completely forgot about her date: "*So, date was OK but nothing amazing! No chemistry just good conversation! I guess I made a new friend! Call me when you get up! Xoxo*". Of course it didn't work out! Naomi was hard to impress and her kind of man was rare on the current singles market! Except for Ian of course, but she wasn't ready for him yet. I changed my mind and decided to text her and use the early time of day to emphasis my excitement: "*Hey hun! Somehow, I am not surprised! BTW, incredible news to tell you. I'm so excited! I'm already up, so call whenever you're ready! XXX*".

While I was on my phone, I checked my emails and found a few from colleagues who were wishing me a swift recovery. It was nice to read them. A few minutes past seven, my phone rang:

"Morning Naomi!"

"Hey girl! Don't mind my eating noises – I am having break-fast. I am quite tight on time this morning as I have to be at work early!"

"No worries, so since your mouth is busy, I'll start and you can finish!"

"Yep!"

"You will never believe what happened! I was contacted by a couple out of town, who saw some of my furniture work at a previous client's place and really loved it. They would like to meet me and hire me to refurbish an old family chest of drawers! I am so thrilled!"

"That's awesome! Are they far away?"

"Some town an hour or so away. I am supposed to call them at lunch time to sort everything out. They want me there in the evening after they finish work. I will travel by train I guess."

"Will you come back after?"

"I am not sure yet! It will depend on the length of the meeting. However, since they are tight on time and can only meet me in the evening, they have already offered to pay for a hotel should we not be finished before the last train back to London."

"That's really nice of them! Perhaps a little too nice!"

"Really Naomi? Don't kill my buzz!"

"Sorry. How about I come with you?"

"Erm, I don't mean to be harsh but no. That would just be plain awkward!"

"Fair enough! It's just I have never seen you so ill, so I worry!"

"I am fine, I feel much better by the way, resting and eating seems to be working!"

"Alright, I'll stop being clingy!"

"Yes please! Not loving that Naomi!"

"OK! Sorry. So, you think you will sleep there?"

"I am not sure. I don't mind, I don't want to rush my meeting with them."

"OK, you're right, go with the flow!"

"I will keep you posted."

"Cool! Yes, please do!"

"So, what about last night's date?"

"Well, I pretty much said it all in my text. The guy is nice and funny but that's it, I don't fancy him basically. Good mate material though!"

"OK, did he ask you out again?"

"Well, no, I basically made sure he wouldn't!"

"What?"

"I told him before we parted that he was nice but I was not attracted to him!"

"Ouch! How did he take it?"

"Better than I expected, he told me and I quote 'my honesty was refreshing'!"

"Excellent! Sorted then!"

"Couldn't be better! Anyway love, I'm sorry but I have to run now or I will be late! We'll speak later."

"Sure! Bye!"

Naomi was very straightforward and upfront, we had that in common and it made our relationship work very well. However, today was a new milestone for us: I had deliberately lied to her for the first time in my whole life! It did not feel good. I was surprised at how easy it was for me to make up a story, I didn't hesitate and the words came easily. I could be a good liar, but not when it came to Naomi, as she knew me too well and it was always odd not to share everything with her.

I spent the rest of the morning cleaning the flat and preparing an overnight bag for the mysterious trip. I had no idea where we were going or what to take, so I chose a couple of outfits and a warm jumper in case it was cold. I packed it all in a leather duffel bag and added a few toiletries.

By lunchtime, everything was done and I could not stand having to wait several more hours to meet Aiden. There was one thing I really wanted to do before I stepped into the unknown: to visit Karuna and her son Rasul. It had already been a few days since I passed out in her shop, so greetings were long overdue.

A short bus ride later, I was outside the shop. I looked decent – thanks to a fair amount of makeup – and happy, since convincing everybody I was fine was my challenge for the day. I have always been good at acting, my grandparents always wanted me to take theatre at school to practice this useful – or evil – skill. Instead, they got a fighter.

I entered the premises and saw Karuna standing behind her counter, just like the first time I had met her. Her eyes sparkled when she saw me. She called Rasul and he came forward shyly. We spoke for a bit and I thanked them again for helping me. I told her I had seen my doctor, who found I was overworked and needed to rest. I did not go into detail as I wanted her to focus on me feeling great, rather than me being ill. Throughout our chat, Karuna kept looking at me keenly, almost as if she was looking right into my soul; but she kept smiling the whole time and was very warm. When it was time for me to go, we hugged; she wished me all the best; gave me a reassuring look and smiled. I walked away thinking I had met a lovely family.

The time was approaching 7pm, the sun had already disappeared over the horizon and my excitement was growing. Finally, I would get some answers. A part of me was worried to go with Aiden, while another part was inexplicably dying to see him. I took a shower and dressed in black skinny jeans, a green shirt and trainers. By the time Aiden arrived, I was already waiting for him downstairs.

Chapter VIII

I dozed off within the first ten minutes of the car ride. Sometimes, I briefly opened my eyes and then went back to sleep. For some reason, all tension in my body and mind had lessened, Aiden's presence made me feel better. I woke up as he was slowing down and entering a private road. It took me a few seconds to realise we had arrived. At the end of the lane, there was a gate dimly lit by two solar powered post lights on each side. We stopped in front of it, and Aiden used a tiny remote that controlled the opening of the gate, revealing an old mansion. He shifted to first gear and drove carefully towards the property, until he parked near the house. We got out of the car, picked up our bags from the boot and made our way to the main door. I looked around – it was dark and since there were no lights or noises coming from any other neighbouring houses, I presumed we were in the middle of nowhere. I could only hear the light autumn breeze and some things or animals moving in the nearby woods.

Aiden pushed open the unlocked door and we went in. I was surprised to feel the warmth of a fire and to smell burning wood. We were standing in a spacious square foyer, facing an old half-landing wooden staircase going to the first floor. Underneath the stairs was a door, probably leading to the basement. On the right side, there was a large dining room, while the living room and kitchen were accessed on the left side.

Aiden took me to the living-room where a magnificent fire was burning.

"Is there somebody else here?" I asked.

"Not right now, but there was someone earlier to prepare the house for us."

"I see. By the way, before I forget, I have to be back in the city by tomorrow night."

"Why?"

"I made a commitment to Naomi. I am sorry I didn't tell you sooner, I didn't expect to pass out so fast in the car!"

"You won't be ready by then."

"Ready for what?"

"For what's coming!"

"Can you please stop talking in riddles and get straight to the point?"

"I am afraid I can't, not yet. This is up to you, you already have enough clues. It is up to you to accept the truth, only then—"

"We can move forward. I heard you the first time! I can't pull out of this, Naomi will know something is up."

"Listen Louise, what is going on right now is more important than anything else. Once, we are over this part, you can party as much as you want!" For the first time, I discerned a hint of distress from him.

"How do you know it's a party?"

"I just guessed. Come on, you and Naomi on a Friday night ... Look, I have a proposal, why don't we settle down, make ourselves comfortable and start getting to the bottom of this. We'll see how you feel about going back to London tomorrow." I could see Aiden was serious and I nodded in agreement.

The living room was huge and had beautiful antique furniture, a black upright piano and loads of paintings – I was mesmerised. Then, my host showed me upstairs to my bedroom. The bed had been made recently; I could still smell the freshness of the laundry products. He put my bag on the bed and said:

"Make yourself at home, if you want to freshen up there is a bathroom behind this door."

"Thanks, where is your room?"

"You see that other door over there?"

"Where?"

"Look closer!" There was only a wall, but when I inspected it, I saw two vertical lines connected with two horizontal ones at the top and at the bottom.

"Is that a door?"

"Yes, it is!"

"Isn't it a bit creepy?"

"Well, it can be, but if you know it is there, it's fine!" His smile eased the mood.

"I guess so!"

"So, there is my bedroom, a replica of yours in perfect symmetry." Aiden opened the door so I could see it. It was true, the rooms were perfectly symmetrical; the only difference was the colour theme. Mine was a dark sea green and his was navy blue. He disappeared into his own bedroom and closed the door, which allowed me to analyse mine thoroughly.

There was a king size four-poster bed, accompanied by two identical French Louis XV style elm veneered night stands decorated with gilt metal drawers pulls. I walked towards the window: a beige Victorian chaise longue made with carved rosewood was facing two twentieth century tawny brown leather armchairs. Plus, there was a Chippendale style English tea table in mahogany that complimented the seating area. The thick velvety curtains were double layered; I peeked through, only to see the darkness of the woods outside. In front of the bed, was another grand fireplace and some logs had been arranged, so we could start a fire should we want to. Above the mantelpiece, there was a large painting representing a sailing boat at sea that looked like an English merchant ship. I looked on my right and saw a very cute dressing table with a mirror, but there was nothing on it. Actually, the whole room was bare of personal objects, almost as if it were waiting for somebody to settle in. I went to the bathroom to freshen up and discovered another world of antique beauty. It had one of those vintage bathtubs with gilt metal feet, a huge sink where a gold framed mirror was hanging and a toilet. All taps and handles were of brass. I went to the sink, threw some cold water onto my face and dried off with a hand towel. I looked at my reflection, it was awful!

I decided to go back downstairs. I was expecting the wood of the staircase to creak under the weight of my footsteps, but it did not, not a sound. Aiden was there, waiting in front of the fire – he looked distracted. Not looking at me, he said:

"How do you like your room?"

"For an antique maniac like me, it's like a kid being in sweet shop! Did you hear me coming down?" I asked, surprised he noticed I was there.

"Yes, I did. Are you hungry?"

"As a matter of fact, I am famished! And thirsty too!"

"I have just put a roast beef in the oven, it should be ready soon!"

"Roast beef? Soon?"

"Trust me, I know how to cook it right!" As he answered, he reached for a nearby bottle of water and handed it to me very gently; his eyes were soft and kind.

"I took the liberty to pick a bottle of wine from the cellar, I think you will like it," he said, walking to a retro home bar where he had left the bottle.

"I think I will after I finish the water."

Still standing by the bar, he opened the bottle. The sound of the cork popping pleased me – it has always had a good effect on me. He poured two glasses and brought me one. We toasted each other and I tasted the flavoursome wine. I recognised certain very specific notes that I had definitely encountered before. I inspected the bottle and confirmed what I thought. It came from my great-grandfather's vineyard. How could he possibly know that? My family kept very few of the last bottles, so we never forgot where we came from. Since my grand-parents passed, only five bottles remained and they now belonged to me. This vintage was more recent, it came from the new owners' domain; however, the soil on the land was still the same. I turned my head and body towards him; our eyes met and we shared an intense gaze.

"How did you get this wine?"

"I bought it. And no, this is not a coincidence, I know about your family history."

"That is so scary. How do you know all these things about me and I know almost nothing about you!"

"You know so many things about me. You will remember – that is the goal of this little escapade."

"I hope you are right. So, when do we start?"

"We already have."

"Have we?" I looked a bit puzzled.

Aiden smiled and explained, "First, I needed you to relax and rest, which you did in the car, and now we are waiting for dinner. It is never good to work on an empty stomach!"

"What work?"

"You are going to explore your mind. I am going to help and guide you."

"OK, I am ready."

Aiden sat next to me and hesitantly reached for my hand. It surprised me, but I let him. I shivered at his touch. I could feel our connection: it was like an energy was going through our bodies and my heart beats accelerated. I held his hand tighter and looked him right in the eyes; our stares locked; a flash hit me and in a fraction of a second, we were taken elsewhere.

Aiden and I were running through some kind of tunnel where something or someone was chasing us. Although the picture was clear, this flashback was not about what I saw, but rather how I felt. Despite all the adrenalin and fear, I felt I wanted to protect Aiden more than my own life and that he felt the same way about me. The short flashback ended and I leaned back on the sofa.

"Did you make me see that?"

"No, but I can sense what you feel."

"So, you know what I saw?"

"I know what you felt."

"If we are connected, can I do the same to you?"

"Yes, but you are a beginner, give it a little time. You already perceive some things about me, but not as much as you will soon."

"What is, or was after us?"

"Not what, but rather who was after us. We had to answer to some people, but at the end we fixed it."

"Did we beat them?"

"I wouldn't put it exactly that way..."

An alarm rang and I jumped. We both laughed at my reaction, as once more it was just the oven timer. I guessed dinner was ready – this was definitely a quick roast! He came back few minutes later with a tray of red meat and a simple green leaf salad. He asked me if I would prefer to eat in the dining room, but it was just fine where we were. As he put the platter down, I stared at the meat and brought to his attention that it was still raw.

"It is a little cooked!" he defended himself.

"Barely, you mean! It is not even blue!"

"Trust me, I am an excellent cook!" he smiled reassuringly.

I didn't argue further. Beef carpaccio was one of my favourite meals after all, and I did enjoy a nice piece of beef cooked somewhere between blue and rare. This one was not too far from it! I dug in and started eating. As soon as I swallowed the first mouthful, I felt an uncontrollable need to eat more and more. The past few days had been horrible – I was constantly thirsty, hungry and my gums were killing me. Although I was getting used to these symptoms, they had not diminished.

Aiden was watching me devouring the meat and I noticed he was not eating.

"Aren't you hungry?"

"Not so much actually, but it looks like you are."

"I'm sorry, I did not mean to be rude. Eating has been tricky recently. Please take some."

"OK, I will have a little piece, but all the rest is for you." He took a piece while I resumed eating. After I finished the platter, I felt slightly buzzy and euphoric – it was great! Aiden was looking at me closely.

"Did you enjoy the dinner?"

"Very much! Sorry for doubting your cooking skills! I feel awesome and I am full which has been hard to achieve lately."

"That's because you didn't eat nourishing food!"

"What do you mean? Of course, I did!"

"Pizza, burgers, bread, pasta whatever, they won't fill you up!"

"I don't understand, are we here on a healthy food retreat?"

"Sorry, no, I did not mean junk food specifically. You need a new diet based on a very high protein intake."

"Why?"

"It is what you need to get better – we'll get to the why later."

"Are those half answers supposed to help me?"

"I am sorry Louise, I promise everything will make sense!"

"When?!"

"Soon. Trust me."

"You keep telling me to trust you, but don't you think I already do? I would have run away if I didn't. I am in the middle of the woods in a deserted mansion with you."

"You make a fair point! Let's take a walk outside." He didn't wait for an answer and led me out, holding my hand. Every time Aiden touched me, I shivered, and it seemed to intensify each time he did it. We walked around the house and into the woods following a little path.

"Aiden, there is so much life out here, I feel it, it is incredible!"

"You don't feel it, you mostly hear and smell it."

"I am not an animal."

"No, but your senses have changed, everything is more ... heightened."

"That's why I could hear you in front of my flat?"

"Yes."

"Aiden, what have I become?" Suddenly, I felt really miserable.

"You have the whole night to figure it out."

We kept walking in silence, and my mood kept swinging between euphoria and sadness. There was so much going on in that forest; I could hear many animals and I was really intrigued by this new awareness. However, it also upset me – it was not normal and I had no idea how it would affect me. I was changing, unable to stop it or even comprehend it yet. After a while, I felt a bit chilly; Aiden noticed right away and showed the way back to the house. It was already really late.

"Do you want to go to sleep?" he asked softly.

"No, I did not follow you here to sleep! Are you tired?"

"I was hoping you would say that! No, I usually go to bed very late or rather early morning and then sleep in. Shall we go back to the fireplace?"

"Yes." We sat together and Aiden gestured towards the empty bottle of wine. My eyes travelled to the bar and saw an X.O bottle of dark rum. He picked up on my gaze and went to get it. He brought two glasses, poured the light brown liquor and we took our first sips.

"This is delicious! Where does it come from?"

"An old trip to the Caribbean. You can't find this anywhere else."

"Aiden, how long were we together?"

"Pretty much since we met, for about seven months."

"So, we split up only a few months ago!" I said, thinking about the picture in my flat.

"Yes."

"Who broke it off?"

"I guess it would be me, kind of..."

"Why?" He kept silent. "Did you lose interest? Or did you find somebody else?"

"No..." His face was serious.

"You can tell me, you know. I don't remember any of it, so I guess it's OK." I gently took both his hands and as we touched, a new flashback struck me.

***

Aiden and I were in a square near my house, which in fact was the same one I had stopped for lunch in earlier this week, and that is probably why it felt familiar. We were facing each other and I was crying and begging:

"Aiden, you can't do this, we can fight them!"

"No, we can't! They will keep coming after us!"

"It can't be the only way!"

"It is, I have been thinking over and over and there is no choice, I will not let anything happen to you." As he finished his sentence, he put both his hands at the back of my neck and tilted up my face so our eyes met. He gave me a long lingering kiss, looked right into my eyes and said:

"Louise, I love you like I have never loved anyone; I am so sorry for what I am about to do, my heart is tearing apart. Now, close your eyes ... and forget about me – forget I ever existed, forget everything about me and my scary world. To-night, you came here by yourself to star-gaze. In five seconds, you shall open your eyes and be free of me and happy."

I did as instructed, I was under some kind of hypnosis. He kissed me one last time and when I opened my eyes, he was gone and I happily resumed gazing at the stars in the night sky.

Chapter IX

The flashback ended, leaving me speechless. This time, Aiden knew exactly what I had seen and he wouldn't look me in the eye.

"Louise, I am so sorry."

"How dare you mess with my head and take away my free will?"

"I had no choice!"

"Again, with the 'I had no choice' card – there is always a choice, even if you don't like the outcome! And what about my choice?"

"I ... I don't know what to say – at that moment, it seemed to be the best option."

"According to who?"

"Some people."

"Does that include me?" Aiden was visibly upset and did not respond, so I carried on, "you have no right to make decision for me! No right!"

I was furious and violently threw my glass of rum in the fire, which created a huge blaze. I had never been that angry before, and my rage kept growing. It started to feel exactly like the burst of fury that made me run in the middle of the night and faint in Karuna's shop. I was pacing back and forth energetically. Aiden was not impressed, he got up and walked serenely towards me.

"Please leave me alone, don't come near me! If you come any closer, I will hurt you!" I warned him, but he did not heed my threat and advanced further towards me.

"I deserve it! Look, I understand you're upset, but you don't have the whole picture yet!"

"I don't need it, I don't care!" I was almost hysterical.

"Wait, please Louise, calm down. You have to relax," he advised calmly.

"No! I don't have to do anything. I have had enough of you telling me what to do and not what I want to know! What about what you did to me after that wacky woman assaulted me! What about that?"

"I can't tell you now."

"Why? Is it because I will not like your answer or because you made a decision for me? Again!"

"If you had the whole story, you would know I did what I had to."

"Says you! What about the whole story, why don't you tell me?" He reached for my arm in an attempt to calm me down, but I pushed him away. "I am warning you, I am not joking, stay – away – from – me!"

He stared right into my eyes and tried to touch me again. I thought he was defying me, so this time, I aimed my fist at his handsome face. To my amazement, he effortlessly stopped my fist mid-air, completely immobilizing my entire arm. His strength was extraordinary, just like my night attacker. In a second, he had me against the wall and was holding both my wrists up, protecting himself from a second punch. It infuriated me even more. It was clear he didn't want to harm me, but he wouldn't let me lose my temper either. Our bodies were close against each other and my blood was boiling, but our physical closeness had also awakened a disturbing sense of desire. He held me like this until I relaxed. When our eyes met again, Aiden whispered, "See for yourself!". Then, another flashback hit me.

Part 1: Becoming

***

Aiden and I were entering a kind of citadel, which I recognised from a previous flashback. We walked through several narrow alleys – it almost felt like a maze – until we reached the entrance of the building. We opened the door and found two guards protecting another gate ahead. When they saw Aiden, they nodded and moved aside, letting us pass. They obviously knew and trusted him.

We stepped into a long dark corridor that sloped underground. I was holding Aiden's hand and felt invincible with him.

Finally, we arrived in a bare room, lit by fire torches. Aiden told me we had to wait here. After a few minutes, a young man came in and said: "Aiden, Miss Bailey, you may follow me. He is expecting you now." We complied and all this time our hands had never parted. We arrived in front of another door where the messenger knocked lightly; he opened it for us and walked away. We entered and found ourselves in quite a large office: there was a stunning antique oak desk and a seating area that looked cosy but more modern. The walls were covered with paintings, all portraits of different people. The lights were so dim, I did not realise a man was sitting at the desk. However, Aiden did; he stood still and seemed to be waiting for something. The man rose from his chair and walked towards us in a friendly manner.

"Aiden! Finally, you accepted my offer to visit!"

"Hello Robert."

"It took you long enough!"

"Well, we have been busy."

"Busy trying to ignore me!" he said with a light laugh. I remained silent. He turned towards me, examined me for a split second and carried on, "And you must be Louise, what a delight to meet you!"

"Nice to meet you Sir," I responded politely.

I walked up to him and offered a formal handshake, which he accepted. He was about 5'8 and appeared to be in his fifties. He had short black hair flecked with silver, dark eyes and his brown skin looked like silk. His stylish salt-and-pepper moustache enhanced his natural elegance while his smile revealed impeccable teeth. He spoke very clearly and had an air of authority. Aiden had briefed me not to challenge him. There was a tension in the air – this visit was not a friendly gathering and serious matters had to be discussed. Our host offered us some wine, but I noticed my glass was poured from a different carafe. He passed us the glasses and gestured to the sofa.

"So, you are the reason why dear Aiden has lost his sanity." He stopped as he noticed I was about to put my glass down on the table. "Don't worry my dear, I am not going to poison you, not my kind of game, but I believe you are aware we follow different diets." He winked at me and I took a sip as a token of my trust.

"I like her confidence!" he said looking at Aiden, who still had not moved, in fact he did not react at all. "What is it Aiden? I am trying to be pleasant, so should you, especially considering the situation."

"Louise already knows who you are. She knows everything about me." Aiden was not at ease.

"Does she now?"

"Yes, and I am fully aware you disapprove of our relationship, which is probably why you ordered me here."

"Aiden, everybody disapproves! It is bigger than me and you should know better! I won't be able to let this go on for long. At some point you will have to face your responsibilities." Although Robert was polite, I could not brush off this feeling of threat.

"I am, which is why I came here with Louise, we don't want to be fugitives."

"Well, there is only one way then, you'll have to part."

"We don't have to do anything we don't want to. We are free—" I tried to intervene.

"Excuse me for interrupting you my dear, but may I ask on whose behalf are you talking?"

"Ours."

"I think you mean yours. You see, Aiden is not free to do whatever pleases him, in fact he has duties to fulfil to our people and also to me"

"I don't understand how our relationship is affecting yours," I continued.

"In our world, there are certain laws and our existence depends on respecting them. I am sure you are familiar with such a concept."

"You can't make laws against relationships!"

"Can't you? Is that why people in gay communities cannot marry in some places or even show themselves together, or why inter-racial relationships can also be problem?"

"Yes, OK, but I will always condemn such rules!"

"Understand that it is nothing personal. We will take drastic measures if you decide to ignore us. Such interbreeding relationships are forbidden by our laws."

"These are our lives we are talking about here, you cannot control us," I insisted.

"We are not trying to control you Louise, quite frankly we have no desire to interact with you. However, Aiden belongs with us."

"What if I don't want to be part of this?" confronted Aiden.

"You cannot possibly be serious, we have survived so long because we have always stayed together and respected our laws."

"Sorry, we cannot abide by that. Louise is too important to me."

"What about your people who always had your back during all those years?"

"I love them too, but if you force me to choose, I choose Louise!"

"Aiden, you are making a terrible mistake to assume you have choices. There is only one choice. If you decide to renounce your status, you will be disowned and you know very well what will be the result of this. Don't say I didn't warn you. If you go through with it, your relationship won't stand a chance. Disrespecting your leaders will be perceived as an act of defiance and they will unleash their wrath on you, Aiden, as an example."

"I am ready."

"And you Louise, are you ready?"

"I am."

"Well, it strikes me there is something that you don't quite comprehend. As I said, we are not so much concerned about you Louise, you can very easily be dealt with. However, Aiden will pay a very high price and I can assure you both, you will never meet again." His threat first upset me and then it made me furious. I stared at him meaningfully and said:

"Sir, are you threatening us with harm?"

"My dear, I do not like the term threat, it is rather a fact."

"Robert, please, drop the diplomatic act and—" Aiden started, but was sharply interrupted by Robert.

"You will not speak to me that way Aiden. I have put up with your behaviour long enough!" His tone had changed; he was getting frustrated.

"What are you talk—"

"Do not interrupt me! Do you think I have just found out about this little exotic experiment of yours? I was about to call in on you in order to sort it out and resolve this unlawful situation at once. Unfortunately, your lack of discretion gave you away, as somebody caught you and exposed your prohibited relationship. Now, our leaders know and I can no longer protect you, it is bigger than me!"

"Louise is not an 'experiment'! And what do you mean we have been caught? Did you have us followed?"

"Of course I did not, but somebody else raised their concerns. You know this is forbidden – we cannot create relationships with them."

"Who was it?"

"I am not sure, it was an anonymous tip."

"Robert—"

"No Aiden, I tried to protect you, but my hands are tied. Out of respect for my position, they have given me the chance to get you to change your mind and split you up before they take action." I froze at this revelation.

"What do you mean, take action?" I demanded.

"My dear, I know you are aware of Aiden's physiology, but our community exists and relies on very strict rules. If we want to remain in this world, there are limitations to what we can do. We have abided by those rules for a very long time and we are not prepared to risk our existence for the sake of your forbidden romance. Nobody can know we walk this earth too – it would be a disaster, a gruesome witch hunt. Therefore, we will do anything in our power to protect ourselves. I think you can understand that."

"Anything?" I asked.

"Indeed, if you decide to continue on this road despite our warnings, we will have to take the matter into our own hands." Aiden and I exchanged a look. Robert's warning was to be taken seriously.

"It may be unfair to you both, but you have to see the bigger picture: centuries of peaceful co-existence, why would we start a war now?"

"Sir, I promise I will never put your community in danger and will never reveal any information about Aiden, you or anyone."

"It is not enough my dear. Aiden should not be mixing with your kind, it will not end well. We are not the same, we don't eat the same and we don't have the same needs or abilities. It is not personal – it is for the greater good."

"Robert, I can't live without her."

"Sir, me neither," I added.

"Well, that is not entirely true, Louise can. Aiden can help you." He glanced at Aiden who was staring at the floor anxiously. I did not understand what he meant; how could Aiden help me live without him?

"I won't!"

"Fine, we'll do it ourselves! It all depends on you Aiden, you can still fix this and that is the only thing I can do for you: give you a chance to fix this mess." We both stayed quiet, we did not know how to react. Here it was, the brutal truth, end it or be ended. I felt like a prisoner, we could not look at each other – our hearts were breaking.

***

I opened my eyes; Aiden's face was only a few centimetres from mine. He had finally released my arms and was staring at the floor. He took a step back and said:

"It was not my choice either." I did not respond, I was speechless. "Louise, forgive me, I just couldn't stand the idea of them making us disappear, like we never existed. At least, in this scenario, I could say goodbye, even if it meant staying away from you."

"I understand," I said, still processing what I had just witnessed. I walked back to the sofa, sat down and took a sip of the rum in Aiden's glass. I wasn't sure how to react to this latest revelation and needed to regroup my thoughts.

Chapter X

We remained silent for a while, then Aiden, anxious to discuss the flashback with me, softly took my hand and asked:

"Louise, are you OK?"

"I'm not sure ... this is surreal."

"I know. What can I do to make it easier?"

"Just let me process this. I am going to get some fresh air." I let go of his hand, got up, took my jacket and walked out.

It was a beautiful night with no clouds and thousands of stars. The temperature was neither hot nor cold but to be honest, I could not really feel anything. For the first time since I became ill, the night felt welcoming and safe. As I walked on the lawn, I could hear the blades of grass bending under my shoes. I was totally aware of everything around me, although I could not see much. Again, I could hear numerous animals roaming or hunting.

This situation was bizarre, but I had to keep my cool if I wanted to discover more. I breathed in and breathed out half a dozen times and managed to convince myself I was going to be fine. I was looking at the illuminated night sky, trying to make sense of all the information that I had gathered these past few days.

According to what I had seen and felt, it was obvious Aiden and I were deeply in love, but why couldn't we be together? And what did Robert mean by saying that Aiden could not mix with 'my kind'? What was he then? Apparently, I used to feel perfectly fine with the 'kind' of person he was, so, why would it be a problem now? He obviously had some sort of psychic abilities like hypnosis: he was able to feel me, read me, make me see things and always knew when to comfort me. He did say we were connected, but how? If we had been together for more than half a year, how could we have managed this without Naomi knowing I was in a relationship? There was no hiding from that girl!

Was I going crazy? Maybe I was already in a psychiatric hospital and was just hallucinating before or after my treatments. Or, perhaps I had never come down from an old LSD trip and was still high as a kite? Or, he was the lunatic, trying to take me down with him in his world of despair!

I was lost and didn't know what to do. I remembered Aiden telling me not to fight my mind and let it do the work, but honestly, I wasn't sure I was ready to face the rest – there was already a lot to take in. However, he was right: accepting the truth – no matter how messed up it was – would allow me to understand, move on and live with it. At least, I wasn't alone; Aiden was here and it seemed like he was not going anywhere. I knew that, because I could feel certain sincere things, like his compassion and good will, as well as his love and devotion. On my side, it was very strange: although I knew I was in love with him, I couldn't really feel it yet. My attraction for him was undeniable, and sometimes I felt some spark of arousal, but it was not completely clear. It probably did not help that I had just found out my feelings for him – it was still pretty fresh.

Seven months erased... I wondered what had happened... I could not wait for the next memories to fill the blanks. I was curious, how had Aiden spent his time since we broke up? He said we were connected, so surely I could sense what he felt – but how? I had no idea how to proceed. I sat on a rock, fixing my eyes on the sky, trying to empty my mind and focusing on Aiden. I could easily picture his face. I was usually considered very empathetic, so I thought concentrating solely on him might help me.

"It doesn't work like that!" I jumped at the sound of Aiden's voice and was embarrassed that he knew what I was up to. I stayed silent and he continued, "Moreover, if you want to know how I feel, you can ask me, I can't wait to tell you!"

"Sorry."

"I don't mind, I have no secrets from you, but it is too early for you to manage this on your own. Plus, it does not work long distance, you need some kind of contact. Soon, I'll teach you."

"Are you saying that at some point I will be able to feel you, as much as you do me?"

"Yes, even more, a shared bond is incredible! Look Louise, I know this is a lot to take in and you must be fairly freaked out. Nevertheless, I am on your side and I am just trying to make sure your transition occurs in the best possible way and more importantly, on your terms."

"Transition???" I stared at him with concern.

"Yes, well, let's call it adaptation if you prefer."

"Am I to expect further upheaval?"

"What do you think?"

"I don't know what to think. I am very confused. I have tons of questions popping into my head every minute!"

"How did you feel when you were back in London?"

"Awful – hungry, thirsty, sometimes in pain, weird blood incidents and I had trouble sleeping, which is very unlike me."

"And how do you feel tonight?"

"Actually physically, I am good – satiated, hydrated, pain-less, blood incident free and rested."

"Why do you think that is?"

"I don't know. Why don't you tell me?"

"Your body is changing and you are going to function dif-ferently. One example is your new diet, as I told you, the old one is no longer suited to your needs." He came closer to me and looked me straight in the eyes, as if he was inviting me into his mind. He gently held my hands and I closed my eyes.

***

We travelled to one of Aiden's memories. This time, it was personal, from his point of view only. I was not there, but I could read Aiden's thoughts as if they were my own. The scene was taking place in some sort of warehouse, where Aiden and another man were in the middle of a confrontation.

"Was it you? Did you give us up?"

"What do you think?" the man replied maliciously.

"Tell me the truth, I don't have time for your games." He was smiling cruelly, enjoying the situation, "stop it, why did you do it?" I persisted.

"It is not permitted, as simple as that! Why should you, Aiden the good boy, be allowed?"

"Spare me please, it is none of your business anyway. What is your agenda here?"

"Well, let's say that now you won't be in my way..."

"What are you even talking about?! Do you realise you have put people at risk?"

"I am not responsible for that Aiden, you did that all on your own!"

"What is your issue with me Kyle? Why don't you deal with me and only me?"

"That, Aiden, would not be as much fun! Actually, I thought they let you get off too easily, as she was allowed to live after all!"

"That's enough! You are so miserable and bitter."

"Let's see what the future holds for you! You might just find yourself as miserable and bitter. Who knows?!"

I left, I did not have time for Kyle's sheer foolishness and jealousy. Ever since he was denied a position on our rulers' council, Kyle had changed. We saw him less and less and he seemed to have lost interest in our cause. His attitude tonight was odd – our conversation did not make much sense, but I could perceive the hatred in his eyes and the cruelty in his voice. I did not enjoy this encounter at all and left, went back to my car and drove to Louise's.

My heart was already broken since I had to leave her, but I was relieved to see her carrying on with her life and be her usual happy self. I was never far away from her and I could never let her go completely. I had to make sure she was safe. I arrived, parked near her house and got out of the car.

The lights in her flat were off. I was trying to figure out if she was home, when I heard her approaching. I recognised her walk, then I caught her scent. I was waiting by my car, I just wanted to watch her get home safely. I was listening and detailing her movements in my mind, waiting for her to appear.

Out of the blue, she stopped and it sounded like she was helping someone in distress. Suddenly, I heard her falling to the ground and letting out a scream. This was not good and I started running towards her. As I arrived at the corner, I saw her laying on the ground between two cars. I was so worried and scared.

By the time I got to her, Louise was already losing consciousness. I just had time to snap her attacker's neck so Louise's arm was released, but it was too late. I tried, I told her not to close her eyes, I begged her to stay awake, to look at me, but she didn't! I could not let her go! I only had a few seconds to think! In the distance, I could hear a police siren, so, I quickly hid the assailant's body in the nearby bushes, before I ran up to Louise's flat and put her in bed. I bit my wrist hard, took it to her mouth and made her swallow some of my blood while I delicately sucked some of hers from her wound. I had done the unimaginable – I took death away from her. She was soon to be part of my world. At the crack of dawn when I could no longer stay, I whispered in her ear, "Forgive me" and left her.

***

When I opened my eyes, I was outside, still under the stars, still holding Aiden's hands. I was back in the real world, or at least what I thought the real world to be. He was so sorry, devastated and said again "please forgive me". I was sad, but could not imagine what I would have done had I been in his place. We went back inside and poured two glasses of rum, sitting next to the fire. Aiden was apprehensive, waiting for me to react.

"Aiden, when that woman attacked me, I died didn't I?"

"Yes, you did."

"Why am I still here then?"

"You were sort of reborn. It is still you, but you are different now."

"Different like you?"

"Yes, like me."

"Who was that woman?"

"Like us I am afraid."

"Who is this Kyle guy? How do you know each other?"

"We have the same Maker, Robert. Kyle wasn't always like that you know."

"Maker?"

"Yes, let's say my transition guide. Louise, I am so sorry we intruded in your life."

"So, was Kyle the 'somebody' who told your people about us?"

"That's what I think."

"Why?"

"My guess is to undermine me and ruin my reputation."

"I see. Do you think Robert ordered my murder?"

"Definitely not Robert. It is not his style – he is a diplomat. I don't think he had a clue. Kyle, however, may have gone rogue, and at worst he might try to make this look like he did it for the well-being of our community."

"So, you think Kyle is behind my death?"

"I think so, but I cannot prove it yet."

"But are you allowed to make your own decisions when it comes to murder?"

"Definitely not, but this is politics and he is very smart at manipulating people."

"Aiden, what are we?"

"We are people of the night. You know what we are, it is just too surreal for you to say it now, but it is important that it comes from you. Only then, you will be able to do the last transition phase."

"Am I still transitioning now?"

"Yes, bit by bit, can't you feel it?"

"Sometimes. When I went outside, I was even more conscious of the wildlife around me than when we arrived."

"Your senses will keep heightening for a while. It is actually a beautiful skill to have and you will experience amazing sensations."

I was still deep in thought when I heard my phone ring. I snapped out of it and looked at the time on the clock above the fireplace, it was past 3am. It could only be one person: Naomi. Of course she was worried, probably imagining I was being cut into small pieces in my fabricated clients' basement! Considering what was really going on, she wasn't too far from the truth. I did not know what to do. Indeed, I had to talk to her but to tell her what? I did not want to lie to her again, even though it was simply impossible to reveal the truth. I had to be smart. I understood then why Aiden wanted me to stay more than a day here. I still had a lot to work on. Was I ready to go back to my life as if nothing had changed? Actually, what about my life? How was it going to work now? I shivered. My mind was racing and I started to feel overwhelmed and hot, until I heard his voice:

"Louise, calm down, breathe... I am here and we have time to figure it all out. I promise we will, I won't let you down." I turned to him; his voice was soothing, but the sight of him was even better. It took me a minute to get a hold of myself and decide how to deal with Naomi.

"Aiden, I need to call or text Naomi – I have to let her know I am fine."

"OK, sure."

"But what should I tell her? By the way, how did Naomi handle our relationship? Did you erase her memory too?"

"Naomi was never a problem for us – we found a way to explain our relationship so she knew you were involved with someone. However, as soon as I removed myself from your life, I had to do the same to her. I am sorry."

"It makes sense I guess, remove all ties…"

"Yes," he murmured full of remorse.

"But actually, Naomi said she saw you last Saturday, when we were about to go into the club."

"Yes, but in her eyes, I was just another random person in a group of clubbers. Maybe she realised I was looking at you, which I was."

"Of course she did, Naomi is always alert when it comes to hooking up! Anyway, I need to be able to talk to her and find an excuse not to attend her party tomorrow night. She will be disappointed."

"You want to stay here with me then?" he asked with a shy smile.

"Yes, I do. We still have so much to explore."

For the first time since he had come back into my life, I saw what Aiden looked like when he was happy. We agreed on a believable story to tell Naomi: I was going to call her back and tell her that my clients had invited me for dinner, and that the evening went on for a long time before I got back to my hotel and passed out on my bed, slightly drunk. Ironically, this was totally feasible! As for tomorrow's party, I would tell her that I had to meet with another couple, friends of my clients, who were also interested to work with me on several pieces of furniture. I was going to say the meeting was planned for

7.30pm and as I was still tired, I would stay one more night at the hotel, which I found really relaxing.

As soon as I was ready to tell my story, I called Naomi back. Lying was once again my only option. I apologised for not calling her before and explained to her my fictitious situation. She said she understood and all was sorted, at least until Saturday. I had to come back to my life sooner rather than later. Naomi was not an idiot – I would not fool her for too long and was reluctant to do so anyway. While I spoke with her, Aiden went out to get logs and fed the fire. When I hung up, I looked towards him; he was sat down, smiling, waiting for me to join him.

Chapter XI

The last flashback had not only shown me what had happened on Aiden's side of events that night, but it had also revealed how he felt about me. Watching me die had ripped his heart out and broken his will to live. He blamed himself for selfishly not letting me go, but his determination to have me alive, no matter what the cost, was stronger. Evidently, he wanted me to know that. So much had happened over the course of the last few days, it was very disconcerting. However, one thing remained clear, I could not be more certain of our feelings for each other. We had obviously been through some serious stuff together, both good and bad. Fortunately for me, I couldn't fully remember the hard times yet, except for the day he had removed himself from my life. Aiden, on the other hand, had to live with all of that and be responsible for both our lives.

"Aiden, how are you?" I asked after a long silence.

"I ... am OK I guess."

"I mean, this could not have been easy on you."

"It most definitely has not, but don't worry about me."

"I don't worry, I am just sorry for what you had to endure all by yourself: decisions you had to make and not easy ones – the life-or-death kind; as well as jeopardising your community and being given a terrible ultimatum."

"Louise, this wasn't the hardest," he paused, full of emotion and continued, "nothing compares to that last moment we shared: one second, you knew me and the next you had no idea who I was, like I had never existed in your life. Letting you go was the hardest thing I've had to do in my whole life. The second was to make you into something you might not want to become..." He looked at me, waiting for some kind of approval.

"Listen, there are still many things I don't know, but for sure I wasn't ready to leave this world yet. I need to thoroughly understand what me being here precisely means and how my life is going to change, before I thank you," I said jokingly to lighten the mood and he chuckled. The sound of his laugh was familiar and warm.

"Louise, you should be prepared to face choices of your own too, very soon," he said on a more sombre tone.

"Do you mean how I am going to live my new life?"

"Well, first and foremost, do you want to commit to this new life? And if so, are you ready to accept the changes that come with it?"

"What do you mean? Is there even an option not to accept this life? And what other changes are we talking about?"

"Yes, you can still decide to live or ... die." I stared at him, speechless, unsure of what he meant. "As for the changes, we are nocturnal beings, so your day-time job for example, will not be an option. Your life as you knew it will be over and the hardest thing for you will be—"

"Naomi!" I cut in.

"Yes."

"I don't want to lose her. Just the thought of it is unbearable."

"I know, I want you to understand exactly the outcomes of your decision. Louise, I promise, we will make the best out of this situation and we will do our best to keep Naomi in your life – just maybe not exactly as it used to be."

"I cannot and will not lose her – we are like sisters. She is everything that I have left in this life or the previous one, and without her I would not be who I am and vice versa."

"I know very well how much you mean to each other and I will do everything in my power for you to keep this relationship."

"Really? Do you think we can work around it?"

"I am hoping so, but it won't be as it used to be."

"I am ready to compromise if she is still a part of my life. Thanks for being so honest with me."

"I want you to be prepared when the time comes."

"You didn't have this chance, did you?"

"Not really, but it was a tougher time and you don't deserve that – you don't deserve any of this."

I reached for his hands. I felt a passionate warmth running through me and I wanted to be close to him. My heart was beating faster and I couldn't stop staring at him. After a minute, I realised he probably knew everything that was going on in my body or mind and I was slightly embarrassed, I blushed. He smiled and gently squeezed my hand as if he wanted to reassure me.

It had been a stressful night and I was exhausted. I told Aiden I wanted to call it a day and go to sleep. He accompanied me to my room. At the door, Aiden gave me a comforting look and I opened the door. Then, he gently touched my shoulder – my whole body shivered and my arms showed goosebumps. He hesitantly took me in his arms and I hugged him back. He held me tight and I did not want to let go of him. He brought his mouth to my ear and whispered "I missed you". The sensation of his almost non-existent breath on my skin was thrilling. We let go of each other and said goodnight. I walked in the room and closed the door. Still confused by our embrace, I did not immediately notice there was a welcoming fire burning in the hearth; I guessed Aiden must have taken care of it at some point. I was so tired, I went straight to the bed and climbed under the sheets. I fell asleep hypnotised by the dancing flames of the fire.

***

I was in yet another time and place. It was the beginning of the evening, the sun had just set. I was sitting on a bench, apparently waiting for someone. I was very happy and excited. A tall man came and sat next to me – it was Aiden – but his body language was distant and he would not look at me. I put my hand on his and asked what was wrong. He gently removed it and took a deep breath.

"Louise, I am sorry but we have to stop seeing each other."

"What? Why? What's happened?"

"I am sorry, this went too far already and I shouldn't have let myself get carried away."

"I don't understand, what has changed?"

"Reality caught up with me."

"What are you talking about Aiden?"

"We cannot be together."

"Why is that?"

"We are not suited to each other."

"What do you mean? I thought you wanted this relationship."

"I did, but it was a mistake. I cannot go further, it's over."

"Was I a game for you? Don't you care about me?"

"No, please don't think for a minute that I wasn't truthful with you."

"So, you just decided this morning that you had enough of me."

"I can never have enough of you, I just cannot have you."

"Aiden, you don't make any sense – do you want us to be together or not?"

"It doesn't matter what I want."

"And what about what I want, does that matter to you?"

"It's not that…"

"I don't want us to stop seeing each other, I … lo… like being around you."

"So do I, but we cannot carry on, I should have never pursued you in the first place."

"Well, yeah, you should have at least said you wanted to keep it casual."

"It wasn't that ... I ... I did fall ... for you, almost instantly actually, but it was not reasonable to ignore my limitations."

"Who cares about being reasonable? Life has to be lived! Look Aiden, I don't understand where all of this is coming from, but obviously something is eating you up, what is it? Are you hiding something?"

"I am sorry Louise. It's over."

Aiden got up and left me – alone and confused. What had just happened? I had met Aiden in a botanical garden almost two months ago. As soon as we met, something I cannot describe happened: I was fascinated by him and within a few days we were completely infatuated with each other. He was so gentle, kind, smart and thoughtful, selfless, funny and truly handsome. He was very observant and would always know what to do or say. I had never met anyone like him. The more time I spent with him, the more I wanted to be with him. Although I was able to control myself and not behave like a possessive girlfriend, when I was with him I lost complete track of time and felt so fulfilled. He seemed to feel the same – his eyes were always focused on me and he was always attentive.

I just did not understand where this sudden change of heart was coming from. In truth, our relationship was special, very different from anything I had experienced before. We seemed to connect on every level and the physical attraction between us was powerful, but Aiden was not ready to go further. We had been taking it slow, and by that, I mean extremely slow. He told me he needed time to get to know me. I thought that was strange at first, but also so unusual and intimate that I went with it. Sometimes, just looking at each other was so profound that it felt like a tantric experience.

Following the initial shock-wave, I felt devastated. But after replaying the break-up scene in my head, I was more upset and outraged. How could he treat me like this? I didn't even get a proper explanation, only a very muddled conversation. Obviously, he was hiding things from me, which realistically was fair as I had only met him a couple of months ago. But why couldn't he tell me why he wanted to end our relationship?

I had noticed on a few occasions, certain strange facts: for example, he was never ever available to have lunch, even on the week-ends; also he didn't eat much, yet he was very athletic. His job seemed very vague: from what I gathered, he was a consultant for a company operating all over the world and sometimes he would disappear for a few days. He never spoke of his family. Aiden was a sort of mystery man. I was trying to connect the dots; I could never bear not to understand people's reactions. The more I reflected, the more I was compelled to find out the truth. I went home and couldn't shake the feeling that something else was going on.

That night, I was so agitated, I couldn't find the peace of mind I needed to fall asleep. I kept replaying my last moment with Aiden. What did he mean by this has gone "too far already"? It had gone literally nowhere! Maybe he thought we were getting too attached ... but what was the point to getting to know each other then? Also, who says when breaking up with someone "I can never have enough of you"? Plus, why did he say it was not reasonable of him "to ignore his limitations"? What was he talking about? I felt I was drowning with hundreds of questions.

I remembered Aiden liked taking me to different places: on our first date, he took me to his friend's secret botanical lab; then, we had gone to his family home in the country. He told me that he enjoyed going there when he needed to regroup and recharge. I also knew he had a flat in the centre of London, but I had never been there so I was looking for a needle in a haystack. However, I more or less knew how to get to the family mansion. I tried to retrace the way there in my head. I have always had an excellent sense of direction, plus I did pay attention to the road last time he drove there. A plan emerged in my mind: tomorrow I was going to rent a car and try to get to the mansion. With any luck, Aiden would be there and I could talk to him, or if he wasn't, I would probably be able to find some clues. The plan put my mind at ease and I went to sleep.

The following morning, I woke up motivated and ready to investigate. When I tried to book the car rental, nothing was available before 2.30pm. By 2.45, I was behind the wheel, leaving London and driving towards Kent. It took me some time to get there – I had to drive slowly to find my way and spot the signs for the towns and villages. Finally, I saw a familiar feature: I recognised the huge oak trees that had stood for many years. I turned left and drove down a narrow and meandering road crossing a number of fields. Despite the cloudy weather, the scenery was stunning in the day time, as last we came, it was night so I couldn't see it. Eventually, the road straightened and I arrived at a crossroads. Instinctively, I went right and shortly after ended up on a private road surrounded by trees. At the end, was the entrance to a property; I slowed down and could see a magnificent mansion ahead. I decided to park the car a few metres away and explore by foot.

I took my phone, locked the car and made my way towards the house. I recognised the gate, so I was in the right place. It was a very bizarre feeling to spy on Aiden and I didn't like the sensation, but my curiosity and determination to understand everything was much stronger.

I climbed over the fence and headed to the mansion; all the curtains were closed on the first floor but not on the ground floor. When I reached the front door, I found myself not knowing whether I should knock or not. I looked around, there was no sign of a car; however, it could simply be in the garage. I took a deep breath and knocked on the door. There was nothing but silence and the sound of my heart pounding. Impulsively, my hand reached for the door knob and turned it, but it was locked. Disappointed, I decided to circle the house – maybe I would find some kind of entrance or let's call it what it is was: a weak spot to break-in. At this point, I was led by my need to find out the truth. One by one, I tried to open the windows, until luckily, I found one that was not locked and that I could lift up. I looked inside for a few minutes in case somebody was there. I did not want to find myself in a very awkward situation and end up face to face with Aiden – or anyone else for that matter – and having to justify my presence here.

When I judged it was safe to get in, I hopped onto the windowsill and climbed in very quietly. I tried to stay really focused and overcome the incoming adrenalin rush. I started by observing my surroundings: I was in the living room with a majestic fireplace. I knew this place – we had definitely been here.

I noticed glowing embers in the ashes of what had been a fire. The idea that someone – hopefully Aiden – had been here earlier and that I could get caught at any moment, was a little unsettling. It became even weirder when I realised there was an empty glass of what seemed to be red wine on the table – somebody had clearly been here recently. Out of curiosity, I went to smell the wine glass, it was after all my speciality. Oddly enough, it didn't smell like any grape variety I knew, but rather it had a metallic tang and the consistency looked much thicker than usual, which made me feel uneasy.

I continued on to the next room, a large kitchen: it was impeccably tidy, not a stain nor any mess. Instinctively, I went to the fridge, opened the door and could not believe what I saw – I was aghast. There was about a dozen blood bags carefully stacked up. I was horrified; was it blood in the glass? I went straight to the rubbish bin and opened it to find an empty blood bag. I picked it up – it had been precisely cut. I smelt the hole and recognised the exact same metallic odour that I had smelt a few minutes ago in the wine glass. I was completely freaked out and disgusted. Why was Aiden, or anyone, drinking blood? Was he ill and trying some kind of experimental blood treatment? Or maybe he was part of some kind of cult like a satanic secret coven? The thought of these theories frightened me and if the second one turned out to be true, I was probably in serious danger. How could I not see that? I could not get my head around it. Even though he was a bit of a mystery man – I liked that in him, it usually took me some time to open up too – he definitely did not strike me as a psychopath in the literal sense. There had to be another explanation, a less dreadful one.

My phone vibrated and cut through my thoughts. I decided to ignore the call, but the time on the screen got my attention: it was almost 6pm and very soon the sun would be setting. The idea of being in this bloody house – literally – at night made me feel like I was in a horror film, but I couldn't leave quite yet. The damage had been done; I was now looking for more information, something that would reassure me. There were a lot of paintings on the living-room walls. Many different scenes of war, love, hunting, battleships and a few portraits that I did not recall seeing on my previous visits. Some of the faces were very similar to Aiden, presumably his ancestors. One picture particularly stood out: it portrayed a tall handsome man with his splendid black horse. I loved horses, they were my favourite animals along with dogs and my first love as a child.

I was drawn to the portrait and studied the face of the man. He looked exactly like Aiden but from another time, probably the nineteenth century considering his clothes: he was wearing a long tailed dark blue coat, straight dark grey trousers, a white waistcoat and a high stiff collar. A classic top hat polished off his impeccable style and he had a well-groomed moustache. I went closer to the painting to analyse it further when I suddenly heard my name; I jumped as I turned around.

"Louise! What are you doing here?" Aiden was in front of me, looking very surprised and uncomfortable. His eyes travelled to the glass on the table and awkwardly came back to me. He was definitely not expecting to find me here and was not ready for this impromptu encounter. I was not very proud of myself; I had invaded his privacy and had surely crossed a few boundaries.

"Aiden, I'm sorry, I ... I ... had to understand! You left me with so many questions."

"And? Did you find your answers?" He was quite rightly irritated. It was the first time I had seen him like this.

"I hope not..."

"What do you mean?"

"I just have more questions." He didn't respond so I carried on softly, "Are you sick?"

"No." He was not going to make this easy.

"Are ... you into spiritual stuff?" I inquired apprehensively.

He lifted one eyebrow. "Not really," he replied, uncertain of what I meant.

"OK, look, I am here now and I understand you weren't expecting me, but think about it this way: the sooner you tell me the truth, the faster I'll leave. Plus, for future reference, if you want to be left alone, you should avoid mixed messages when breaking-up with someone." I was slightly annoyed at his lack of cooperation. His attitude challenged my patience, so I decided to change my strategy and opt for a more straight-forward approach. "Aiden, is that your glass on the table?" I gestured towards it.

"Yes, it is."

"Why are you drinking blood? Are you part of a satanic cult?" As it came out of my mouth, I realised it sounded completely insane, but the situation was so peculiar that everything had to be considered. He frowned but also looked slightly amused by my theory. "Ah! You think this is funny, great!" I carried on.

"Sorry, I just somehow never expected anyone to ask me such a question, particularly you!"

"Frankly Aiden, I wish I did not have to go through all this questioning and confusion. I wish you would have the decency to be honest with me, but I am glad that at least I entertain you!" I started to get really annoyed with him. I stared at him severely and he could not look at me. I paid attention to the portraits in the background and all of sudden I thought, what if these ancestors were in fact him but at different times? I decided to pursue this theory and asked: "Is it you in the paintings?" He looked at the diverse pictures and sighed as if he had resolved himself to surrender.

"Yes..."

"Are we dealing with something bizarre here?"

"Inconceivable would be more accurate."

I paused my interrogation and took a minute to think. I analysed all the elements I knew: only evening dates; time traveller; blood drinker... No... This was impossible and I was probably going insane just thinking about it, although it did make sense. I have always considered myself as Cartesian – I believe in facts. The expression of my face must have shown turmoil as my thoughts developed, and Aiden picked up on it. He did not move and seemed to be waiting for me to proceed with the inevitable conclusion. I took a deep breath and finally managed to use words I never thought I would put together, except at a Halloween party:

"Aiden, are you ... are you a ... a ... vampire?" I stuttered unsure of how such a question should be worded.

"This would be how your society folklore named my kind, but yes I am." I was in shock and remained stunned for a few minutes. Aiden walked slowly towards me and I backed off, so he stopped and said, "I am not going to harm you, I never have and never will. I guess it is my turn to talk now."

Chapter XII

I was unable to move or say anything. Aiden's last words were still echoing in my head. Was he insane or was I? How could this be real? Wouldn't the world know if vampires were a part of it? I just couldn't see how it would be possible to hide such a thing these days, especially with the internet and social media allowing people to share anything and everything. Perhaps Aiden was mentally ill. I wasn't sure which was the most disturbing: option one – Aiden is a vampire, or option two – Aiden thinks he is a vampire. If it was true, I was definitely in danger of being served up for dinner. But even if it wasn't, I was probably not safe all alone with a nutcase in the middle of nowhere. He looked at me tenderly and began to talk:

"Louise, I imagine this must be disconcerting and extremely frightening, but like I said – I will never hurt you." I realised that if he wanted to hurt me, he probably would have already done so, unless he was a very cruel sadist. I looked again at the paintings in the room: Aiden was pictured in different set ups, places and times; sometimes with other people.

"As you can see, I have been part of this world for a little while, and lived several lives," he paused, "I sound completely insane!" he said shaking his head.

"You do..." I replied, stepping back warily. This turn of events was so surreal, I did not recognise the Aiden I had met only a little while ago. The thought of running away crossed my mind – if he was a vampire, I would not make it very far; however, if he was a lunatic, I had a chance to escape!

"I know you must be afraid and shaken up, but if you just open your mind to the impossible and let me tell you my story, you will get the answers you came looking for."

"If I wanted to leave, would you let me?" He looked at me slightly disappointed, as if now he had the opportunity to reveal his truth, but would not be allowed.

"It's fine, I am not holding you here, you can go... However, please acknowledge the fact that by the time you reach home, you will have hundreds more questions, which you could get the answers to right now." He was completely right and how clever of him to use my own obsessive mind against me! As much as I wanted to get out of here, I had to admit he had seen right through me. I would indeed be a complete mess if I gave up now and left when I was about to get my answers.

"OK! But you stay over there and don't come any closer!"

"As you wish!"

I could see that Aiden was slightly amused by my caution. He was probably not used to seeing me like this. I wasn't usually a play it safe type of person, but right now I knew very well I was not in control. I had put myself in a very unpredictable situation that could go wrong at any point. In spite of myself, I could not resist hearing Aiden out and hopefully discovering his true self. Aiden sat down on a leather armchair and looked at me, indicating he was about to start his tale:

"My father was an intelligent English man with many talents: trading; negotiating; exploring; city planning, amongst other things. At one point, he stayed for a year in Calcutta and got romantically involved with a local woman, her name was Jaya. Soon after, she got pregnant and nine months later I was born – this was in 1841. Unfortunately, my mother did not survive childbirth. My father was devastated, but had sworn to her that he would provide for me and take me back to England, which he did a few weeks later.

My father travelled a lot – he was always being sent to different places mostly in England and Europe, but sometimes he would take on missions to the other side of the world. He loved sailing, exploring and encountering new cultures. In that sense, I was raised in a relatively relaxed way and I did not follow the traditional Victorian upbringing. My father took me along on all his trips and he hired a teacher who travelled with us and schooled me.

When we weren't abroad, we lived in Richmond, on the edge of London. My father was involved in the construction of Kew Gardens: in the early 1850's, he participated extensively in the conception of the Herbarium, which today holds millions of botanical specimens from all over the planet. Whenever I feel nostalgic, I like to stroll in botanical gardens and have visited many around the world. Last time I went to one, I met you.

If we were travelling or if we were at home, my teacher, Philip, stayed with us. My education was very advanced and our unsettled lifestyle didn't allow me to follow the customary school curriculum. But frankly, it was not a problem, as I was learning so much by my father's side. I grew up in different places, so I developed a good ear for languages and by the age of fifteen I was proficient in Latin, Greek, Hebrew, French, Spanish, Portuguese, Italian, German, Arabic and Cantonese. I wanted to be an explorer; as like my father I loved discovering new places and people, so we focused my studies in history, geography, natural sciences, technology and of course languages.

My father was taking me to every important professional and social gathering he attended. He was preparing me to take over from him, but I wanted to explore the world at my own pace and spend as much time in new places as I could. I did not want to go anywhere on behalf of someone – I wanted to choose my own destiny. My father was aware of my ambition, but he still wanted to introduce me to all the high profile people he knew. By then, although I was not aware of it, he knew he was ill and would not be able to take care of me for much longer. Three years later, he passed away. I was alone in the world, except for my great teacher Philip, always by my side.

We decided to start a world expedition, beginning in the West Indies. We travelled for a good ten years, regularly sending scientific reports to the Universities of Oxford and Cambridge, as well as the British Museum. When we eventually returned to London, we found it a changed city from the one we had left – or perhaps we were changed men – and couldn't wait to leave for another expedition.

One night, after celebrating our new departure date, we left the pub rather intoxicated. We took a few wrong turns and ended up in a backstreet alley. We realised we were not in a safe place and we tried to head back. Unfortunately, a group of hostile men had already surrounded us and were closing in. They ordered us to give up all our valuables. I was wearing my father's family ring and it was out of question to lose it, so, while Philip was trying to keep them calm, I tried to hide the ring. One of the men saw me and snatched it out of my hand. The atmosphere turned ugly and I just had time to give an apologetic look to Philip before they had him thrown against the wall, knocking him out. The others jumped on me and I felt excruciating pain in my chest and back. I fell onto the filthy paved street, when suddenly, somebody arrived and fought them off until they all ran away.

I looked for Philip – the poor man was unconscious but still breathing. I, was not so well: I was covered in my own blood and found it really hard to breathe and not to fall asleep. Our rescuer came towards me and leant over my dying body. I dimly heard the words he spoke to me – he said he had been watching me since I was fifteen and had bigger plans for me, but I had to do something strange to get there. I nodded. I knew I was dying; I could feel my body shutting down and was starting to lose consciousness. I just had enough strength to mumble Philip's name. The stranger hastily glanced at him before returning his attention to me. He bit his own wrist until he bled and placed it into my mouth; he then grabbed my arm and I felt a light prick before he drank my blood. As I was drifting away, a metallic taste developed in my mouth, then all turned black."

Aiden paused his narrative and looked at me. I was completely hooked by his story and was thinking that if he was a lunatic, then he was a hell of a creative one! The more I listened to him, the more I was inclined to believe he was telling the truth. Instinctively, I went and sat on the sofa next to the armchair, but still with a bit of distance between us. Aiden smiled and carried on:

"That night, I died and was reborn. I was no longer part of the Human world and was about to start a new life. The stranger who saved me was Robert, he is my 'Maker'. He was kind enough to help Philip too, and I am thankful he did. I mean, I would have been devastated if Philip had died just because I did not want to lose my family ring. Like he said, Robert had been following the course of my life, so he knew how much Philip meant to me. Robert hypnotised him and made him think that we had decided to part and go on our own adventures. Robert told him to return to whoever was special to him: the following day, Philip was on a vessel to South America, where he had fallen in love a few years previously. At least, he got a happy ending. For me however, it was hard to accept my fate once I understood exactly what it entailed, but eventually I came around and decided to make the most of it.

Vampires, as you call us, have been around for a very long time and we have learnt to live within society. For that, our true identities have to remain hidden. Therefore, we do not have personal relationships with Humans – what you and I have been doing is completely forbidden by our laws. Our community works according to a well-defined scheme – each member is of service, or has a particular skill which makes us powerful and self-sufficient. The main reason Robert had already chosen me, was because of my ability to speak many languages and travel around the world. By the time I died, I was thirty and had learnt lots more foreign languages and dialects.

Even though we live secretly, we still share the same world: we run corporations, we arrange deals, we attend social events, we travel and so on... But no Human can ever know our kind exists, therefore every interaction is controlled and minimised. Back in the early days, we had no choice but to feed on animals and occasionally on Humans, but even then, we only picked the worst of the worst scum. Nowadays, we have found new ways to feed without having to harm Humans or animals – the blood is supplied willingly or naturally: we have created blood banks, where people can sell their own blood and we also own corpse disposal companies. We are basically a minority people with our own economy."

He paused again; I thought he was giving me time to take in this incredible information. I was still speechless – I could not believe Aiden was a vampire. Just the thought of it did not feel healthy. I had always been fascinated by fantasy worlds, and it was exciting to know the world had more to offer, but also frightening to think vampires were actually real. His version of vampirism was quite different from the famous Count Dracula and the old folklores of the undead coming back to eat us – it was comforting to know he did not see me as a snack! After a minute of silence, I realised Aiden had finished his story and was waiting for me to react.

"So, you don't kill people?"

"Not any longer."

"What changed? How did it start? Who was the first vampire and how did he become one in the first place?" Suddenly, I was full of questions.

"First, we don't call ourselves vampires but rather Kindreds. As for the rest, I cannot go into too much detail."

"You said you would tell me the truth."

"The truth about me and how it relates to you, which I am doing. I am not at liberty to reveal all the details of our history, but I am prepared to give you some sort of summary with the main events. But Louise, this is top secret. I trust you, but you can never repeat this to anyone, not Naomi and specifically not to my people should you meet one, I would be considered a traitor."

"I promise I will not say a word to anyone!" I understood how much it had cost him to be honest with me, it was much bigger than just us and involved many other lives.

"A long time ago, a battle resulted in the long and painful death of an army general. The alignment of several unpredictable factors caused his rise from the dead as the first Kindred. He came back savage, strong, fast and thirsty for blood. For a while, he went on a killing spree and 'turned' other people into the same monster that he had become. Eventually, he was destroyed by his very own undead victims, who started a new order – they understood that they would always be hunted if they did not change and decided to re-imagine their way of life. They slowly disappeared from mainstream life and stories about them became legends and myths. In the meantime, they defined their ideology of a world where the Kindreds could exist and be harmless to others. They initiated our first code of conduct, laws and rules. Over the centuries, we evolved and became what we are today: organised, disciplined and self-sufficient on every level."

"That is amazing! But, I am curious, how could you fly under the radar for so long?"

"We simply don't bring attention to ourselves."

"And you really don't kill anyone?"

"Yes, that kind of guarantees that nobody pays any attention to us – a very good incentive that was used by Ordinem to convince their comrades."

"Ordinem?"

"Oh, sorry, that was the name of the first circle of Kindreds who set up our community. We kept that name and today, it defines our Council of leaders."

"This is unreal Aiden... I mean, very scary but I must say also fascinating!" I then realised that this was the reason he broke up with me and my face darkened. "So, is this why you had to leave me? Because you cannot be with me?"

"Yes, it is the only reason and believe me, I hate it."

"And now what?"

"I don't know – aren't you repelled by me?"

"No, I am not repelled." As I said that, I moved closer to him and reached for his hands. We still had an amazing connection and by sharing his extraordinary secret, Aiden had only made it stronger.

"You don't think I am mad?" he asked with a cheeky smile.

"I did think it could be a plausible explanation... But I believe you, don't ask me why!"

"I am glad you do."

"You mentioned that Robert had hypnotised Philip, do you have the same ability?"

"I do, we all do."

"Aren't you going to use it on me?"

"I like your bluntness! Well, no, but if you had started freaking out and running away from me, I would have done it instantly. I could not have possibly taken the risk that you would expose us and yourself."

"Fair enough! Look, Aiden, although there are a few things that I am still unclear about, I am pretty sure that you wouldn't hurt me and I understand how much it must have taken for you to tell me your secret." For a minute, we were quiet, but

I noticed Aiden was becoming nervous, until he finally found the courage to ask what he had been wondering:

"Now that you know the truth, do you still want to be with me?" I knew the answer to that question: hell, yeah! But I also appreciated what he really meant – it was not just a matter of our relationship or accepting the fact that he wasn't Human; in fact it had a broader scope of issues specifically regarding his community and its rules.

"The answer to this question is not only up to me, right? If I understand, you are not allowed to be with me."

"Yes," he admitted, head down.

I wanted to fling myself into his arms, but I restrained myself. I understood this relationship would bring certain unavoidable complications. The fact that Aiden had told me the truth was huge: it first proved he trusted me with his biggest secret and second, that he wanted me to be part of his real life. I have always thought life had to be lived to the full, with its highs and lows. Taking risks could be a scary move, but at the same time, life wouldn't be as much fun without them. I have often fantasised that my life would be more than just what it was now: a pretty ordinary life, even if it was an entertaining one. Aiden and I had such an intense chemistry, I was not willing to let him go. He swept me off my feet just by looking at me and such passion could not be ignored. I definitely wanted to live this adventure with him. But did I really understand all the risks? Was I supposed to go back to my normal life and just move on as if nothing had happened and ignore my true feelings? No, I would rather live dangerously than feel dead inside. I looked at Aiden who had been staring at me during my reflections. I liked that he never pushed me and understood how much of a thinker I was.

"I want us to be together." Aiden let out a slight sigh expressing his relief and he smiled briefly.

"Louise, I feel it would be dishonest not to impress on you the fact that our relationship can never be a normal one. Are you sure you are fine with this?"

"Yes. What is going to happen to us now?"

"I don't know, I have never encountered this situation before... My guess is that eventually, 'They' will find out about us and will try to interfere."

"How?"

"I don't know, but I guess by ordering me to disappear from your life."

"Will you obey?"

"I don't want to ruin your life, not even a tiny part of it. I would rather not have you."

"I need to know you are in this as much as I am!"

"I am, but I will never risk your life." His selflessness was irresistible. I got up, still holding his hands and he followed my lead. I came even closer to him, pressing my chest against his. I tilted my head back and our eyes met. There was so much electricity between us and I had millions of butterflies in my stomach. I moved forward to kiss him, but he stopped me just as our lips were about to touch:

"Are you su—"

"Yes!" I interrupted.

He brought his mouth to mine and finally we kissed for the first time. It was wonderful. Our hands parted and our arms wound around each other's back forming an intimate embrace. My lower limbs started to feel numb until the only thing holding me up were Aiden's arms.

Chapter XIII

I woke up and could still feel Aiden's embrace, which both aroused and disorientated me. It took me a few minutes to cool off. I looked around and was immediately brought back to reality. I was in the guest bedroom at Aiden's, in the same mansion I had just been dreaming about. There was not much light piercing the thick curtains, so I took my phone and read the time – it was 4pm. I had slept a long time and felt rested.

I went to the bathroom and drew a bath. While the tub was filling up, I prepared clean clothes to wear and went to the mirror. I was pleased to see that finally, my face had recovered its natural glow and I looked almost like my usual self, which definitely put me in a good mood.

A few minutes later, I entered the warm water. I could not stop thinking about our first kiss – my mind was re-enacting it so well that I could feel every brush of Aiden's lips on mine.

All of sudden, other images came rushing back and I re-membered the whole dream: Aiden finishing with me; the drive to the mansion and Aiden's revelation to me about what he actually was. I remained shocked for a few minutes, not knowing what my next move would be. The truth was scary and seriously unsettling, yet, it made sense.

I got out of the tub, got dressed and made my way down-stairs. Aiden was there, sitting on the armchair next to the hearth and reading a book on advanced biology. The curtains were closed and the room was dim. His eyes left the pages he was reading and moved up to me. He was waiting for me to say something and seemed quite apologetic.

"Hi!" I started.

"Good after—"

"Did you make me a Kindred?" I cut in.

"I guess you've got to the most important part of the puzzle," he said as he closed his book.

"I don't believe it! This is absolutely bonkers!"

"Do you understand why it had to come from you?"

"I guess. If you had just told me I would have thought you were insane!"

"But you know it is true, don't you?"

"Yes. I dreamt about the day I found out the truth or at least a big part of it."

"Soon you will recover all your memories."

"Will it keep coming the way it does now, in my dreams and random flashes?"

"Mostly. Does it feel like the more time passes, the more intense they get?"

"Yes, definitely, the dream I had was long, detailed and much more profound. I have noticed the recent flashbacks seem to be closer in time too."

"It is normal, the hypnosis I had to perform on you a couple of months ago is wearing off as your transitioning process proceeds and intensifies. When you are finished, you will remember everything."

"All at once?"

"It is difficult to say, it depends on each individual and how well their transition is managed."

"Are you managing me right now?"

"No, I am managing your transition, you manage yourself!" We exchanged a smile.

"Is this why you took me away?"

"Yes indeed. Louise, you, or anyone else for that matter, cannot deal with this on your own. You need to be guided properly to understand fully what is at stake and most importantly to decide whether you accept your change or not. It is part of our duty as Makers, when we turn someone, to care for them until they are ready. They must know how to control their urges and behave in the world as part of our kind. You see, before we came here, you knew something was wrong but had no idea what and you would have never guessed. I mean, it is very unlikely anyone simply says, 'OK, cool I must be a vampire, great, let's go eat!'"

I smiled at him. "For sure. So, you will stay with me?"

"Always."

"So, what comes next for me?"

"Well, now that you know what you are becoming, one of the key issues we have to get to grips with is feeding." I shuddered at the thought of drinking blood. Although I was fairly disgusted, it also felt strangely comforting.

"You mean drinking blood?" I asked unable to hide what was left of my human repugnance.

"Yes. It has to be done properly and regularly enough to never be hit by a hunger urge."

"Are you going to make me drink it?"

"I am not going to make you do anything. It is your decision and yours only." His mood darkened slightly.

"Do I really have a choice?"

"You do."

"Is that one of the choices you mentioned last night?"

"Yes, you can choose not to feed and die for ever. However, if you drink blood, it will seal your fate as one of us and you will live." As Aiden finished his sentence, I started to feel a little uneasy and my gums ached slightly.

"How long do I have?" I asked, even though I somehow knew I did not have much time.

"Are you hungry?"

"I think so..."

"OK, we should start exploring your options," he said in a serious tone.

I walked over to the sofa and joined him showing my approval. My phone was in my pocket and I removed it to place it on the table. I saw the screen was flashing, which got my attention. I had received several messages, including one from the GP's office stating that my blood test results were ready to pick up. I froze. I had completely forgotten about the test. My blood was so thick that day, I couldn't imagine what the samples had revealed! Immediately, Aiden picked up on my distress.

"Are you OK?"

"I... I... completely forgot! Dammit! Aiden it's bad! Really bad!"

"What is it?" he asked calmly.

"I had a blood test done on Wednesday afternoon! Can they see what I am?" I panicked.

"Louise, calm down..."

"What will they find? It's bad, I am finished, aren't I? I—"

"Louise, stop! Don't worry it is not a problem, I took care of it!"

"What are you talking about?"

"I intercepted your blood samples before the lab analysed them."

"What... How?"

"Well, I—"

"How did you even know I had a blood test done? We hadn't talked then!" I cut in. My thoughts were all over the place. "Did you follow me? Yes! You did! I saw you at the café, then outside my window!"

"May I please have the chance to answer your questions?" I nodded silently. "Louise, since the night of the accident—"

"The night I died you mean!" I was still very agitated.

"Yes, since the night you passed and I... intervened, I stayed close to you. I knew what was coming to you: disorientation, agitation, sickness, uncontrollable rage, incredible hunger and thirst, painful gums, eerie bloodlust, strange dreams and weird feelings. As I said earlier, it is our duty as Makers to supervise the transition. You woke up alone the following day at home, not having a clue what had happened to you, or how to interpret your symptoms. I knew it was only a matter of time before you visited your doctor. So, I had it sorted and simply swapped your blood sample for another. Blood supply is not a problem for us."

"So, it was not a coincidence when you interrupted my freaky bleeding episode?"

"No, I felt your distress, so I tried to divert your attention, and it worked."

"What about the nurse who took my blood? She realised something was weird."

"Don't worry about Nurse Lacey, I just paid her a visit and rearranged how she remembers this specific event. To her knowledge, nothing was wrong that day."

"How can you say such a thing so casually? It's not OK to tamper with someone's mind!"

"You are right, but the fact is, I had no choice. We sometimes have to use our ability to hypnotise to keep our identity secret. Legally speaking, we are only allowed to use it when absolutely necessary for the good of our anonymity."

"Our two worlds are really separate, aren't they?"

"It is not quite so black and white; we are somewhere in the grey area. Basically, our peaceful world can only exist if Human kind does not suspect the truth about our existence."

"Yes, I can imagine that if the truth about you came to light, you would all be hunted down, killed and/or experimented on. I understand what you mean, but how can you be sure that all your people respect the rules?

"Our laws define our existence – it sounds a bit severe, but the rules are clearly intended to preserve our identities. They are only restrictive when it comes to being a part of the Human world. Apart from that, we are free to do what we want. We all have different skills, so we can help each other out."

"But how can you be sure nobody uses their ability to serve their own agenda? Has it ever happened?"

"I have not witnessed such a thing since I was reborn. I heard vague tales in the past, but a very long time ago, before we became what we are now. Our laws have actually enabled us to develop and set up a system that works. They have evolved with time and we have found a way to live peacefully through the centuries. Part of the process is to care for our pupils: teach them our code of conduct; how to use their new abilities and guide them to avoid a traumatic change that could impact them negatively. Also, we have rules regarding who we can turn, it cannot be done to just anyone. It has to be discussed and accepted."

"Accepted by whom?"

"Ordinem, our board of leaders: it holds the six oldest Kindreds, 'the Elders' and three 'Youngers'. The Elders keep their seats for a very long time, while the Youngers are re-elected every twenty years."

"Oh yes, you mentioned them last night. Did they accept me?" Uncomfortably, he looked down. "Did they?" I insisted.

"I... I did not ask..."

"So, what does that mean exactly?"

"I don't know – I have never encountered this situation before... For sure, I will have to answer to my Maker, Robert. He is also one of the Elders of Ordinem. The only reason we are in this position is because you were murdered by one of us, which is not allowed either. We are completely forbidden to kill anyone. So, in a way we aim to restore the natural order of things."

"Hopefully they will see it that way. By the way, if you saw me at the club and then managed to be at my place the night of the attack, does it mean you were already following me? Not just after you turned me."

"You caught me."

"How long were you following me for?"

"Since I hypnotised you. I struggled a lot..."

"I see... By the way, I have been having confused episodes, that Naomi likes to call 'blackouts', could they be the result of your little mind trick?"

"What kind of confusion?"

"Sometimes, I couldn't remember the exact date or names of places I had been to."

"It's probably when you were with me. I just removed myself and certain locations from your memory, but your mind remembers the rest and forgets about the little inconsistencies, except when you think about those specific moments. For example, if Naomi asked you what you did on a particular day that we had been together, you would struggle to recall everything that happened, because all the moments related to me were erased. Do you understand?"

"Yes, I do."

"I am sorry Louise."

I felt the pain in my gums was intensifying and my stomach started to hurt. Aiden could see the state I was in and we both knew I did not have much time left. Honestly, I was not ready to disappear from the world, but I wasn't sure I could handle this surreal new lifestyle either. I had more questions though:

"Earlier you said that you knew what was going to happen to me when I woke up, the morning after I died, but you left me alone. Why didn't you just whisk me away at the time and bring me here for example?"

Aiden shook his head. "I couldn't. First, it happened quite late at night, so I couldn't make you disappear and have time to visit everybody from your life before the morning. Permanent mind hypnosis is serious and cannot be rushed. Like you said earlier, tampering with someone's mind is not OK and even if I wanted to, I would not be allowed to enter that many people's heads in such a short time. Secondly, can you imagine what your reaction would have been if you had woken up here, not remembering me? You would have freaked out and been so scared. These sorts of feelings have to be avoided at all costs during transition. Resentment is the worst emotion and it can lead to evil behaviour later on, which is why the acceptance of your new condition is the key to success. In order to have a successful result, the transition needs to be as smooth and gentle as possible, but above all it must be done with consent. To put it in simple words, by the end of the transition, you should want to change and be a part of our community, if that makes sense."

"Yes, it does. Resentment certainly does not inspire genuine cooperation. How do you choose people? From what you've told me, it seems that you pick a candidate and follow them until the right opportunity presents itself."

"Not exactly, we find people with profiles that we need, or even like sometimes and we keep more or less close to them until they meet their death. We used to pay greater attention to the unfortunate adults with illnesses, as it is clearly easier to anticipate an impending death rather than a natural one. These days, our community is not really expanding."

"How many people have you turned?"

"Only one..." He stared at me meaningfully and I realised he meant me.

I needed more information. "What is the connection between the Maker and the pupil?"

"It is difficult to explain, it depends on each case, but there is always a special bond and we can feel each other's emotions. The bond is created by the exchange of blood between Maker and pupil at the moment of death. The more profound the relationship, the greater is the bond. It can develop in many different ways. For instance, we can invite each other to private past memories or even fantasies."

"Like you did when you showed me your argument with Kyle?"

"Yes exactly."

"I know you can read or feel me, but why can't I do the same?"

"I don't read your thoughts or mind, I just feel your emotions. You will be able to do it too, but it is very subtle and new right now, so it feels more like instinct. Time and experience will enable you to manage this skill like we do."

"Is that why I trust you and feel safe by your side, even when I was not sure who you were?"

"Yes and that could not be more right."

"And are you sure I won't turn rogue and go on a killing spree?"

"I am sure."

"How can you?"

"One of the vital elements in the choice of a new recruit is that they are sane, as we keep our Human character once reborn. The First Kindred was nothing like us. He was wild and came from a much cruder time. He had no control over his emotions, so of course when the first blood lust occurred, he just went for it."

"In my dream, I remembered you mentioning something about unforeseen elements that made the First become a Kindred in the first place."

"Yes, we think it was an accident, or a freak of nature. But we will get to that later, as there is a special place I would like to take you to. There, you will understand where we come from."

The way Aiden was describing his world sounded like they had created a new peaceful society, a 2.0 version of our world. I liked his honesty and transparency. I was mesmerised and his world seemed much nicer than the Human society I knew. I was very hungry and my discomfort was intensifying, but I still had more questions I couldn't ignore.

"Aiden, are we immortal?"

"There are specific ways we can be killed. But we never die of old age, you will remain as you are now forever."

"I see, so a good old spike in the heart would kill us?"

"Yes, as well as beheading and immolation."

"So what happened to the woman who attacked me? You broke her neck, didn't you? Is she dead?"

"Yes I did, but it did not kill her – she was only asleep for a little while."

"I see. What happens if we get hurt?"

"We heal, some sort of super-fast tissue repair."

"Incredible! You must be fearless!"

"Don't forget, there is no reason for us to get hurt in the first place, except for collateral damage that can occur on very rare occasions."

"Of course, but I mean you can pretty much do anything!"

"Yes, with skills and training, I mean, don't think that if we plunged off a skyscraper, we won't end up smashed on the ground like any Human would! However, we can control our speed, so we can jump and catch things to ease our descent, a bit like parkour basically but faster."

"I have always admired people doing parkour!"

"Soon you can try!"

"What other abilities will I have?"

"We all have enhanced senses like you've started experiencing with your hearing and smell. You should also have noticed an improvement of your visual perception, which is why your pupils are slightly more dilated. We are also almost effortlessly faster and stronger. As you already know, we don't die of natural causes, nor do we age and we have some mind control abilities that allow us to hypnotise Humans. These are the core ones and then, some individuals have specific extra skills that develop depending on what they were able to do as a Human."

"Do you have any?"

"I always know where I am, as I have a heightened sense of direction – it probably comes from all those years I spent exploring and navigating the world. Plus, I run very fast and I can sprint about three times faster than Usain Bolt!"

"Whoa! That is amazing! Why are you much faster than the others?"

"Oh, very simple! I was always fast, even as a kid; I would outrun every one of my own age and half of the older kids. By the time I reached adulthood, I was almost unbeatable."

"What about your language skills?"

"That transferred from my Human life too, and I suppose becoming a Kindred has enhanced my fluency in all languages."

"What about me, do you think I will have a specific skill?"

"We shall see, but it is very likely that your fighting skills will develop."

"OK. Aiden, how does it feel almost two centuries of living?"

"Well, it has gone faster than I imagined! I am still quite young in comparison, but there were cases of very old Kindreds who had enough after living a long while."

"Does suicide have to be approved by Ordinem too?"

"When it comes to that, there is no discussion, we don't want a resentful old Kindred going rogue. If one of us wants to die, then it is just a matter of organising his own permanent departure and finding his replacement, should we need one."

"How organised!"

"The reason we manage not to interact too much with Humans is because we have everything we need amongst ourselves."

"Fair enough." My hunger was growing, my gums were killing me and terrible hot flushes hit me all at once. This vicious combination gave me such pain, I could already feel a burst of rage building up inside me.

"Louise, you are starting to get sick, this is not good..."

"I know, why is it happening so fast? I was feeling just fine when I woke up!"

"The fresh blood from the meat yesterday helped to put you on standby, but that was just temporary. I guess it is now catching up with you. Your body is stuck in-between two states, your Human one and the Kindred one, which is why you are struggling. All of your symptoms are coming from your Human physiology fighting your new self. For example, you were able to be in the sun during the first days of your transition, whereas now, you would start to find it difficult. Slowly, your new self is taking over. The more you wait, the more unbearable the symptoms will get. They will stop only after you entirely turn... so, once you accept you must feed."

"OK, we should speed this up then! I still have so many questions."

"You do know that we won't have the time to go over everything – I need you to be able to stand and think for yourself when... I mean if, you feed."

"OK so let's skip to the fundamentals! What is my life going to be like? I mean how is my old life going to be a part of the new one?"

"We have to figure it out and I promise, we will do our best for you to stay in touch with Naomi." I smiled – Aiden knew my real concern. There was no way she would miss the changes in me. Aiden continued carefully, "But Louise, we may have to ... remodel her mind."

"Hell no! We are not doing any of that!" I reacted protectively.

"Louise! Stop! This is the first time you have to think of our community and not just for your friend. More of these choices will come your way in the future, so you have to be sure that in every case you will choose what is good for our people!" I was very frustrated and the ball of rage inside of me was growing. "You have to control this rage, do not let it out. What I meant by remodelling Naomi's mind, was to simply suggest to her that she doesn't care about your new lifestyle and doesn't think it is odd. At no point do I mean to make her disappear from your life. I already promised you I will do all I can to prevent this."

"It doesn't mean you will be able to!"

"Louise, I would rather die than hurt you again – how is that for commitment?"

"I am sorry Aiden, I must sound like a spoilt brat, but you have to understand she is the only family I have left!"

"I know exactly what you are to each other and I was expecting Naomi to be hardest change for you to deal with."

"OK..."

"Now, I am sorry to insist but you need to make up your mind, what do you want?"

"What if I don't feed?"

"You will die of starvation and dehydration, at least that's what it will feel and look like."

"And if I feed, I will live happily ever after?" I said annoyed at the lack of time I had left to decide.

"No, you will live as a member of our kind, which means that you must accept all the conditions and the code of conduct."

"And if your kind rejects me?"

"They won't, they cannot leave you abandoned to nature."

"They could kill me though."

"That would be very extreme."

"And also, a good opportunity to remind everyone not to mess with the rules!"

"No, I don't think so. However, we will have a tough time explaining what happened, but I think it will be fine, Robert is a reasonable man."

"I could die tonight, in a few days or centuries, it is very odd to think about!"

"I know, but we are in this together."

It was not easy to process my thoughts, while trying to contain my rage and pain. I knew what I wanted and I was not scared to become something else. To be honest, in general terms, Aiden and his people's lives seemed simpler and peaceful, so I was quite keen to discover this new world. It was hard to admit it, but actually, his idea to remodel Naomi's mind was not that bad. If it just made her not ask questions and trying to figure out what had changed, I could roll with that. I guessed I could live with the guilt if that was the price of everyone's safety.

I had made up my mind and did not want to wait any longer – I could not stand the agony I was in. "Aiden, I want to live."

"That's great! I don't want to lose you again!" he said, obviously relieved after getting to the limits of his patience.

"I am not ready to go! How do we do this?"

"I am going to prepare you a glass of Human blood from one of our supply banks. This first time, you may feel extremely distraught. If so, please tell me, as this is not a good state to be in while turning. I thought of using a take away cup with a lid, so you could not see what you are drinking – I think it will make it easier. Try to feed slowly, considering how hungry you are; I know it will be tough to control, but do try. I will be with you every step of the way to help you. After, you will feel much better and your transformation will be complete." I nodded in agreement.

He got up and went to the kitchen. I could hear him opening the fridge, the noise of the plastic blood bag being taken out and cut and the thick liquid being poured into a cup. It was so bizarre! Even though I was accepting my fate, it was hard to admit this was the new reality. It still felt unreal. After sealing the cup with a plastic lid and piercing it with a straw, Aiden came back to the sofa and sat next to me. He held the cup towards me and waited for me to take it. The smell of the blood coming through the straw was so tempting, it freaked me out. Aiden gently told me to relax and keep my mind free of thought. I tried my best, but I was torn between my old and new self. A part of me wanted to devour the contents of the cup, while another part was horrified. My heart was pounding. For a second, I was completely lost and doubted I could go through what I had resolved to do a few minutes ago.

Chapter XIV

Aiden had his eyes focused on me, waiting for me to take the cup. I recalled everything he had told me. He had been very clear and I understood what I was signing up for – even if I knew there were plenty of other things, good and bad, that I could not begin to imagine. As I was staring at Aiden, I remembered our first kiss that I had dreamt about and it gave me goosebumps. Slowly, I leaned towards the cup and took it. Aiden's eyes did not leave mine and he said:

"OK, now remember, drink slowly." I nodded in agreement. As I brought the straw closer to my mouth, the delicious smell of the blood grew stronger. It was compelling, almost as if the attraction was magnetic. There was still a small part of me that was repulsed, but it was fading as the desire to drink intensified. Aiden whispered, "Slow."

By the time the straw touched my lips, I was completely hooked. The only thing in my mind was how much I wanted to drain this cup dry! I took a hesitant first sip and I instantly felt overwhelmed by a rush of energy; it was so delightful that I wanted more and more. I could not resist the urge and I drank faster and harder. Aiden tried to calm me by touching my hand that was holding the cup, but I tightened my grip tenaciously. As a result, he let go of me; he probably did not want to frustrate me. He had said that negative feelings, such as anger or resentment had to be avoided during transition. Within a few seconds, the cup was empty. I closed my eyes and felt like I was on a cloud – so light and happy. Then a blast of energy and euphoria hit me – I was ecstatic and felt so powerful.

"Oh man! I feel awesome! Let's do something, let's go outside!" I said, getting up and grabbing Aiden's hand.

"Easy Louise."

"Why? Let's go! I am fine, even more than fine, I feel marvellous!"

"Of course you do! You are high!" he said with a slight grin.

"Am I? I don't mind! That, I can handle!" Aiden was staring at me trying not to laugh, but he was barely concealing his amusement. I pulled him outside and he didn't resist. The dusk was disappearing, allowing the night to settle in.

"I feel so alive! I want to run! You think you are so fast, can you catch me?" I ran off into the thick forest without giving him a chance to respond.

He had no choice but to chase me and I was so spaced out that I did not realise how fast I was going. I didn't need to look back – I could hear Aiden's breathing and the sound of his limbs landing on the ground, and with each of his powerful strides, he was getting closer. I was hit by some sort of adrenalin rush and sped up. I didn't know where I was going but Aiden did, so I kept running. Eventually, the effect of the stimulant lessened and I stopped in a little glade – Aiden was right behind me. I suspected he had let me stay ahead, so he could always see me.

"This is wonderful..." I started before a whirlwind of mixed emotions suddenly brought me down from my happy trip.

I burst out crying but had no idea why. This abrupt and unexpected mood swing confused me. Aiden intended to reassure me, but as soon as his hand touched my shoulder, I pushed him away. Astonishingly, he flew through the air and collided against a nearby tree before falling down on the grass. I was horrified, how did I get so strong? I did not push him hard, I just needed him to back off and had no intention of harming him. I panicked at the idea of not being in full control of myself. Aiden got up slowly, shaking his head and said gently:

"OK Louise, keep calm. Everything is OK, I am OK, you are OK, all is fine."

"I am so sorry, I don't know what happened!"

"Don't worry, your reaction is completely normal. Now, will you let me come to you?"

"Yes, I think so... I am not sure, what if I hurt you?"

"Do you want to hurt me?"

"Of course not!"

"So, you won't. You were out of control and you panicked, but if you want me next to you, it will be fine."

"OK... Yes, come," I said, getting a hold of myself. He walked towards me and I could see he was not scared – he knew I was disorientated and struggling to comprehend my situation. Once he reached me, he asked if he could take my hand and I agreed. As soon as our hands came together, I felt he was trying to share his calmness. He squeezed my hand to encourage me to follow his lead.

"You are doing well Louise, relax!"

"What was that?"

"You are stronger."

"Stronger than you?"

"Perhaps. We shall find out soon!"

"What if I can't control it?"

"You will, you were taken by surprise and so was I, that's all. Now that you are aware of your strength, you can anticipate and control it. Most of us went through the same thing at the beginning!" I nodded to show I trusted him. I started to feel calmer and a few minutes later I was at peace.

"This is so weird..."

"You will learn to manage your abilities as you discover them."

"No, I was talking about how I felt before I pushed you."

"How did you feel?"

"I went from complete joy to absolute despair – I don't understand why?"

"Probably because everything happened very quickly – too much, too fast!"

"Can we talk about it on the way back to the house? It always relaxes me to walk."

"Sure!" We started heading back.

"Is this going to happen every time I feed?"

"No, not if you do it properly."

"Did I not?"

"It was your first feed, so there was little chance it would go smoothly! But, if you want my honest opinion, it went fairly OK."

"Except for the freak out!"

"It happened because you drank too quickly, your old and new emotions got thrown together all at once, without being processed."

"I see, so that's why you wanted me to drink slowly?"

"Yes. The first feed is tough. I remember mine, the attraction to the blood is as fascinating as it is repelling. It also marks a very important stage: it is when you accept your new fate and let go of your old self."

"I see, so how do I feed properly then?"

"As a beginner, the proper way to feed is to drink one or two bags a day, every day. Once you are in total control of your urges you may change your diet, but until then you can't."

"What will happen if I don't follow this?"

"In a nut shell, you will have a very tough time and possibly be harmful to others."

"Sounds terrible!"

"Drinking blood used to be our main weakness. We had to understand how to master our feeding schedule so we could be free from this craving. The more consistently we fed, the fewer impulses we got. If you feed every day, you won't be hungry and won't crave for blood."

"Are you saying that a malnourished Kindred may end up killing innocent people?"

"It is possible, hence the importance of the training with the Maker. In addition, we have to be very informed and aware of those we choose to turn: as we keep our Human temperament, some personality traits can be harmful to have when becoming one of our kind."

I was quiet, trying to ignore all the noises coming from the fauna and flora of the forest, so I could focus on Aiden's explanation and guidance. He noticed I was having difficulty concentrating and asked me if I was OK.

"These woods are so lively! It is a bit distracting!" I replied.

"Yes, I know, we will also work on your heightened senses. Everything now is pumped up, but it will smooth out. You will be able to use your abilities on your own terms and tune them as precisely as you need them to be, at any given time. Although it requires some preparation, it is not as arduous as it seems and I don't doubt you will manage just fine!"

"You will teach me, won't you?"

"Of course, we have already started!"

"So, back to the blood. You are telling me that by feeding regularly, I will be in control of myself and will be able eventually to feed when I please, but without ever regarding a living being as 'food'?"

"The frequency of our feeding is the key to our stability, health and control. If you fail to feed regularly, you will have a really hard time handling your abilities and cravings. Everything is connected, exactly like Human physiology."

"It makes sense. So, will my next feed be tomorrow?"

"We shall see, you have been unknowingly craving it for days, so you might have to feed once more later tonight." I did not feel at all disgusted at the idea of feeding again, I was actually looking forward to it.

I asked Aiden how far from home we were and he said we still had quite a long way to go, so we decided to run back to the mansion. By the time we arrived at the house, night had completely fallen, wrapping us in a dark blue blanket. We entered the living-room where the fire was no longer burning, only red embers remained. Aiden put a new log on them, while I looked at the paintings I recognised from the last dream. I stopped in front of the same portrait that had got my attention when I came here uninvited.

"Magnificent, isn't he?" said Aiden looking at the painted black horse.

"Yes, very, what was his name?"

"Shadow, he was my best friend for a long while."

"Do you still miss him?"

"Indeed."

"Is this painting from before or after Robert turned you?"

"Shortly after," he replied, smiling slightly.

"Are you wearing your father's ring?" I said, pointing at his hand on the canvas.

"Always observant! It was stolen from me the night I died, but Robert hunted down the thieves and returned it to me later, after my transition," he said as he pivoted the ring around his thumb.

"Yes, I remembered your story in my last dream, but it didn't cover the part when you got your ring back. Talking about being observant, the portraits weren't here the first times you brought me here, before I knew the truth about you, were they?"

"I did not see that one coming!" he said taken by surprise.

"Some of those dreams are extremely detailed!"

"You are right, of course. When we started dating, I removed them. I didn't want to have to lie to your face if you started asking questions."

"Fair enough! Aiden, I am going to my room for a bit, I would like to freshen up and talk to Naomi."

"Sure, good thinking, she must be waiting on your call!"

"By the way, when will we be heading back to London? I am running out of excuses to postpone my return home and she will definitely ask!"

"Since we tackled the first feed, I guess we could drive back tomorrow."

"That's great, thanks. I might use a fake lunch date to justify my late return, I guess that could work!"

"Yes, sure, whatever you think is best to avoid raising questions."

I left Aiden in front of his portrait with Shadow and went upstairs. Although there was no fire, I did not feel cold. I drew another bath, since the one this morning had been unexpectedly short! I looked for my headphones, plugged them into my phone and sat in the tub. Once I was comfortable, I called Naomi. The clock showed 9pm, which was a perfect time to ring her, since officially my second fictitious client meeting had started at 7.30pm.

"Hi girl!"

"Hey Naomi! How are you?"

"I am fine, and you? Are you done with your meeting?"

"Yes, we finished ten minutes ago, I just got in my room!"

"So, how was it?"

"It was great, they showed me the few pieces they have here and pictures of some others that are in their second home in Spain."

"In Spain? Does that mean they will ship them over or will you go there?"

"I told them I didn't mind going there to work!"

"Fantastic! Does it mean we will soon have a city break in Spain?"

"Maybe! So, what about your after-work party? How is it going?"

"Fine, but I might dash soon."

"Why? What are you up to next?"

"Some of our friends are heading to a bar later. Gorgeous Ian texted me, but I don't know why he thinks I am interested!"

"You are so mean! He just likes to be around you!"

"I know, it's like he is waiting for me to fall into his arms! Like that's going to happen!"

"Ian is awesome! Perfect for you!"

"A little too perfect! Suspiciously perfect, if you ask me!"

"You may not be ready for him right now, but one day you will see it!"

"Maybe! He is so hot! So anyway, when are you back tomorrow? I could do a very late brunch?"

"Too early, I will be back in the evening! How about dinner?"

"OK, sure! What are you doing tomorrow then?"

"I didn't want to say anything before I see you, but I have to confess something..."

"Please do! I am all ears!"

"I met an interesting guy."

"Awesome! What's his name? What does he look like? How did you meet?"

"Way too many questions hun! I will tell you all tomorrow. For now, just know that we met this afternoon while I was strolling in the town. We ended up having a coffee together. Anyway, I am meeting him tomorrow for a late lunch!"

"Great! I can't wait to hear it all!"

"You will! In the meantime, enjoy your evening and say hi to the gang for me, especially Ian!"

"Maybe! Thanks, have a good one too, see you tomorrow!"

"Bye!"

It was quite startling how fast and flawlessly the lies had come out of my mouth. Yet, I did not feel bad – I knew it had to be done. Also, I wanted to be able to use these lies in the very near future when I needed an excuse to leave London on my own. Work and love were the best no-questions-asked reasons.

Chapter XV

I was getting ready in my room when I thought I heard Aiden on the phone: it sounded like he was talking to someone and I doubted he was having a conversation with himself. Once I reached the ground floor, the discussion had stopped and Aiden was not in the living room. I heard noises coming from the kitchen, where I found him with two blood bags in his hands that he had just taken out of the fridge. My eyes fixed on the dark red pouches and would not look away. My senses intensified and the same attraction that had struck me earlier, returned. Aiden took my hand and pulled me back to the living room.

"Sorry about that, it is better at room temperature."

"It is happening again – I want it now!"

"Not now!" He took me outside so fast, I did not have the time to react. The change of scenery helped: out of sight, out of mind.

"Louise, I was thinking we could do something fun!"

"Am I not fun enough?" I asked daringly.

"Good one! How about a little hide and seek in the forest now?"

"Hide and seek? Is that a code name for something?"

"Ah! No! The game we used to play as kids!"

"OK ... A bit... childish!" I teased.

"Don't mock me! It will be nothing like the game you used to play. Now, you are different and you will hear, smell, see things you couldn't before. Take it as an exercise to appreciate the extent of your environment so you can focus on specific noises, scents or sights."

"Now you're talking! Game on!"

"Great! Go hide, you have thirty seconds! Go!"

I darted towards the thickest part of the woods. I still could not believe how effortlessly fast I was able to run, although Aiden would probably catch up with me twice as fast! I realised that although it was dark, I could see through the pitch-black forest. It was incredible – similar to the images of a night vision camera used in animal documentaries, with the same tones of black, grey and white, but not as sharp. It explained how Aiden found his way in the dark so easily when we visited his friend's greenhouse on our first date.

Rather than just running, I decided to climb up a tree. I stopped for a second and looked for the tallest one. About ten metres away, was an imposing English Oak, but I could hear Aiden counting "21, 22, 23" in the distance, so I had no more time and had to climb now. I grabbed the lower branches of the nearest tree with my arms while my legs pushed against the trunk. Amazingly, it was very easy and within few seconds I was at the top of the tree. I moved from one tree to another until I reached the Oak I had chosen. It must have been twenty metres high. I then settled on a strong branch and waited quietly for Aiden to find me. I knew I stood no chance, as he was much more experienced and efficient than I was. Having nocturnal vision was very disconcerting, sometimes it was better not to see what was in the dark! I was expecting something scary to pop up from anywhere.

As I was busy looking around for monsters, I lost track of Aiden. When he stopped counting, he had headed in my direction, but now I could not see or hear him. I was trying to pay attention and locate him, but the sounds of the owls, insects and rabbits, among all the other inhabitants of the woods, distracted me. They were so loud – I could not hear anything else.

Suddenly, I felt a tap on my shoulder; I turned around swiftly and lost my balance in the process, slipped and fell off the branch I was sitting on. Luckily, it was Aiden; he just had the time to promptly catch me by my ankle and pull me back up.

"Got you!" he said as I found my balance again.

"You scared the shit out of me!"

"I know!" he said, amused.

"How did you even manage to get up here without me noticing?"

"I was extremely quiet!" he joked.

"Don't play smart with me when you know you have the undeniable advantage of being much more experienced, than young and fragile me!" I said in the same jokey tone.

"Fair enough! I have to say, it took longer than I thought! Well played on climbing and moving up, I would have found you earlier otherwise. I lost your scent a few metres away, so I ran around and came back to the same spot and figured you could have only gone up. Then I climbed and picked up your scent! The stronger it was, the slower and quieter I approached, until you were so focused on the forest life that I could sneak up on you."

Before I had time to reply, he stood up and glided down gracefully from the branch. We were a long way up, but Aiden caught some branches on the way down and effortlessly landed on his feet. He looked up and invited me to join him. I stared down, stood up and assessed the distance between Aiden and me. Uncertain, I held on to the Oak trunk.

"You can do this, jump and catch some of the branches on your way down. We can jump from pretty high up and control our descent. Just do like I did," Aiden encouraged me.

I worked up the courage to let go of the tree. I looked carefully at the branches below me to plan my way down. I was not sure how, but my brain registered the obstacles and identified the branches to catch. I jumped straight down, grabbing a couple of branches on my way, but my landing was much messier than Aiden's. I came down with so much force that I fell and rolled a couple of metres away.

"Oh damn! Are you OK Louise?" Aiden came running over to me.

"I'm fine!" I responded, annoyed at my clumsy touchdown.

"Well done for a first time!" he said sounding impressed.

"Really?" I said sarcastically.

"Yes, not everybody actually jumps the first time!"

"I have to admit it was awesome! I thought I would be scared but once I looked down, it was like I knew what to do."

"You are discovering your new instincts."

"I think I am going to love them!"

"With experience, you will be able to do really high jumps – up or down – and control the speed of your descent, but for now let's take one step at the time."

"Fantastic! By the way, earlier you mentioned 'my scent'... What do I smell like?"

"Aha! You smell like you, everybody is unique."

"And what do you smell like?"

"I don't know, you tell me!" he said, while pulling me towards him. As our bodies met for an embrace, I breathed him in. It was really hard to specify the odours emanating from him, although I could distinguish subtle bergamot and woody fragrances.

"Now you know!" he whispered.

I didn't have the time to react; he was already gone. I was left alone in the middle of the woods, recovering from the effects of his soft words brushing the skin of my neck. It took me a few seconds to snap out of it before I started counting. I could not imagine how far Aiden could go in thirty seconds.

When the time was up, I tried to identify where Aiden's scent was the strongest, but I could not. He was probably too fast. I decided to use my common sense and find some kind of footprints that would indicate what direction he went to. I managed to find his prints and follow his tracks. The marks were very faint and far apart, which made the task quite challenging. I finally reached a point where they disappeared. I guessed that just like me, he must have moved upwards to cover his tracks. I focused on my senses, hoping to hear, see or smell something, when I felt a gentle breeze. I knelt down facing the light air and inhaled deeply. Gradually, different scents came to me, including a hint of bergamot – I was onto him. I followed Aiden's fragrance, and with each step, it intensified – I was getting closer. At last, I was able to locate him hiding inside the hollow trunk of a dead tree. I advanced quietly towards his hideout, although I knew he could inevitably hear and smell me.

"Found you!" I said excited and proud of my success.

"You sure did! Took you long enough though!" he teased.

"Yes, because somehow, no scent was to be smelt, Mister Smarty-pants!"

"OK, I am busted! I ran very fast and away from you so my scent would be concentrated in one place, well away from you! But to be honest, it only worked because you are a beginner. It would not have kept any others of us away for very long!"

"Ah, so you cheated!" I said jokingly.

"No, I benefited from your lack of experience! But how did you know which way to go?"

"Good old Sherlock style: I looked for footprints! OK, my turn again!"

I ran and did the exact opposite to Aiden. I ran around him a few times so I could spread my scent all over him, hoping it would confuse his expert nose. I then disappeared into the woods, looking for an empty fox hole to hide in. These wild canines have the habit of peeing all over their territory and also have scent glands under their paws to mark their way. I finally caught the distinct odour of one, which I had noticed from my previous hide-out, and raced to it. Luckily, it seemed to be abandoned. Before I hid in it, I took the time to roll on the ground to get covered in the fox scent. The entrance was so tiny, I had to punch my way in. Just as I managed to crawl in, I heard Aiden finishing his count. I tried to quiet my breathing so I could remain cloaked. At this point, I just had to use my ears to follow Aiden's route.

For a while, I didn't hear a thing, which could mean my scent trick had worked. I stayed focused – I did not want to get complacent, let my guard down and be found. I wanted Aiden to really have to hunt for me, even if it meant I had to reek of animal urine! Eventually, I heard the vegetation crackling under the weight of Aiden's steps. Then, I could distinguish his breathing and even the way his body moved – he was nearby. Slowly, a slight scent of bergamot hit my awakened nostrils. I could tell by the way he was moving that he still had no idea where I was. He seemed to be turning around in circles. I was very satisfied with myself. As he was getting nowhere, he climbed a tree and went up looking for me. How foolish of him, I would never use the same trick twice! He ran through the trees so rapidly, the branches barely moved. Soon after, he came back down to ground level. He sounded disappointed when he called:

"Alright Louise, you win!" I did not respond. "I don't know where you are, can you please come out?" he pleaded. I kept quiet. I thought of giving him a hint as I had won anyway! He couldn't see or smell me, however he could still hear me. I was hundred percent sure he was fully alert, so I whispered:

"I'm here."

"Oh, I see, you want to play!" he said, reassured I was nearby.

"Come get me smarty-pants!"

"Oh, trust me I will!" he answered confidently.

He started moving around again, but slower and closer to me. He was scanning the ground, but still he couldn't catch my scent and since I was underground, it could take a while.

Plus, I had thought to cover the entrance of the burrow with branches just as I crawled in. Honestly, I was enjoying being the smartest one. Aiden was getting closer; I could see his legs. I waited for him to move very close and suddenly grabbed one of his ankles before I pulled him sideways on the ground. I then jumped out of the hole and put my shoe on his stomach like I had won a wrestling match. Without hesitation, he grabbed my calf and pulled me down too. I ended up right next to him.

"Oh, Louise you smell so bad!" he said amused and disgusted at the same time.

"I win!" I cheered, ignoring my filthy state and overjoyed by my victory.

"Yeah! Such zealous efforts have to be rewarded!"

"I can't believe it worked! I fooled you!"

"Indeed! You did go all in! I mean all the way in!" he said gesturing to the fox hole.

"So, it looks like Mister Smarty-pants has been beaten!" I joked.

"Well played, looks like you are the new holder of the Smarty-pants title!"

"Thanks! Do you reckon we could go back to your place and eat? I think I'm hungry."

"Sure, I am famished myself. How about a race to get back to the house?"

"You mean a race that I can't win?"

"It's not always about winning! And by the way, as you so cleverly demonstrated, you can win even if the odds seem to be against you!"

"I guess so, but I don't know what direction to head in."

"You will find your way, that's part of the learning process!" he said in a challenging tone before he disappeared.

Chapter XVI

Aiden had departed so fast that I had no clue which direction he had gone. The only way to locate him, was to catch his scent and follow his tracks. I focused and identified a trace of his essence. I thought to myself that he intentionally did not run as fast as he could so that I could locate his trail. Or, maybe after a little practise, my olfaction had already sharpened. I sprinted after him, concentrating on his fragrance and I soon found myself in a familiar part of the forest. I went down the little path that we had taken on the previous walk, but I noticed Aiden's scent was fading, which meant he had not taken that same path. I looked around, quite surprised as the mansion was only a few minutes walk away. Where had he gone? I kept smelling the air and eventually realised he had gone through a secret passage, well hidden behind a thick bush.

At first, it looked like it could be an animal den, but as I investigated, it turned out to be a tunnel that seemed to lead straight towards the house. Aiden was full of surprises, although he did not need any tricks to win the race, so what was the real purpose of using this passage? Did he want me to find it? Or, maybe I already knew about it and he intended to refresh my memory. I was not sure which way I should choose to get back to the house. My curiosity got the best of me and I let myself into the dimly lit tunnel.

After a couple of minutes, I ended up in the basement. I remembered this place; it had appeared in a brief flashback yesterday, soon after we arrived at the mansion. There was no doubt Aiden had used this route as his scent was all over the place. There was not much down here, only a few cardboard boxes and a staircase leading to the ground floor. I went up the stairs and quietly turned the door handle. I was in the hall, advancing silently, trying to locate and spy on Aiden. He was not inside, so I peeked discreetly through the window and there he was, waiting for me at front of the house. I opened the door and said out loud:

"At last! I have been waiting for you forever!"

"What!" He turned around, looking like a rabbit in headlights. "How did you pull that off?" he asked.

"Looks like someone tried to cheat by using a secret tunnel..." I joked, walking to him.

"Looks like two somebodies tried to cheat!"

"But why, when your victory was a sure thing?"

"Well, it is simply habit for me to use the tunnel. Did you remember it was there?"

"No, I had a very brief flashback of a tunnel yesterday, but I didn't realise it was this one until I was in it!"

"So, how did you figure out the way in?"

"Your scent led me to it! By the way, how come I was able to smell you more than before, did you go slower or have my senses enhanced?"

"Both, the exercise here was for you to track and find me and you passed!"

"Yay me!" I said cheerfully. Then, I recalled the dream when I broke into the house, how Aiden had not heard my knock on the door and appeared out of nowhere a moment later.

"Were you in the basement or tunnel when I came here uninvited, after we broke up?"

"I had trouble sleeping that day, so I went into the woods through the tunnel. I guess when you arrived, I was still there.

The main purpose of this tunnel is to provide a direct and sun-free access to the forest."

"I see, so you can go to the woods any time of the day?"

"If the weather is cloudy, yes. However, if it is a sunny day, we need to wait until dusk. The trees only protect us from the UV light to a certain extent."

Aiden led me back inside the mansion and I went straight up for a shower. I was still covered in foxes' pee and probably other stuff I did not want to think about. A short while later, I came back downstairs, all clean from head to toe and joined Aiden in the living room. He was sitting at the piano, ready to play.

"Sorry, I thought you wouldn't be down for a while!"

"No worries, I would love to hear you play."

"Sure, but we should eat first," he said, as he walked to the kitchen.

I sat down on the sofa and waited for him to prepare our 'dinner'. Within a few minutes, Aiden came back with the same kind of cup he had previously given me. Before he handed it to me, he told me to try pausing for five full seconds between each sip. I promised I would try and he gave me the cup. This time, I did not feel as heavily compelled as I did the first time: I really wanted to drink, but I was able to anticipate my craving and control myself.

In a gesture of trust, Aiden went back to the piano, drank a little blood and set his crystal glass on the lid of the piano. He turned his back and began to touch the keys before I had the chance to start drinking. He played one of my favourite piano pieces. Evidently, it was not a coincidence – he knew my taste in music. Actually, he knew a lot of things about me. The mellow music soothed me and I proceeded to drink. I took a first sip and waited five excruciating seconds before I took the next one, as I had been advised. It was going to be hard. I repeated the process successfully, until the cup was empty. Each time I drank, the wait in-between the sips felt easier. Aiden kept playing, undisturbed. He seemed focused on his own thing and I listened, fascinated by the sound of the music. I could also sense the gentle vibration of the musical notes brushing the skin of my arms. I was not high like the last time, instead, I was very aware of everything around me. I did not realise how long he had been playing, but it was an hour and a half later when Aiden stopped.

He came and sat next to me, stretching his fingers. Aiden told me he had learnt to play the piano when he was Human and at a young age. Philip, his teacher, used to play and taught him. Aiden could pretty much play anything, he was even a bit of a composer and sometimes was called upon to entertain the guests at parties amongst his people.

We decided to call it a day and went up to our rooms. Aiden told me he was proud of me for controlling my urges while feeding. We parted at our respective doors. I brushed my teeth – although I was not sure it was still customary, a minty breath always felt good – and went straight to bed. All this running around and this constant state of alertness, made me really exhausted. However, despite my genuine fatigue, I could not relax my mind to sleep, I could only think about Aiden. The training and the novelty of my new state had kept me busy, but inside, I was very much attracted to him. Even though I was frustrated to be missing all of our memories together, I just knew I was in love with him and obviously he was with me too.

I wondered how long this partial amnesia would last – I was never the most patient person. Restless, I got up and walked towards the disguised communicating door between our rooms. I could sense him feeling my presence behind the door, which was weird. I knocked before I opened the door, but went straight in. He looked at me, motionless, unsure of what to expect. I climbed into his bed and curled up next to him. I told him I wanted to be with him and he smiled. Being next to his body gave me shivers and aroused me at the same time. I understood what Aiden had meant by saying that the key was controlling our emotions and that was probably why, so far, he did not show any interest in getting physical with me. I tried to focus on calming down and thinking about something else helped: I remembered the last time Naomi and I went on holiday together; we had so much fun then and still had so much to come!

***

That night, everything came back to me in a flood of images and a recollection of new memories. Aiden and I had been through a lot to stay together. From the moment we met, we were infatuated with each other. We had a few intense dates before he broke up with me out of the blue, which I had already dreamt about. I did not let him go easily and went after him at the mansion, which is when I discovered the truth about his real self. I re-lived our first amazing kiss that had already sparked my imagination. Up till that moment, I knew more or less what had happened, but after that I had no clue, except for short flashbacks of unknown events. Once I had learnt about the real Aiden, I had no doubt I wanted to stay with him. I was not scared at all of what he was, but rather curious and eager to know more. The idea of another community of people living a different way of life with different customs was simply fascinating to me.

We kept seeing each other and the meetings were more and more intense. Aiden took me to beautiful places: one day, he gave me GPS coordinates with very precise instructions to meet him at a specific place, which turned out to be the very same pond I had dreamt of before. He arrived only a couple of minutes behind me, just after sunset. We untied the small dory boat from the old pier and rowed away from the bank. We had an amazing view of the colourful sky. We stayed on the water until the moon rose high and we gazed at the stars.

The next scene took place in a different location in early evening. We were on the monumental cliffs of Seven Sisters, not too far from Brighton.

Then, we were somewhere else, in the Scottish countryside. I recognised the landscape around us and my appearance from the curious photo I had found at home, but unable to identify it then. There were also a lot of dinners, drinks, walks and passion. I guess we did have a normal couple's life. Yet, the common point of all these scenes, was the fact that we never seemed to interact with other people, we were in a world of our own.

Later, the atmosphere in the images darkened. I was again talking to Robert in his office, but the scene then continued to reveal what happened after: we left the Ordinem headquarters and went for a night walk on the beach, where we discussed our next move and what sacrifices it would entail. We decided we would stay together but hidden from public view.

From that moment, we often met at the mansion, but it was only a matter of time before we got caught. One night, Aiden and I were lying in his bed, chatting and messing around when suddenly his behaviour changed. He said that he sensed some Kindreds were at the house and that he was not expecting anyone. I picked up on Aiden's urgency to get out and we dressed quickly. He gave me a large blanket to cover myself and also one for himself. I was not cold and did not understand why so much preparation was needed, until I smelt the blanket. It had a very strong smell, which could disguise our scent. Aiden opened the window very wide, so it looked like we had just jumped out and we went quietly through a secret door leading straight to the basement. He then told me two Kindreds were about to enter our room and we needed to go to the underground passageway accessed from the basement. We locked the secret door behind us and advanced to the tunnel. Aiden walked ahead of me and led me through the dark. His senses were on very high alert, focusing on every detail that could hint at the location of the intruders. At some point, he stopped and gestured me to stay quiet.

"They took the bait, they have just jumped out of the window." I guessed he could hear the thumping sound of people landing after a high drop. He whispered in my ear to stay as still as I could and not to move while he would go out and distract them. "Don't leave here unless I – and only I – tell you."

He carried on in the tunnel until he reached outside. Then, I was seeing the events not from my point of view, but from Aiden's. Our physical contact must have been reinforcing our bond, allowing me to see from his perspective.

I decided to run but not as fast as I could, only fast enough so it would appear like I was trying to escape. It did not take long for two men that I recognised to surround me:

"Where is she" the smallest man asked.

"Who?" I replied innocently.

"Don't play games Aiden, you know exactly who I am talking about!"

"No."

"I am going to give you a chance to respect my intelligence, as you reek of her!"

"Leave her alone!" I said angrily. I knew I was trapped.

"Right back at you! I wish you had not brought her into our world, then she would have been left alone for ever. But now, thanks to you, she is a liability."

"Deal with me but leave her out of it!"

"Trust me brother, you will have to answer to Robert after ignoring him for so long! Today, we came here on his behalf and this is your last chance to make this right! Do you want her life to be constantly on the run from enemies she doesn't stand the slightest chance against? I'm not a bad guy and I sure don't want to hurt her, but if you carry on, expect Ordinem to take care of the matter."

"You don't intimidate me!"

"It's got nothing to do with intimidation, but everything with facts. You know very well what I mean, so don't be an idiot."

I stopped talking, looked down and thought for a minute. Forced to admit I was running out of options, I said bitterly, "Tell him ... he's won!"

I left rapidly and went to get Louise back. I knew it was safe to return to the house for tonight but not for long.

As soon as Aiden found me, the point of view changed again to me. Aiden told me we had been followed by his Maker's people who he had got rid of, and although we were safe for the rest of the night, we should head back to London the next day.

Two days later, he erased my memory. We had been together for seven months and had been apart for about two months before I was killed.

Chapter XVII

When I woke up, Aiden was nowhere to be seen, but I could clearly hear him downstairs. I was still adjusting to my new abilities growing stronger by the day. In bed, his scent was intoxicating; I reluctantly got up and went back to my room. On my way, I noticed the other secret door revealed in last night's dream that led from Aiden's room to the basement. Today, we had to go back to London, and tonight I was going to see my lovely Naomi. I was really looking forward to seeing her, although I was very frustrated not being able to tell her the truth about my new life. It felt strange lying to her and hiding what was truly happening to me – I could not play this game for long. I got ready and packed the things I had brought with me. I took a last look around; all was in order and I placed my duffel bag on the antique dresser. I made my way downstairs, feeling ecstatic. As I entered the room, Aiden turned around with a radiant smile, one that I had not yet seen since we arrived here. He was so handsome.

"Afternoon early bird!" I said joyfully.

"Hey! How are you?"

"I feel fantastic! The night was ... inspiring!"

"Was it? I take it you slept well then."

"I remember everything, Aiden!" I exclaimed in relief.

"And how do you feel about that?"

"Isn't it obvious? I am really happy, finally everything makes sense!"

"Yes, I can see, but I just wanted to hear it!"

"And ... it was really good being close to you..." I shared, blushing.

"Yes, it was!" he responded in the same manner.

"It's a shame that we have to leave now, but I am happy to go home and see Naomi. It feels like an eternity, even if it has only been a couple of days."

"I have been thinking about our return to London. If we leave in an hour, we should be there around 7, what do you think?"

"It's perfect!"

"I will drop you off at your place and leave you to your evening with Naomi, but I will still be around."

"OK. Will you come to my place afterwards?"

"Would you like me to?"

"Of course! Come on Aiden! Don't be so shy, I told you I remember us, I feel us and I need you! I cannot mess up in the city."

"Don't worry Louise, I will always be close by. I would never leave you alone for your first night out in public as your new self."

"Thanks."

"First thing first: feeding. You are going to drink a full bag now, half of another one just before you go out and the remaining half when you get home. Alright?"

"OK, I will. Can we go for a last stroll in the woods before we go?"

"Good idea!"

Aiden prepared our food and we went on our last walk in the Kent woods. He suggested we played a little game while we wandered. The concept was easy, one of us would say a word related to the woods and the other would have to say if it could be heard around us, right now in the forest.

"Let's start with an easy one – how about water?" Aiden began.

"Yes, I can hear small animals drinking from a puddle of water. And of course, the Great Stour River is a little further away."

"Well done, what about squirrels?"

"That's amazing – I think I can actually hear two of them squeaking. They are far away, but it sounds like they are having an argument!"

"You are good at this!"

"I will take your word for it, but what is the real point of this exercise?"

"I just want you to be able to isolate specific sounds and identify them. This will help you, particularly in a crowded area, perhaps like tonight!"

"Always one step ahead!"

"Anticipation is the key!" he responded wisely.

We carried on playing until came the time to leave. We loaded the car with our bags, locked the house and drove away towards the city. Aiden was behind the wheel while I was admiring the view through the passenger seat window. I usually liked to drive, but this time I was perfectly fine fantasizing about the disclosures from last night's dream. Before, I knew I loved Aiden, but now that I recalled everything, I knew why I did. Some of the images came back to me now as vivid as they were and I could not resist exploring them. I closed my eyes and invited the sensual flashbacks in. Being with Aiden was nothing like I had experienced before. He could be as wild as tender and always seemed to know what to do at the right time. Our connection was profound, both emotionally and physically. I was visualising the images and I could feel his touch and his lips, arousing my body. Then, I remembered Aiden was right next to me while I was having erotic thoughts about him. I opened my eyes suddenly and straightened up in the seat. He looked at me, surprised at my abrupt move.

"Is everything OK?"

"Yes..." I replied self-consciously.

"Are you sure? You seem a bit startled."

"Don't you know?"

"Why would I?"

"Can't you tell?"

"Not really."

"Can't you tell how I felt just then?"

"Just because I can read your behaviour and feelings, it does not mean I am constantly analysing you – I respect your privacy. On top of that, reading people is not so easy when we are distracted doing something else, like driving for example!" he teased.

"Good, so I know when to keep you busy!"

"Do you have something to hide?"

"Nope!"

"So, tell me then!"

"Erm, I was just thinking about last night's dream and remembered that I was not alone!" I said, winking at him.

"You said you had all of your memory back..." he figured out.

"Yes, everything!"

"Everything of everything?"

"Yes, every little thing!"

We exchanged a passionate glance, Aiden put his hand on my thigh and I ran my fingers through his hair. Unfortunately, the precious moment was interrupted by my phone ringing. I picked it up:

"Hello Naomi!"

"Hey, how are you?"

"Fine, thanks, I should be home soon. And you?"

"Great, I am really looking forward to seeing you tonight!"

"Yes! Me too! Where do you want to meet?"

"I can come pick you up. I was thinking of hitting Shoreditch tonight, food and drinks!"

"OK, sounds good, what time will you arrive?"

"8'ish."

"Ideal! OK hun, I see you later then," I concluded.

"See you!"

I put my phone back in my bag and was happy to see that Aiden had not moved his hand. For a micro-second, another arousing flashback went through my head, but Aiden's voice interrupted me:

"It is nice to see you happy!"

"I am! There are still a lot of things to figure out, but right now I need to see Naomi."

"Yes, I know what you mean!"

"Do you have a Naomi?"

"Kind of, I have a Luca!"

"Oh, yes, Luca, of course! I remember you mentioning him before you removed yourself from my life!"

"I have not seen him in a few months, but I guess for us eternal beings that means nothing!"

"Will you introduce me one day?"

"Of course, you will officially meet everybody!"

"That many?" I teased.

"Luca is my best mate, but you also have to meet Clara, she is the final part of our trio! And we have other friends you know!"

"It's odd to think that we can now be out in the open, at least in your world."

"It's our world now!"

"I am still getting used to it!"

"Fair enough. You know Louise, I meant to tell you, I spoke with Robert yesterday and told him we needed to see him as soon as possible."

"I thought I heard you talking with someone, when I was upstairs."

"From your bedroom?"

"Yes, I wasn't eavesdropping, I just heard your voice."

"That's good, I mean that you were able to hear me."

"So, he knows what happened to me?"

"He knows that what happened to you was because of Kyle's wrong-doings. Robert never wished you harm even in the worse times!"

"Do you mean even when he sent his men after us? I saw what happened after you left me in the tunnel, in my dream last night."

"When they chased me?"

"Yes, they were pretty clear about the consequences should we continue to see each other. What would Ordinem have done to us?"

"I don't know, I guess they would have forcefully removed me from your life, by erasing your memory themselves without any warning."

"And you? What would have been the price to pay?"

"Some kind of punishment. I am not sure what, but they would have kept me very far away from you and made sure I didn't try to come back."

"So, it was not a life-or-death matter?"

"I don't think they would have physically hurt us, but they certainly would have solved the problem rather efficiently."

"So, they just wanted to split us up for good?"

"Yes, as well as making sure it would not recur!"

"So basically, Robert wanted to let you handle your own mistake."

"I don't see you as a mistake, but in a nut shell, yes. Robert is very respected among us, if it was not for him, Ordinem would have acted immediately."

"I suppose so. He did give you a second chance to do right by him, after we ignored his first warning. Do you think he is going to help us now?"

"He could be very helpful to convince the other Elders that you were a good choice, though we might have to alter some part of the story, like the fact that it was more saving you than choosing you!"

"I just want us to be free!"

"Me too, and eventually we will be!"

The rest of the way, we talked about random stuff. Like me, Aiden liked to crack jokes here and there and he was very funny, we always exchanged good humoured banter. Before I realised it, we were entering London – time had flown by. Once we arrived at my place, Aiden pulled over and accompanied me upstairs. He smiled as he entered the flat and looked around. He hadn't been here for a while, except for the night I died. We had hung out a couple of times here, however it wasn't usual.

"Aiden, I don't mean to be rude but I should get ready, Naomi will be here in about forty-five minutes."

"Sure, I will leave you to it. Before I go, I do have one instruction for you."

"Instruct me then!"

"I have prepared your dinner in this cup. You will have to drink all of it just before you go. It is only half a bag."

"OK, sure, I like your cautious thinking!"

"I just want you to be fine and relaxed!" he said gently.

"I know and it is very sweet of you!"

"OK, I am leaving now, don't forget I am only a phone call or text away!"

"Thanks Aiden, I will call if anything is troubling me."

"At the first sign – don't wait or try to be tough!"

"I promise!"

"Alright, see you later!" he said while walking out of the flat.

"I will text you when I am on my way back."

"I can even pick you up if you need!"

"We'll see!" I said before he left and I closed the door.

Chapter XVIII

After Aiden left, it was strange being alone in my flat, but I quickly got into my old routine. I just had time to toss my worn clothes in the laundry basket, style my hair, fix my face and get changed. I looked at the time, it was 7.47pm. I walked towards the kitchen where Aiden had left my food. I started taking the first sip, then waited five seconds and took the next one, when suddenly I heard three knocks at my door. It could only be Naomi, who had decided for the one time in her life to be early! I panicked and ran to the kitchen sink where I poured out the contents of the cup. I cleaned rapidly, put the lid back on the cup and threw it away. I took a last look around and all was as normal. Naomi knocked two more times just as I opened the door.

"Louise! Finally!" she exclaimed.

"Yeah, sorry I was in the bathroom!"

"What's this on your lip? I think you are bleeding." I was devastated inside, but I knew I could not show any sign of it.

"I must have cut myself, my lips have been so dry lately!"

"Nothing lip balm can't fix!" she said as she sat down on the sofa.

"I am not quite ready and frankly I expected you to be fashionably late, not early! That's a side of you I never knew existed!"

"Aha, mock me if you must! I simply could not wait any longer to hear about your country adventures!"

We kept chatting until I was ready and then we left. After a short taxi ride – when I took the time to text Aiden our destination – we arrived at the restaurant and it was buzzing! There was a line of people who had not made a reservation and the bar was full of guests. Naomi knew the doorman and had booked a table, so we got in easily. A lovely hostess led us to our table, where we were greeted by our waiter. We ordered drinks: a Gin and Tonic for Naomi and an Old Fashioned for me.

At first, I was fine, but as I looked around, I started to hear different noises coming from all around the restaurant. The more I looked, the more sounds I could distinguish: from the bartender using a long cocktail stirring spoon in a mixing glass; the bank cards being swiped; to the other customers chewing and swallowing their food. I closed my eyes and focused.

"Louise, what are you doing?" asked Naomi.

"Nothing, just one of my eyelids is trembling, it does this when I am tired – I hate that!"

"Ah yes, me too!"

Our drinks arrived and I managed to concentrate on Naomi, but it was tougher than I expected. Shortly after, we ordered our food. Luckily, they had Beef Carpaccio, so I could use the help from the raw meat. I only ate one course as there was no point in me eating, apart from looking normal to other people. Naomi inquired about the fake date I had when I was away. I told her we had met a couple of times, had good fun and exchanged phone numbers. I did not want to go into much detail, as I was not comfortable lying to her. I knew I had to, but it didn't mean I had to exaggerate the stories. We also talked about the fake job in Spain; it would be the perfect excuse for Aiden and myself to escape and go visit Robert.

I told Naomi that this last trip to see the new clients had broadened my perspective and made me realise I was no longer happy in my current job. We discussed the possibility of me quitting and focusing just on making furniture. She, as always, encouraged me to follow my passion. Her advice could not have been more accurate!

We paid our bill and moved to a bar around the corner. We ordered more drinks and found some friends on our way to a table, so we sat with them. Ian walked in with one of his mates a little later on. I found the coincidence a little too convenient and teased Naomi. Whatever she said, she was definitely into him but scared of commitment. I also believed Ian knew very well who he was dealing with and decided to remain within her radar until she finally was ready to admit her feelings. As they started their usual flirting display, I chatted with his friend Joe. We were quite well acquainted, since every time Ian and Naomi were around, Joe and I ended up being each other wing-wo-man.

Suddenly, I heard loud pulsing sounds that I did not recognise at first. It took me a minute to realise they were the heartbeats of everyone in the bar, which didn't seem to be a good sign. Then, my gums started to ache and I understood what was happening – soon I would be craving blood. I apologised to Joe and went to the toilet where I hid in a cubicle. I texted Aiden right away: "*I can hear people's heartbeats and I've got sore gums.*" He answered immediately, saying he was on his way to pick me up, which reassured me and helped me to chill out. I slowly breathed in and out, and told myself to use whatever I had in me to hide my discomfort. When I was calmer, I went back to our table and softly took Naomi's arm. I explained that I was very drunk and tired, so I wanted to go home in a taxi. Luckily, she was so busy with Ian that she didn't worry that I was going to leave without her.

Five minutes later, I was getting in Aiden's car. As soon as I closed the passenger door, he drove away and I was relieved not to have to pretend I was fine any longer. The sound of the heartbeats disappeared, but my gums however, remained painful and my frustration grew. Fortunately, Aiden was not a slow driver, so the ride home was short. On arrival, he parked near my house and we went up. As soon as we were through the door, Aiden took out a blood bag and poured the contents in a glass. He insisted on holding the glass for me so I couldn't go crazy with it. I drank slowly and paced myself. After a few sips, I already felt better and once my glass was finished, all my problems were gone.

"What happened this evening?" he inquired, leading me to the sofa.

"I think I didn't feed well enough before I left," I confessed.

"Didn't you drink the cup I left you?"

"I started but Naomi came early, I panicked and threw everything away as fast as I could!"

"That explains it! You could not possibly have handled tonight without feeding properly first!"

"I had a couple of sips!"

"A couple of sips won't cut it!"

"Are you mad I messed up?"

"I am not mad – you are still learning."

"That was a silly mistake though!"

"Let's say it could have been avoided, but don't beat yourself up! Sometimes the best way to learn is the hard one."

"If I cannot handle a simple evening with friends, how am I supposed to handle secrecy and an eternal double life?" I asked, disappointed with myself.

"Louise, it's only been 24h since you turned! Maybe you should give yourself a break!"

"I am sorry I messed up tonight at the risk of putting my friends and our people in danger."

"Our people?" he echoed with a spontaneous smile.

"Yes!" I smiled back.

"This is the first time you have said it!"

"Well, there is a first for everything!"

I texted Naomi that I was home safe. Whenever one of us headed home before the other, we would text once we reached home. Contrary to what I had previously told Naomi, I was not tired and now that I had recovered from my troublesome episode, I was full of energy. I opened my window and invited Aiden to join me. We listened to the sounds of London and tried to identify what we heard, a metropolitan version of the game we had played earlier in the woods before we left the mansion. A little while later, we went back to the sofa and I instinctively leaned on Aiden.

"Aiden, what's next?"

"Well, we will have to take it one step at the time. First, we should arrange a visit to Robert, the sooner the better."

"Yes, I agree. I mean, I don't want to live hidden like we did previously. Surely, the fact that I am like you now should help, if not actually sort it all out."

"It might not be very easy, but I trust it will be OK."

"I already kind of prepared the way with Naomi for us to leave."

"How?"

"Well, you know the story I told Naomi about this little getaway, the fake clients and the fake date? I also told her that the trip helped me figure out that I was no longer happy in my job and that I wanted to quit. Anyway, I will have to! Plus, I told her that the new clients had asked me to work on some of their furniture in Spain."

"Look who is one step ahead now?" he teased.

"I know, I told you, I am really OK with all of this! So, when do you think we should leave?"

"As soon as possible."

"How does Monday evening sound?"

"Are you sure?"

"Yes, I would like to resign first thing Monday morning. Can I do it in person?"

"It depends on the time, the weather and the position of the sun."

"A lot of unpredictable factors!"

"Yes, I am afraid when it comes to daylight, we are limited, but you will learn to move safely during the day! Luckily, tinted car windows do help!" he said while checking his weather app on his phone. "So Monday, the earlier you go the better – the weather should be cloudy, so you will be fine for a bit. How are the windows set up in your office?"

"Actually, not that great, we always complain about the lack of natural daylight. We are located on the side of the building which faces another one, so it is actually pretty dark without the ceiling lights."

"It sounds great!"

"Yes, we used to have an awesome office back in Alastair's days, but our new boss moved us to a cheaper location. But at least now, I can speak my mind to her face."

"About that, try to keep it short and don't let it build up to an argument! You might not be able to handle your emotions and rip her head off!"

"What?! Are you serious?" I asked, freaked out.

"I exaggerated a bit, but do always be careful with strong emotions!"

"OK. What about income? I mean how do we support ourselves?" I wondered suddenly.

"You don't need to! Being part of an almost two thousand year old community has its perks. We own a lot of properties and companies and we all have a monthly allowance. We can also request special funds for specific occasions. In exchange, we just need to play our part and be useful to our community."

"I own my flat and the family country house that is currently rented, does it mean that they now belong to the community?"

"It depends, we will have to see with Robert. Your case is a bit different."

"How so?"

"We all died at least hundred years ago and have been taking different identities since then. We move around so people do not notice we don't age. In your case, you are not officially dead – you are alive to everybody's knowledge."

"I understand. Look, for now, I could tell Naomi and everyone that I am going to Spain for the refurbishing job, couldn't I? It would work as I travel a lot and it would not surprise anyone. Not even Naomi."

"Sounds feasible."

"Should I meet Naomi tomorrow night and tell her our plan?"

"What would you do normally?"

"We tell each other everything, or at least we used to!"

"Alright, so do it!"

"I can meet her for drinks in the pub like we often do on Sundays! I will start organising everything on my side for our trip before I see her."

"And I will take you to your work on Monday morning and back home after. I will arrange the visit to Robert as well. I hope your passport is up to date!"

"Yes, it is! Aiden, why do you trust me so much? I mean it is safe to go to the office, isn't it?"

"I am not going to lie to you, there so many ways this could turn to a disaster, but you know what you are doing, don't you?"

"I thought I knew what I was doing tonight and look what happened!"

"Louise, you have always been a sensible person, there is no reason for this to change!"

"I can also be feisty as hell!"

"That too yes! You have to know your limits. The only difficulty with Monday will be the daylight and making sure you manage your temper with your future ex-boss. I am just going to ask you one thing: make it short! It is only about quitting not arguing!"

"I think you're right. I don't need to make a scene, me leaving is enough! Thank you for believing in me."

"My duty as your Maker is to make you responsible for yourself and learn how to control your emotions. I don't believe that can be achieved by keeping you hidden somewhere. The more exposed to these situations you are, the better and faster you will handle yourself. Plus, it is much more realistic if you go back to the office before you leave, otherwise it will look like one of those unresolved mysteries where people disappear and simply leave a letter behind."

"I understand."

It was 4am and we decided to go to bed, but Aiden insisted on staying on the sofa, which annoyed me. Now that my choice was made and that I remembered everything, I did not understand why he was still holding back so much when it came to physical contact. So, I decided to ask him directly:

"Aiden, why don't you want to sleep together?"

"What do you mean?"

"Aren't we a couple?"

"Yes, at least we were..."

"Aren't we still? I thought we felt the same for each other."

"Don't get me wrong Louise, I feel the same way about you, if not more so, but we have to deal with our emotions carefully. You and me ... it is ... intense. We have to disassociate our feelings for each other, until you are completely in control of yourself. Plus, you have currently enough to deal with, such as Naomi and your workplace. We don't need to add more pressure."

"I understand. How long do you think that might be for?"

"I don't know. But believe me, it is hard for me too, I found you, then lost you and now we are reunited again. There is nothing more I want than being close to you."

"But what about last night?"

"It was an exception, a lovely interlude." He smiled. "You becoming one of us should not be linked to our feelings for each other. You need to find yourself first. And believe me, I can't wait for this to happen."

"Fine, I guess I will have to remember our past instead!" I said provocatively.

"I'm sorry, I do love being next to you and restraining myself is harsh, but unfortunately we must."

"And I love that sense of duty of yours!"

I went to bed while Aiden settled on the sofa. He was not tired and read the same book I had previously seen at the mansion. Laying in my bed, I could not stop tossing and turning. The fact that Aiden was so close, yet so far was killing me. I thought about our last conversation and had to concede that Aiden was right. I was still having a hard time to control my emotions and I wasn't sure what an avalanche of lust, love and passion would bring about. Although I was preoccupied, I managed to fall asleep and I woke up naturally a few hours later, around midday. Lazily, I took my phone and called Naomi:

"Good morning sunshine!" she said happily.

"Hi, you sound in a very good mood!"

"Yes, I had an awesome night!"

"Let me guess! With Ian!"

"Yes!"

"Whoop whoop!' I exclaimed.

"Calm down, don't get your hopes up!"

"Sorry, are you still at his place?"

"Yes, he would not let me go this morning and he is making us breakfast."

"You see, he is nice!"

"Louise, seriously don't ruin it!"

"OK, OK. I'll shut up! Can we meet up tonight?"

"Yes sure, at the pub?"

"Yes, I have exciting news!"

"I am not sure I like the sound of that!"

"Don't worry – you'll be happy!"

"OK then, if we keep surfing on the happy vibe, I am up for it!"

"Shall we say 6?"

"Perfect! Gives me time for a little recovering nap!"

We said our goodbyes and I went to the bathroom to get ready and start pack for our upcoming trip. Aiden came through the half open door, holding a wine glass full of blood that I took happily and drank slowly as he taught me.

We spent the afternoon organising our trip. I had no idea how long we would go for and when I asked Aiden, he didn't seem too sure either. That afternoon, he made quite a few calls and spoke to Robert, who had arranged a private jet for us. He also rang his friend Luca and it sounded like I would meet him soon.

For my part, I wrote my resignation letter to work and gathered information on all kinds of ties I had to this world: bank, insurance, work, national insurance number, household bills and so on.

Chapter XIX

The alarm I had set for 5.30 went off. I put a jacket on, made sure I had some cash and was about to leave for the pub when Aiden stopped me. He told me to hang on a moment and very quickly prepared a glass of blood. "Let's not repeat the same mistake," he said with a teasing smile. I ate and left. Aiden stayed at home; I wondered what he would spend his time doing. On my way to the pub, I could not stop thinking about him: I was longing for him but could not have him, it was so frustrating.

Naomi and I arrived in front of our regular pub at the same time. We went inside, ordered two Bloody Marys at the counter and found a table to sit at.

"Are you hungry Louise?"

"Oh no, I am fine, I had a little snack before I came out!"

"I am not hungry either, my metabolism is still working on Ian's breakfast!"

"So, how about that?"

"He really is adorable you know!"

"We all know that! You, on the other hand, you've put so much energy into overlooking it!"

"I know, but you see I wasn't ready to be involved with him then."

"Why are you talking in the past? Are you now?"

"I am not sure, but I cannot deny how much chemistry we have. Every time! And he wants to be around me, I mean even the not-so-charming sides of me."

"Well, if you ask me, you are past this stage! He's already seen you at your best and worst, so he knows what he is signing up for! And so do you by the way!"

"That's true!" she chuckled. I was so going to miss the sound of her laugh.

"Yes, I think you guys will be just fine!"

"He invited me out to dinner tomorrow night."

"Nice! Where are you guys going?"

"Well, I did not actually say yes," she confessed.

"Why? Are you busy?"

"No..."

"So why?"

"I don't know! I just told him I would text him!"

"So, no change there then! You know Naomi, I love you, but if you keep playing this game, you might lose him. He is not going to wait forever!"

"Look, I know how I feel about him, I am just scared that it gets too serious too quickly, that I love him too much or worse he could break my heart!"

"We don't know what will happen, but stop worrying about what the future could hold and live in the present! Anyway, you can't keep pushing him away because of what might or might not happen!"

"Louise, I am not made like you, you live for passion and I am a bit more cautious!"

"Naomi, I think we are past caution."

"Are you saying I am a coward?"

"You're not normally a coward, but in this instance, you are behaving like one, pardon my bluntness."

"I know, I can't deny it."

"What is so bad about having a relationship with someone to its fullest?" I asked her.

"Well, nothing, as long as everyone is happy!"

"The low points of a relationship, either end it or make it stronger. Don't you want to have someone by your side that you can go through anything with?"

"What if he leaves me while I am so in love with him?"

"Well, that's a risk you have to take! I mean, it's a risk that everybody takes when they start a serious relationship!"

"But what about after, when we live together and we get annoyed with each other? Maybe he has nasty habits!"

"Naomi, you are over-thinking this! Date the man first and then we'll see about moving in together! You don't have to rush into anything! I am just telling you to give him a chance if you really like him."

"I guess you're right," she finally accepted.

"And, you can discuss all of your fears with him when it gets more serious."

"Thanks, you're the best! Moving on, do you have news for me?"

"Ah yes! You remember our chat last night about me quitting my job?"

"Yes."

"Well, I am doing it!"

"What? Like now? I thought you meant in the near future!"

"Yes! I had a call today from my clients, they told me they were heading for their house in Spain tonight and would stay there for at least six months. They asked if I could start with their furniture over there."

"That's great!"

"Yes, they have six pieces waiting for me!"

"OK, it does feel a bit sudden though!"

"True! But why would I waste any more of my time at work, when I have no ambition to have a career there. And frankly, I am really happy at the idea of removing negative people like Eleanor from my life! Do I need to remind you how she treats people?"

"No, she is a devil! And money wise?"

"Well, they are paying customers. I have to give them my final offer today and if they agree to it, I can go there tomorrow!"

"What! You are leaving to go to Spain tomorrow?"

"Yes, I hope! I am really excited about this!"

"That's just like you! How long are you going for?"

"Well, depending on the size of the pieces, two to four weeks I guess."

"And what about money after you come back?"

"I have the first customers who did not mind that I took care of their friends' pieces first, and hopefully by then there will be others! And anyway, I don't need much to live on: I have savings, my parents flat and the rent from the country house, so I think I am pretty good!"

"But I don't understand why so soon!"

"This is what you call an opportunity hun! Come on! Don't be so negative! It's great!"

"Yes, you're right. I'm sorry, I am being selfish here! I'm going to miss you that's all!" She had no idea how much her words broke my heart.

"I will be back before you have time to notice I've gone and seeing Ian may occupy your time just when you need it!"

"Smart girl, you never let go!"

"Not if it's for your own good!"

"If you are leaving tomorrow night, are you resigning tomorrow morning?"

"Yes!"

"Nice! By the way Louise, you never told me the result of your blood test!"

"Ah yes! Well, I got a text on Friday to tell me the results were ready, so I will pick them up tomorrow before my flight. I am sure everything is fine. I feel so much better. I think I started a mini burn-out that motivated me to quit."

"You have been unhappy lately at work and you do look much better, so that makes sense."

"Yes, since I have taken on all these projects, I feel great! I am so looking forward to exploring this new path!"

"Well... I'm thrilled you are finding your way! What time are you leaving tomorrow?"

"I'm not sure, we haven't discussed details yet. I don't want to jinx it before I give them my offer. But I will text you as soon as I know. Hopefully we will have time to meet for a last drink before I go!"

"Sure, whatever time, I will make it happen! Do you want me to go to the airport with you?"

"No, thanks, you are sweet but I will order a taxi to pick me up, it shouldn't be too much of a hassle!"

We continued chatting for a bit about our friends, work and Ian. By the end of the evening, Naomi decided to start dating him seriously. I was relieved: if I was to disappear from this life at some point, I wanted Naomi to have someone trustworthy like Ian to rely on. Since I wasn't sure when we would meet again, I insisted on walking her home before I went back to my place.

When I arrived, Aiden was reading on the sofa, a glass of blood in his hand and the absurdity of the scene made me chuckle! He had already prepared a small glass for me and invited me to join him. Then, we decided to go for a night walk in the city. Surprisingly, he took the initiative to hold my hand. As usual, I shivered at his touch. We talked about the plan to leave tomorrow and I recounted all of my conversation with Naomi. We got home around 2 in the morning and went to sleep straight away – me in my bed and Aiden on the sofa.

In the morning, I heard a gentle voice calling my name and telling me it was time for me to get up. Aiden was seated at my side and an appetizing metallic smell hit my nostrils: breakfast! I opened my eyes wide, ready to drink. This glass was a big one! Aiden said he would rather me be over-fed and slightly high, than under-fed and potentially too aggressive.

He checked through the blinds and judged the weather was cloudy enough for us to drive to my work place.

We arrived at 9am, Aiden pulled up right in front of the entrance. I put my cap on – fortuitously, it was not unusual for me to wear one – and made sure all of my skin was properly covered. Before I got out of the car, he reminded me to keep calm and that my only aim was to make my departure publicly official. Eleanor usually got in the office around 9.15am, which gave me just enough time to give my friends a heads up and collect the things from my desk. By the time she arrived, I was sitting on my chair.

"Louise, how kind of you to show up—" she started before I cut in and said calmly:

"Eleanor, allow me to tell you what a horrible person you are! You are the worst! Working for you has been such a bad experience and Alastair would be so upset if he saw what you have done to his legacy. You are a bitter lady who does not respect anyone and dramatically underappreciates all her employees. Everybody here deserves someone much better than you and more importantly you don't deserve any of our energy. On that note, you will find my letter of resignation on your desk. Goodbye!"

I was so proud of myself and almost felt like 'dropping the mic', as I had always dreamt of shutting Eleanor up publicly. She was gob-smacked – could not believe what she had just been served! I walked away towards the exit with a large smile on my face. All my co-workers were looking at me enviously. I gave them a nod and wished them luck.

On my way down, I texted Aiden that I was about to come out and when I walked out of the door, his car was there. I hopped in and told him all about my speech while he drove back to the flat. I was so excited and I could feel Aiden was proud of the way I handled the situation. As we drove back, the weather darkened and it started to rain. We saw the perfect opportunity to go and pick up the blood test results.

Twenty minutes later, we were at the medical centre. I had called the desk from the car, to let them know I was coming to pick up my blood test results and that Dr Madison had asked to be informed, so she could read them.

Aiden waited for me outside in the car and I went inside. It didn't take long for me to retrieve the results and see the doctor. She was happy to see how much better I looked, as well as to discover the positive results. I told her that I had just resigned from work and was figuring out what was best for me now. We said our farewells and I went out to the car.

Back in my flat, I texted Naomi that I had quit my job and invited her to come over around 6pm – by then, I would be able to open the blinds – as I was supposed to leave my place at 8pm. In the meantime, Aiden and I decided to watch a film, but we were so comfortable that we dozed off. Fortunately, Aiden had set up an alarm for 5.30 that woke us up. He took his bag to the car, but left mine in the flat so Naomi would not ask where my luggage was. Before he left, we agreed on a meeting point at London City airport – I knew Naomi was going to wait with me for the taxi to arrive and wave me off.

Naomi arrived on time, looking effortlessly superb for her first real date with Ian later. I gave her a pep-talk to encourage her in the right direction – I didn't want her to change her mind – but she was not nervous. We talked about my resignation and the good results from the blood test, which she was delighted to hear about. We kept chatting, joking and laughing until it was time for me to go. As I predicted, she helped me down to the taxi and I waved goodbye to her through the rear window.

Forty minutes later, the taxi arrived at the main departure building. The driver took my bag out and I paid him. I waited for him to leave and made my way over to Aiden who was standing next to his car in the same drop off zone. The departure area for private jets was a little further away, so we had to drive a bit more. We parked in a covered car park and Aiden gave the car keys to a man. After we had gone through Customs, he led me to the tarmac where our plane was awaiting us. We looked at each other for a second and walked towards the aircraft holding hands, determined to find our freedom together.

Chapter XX

An hour after take-off, I realised I had no idea where we were flying to. When I asked Aiden, he told me with a smile that we were on our way to Madrid. This was great, I would be able to send Naomi real pictures, and it made my lie a little bit less of one! I sat back to relax and felt a slight burn on the nape of my neck. I touched it softly: the skin was a little rough and quite warm. I asked Aiden to take a look.

"You got sunburnt, I guess from this morning."

"Really?"

"Yes, this is just a prelude of what can happen to us if we aren't properly shielded from the sun. Does it hurt much?"

"No, it's OK. So basically, we cannot handle direct sunlight, however should a day be cloudy and grey, we could be outside, couldn't we?"

"For a very short time yes, provided our skin is properly covered. Plus, we can handle the hours of dawn and dusk. It's not that bad, just as if we had night jobs!"

It was surreal to have such an extraordinary conversation in a middle of a private flight. Shortly after, we started our descent to Madrid-Barajas airport. The night sky was clear and we could see all the city lights.

Upon our arrival, a man seemed to be waiting for us, which was confirmed by Aiden's expression when he saw him. They hugged each other before Aiden then introduced me to Luca. He was not tall, around 5'7; he looked quite muscular but not excessively and had a smooth, naturally tanned skin. His hair was black and his eyes brown; he also had a very slight Spanish accent.

"Pleasure to meet you Louise. Sorry for showing up out of the blue, but I could not let you guys take a taxi!"

"What are you apologising for? It's so nice to finally meet you! Thanks for coming to get us!"

"No problem at all! OK, follow me guys, let's go straight to the house?" he suggested.

"Yes! Louise, you are going to love this place!" said Aiden.

In the airport car park, Luca stopped in front of a black sedan with tinted windows and unlocked it. It took us half an hour to leave the busy area of the city and reach quieter streets. In the meantime, I read text messages from Naomi telling me about her date with Ian. It looked like it was still going on. I replied and told her I had landed safely, but was going to bed soon and would call her the following day. Luca had stopped the car and was waiting for an automatic gate to open, but I could not see any house yet. We entered a property that was surrounded by a lot vegetation. Luca drove slowly, until finally, behind some more bushes and trees, I could distinguish a huge villa. The front entrance had a remarkable wooden door, probably from the eighteenth century by the look of it.

"Alright, I shall leave you two to settle in. Aiden you know the way!" said Luca as we entered the house.

"Thanks! Have you heard from Robert?"

"He should be here soon."

Aiden nodded and led me to a bedroom. I could not believe the size of it: there was a massive emperor-size bed; in front of it, was an antique mahogany apothecary chest of drawers that still had the old labels. A bit further on, there was a step, leading to a small stage with a lounge area furnished with a banquette seating and a couple of large armchairs. On the left, I found a bathroom made of stunning mosaics with an enormous shower, two imposing sinks and a toilet.

"How do you like your bedroom? I will be next door, by the way."

"This place is superb! Is it Luca's?"

"Only one of his favourites! We used to spend our winters here – Spain is not ideal for us in the summer, with too many sunny and long days. I knew you would like it, I thought it would be a nice break for you."

"The calm before the storm!"

"Don't worry, I think it is a good sign that Robert is getting here fast!"

"I hope so. How long will we stay here?"

"I don't know yet, it all depends on him."

"Alright."

"Don't worry for now, I want to show you the house!" he said excitedly.

He took me to the different rooms of the villa: there were two living rooms; a huge dining room; a kitchen with a stunning terracotta floor; a library filled with what looked like hundreds of old books; six en-suite bedrooms; a couple of offices and a billiard room. Outside, Aiden showed me a well decorated terrace, which led to a semi-covered pool – also accessible from the house – and a summer patio containing a dining area and an outdoor kitchen. The pool was no ordinary pool: a real effort had been made to recreate a tropical environment, with a small waterfall and a lush vegetation.

"I can't believe this place! It's fantastic!"

"Yes, I love it!" Aiden agreed.

"But I didn't bring any swim wear!" I said jokingly.

"Don't you worry love, I can sort you out!" said an unknown female voice.

"Clara! I was not sure you would get here today!" exclaimed Aiden, hugging her.

"I wasn't far away! So, you must be Louise?" she asked, facing me.

"Yes, pleased to meet you Clara!" I offered a handshake.

"Please, don't be so formal!" she replied and pulled me in for a hug.

"Clara is our closest friend! The three of us lived together for a while!" Aiden reminded.

"She can be blunt, but she's a lovely being!" joked Luca. We all laughed, but were interrupted by a familiar deep voice:

"I can see you are all having a good time!"

"Robert! So nice to see you!" said Clara, walking up to him enthusiastically for an embrace.

"And you too!" he replied warmly.

Luca followed Clara's lead and welcomed Robert. Aiden was observing, waiting for some sign of approval. Robert looked at him and started walking to us. Clara and Luca picked up the cue and disappeared. Once Robert and Aiden were face to face, they grabbed each other's forearms and hugged. Aiden was relieved, I could feel it. Then, Robert looked at me and said:

"My dear Louise, our paths meet again!"

"Hello Robert! How are you?" I said cordially.

"Right now, I am intrigued but I hope to be more at ease by the time I leave. Shall we?" he said gesturing to the outdoor lounge.

The three of us sat down and Aiden proceeded to tell Robert our story – the real one: he first reminded Robert how he had finally obeyed and erased my memory; then he moved on to how he suspected that Kyle was behind my murder and Aiden's intervention as I died. He narrated what we had been up to in the last few days and how we handled my transition together. He apologised for not being upfront with Robert immediately after my attack and admitted he feared his reaction. He reminded that instead he had texted Robert to warn him that something was off with Kyle; but he hadn't gone into much details, as obviously, he could not directly talk about me. He had then confessed everything over the phone, only once I decided to turn, as he was not sure how Robert would react and he didn't want to be taken away from me, especially if I was living my last hours. Robert kept quiet the whole time but listened carefully. At the end of Aiden's monologue, he finally spoke:

"I don't understand. If Kyle is really behind Louise's murder, what could be his motive?"

"Kyle has not always been my biggest fan."

"Yes, sure, you two are very different, but I doubt he would take a risk as big as killing someone for such childish reasons!"

"Robert, I am telling you the truth."

"I know you are, but something does not quite add up."

"You think there is more?"

"I have not been able to locate Kyle for a few days now," Robert admitted.

"That cannot be good!"

"If he is responsible for Louise's death, he knows he will have to face the consequences of his wrong-doing. However, acting before thinking is not his style, which really bothers me."

"We should find him!"

"You have other business to attend to – Ordinem will take care of the Kyle investigation. I believe you should stay away from this case."

"As you wish," Aiden conceded.

"As for you my dear, if I understood correctly, you are officially still alive in the Human world?"

"Yes, I have pretended to go abroad for work."

"How long can this excuse cover you for?"

"At least a month, I can always push it back."

"And it doesn't sound out of character for your friends and family?"

"Absolutely not, quite the opposite actually. I travelled a lot both for leisure and work."

"So suddenly?"

"Yes, that's the spontaneous part of me!" I said with a slight smile.

"I like your spirit, Louise!"

"I understand it is rather unusual not to be deceased." I inquired.

"It is, nonetheless, it has happened in the past when we needed to access the Human world in specific ways. As long as the Kyle situation is uncertain, I would prefer you kept your identity."

"I don't mind at all!" I agreed happily.

"I am sure you don't, but do understand Louise, it can only work for a short time."

"Yes, I guess at some point it becomes impossible to justify the non-ageing part."

"Precisely. In addition, you belong to our world now and will have to abide by our rules and regulations."

"I shall do so," I complied.

"How are you handling the changes so far?" he asked, curiously.

"I'm fine – the first few days were definitely challenging. Aiden has been helping me a lot with controlling my senses and emotions."

"Aiden is very knowledgeable, however, considering the romantic nature of your relationship, I would like you to undertake your training with someone else."

"Like whom?" asked Aiden unhappily.

"It depends on her abilities... You are strong, aren't you?" Robert asked me.

"I don't know how to gauge it!"

"She is," Aiden confirmed.

"Anything else intensified recently?"

"Not yet, except for her senses, but you have to know that Louise was a trained fighter."

"Alright, you should be taught by someone with similar capacities..." he said while reflecting, "What about Chhay?'

"Excellent idea! I will contact him," said Aiden suddenly excited.

"Who is Chhay?" I asked curiously.

"A good friend, a good fighter too and stronger than most of us!" answered Aiden.

"He used to be a master of martial arts, so he is definitely up to the task. You should arrange your trip soon," Robert added.

"Where is he?" I inquired.

"At this time of year, he should be in his house in the Cambodian province of Mondulkiri!" said Aiden.

"Cambodia? Isn't it a bit too sunny for us there?" I asked curiously.

"The sun can be strong, but the mountains of the region offer lots of shelter. Moreover, Chhay lives in a remote area, which makes it a great place to train discreetly," explained Robert, "I have one last straightforward question for you Louise and I expect a similar answer. Are you sure you want to be one of us?"

"Yes, I am, Robert. Frankly, I am very much looking forward to control my new self and be a reliable member of our community." Robert smiled when I said "our community" – I knew it was important for him that I was truly committed. It made sense, considering he was going to be the one putting his neck out for us.

"What about Ordinem?" Aiden asked worriedly.

"Leave my comrades to me, it is all about presentation skills. For now, we have to act on the Kyle issue. I have already called on an urgent meeting tomorrow night with the rest of the Ordinem members to discuss our course of action."

"Alright, I will arrange transportation for us for tomorrow!"

"You can have one more day here, as you have literally just arrived. The training with Chhay will be exhausting – have some rest while you can!"

"Sure!" agreed Aiden.

"One more thing Aiden, the training is for Louise only, so I expect you to leave her alone with Chhay during the hours of work. Why don't you ask Luca and Clara to join you? That should keep you busy!"

"I won't interfere in Louise's training. As for Luca and Clara I did think of asking them to come with us."

"Well, all is arranged then, I will return to my quarters for now and will head back to Malta tomorrow evening. Until then, goodnight."

Robert got up and we just had time to wish him goodnight before he left. Aiden and I were looking at each other, quite happy with Robert's reaction. Unexpectedly, Luca and Clara arrived wearing swimming suits.

"Louise, why don't you come with me? I can lend you a swimming suit, unless you prefer going in nude!"

"Nope, but I will gladly accept your offer!" I replied, laughing.

Clara grabbed my hand and led me towards her room. She pulled a drawer and showed me about ten swimming suits to choose from: bikini, trikini, tankini, classic one piece – she had every style! I picked an elegant black trikini that was approved by Clara. She was very friendly and I liked her straightforwardness – it was easy to communicate with her. In some ways she reminded me of Naomi.

When we got back to the swimming pool, we found Luca and Aiden playing and trying to drown each other. At this moment, it felt like we had no problems and I was on a perfect holiday with friends. Both Clara and I jumped in, the boys swam to us and we played altogether. We messed around for a bit until Aiden and Luca went out of the water to get some drinks and blood.

"Can we still get drunk or high?" I asked Clara naively.

"Of course we can, but it takes much more to feel like you used to!"

"Thanks for being so nice to me!"

"Please, we are family here! I have been dying to ask, what is going on between you and Aiden?"

"Don't you know?"

"I know you guys are together and you both have this very intense way of looking at each other, yet you are not so close—"

"Physically! I know it is killing me!" I cut in and confessed.

"Oh, I see what is going on, you are not ready!"

"I am very ready but Aiden..." I stopped. As I spoke, Clara started to very gently caress my arm, I immediately got goosebumps and felt very aroused. As she took her hand away she said:

"Aiden knows what he is doing, don't worry!"

"That touch was very confusing, Clara!"

"I know love, and you don't know or fancy me, so imagine what it could be like if it was the person you desired doing that..." She made her point. I was still trying to block the feelings of lust coursing through my body. Clara carried on, "It must be tough for him too, I see it, you are undoubtedly attracted to each other."

It was true, I had maybe not taken seriously how real the frustration must have been for Aiden too. Perhaps that is one of the reasons why Robert did not want us to be alone. We kept chatting about random subjects, until shortly after, Aiden and Luca came back with the refreshments. We drank dark rum and ate. I supposed Aiden had filled Luca in regarding our relationship, as he seemed to be fully aware of the situation. I could see the two were extremely close and trusted each other very much. Clara also knew about us, but not in so much detail; however, it was only a matter of time before they told her the whole story. I could tell she cared about me and wanted me to feel welcome. She was slightly older than us and looked like she had stopped ageing sometime in her mid-thirties. She was around 5', had long ginger hair, almond shaped green eyes that shone fiercely, perfect eyebrows, pink lips and tiny freckles on her cheekbones. She was gorgeous.

Eventually the first lights of dawn pierced the once dark sky and we left the pool. We all went to our bedrooms and after a quick shower, I went to bed. I decided to send a text to Naomi: *"starting my day soon, will call you tonight xxx"*. Aiden knocked, came in and wished me goodnight. I fell asleep pretty fast; I wanted to avoid the frustration of being away from him. Even though I understood the why of the situation, I was still suffering from it and so was Aiden.

Chapter XXI

After I had woken up from a dreamless sleep, I got up and started getting ready for the evening. I focused on trying to locate Aiden in the house and I heard him laughing and talking in the kitchen. A few minutes later, he appeared at the door with our breakfast.

"Good afternoon my lady!" he said smiling, visibly in a good mood.

"Hello Milord! It looks like you slept well!"

"I did!"

"Great! Me too!" I said while taking my glass from his hand.

I wanted to call Naomi; I was dying to know about her date with Ian. I told Aiden and walked out into the fabulous garden to call her. It was the first time I could thoroughly see our surroundings – the garden looked so dense, as if it had been especially created to keep our privacy. There were so many trees and plants: olive trees, cedar, pines, palm, fruits trees, bamboos, roses, dahlias, day-lilies, lavender and veronicas as well as other species that I was less familiar with. It took me a while to take all that beauty in.

I finally called Naomi. Her evening with Ian had gone perfectly and they had already planned another date later in the week. I made up a story about my fake day of work. We spoke for a while and I was happy to hear her voice. When I saw Robert walking out with Aiden, Luca and Clara, I pretended I had to run an errand, so I could hang up and join them.

Robert was about to leave, as he had to prepare for his meeting with the rest of the Ordinem members at 10 that evening. He told Aiden he would be in touch afterwards. We all hugged, he left me till last and said in my ear "Welcome on-board!". I hugged him back as a warm thank you. It meant so much coming from him. Aiden and I exchanged a satisfied look. We watched Robert walk away and I noticed a huge garage that piqued my curiosity.

"Luca! What do you have in there?" I inquired, gesturing at the structure.

"Not much, just my car and a few motorbikes!" he said casually.

"What kind of motorbikes?" I asked with wide eyes.

"Do you ride?"

"I used to, back in my younger days!"

"Would you like to try one out?"

"If you don't mind, I would love it!"

"Follow me!" he said happily.

When he switched on the lights inside the garage, he revealed, just like he said, his car and five motorbikes for different purposes: one off-road, one adventure type, a couple of retro bikes and a sports one. I had my eyes set on the Triumph.

"Ah you like the Speed Twin – awesome ride!" he said as he threw the keys at me.

"I used to have an old Bonneville, years ago back when I travelled in Vietnam!"

"This is much sportier, I am sure you will love it!"

"Are you guys joining me?"

"Yes, sure!" said Luca excitedly.

He picked a Honda adventure bike, and Clara rode with him. Aiden looked at me, smiled and took the other retro bike, a Ducati. He knew, I would prefer to ride by myself. We put our helmets on and drove off the property. Luca led the way, as he wanted to show me around.

The villa was located near a national park and Luca navigated us through rocky mountains to get there. At some point, he stopped and switched off his engine. I copied him and realised he had brought us to a breath-taking viewpoint, where we could see the whole valley, including the city of Madrid. After a couple of minutes, Luca lit a cigarette and asked if we wanted to go back home or if we fancied a race. The ride up was good, but had triggered a need for speed.

"Race!" I said enthusiastically.

"What spot do you have in mind for this Luca?" asked Aiden.

"You know!"

"*El puente*[1]?"

"*Claro que sí*[2]!"

"We may still encounter other vehicles at this hour! We usually do it later at night!"

"So? A bit of adventure won't hurt!"

"OK, are we going or what?" I asked impatiently as I put back my helmet on.

"You see Aiden, Louise sees what I mean!"

"Alright let's go!" he agreed.

"OK, so here is how we are going to proceed: once we reach the right place, I will indicate with my warning lights so we can all line up on the same starting line. If we can't stop because of the traffic, Clara will give a signal as we go. We turn round at the first fork where it splits to the *Ermita*[3]. The finish is the same as the starting point. All clear?"

Aiden and I both agreed and switched our engines back on. We drove for about thirty minutes; we passed a few towns and the road was almost empty. Eventually, after a bend, Luca switched on his warning lights, slowed down and we all lined up. Aiden went next to Luca on the right and I took his left side. We were in front of an impressive bridge over the water

---

1 The bridge

2 Of course

3 Chapel (shrine)

and in the distance I could see the lines of the mountains. There were no vehicles behind us. Luca looked at Aiden, then at me, before he focused his attention back on the road ahead. Clara lifted up her arms, we all got in position and she dropped them while shouting "Go!".

The sound of the three engines accelerating at the same time was exhilarating. In seconds, we were going full speed across the bridge. It was a straight line, so it was down to the most powerful engine and the smoothness of the rider. I knew the U-turn ahead could change everybody's chance of winning. Surely, Aiden and Luca had the advantage of knowing the road, but at the same time Clara was bringing more weight to Luca's bike. Adrenalin was rushing through my veins and ironically, I had never felt so alive! I have always liked the sensation of speed, whether it was behind the wheel of a car or riding a motorbike or a horse; but before, I would always be limited by, you know, the fear of death! I have to admit, this was to me the most seductive part of being a Kindred, I could finally do it all, even things that used to scare the death out of me.

Comforted in my invincibility, I accelerated again, which put me ahead. In the distance, I saw the fork Luca had told us about, which slightly distracted me as I was amazed I could see so far in the dark, even if it was a bit blurry. I looked in my mirrors, Aiden and Luca were just behind me, catching me up. We got to the fork; no vehicles were coming from the other lane, so they executed two perfect U-turn drifts, while my slower turn made me lose my slight advantage. I accelerated hard and levelled up with them. At this point, it was between Aiden and I. Luca was trailing behind. I did not care so much for winning, but I wanted to go as fast as I possibly could. It was stunning to see the reflection of the starry sky on the reservoir's surface, even at such a high speed. Thanks to the power of my engine, I managed to overtake Aiden at the last minute. We reached our finishing line and stopped at the end of the bridge.

"That was awesome!" I said as I opened the helmet shield.

"Yes, I love this spot!" Aiden agreed.

"Me too! It's one of my favourite!" Luca replied while Clara nodded in agreement.

We rode back to the villa. After parking the bikes in the garage, we were all very excited and I was still shaking from the adrenalin rush! We settled in the living room near the pool and started drinking and feeding as we chatted and laughed. We were having a good time and we got on very well with each other. Now and then, Aiden and I exchanged private glances – he was happy too.

A short while later, out of the blue, Aiden's and Luca's phones rang at the same time. They looked at each other a little taken aback by the odd coincidence. They proceeded to check their phones. Both of their faces darkened. Clara and I exchanged a worried look, we knew something bad had happened.

Chapter XXII

For the first time since we were reunited, I saw Aiden worried and upset, he was very tense and quiet. Concerned, Clara asked directly:

"What is going on?"

"We got an email from Robert titled 'Under Attack'," replied Luca, puzzled.

"That's it? No message?" she inquired further.

"I just need to think!" Luca got up angrily, still trying to make sense of the email. Luca and Robert seemed very close but I didn't think he was his Maker – they had a different kind of relationship. He lit a cigarette and smoked it nervously.

Aiden was re-reading the email, looking for a clue. "It does say something in the message!"

"Did I miss it?" replied Luca, checking the email again. Aiden showed us the message, it had only one written word: "*see*". Robert must have been under extreme pressure and had limited time. Disappointed, Luca continued, "Oh yes, I saw that, but I can't make sense of it!"

"It's from Robert, it means something! Let's think!" encouraged Clara. Luca was impatiently pacing back and forth, until he stopped, lifted his head up and disappeared into his room. He came back a minute later with his laptop.

"I get it now! Robert wrote 'see', because I can see everything that happens there!"

"What? How?" asked Aiden.

"Last month, Robert asked me to install a surveillance system in strategic places all over the premises of Ordinem. He had noticed a few things had been moved and wanted to investigate further."

"And you can access the system?" inquired Aiden.

"Yes, I went there and hid the cameras in different places. I also installed the software on Robert's computer and phone. We did it when nobody was around, so, technically apart from me and him, nobody knows the place has been under surveillance!"

As they were talking, Luca accessed the surveillance system. We were all staring at the screen, waiting for the images that illustrated Robert's alarming email. Luca connected the computer to the large flat TV screen, so we would not miss anything. I recognised the place – it was in the citadel where I had met Robert for the first time.

There were five cameras: one outside aimed at the old building entrance; one in the guarded hall leading to the basement – where the operations of Ordinem took place; one in Robert's office; one in what looked to be a conference room and the last in the corridor. Luca set the time to 9pm, about an hour before the email was sent and played the video recording. Nothing much happened apart from a few people walking through the corridor. We fast forwarded a bit. At 9.50pm, Robert appeared in the corridor with another man by his side, who Aiden, Clara and Luca identified as the Ordinem members' assistant. I also recognised him from our single visit – he was the man who had taken us to Robert's office. They were chatting and the assistant seemed to be giving him some information. Robert looked at his watch, nodded and they both walked to his office. Robert sat at his desk while the helper left closing the door behind him and then waited next to it, which was odd. He seemed to be waiting for something.

Five minutes later, the Ordinem conference room was slowly filling up with its members and at 10pm, all the chairs were taken except for one: Robert's. He was still in his office and seemed unaware that the other leaders were awaiting his arrival. At 10.02pm, we could see three men coming towards the building and entering the front door. The next camera, in the modest entrance, showed them with the two Ordinem security guards and they talked for a few seconds. It appeared they all knew each other, as the guards did not seem to be wary of the newcomers. Unfortunately, we could not see the visitors' faces, as the camera was angled towards their backs.

Suddenly, two of the visitors stabbed the guards simultaneously straight through their hearts. The guards fell to the floor and eight other masked men appeared. The two murderers were wearing black robes that they then removed to reveal identical outfits to those of the slaughtered security guards. Right after, they took their positions in the entrance, pretending to be them.

The other men were carrying three long black cases. It looked like a military operation. They opened the cases and three of the intruders strapped on flamethrowers.

I came close to Aiden and held his hand tight – he was very stressed. Next, the assassins made their way underground to the conference room. Once they reached it, they entered and using the flamethrowers burnt all the members of Ordinem until they were dead. They also threw in the corpses of the entrance guards. They left them no chance. The scene was unbearable to watch.

The victims' screams alerted Robert, who suddenly got up and tried to open his office doors, but they seemed to be stuck; he glanced up at the camera and ran to his desk. It looked like he was watching something on his computer, probably the live stream from the surveillance cameras. Then, he started to write a note, glancing at the computer nervously. He sealed the message in an envelope and hid it under the carpet. On the corridor cam, we could see three other men marching towards Robert's office, who in the meantime was typing on his computer, obviously sending the email to Aiden and Luca. He just had time to get up and pretend to be sitting on his sofa. On the other side of his office door, one of the three men approached the assistant and swiftly cut off his head with a large sabre. He then put the two pieces of corpse into a body bag and took it away. Meanwhile, the two others kicked open Robert's office doors, came in and took him away, rather peacefully considering what had gone on in the rest of the premises. Robert did not put up a fight and followed them. He probably knew he had no chance and if they wanted him dead, he would be. Instead, they had made a real effort to separate Robert from the others and make sure he was not present in the execution room. Just before they left, we chanced to see one of the men facing the camera with a look of triumph on his face. He was the leader and the only one who had his face unmasked: it was the first and only time we saw him face-on, although his body language was very similar to the third guy who was with the two killers at the beginning of the video.

Luca paused the video and looked at Aiden meaningfully. I felt Aiden crumble inside while Luca was cursing away.

I looked at the image again, the man in charge of this massacre was familiar and I had seen his face before. All of a sudden, it hit me – I did not know him personally, but Aiden did and had showed me this man in one of his flashbacks – it was Kyle. We were all shocked, still trying to process what had just happened.

"Who the hell are those guys with him?" exclaimed Luca.

"I don't know, but it's not good!" responded Clara.

"They could be other Kindreds, or hired hit-men... We must find out!" he continued.

"In any case, it's a disaster," replied Clara, devastated.

"The note, Robert left us a note, we need to go get it!" Aiden said, coming out of his silence.

"I'm going to kill this maniac!" Luca was furious.

"Trust me Luca, there is nothing more that I want than finishing Kyle off, but for now we need to get to the note, it is obvious Robert wants us to find it!"

"OK, but after we take care of Kyle!"

"Count on me brother!"

"No – this is exactly what he wants!" intervened Clara.

"Then he shall get served!" responded Luca.

"Guys, I want to see him pay for his crimes too! But let's be smart, we should consider that maybe he was aware of the surveillance, something in the way he was facing the camera. I know we only had a brief glimpse of him, but I have a feeling it was not a mistake, maybe he wanted to be identified, which raises one question: how could he know about the surveillance if it was yours and Robert's secret?"

"Hmm, you're right *Clarita*... However, surely he didn't expect us to watch the video so soon because he couldn't have anticipated Robert's email and note. That gives us an advantage," added Luca.

"The assistant?" I suggested responding to Clara's question.

"Louise is right, he talked to Robert a few minutes before the meeting, accompanied him to his office and waited. I am sure if we rewind the video, we will see him tampering with Robert's doors as the carnage started," said Aiden.

Luca rewound the video and we witnessed the assistant chaining the doors of Robert's office, which confirmed Aiden's prediction. We presumed he had been the one snooping around the premises and probably found out about the surveillance. However, we could not understand what could have been his motivation to betray Ordinem and the rest of us; maybe he had been misled to believe that he was doing something else. And what was he trying to do with the chains that locked Robert's door? These could not possibly have held Robert for more than a few seconds.

We talked through our options and decided to fly to the Ordinem headquarters tonight. It was strange to think that it was barely 10.30pm and that the lethal attack had only just occurred.

Aiden and Luca were very efficient at planning a last-minute trip: Aiden was arranging the flight and Luca focusing on the arrival in Malta. Clara and I decided to go pack rather than feeling useless.

Half an hour later, we were ready to leave the villa. We drove to the airport in Luca's car and like Aiden in London airport, he gave his keys to a man. We got on the plane and took off ten minutes later. On board, we talked about the horrible images we had seen, but I also had a few questions:

"Sorry for asking, it might sound a bit trivial, but why is Ordinem located in Malta, it's super-sunny over there!"

"Strategic location and nobody would think of looking for us there, specifically for the reason you highlighted. Only the members of Ordinem stay in Malta, they aren't there all the time though and no other Kindreds lives on the island permanently," responded Luca.

"Why?"

"It is only an added precaution; in case something went wrong, it could not be related to them. Anyway, Ordinem is under an old fortress, they are well hidden!" he specified.

"But not safe," added Clara sadly.

"They were for centuries, before *ese bastardo*[4] attacked us! We weren't expecting to be attacked by one of our own! But *no te preoccupes*[5] *Clarita* we will get him!" said Luca assuredly.

"So, does it mean a new Ordinem will be formed?" I asked, not having a clue how they worked.

"We have never experienced such an event, I don't know either. I am hoping we will find some answers over there," said Aiden.

---

4 This bastard
5 Don't worry

Chapter XXIII

Aiden had been deep in thought since we had left the villa. Robert was his pillar and his guide – he was devastated and very angry, but kept his calm, Aiden style. It hurt me to see him like this, I wanted to help but did not know how. The image of Kyle's face appeared in my mind and I felt so much hatred. He had taken my life away from me; put Aiden through hell and now had destroyed centuries of work and achievements by murdering the Ordinem members, jeopardizing the lives of our entire community. He had to be stopped.

Aiden looked at his watch and got up from his seat. He came back a couple of minutes later with a bag of blood, poured it in a glass and gently handed it over to me. How could he possibly still be thinking of my well-being at such a time? At this moment, I loved him even more and wanted to do everything in my power to protect him too. No words came out of my mouth, but the expression in my eyes was promising him my eternal loyalty.

Shortly after, the pilot announced we would be landing soon. On arrival at the airport, Luca picked up the keys of a black van and soon after we were on our way to the citadel. The atmosphere was heavy, nobody talked. I took Aiden's hand and never wanted to let go. We parked nearby and walked the remaining distance.

Aiden and Luca led us to a secret underground entrance. We found footprints that indicated a couple of guys had been guarding this exit, probably during the attack. We entered and closed the door behind us. We walked a few metres and were suddenly overwhelmed by the putrid smell of the charred corpses – it was revolting. We moved along the corridor until we reached the conference room and the scene we found was as traumatic as the stench. There were not many remains left of the eight poor Ordinem members and guards. Sick of the view, Aiden closed the doors and turned around to face us:

"We need to sort this place out," he said morosely.

"Shall I call for help?" asked Luca.

"I am not sure, let's first figure out how we are going to handle this – let's go to Robert's office."

I followed him; Luca and Clara were right behind us. When we arrived in the office, all was exactly as Robert had left it. We retrieved the hidden note under the Persian carpet and were impatient to read his last instructions. Unfortunately, we could not read the message, as it was either coded or in a foreign language, one completely unknown to me. By the expression on their faces, I could tell Luca and Clara were as clueless as I was. The three of us all turned to Aiden, hoping he would understand the note.

"So, do you know what it says?" asked Luca.

"I know this... I haven't spoken this in a long time!" Aiden was trying to make sense of the words.

"What is it?" Clara inquired softly.

"Dalmatian, one of Robert's main languages that he taught me a long time ago, at the beginning of my Kindred life."

"From Croatia?" I inquired.

"Yes, well this is an ancient language, which died out at the very end of the eighteenth century."

"Aiden, can you make sense of this?" continued Clara.

"Yes, it has been so long though, give me a minute." We watched Aiden trying to translate the message. Only a couple of minutes later, he was ready to translate:

"Our new addition must proceed with her training.
She is a valuable asset, even more now than ever.
Follow the plan and take her to her teacher.
The three of you have to find the next Elders to reb
build what has been destroyed. You must act fast as
order is important. The source retains the informa-
tion you seek. The key remains where you last saw
it. Do not let revenge fuel your lives and above all,
protect our legacy."

We were all surprised by the mysterious nature of the message. We assumed Robert wanted to be sure only Aiden could read the note and keep our identities anonymous, so he used the Dalmatian language in case it fell into the wrong hands. There was still some ambiguity regarding some parts of the message that we decided to assess later on. For now, we did not have much time until sunrise and we needed to organise a plan to dispose of the bodies and lock the place down until further notice. Clara explained that usually, nobody visited Ordinem; it was more a place you were summoned to, which allowed us to keep this terrible event solely between us for now.

"We need to entirely clear this place. The evacuation cases should still be in the emergency room. Let's use them for everything ... and everybody," stated Aiden.

"*Vale*[6]*!*" agreed Luca.

On our way, Clara explained to me that there was an emergency room containing all the objects they should ever need in order to evacuate in a hurry. The large metal cases were specially kept to be able to empty the spaces of items and <u>transport them</u> rapidly. The procedure was meant to protect

6   Alright!

them in case of a breach of their real identities, but not against their own kind.

We got to the room and carried the cases out. It was very helpful for all of us to be very strong and we managed to have the task done in less than five minutes. We agreed we should split up: two people could empty the offices, while the other two would gather all the remains of the Ordinem members. I volunteered for the gruesome task and suggested that Aiden took care of Robert's office, but he was not sure. I asked him to read Robert's note out loud again, which he did.

"Aiden, do you know what key he's talking about?" I asked.

"I have no idea!"

"Isn't it possible that you will find out while searching his office?"

"Yes, probably, you're right," he accepted.

"I will come with you Louise," offered Luca.

"Are you sure?" I wanted to offer him a way out. It was going to be a horrible task.

"Yes," he confirmed.

With a last look at each other, Luca and I went to the conference room with a couple of cases, while Clara and Aiden went towards the offices. Only when I let go of Aiden's hand, I realised I had never stopped holding it. Clara accompanied him to Robert's office – she knew it would be emotionally difficult.

When we got to the conference room, Luca was filled with sorrow – it was painful to watch. We opened the double doors and the nauseating odour invaded our sensitive noses. The corpses looked like charcoal: there was almost no blood, just black dust and pieces of bones, charred flesh and skulls. I don't even know how I managed to be in this room and in charge of cleaning it, but I knew I didn't want Aiden to suffer this. I supposed the fact that I didn't personally know any of these people made a difference. We started lifting the remains and moved them to the cases. Luca's heart was heavy and his eyes were wet. I offered him to carry on by myself, but he refused to leave me to do it alone. It was a horror show. It didn't take us long to fill the cases, but the cleaning that went after was challenging: there were black burn marks everywhere and the tables and chairs that had once furnished the room, had almost disappeared.

Half way through, Aiden and Clara joined us and helped. They had finished gathering all the papers in every office and had also removed the numerous blood stains left by the macabre decapitation of the assistant. A while later, there were no signs left of the murders, except for the permanent structural damages that could be explained by an unfortunate fire, if needs be. All that was left were the five cases, two full of Kindreds remains and three of papers and books. Robert's belongings had been kept separate from the rest, in their own case.

"Aiden, have you found the key?" I asked.

"No, there was no key in any of the drawers or on his desk," he replied, quite upset.

"Don't you think it's odd? Robert said it's in the same place you last saw it!" Luca insisted.

"I have no idea what key he is talking about!" he answered frustrated.

"What if it is not a key per se?" I suggested.

"Smart Louise! Aiden, please read again the message!" Luca said.

"Our new addition must proceed with her training.
She is a valuable asset, even more now than ever.
Follow the plan and take her to her teacher.
The three of you have to find the next Elders to re‑
build what has been destroyed. You must act fast as
order is important. The source retains the informa‑
tion you seek. The key remains where you last saw
it. Do not let revenge fuel your lives and above all,
protect our legacy."

"So, the key is supposed to open whatever he calls 'the source' to give you the information you need in order to find the new members to rebuild Ordinem. Is that it?" I summarised.

"Of course! I understand now!" Aiden exclaimed.

"Does he mean the source is The Chapel?" asked Luca.

"Yes! I think so! There is a vault down there somewhere. I guess the information Robert is talking about is inside it."

"Do you know the code?"

"I am not sure. I was there once when Robert opened it, but I wasn't supposed to and apparently I did not fool him!"

"What are you talking about? What is the source or The Chapel?" I inquired.

"It is like a place of pilgrimage – it contains all of our history from the beginning. It is the Maker's duty to take their pupil there, at least once after transition," responded Aiden.

"So, is that the 'special place' you mentioned back at the mansion?"

"Indeed, but I was going to take you there after your training."

"I guess we will go before then now," I said, looking forward to discovering our history.

"OK, so are we heading to The Chapel next?" asked Luca motivated into action.

"Yes, the sooner the better, as Louise's training has to start!" replied Aiden.

"Yes, I want to be ready and by your side when the time to take down Kyle comes."

"Amen to that!" said Clara, softly.

"It's 5am, we need to move fast! Sunrise should be around 6.30am and according to the weather forecast, it's going to be sunny!" stated Aiden.

The idea of being stuck underground, with the horrid smell of burnt bodies, did not appeal to me at all. We had to get out of here, whatever it took! Aiden and Luca looked at each other and knew exactly what they had to do – one organised the air transportation while the other handled the land transportation on arrival. In the meantime, Clara and I went to pick up the van and brought it closer to the underground entrance, as we did have five cases to move as discreetly as possible. Quickly, we loaded all of them into the vehicle. Luca waited in the driver's seat while we went back for a last check. Fortunately, we had worked thoroughly! Aiden had one more thing to do: he went back to Robert's office and picked up all the blood bags stored there, planning ahead as usual. We headed back out, trying to beat the clock. We drove back to the airport and loaded the aircraft, after going through the fastest passport check I had ever experienced. They did not even pay attention to the cases. By 6.30am, our plane was taking off. We pulled down our windows blinds and sat down.

"Where are we going?" I asked curiously.

"Poor love, forgive us, sometimes we forget you are a newbie! We are going to the Carpathians Mountains. The Chapel is located on the grounds of a rustic castle that we own." answered nicely Clara.

"A bit cliché if you asked me!" mumbled Luca.

"Maybe it is, but this is where it all started, it's symbolic!" responded Clara.

Aiden got up and brought back bags of blood for everybody. We ate silently and I dozed off. I woke up as the plane began its descent and realised Aiden had taken my hand in his – I smiled at him. I carefully opened the window blind and was happy to see that the weather was on our side: it was very cloudy and dark. Suddenly, I thought of the two cases of body remains that we were transporting. We could not be that lucky twice.

"How is it going to work with Customs or security?"

"What do you mean?" asked Clara.

"Aren't they going to check what we have in the cases?"

"Don't worry about it love, leave that to me," she responded calmly and assuredly.

The lack of concerns from them all reassured me – after all, they were used to traveling around, although two of the five black cases seemed definitely risky to me.

When we arrived, Clara handled the talk with two Customs officials, while we presented our papers. They asked what was in the cases and Clara casually explained that we had to move some important papers from an office abroad to another in Bucharest. She was told to open the boxes, which Clara did without hesitation. The first one revealed stacks of paper, so did the second and the third. I was watching the scene aghast, hoping they would not go further. Clara was very relaxed, she looked so genuine and gentle, her body language was very confident and she was perfectly spoken. When she offered to open the remaining boxes, my heart stopped. One of the officials said it was not necessary, but the other insisted she opened them all. Instantly, she followed the instruction while smiling at him and disclosed the contents of the cases – I was stunned. Aiden glanced at me and smiled. The officials briefly looked inside with no expression on their faces, told Clara we were good to go and thanked her for her cooperation. I was gob-smacked, how the hell did she pull that off?! I tried to remain calm until we got into the car, but I was dying to know the trick. We loaded a dark grey van with tinted windows – Clara drove this time and Luca was in the passenger seat, while Aiden and I were in the back.

"Aiden, sorry I know it's not the best time, but I have so many questions!"

"I can imagine, go on, ask away!"

"What did Clara do to the Customs officials? I thought I was going to have a heart attack!"

"Sorry love, we should have forewarned you! I just convinced them that it was only paperwork in the boxes!" Clara responded before Aiden had a chance.

"Yes, but when they saw and smelt what was contained in the last boxes, why didn't they react at all? It was like they didn't see it."

"That is exactly what happened: whatever I had showed them, they would have only seen what I told them to, in this specific case, it was paperwork," she explained casually.

"Clara has a unique gift of hypnosis, that's her thing. She is extremely convincing and contrary to the rest of us, she can work on different minds at the same time," detailed Aiden.

"Incredible!" I said amazed.

"Yes, quite a cool gift to have," added Clara happily.

"And what would we have done if it was sunny now?" I continued.

"We would have arranged a driver for the van, but luckily it is dark enough. Plus, we will be in the mountains soon which helps!" answered Aiden.

I watched through the window – the scenery was lovely, very green and natural. I was amazed to be able to see so far away: not in so much detail but rather if there was a movement, it would get my attention and I could locate where it came from. It kept me occupied for the rest of the ride. Shortly after, we arrived at a modest castle, hidden in the mountainside behind tall pine trees.

Chapter XXIV

Clara parked the car in the garage and we accessed the castle directly from there. It had retained its authentic and simple look: the floor was made of old oak parquet; the ceiling revealed large wooden beams and most of the furniture was also made of wood. Every window was dressed with luxurious thick velvet curtains, which helped to keep the inside of the house well protected from the sun.

I heard footsteps approaching us, coming down from the first floor. I stared at Aiden and he told me it was only the caretaker. I guessed since this place held some of their precious secrets, they did not leave it unattended. A man seemingly in his fifties arrived in the main room where we stood.

"Hello, you got here fast!" he said.

"Yes, the trip went smoothly," Aiden responded.

The man greeted Luca and Clara and stopped in front of me. Aiden introduced us – his name was George – and told him that I was part of the team, but he did not give him any more information. Evidently, they were all well acquainted, but Aiden would not give George too many details. Aiden was a natural leader and he was well respected, as if he was some kind of important person. I completely understood why he was being secretive – we had been running around trying to keep an advantage over Kyle; but realistically, we did not have the whole picture, had no idea yet what his plan was and how far in he was, or even who worked for him. We had just dutifully followed Robert's instructions. I guessed in order to be a caretaker of such a place, you had to be very trustworthy and discreet, but we couldn't take any risks to compromise our mission.

We pretended we were here for my first pilgrimage to The Chapel and he welcomed me. I noticed Aiden, Luca and Clara exchanging a look while George was busy talking to me. I didn't know what it was all about, but I imagined it was very likely to be about the cases still in the van.

A few seconds later, Clara came up to us and placed her hand very gently on George's shoulder, asking him for news from the area, as well as his opinions on the whisky they should drink. The distraction worked and George followed her obliviously into another room. It was obvious that Aiden, Clara and Luca were used to working together. Quickly, Aiden gestured for me to follow them and the three of us went back to the car to pick up the cases. We managed to take them to some dense woods at the rear of the property and left them behind some bushes.

Luca, Aiden and I came back to the main room, where minutes ago we had met George. When he and Clara came back, it looked like we had been patiently sitting on some of the armchairs, waiting for them. We drank a glass of the whisky they had brought back. Aiden and Luca played their guest roles perfectly and led the conversation with George and Clara.

Fifteen minutes later, Aiden told George we would be going to The Chapel now and that he could finish his work for the day. George gave Aiden a key and left us. The four of us made our way to The Chapel that could not be seen from the castle. We walked under the shade of the trees, towards the thickest part of the forest – the cases weren't too far from us. Suddenly, Aiden and Luca stopped and opened a hidden trap door in the ground. We followed them down and entered a dark underground corridor, leading to the ancient chapel, which was now buried. We found a few torches to light and took one each. It did not take long for us to reach a small room, where we found holders on the walls to put the torches in. The floor was made of stone and the four walls were each decorated with a large painting illustrating a story. Each picture had an inscription written in Latin at the bottom. In the middle of the room, was a simple round white marble table on a platform made of stone. It had several candles on it that Luca had lit from his torch. Aiden was looking at the bare parts of the walls when Luca came close to me:

"These tell the beginnings of our existence. Can you read Latin?"

"I am afraid not. But let me look at the paintings first, see what I can get from them."

"I can help you with this Louise, but first we need to take care of the cases," said Aiden.

"Yes, sure, shall we bury them for the moment?" offered Luca.

"Good idea, let's bury the papers boxes. As for the others … we will have to empty them to properly inter the remains," reflected Aiden.

The three of them looked really sad and the worst is that they did not even have the time to process everything, or even take a minute to mourn their people since we had landed in Malta. I could not help thinking how their dead deserved better and suggested:

"How about we bury the documents cases now, and then find another place – a nice one – to lay to rest your comrades later tonight? You can pay your respects in peace."

"I think it is a great idea!" said Clara.

"Why don't we split up then? Clara and I can take care of the paperwork cases while you guys can get started here," offered Luca.

"Sounds good to me!" confirmed Clara.

"Fine by me too, you guys meet us back here when you are done. Just make sure to remember where you hid the documents!" concluded Aiden. When Clara and Luca left, he turned to me affectionately and said, "Thanks for being so thoughtful."

"How so?"

"It means a lot that you understand our sorrow. I know it is still all new to you and you did not know any of the Ordinem members, but for us we suffered a great loss."

"Aiden, you don't need to thank me, what we witnessed was terrifying and they deserve a proper burial and to be commemorated. Whether I knew them or not is irrelevant to me – you did and that's enough."

"Still, we all appreciate your empathy... Would you like to take a look at the paintings now?"

"Definitely!"

"Go ahead!"

I studied the paintings one by one – there seemed to be an order to follow. One man was present in every one of them and it looked like it was his story: the first picture represented his death, while two other canvases showed gruesome killings and fighting scenes; the last one seemed to depict a new beginning, as the main character was lying dead on the floor and other people appeared to be agreeing on something. The writing at the bottom of each painting was quite lengthy, probably telling the story in detail. I tried to make sense of some words, but I had no knowledge of Latin so did not get very far.

"Can I help you with the translation now?" Aiden offered.

"Yes please. Is this guy the first Kindred?" I asked.

"Yes, Lucius The First. Let's start with the first painting. The text is actually very detailed, you can't get much just from the pictures."

"That is what I thought! Go on, I am all ears!"

"Before we start, I think it is important that I remind you how different our kind was at the beginning. The origins of the story date back to ancient times, almost two thousand years ago."

"So long ago!"

Aiden and I were standing in front of the first canvas. He translated for me while I looked at the scene illustrating his words:

"Long ago, in the first century AD, two soldiers managed to retreat from a battlefield with their dying General, Lucius. He suffered so many wounds and gashes to his chest that some of his organs were visible. His end was nigh. At night, while one soldier was asleep, the other witnessed two bats feeding directly on Lucius' heart as he gave his final breath. In the morning, the soldiers buried the corpse and carried on with their journey. The following night, General Lucius rose from the dead and found his way to his comrades. He could move faster and he was incredibly strong. His senses of smell, touch, sight, sound and taste had heightened, which allowed him to track them. When he found them a few hours later, they were deeply asleep and as he looked at them, he felt overpowered by a terrible urge to drink their blood. While Lucius killed the first man, the second had time to run, screaming it was impossible since he had seen him die. Lucius then realised he had come back from the dead. He caught up with the second soldier, chocked him to death and fed on him. The soldier tried to fight back and bit Lucius' forearm, but he died regardless. Lucius buried the bodies. Later, the second soldier also rose from the dead and joined his Maker."

He paused and we moved to the second painting, where he continued: "For a while, they terrorised the local villagers crossing the mountains for work or travel. The local inhabitants knew that something was hiding in the forest and that people were disappearing, but they had no idea what it was.

Eventually, Lucius understood that the blood exchange was likely to be the key to turn his victims to become like him. Nobody else had risen from their graves, except the soldier who had bitten him.

One day, five of the strongest villagers decided to hunt down the beast that was hurting their people. By nightfall, they had found the lair, but stood no chance: Lucius and the soldier killed them all and buried them too. However, Lucius had not forgotten about his blood exchange theory and tested it with the most courageous villager by feeding him his blood while he was sucking his. As a result, the valiant Mislav also rose from the dead. Then, Lucius launched an attack on a small group of violent mercenaries that he turned too. Lucius was the strongest as well as the most savage and he was commanding his little army with an iron fist. The soldiers were possessed by their darkness; they started coming out of the forest and attacking the villages in the area, sweeping the region with destruction and sorrow. Each urge to feed became a dreadfully violent feast and all their prey were found empty of blood."

Again, Aiden paused and led me to the next picture: "In a last desperate attempt to protect their homes, the inhabitants who were left began to use witchcraft and symbols of the new monotheist God such as wooden crosses and holy water. In reality, their only hope was a group of men and women who had decided to create a secret army to hunt down and destroy the monsters. It took the courageous Humans a little time to understand what could kill a creature for eternity, but after a few attempts they figured it out. Ultimately, they led a massive assault during the day time and managed to kill a quarter of Lucius' army. The vicious General and his disciples retaliated by attacking the village where the vigilantes came from. They killed everyone, drank their blood and piled the corpses up for the brave army to see. When the vigilantes came back from their patrol, they found the heap of bodies and did not expect to find Lucius' army still there; they stood no chance and it was carnage. Lucius wanted the leader for himself: he made the man watch the massacre of his peers, then, he killed him and turned him as a punishment. His name was Borna. When he came alive again and understood what he had become, he hated himself; but Lucius kept him close to him, so he could not take his own life. Borna was disgusted by his new self, until he developed a friendship with Mislav – who had suffered a similar fate. Lucius was merciless with them and Borna never lost his desire to destroy him. However, each blood craving took him further away from his humanity. In his previous life, Borna was a wise man and the respected chief of his village."

I looked at Aiden; his tone seemed to indicate it was time to move to the last canvas. He smiled and finished the story: "Borna knew the only way to kill Lucius was to stand by his side. So, he and Mislav agreed to wait for the perfect opportunity. Until then, they decided to remain close to him hoping to find a weakness to exploit.

Eventually, another bigger group of vigilantes formed. They had found the written reports left behind by Borna's army and benefitted from their experience and knowledge. Borna and Mislav had been observing them and knew how numerous and organised they were, so they informed Lucius anticipating his reaction. He was enraged and ambushed them at night, but the new vigilantes were ready for the blood suckers and a gruesome fight took place. When Lucius was about to execute their leader, Borna jumped into the air and drove a wooden stake right through Lucius' heart. The vicious General collapsed and died. In the meantime, Mislav launched an attack on the rest of Lucius' army, allowing the vigilantes to recover and finally defeat them all.

After his strike, which had saved a Human life, Borna had a chance to talk with the survivors that he knew from his previous life. Mislav, whose loyalty laid with Borna, was spared. Borna and the leader of the brave militia called a truce. It was agreed that Borna and Mislav had to leave forever and could never come back. Before they disappeared, Borna and Mislav removed Lucius' canine teeth. They kept one and gave the other one to the vigilante leader in a declaration of peace. Lucius' corpse was burnt and his ashes were safely locked in a heavy metal box that was thrown out to sea so he could never come back. His reign of terror had lasted half a year.

Borna and Mislav retired to the mountains, feeding on animals. It took time for them to accept their new fate: they were worried that their solitary life would turn them into the same monster Lucius once was, until they realised they were nothing like him. In the end, they thought of a new way of living. This curse for some, could be a salvation for others. They imagined a life where they could peacefully walk the Earth too and be free of their deadly urges. Slowly, they started locating people who were dying prematurely and turned them, giving them a second chance, and created their own community. They are the founders of Ordinem, the new order of the Kindreds."

"Fascinating, I have so many questions!"

"Of course you do! Go on!"

"Why did Lucius and his men turn wild whereas Borna and Mislav did not? Why did they have a conscience?"

"When we become a Kindred, we keep our Human essence. Lucius and his army were men of blood, mercenaries, whereas Borna and Mislav were brave men of peace. We also think Lucius' infection was much stronger than his pupils'."

"Infection? Like a disease?"

"Over the years, we have been able to understand that the bats who fed on Lucius' heart were infected by some kind of mutated strain of rabies. Moreover, we believe the effect of the full moon on the Human body played a part as well as Lucius' blood type. Since discovering this, we are forbidden to turn Humans into Kindreds on full moon nights."

"Are these 'the alignment of unpredictable elements' you told me about?"

"Precisely. Plus, other unknown factors may have dramatically affected Lucius' chemistry too."

"How can you know all of this?"

"Years of research and science."

"Is that why you are so keen on biology?"

"I have always loved it, but yes, it is one more excellent reason to study—' Aiden was interrupted by the return of Luca and Clara.

"All done!" said Luca as they entered.

They had returned quite quickly since digging was not such a hard task for two Kindreds. Aiden looked at me and I told him we could continue our discussion later. I knew we had to prioritise right now and focus on opening the vault to find out what was kept inside.

Chapter XXV

Aiden took Robert's note out of his pocket and read it again out loud:

"Our new addition must proceed with her training. She is a valuable asset, even more now than ever. Follow the plan and take her to her teacher. The three of you have to find the next Elders to rebuild what has been destroyed. You must act fast as order is important. The source retains the information you seek. The key remains where you last saw it. Do not let revenge fuel your lives and above all, protect our legacy."

I wondered what could possibly be hidden in the vault. It was only a matter of Aiden remembering the code and location of the secret door. Luca started to take down one of the large paintings with Clara's help, but Aiden stopped them. The last time he saw Robert in here, the canvases were not moved. We each took one corner of the room and closely examined the walls, looking for irregularities that could indicate some sort of door, but nothing.

"Aiden, what do you remember?" asked Clara softly.

"The one time I came here with Robert, he showed me the paintings and we talked about our history. Then, he sent me away, telling me he would be only a few minutes behind me.

But as I left the room, I heard noises and I turned around to investigate. Robert was facing one of the walls ... this one I think, and he disappeared into another room. I left after that – I did not want to get caught. When I asked him later why he stayed behind, he told me he was not at liberty to tell me everything, but there was another room there, only accessible to the Elders of Ordinem. I have always assumed it held precious documents or archives."

"What kind of noises did you hear?" she carried on.

"I am not sure, it was almost hundred fifty years ago!" replied Aiden, annoyed with himself.

"Aiden, look at me, are you willing to work with me?" she asked meaningfully.

"Yes, let's do it!" Clara and Aiden were facing each other, looking straight into each other's eyes and holding forearms.

"Aiden, Robert said the key was where you last saw it, what was in this room last time you came? Close your eyes. Visualise the room Aiden, and tell me what you see." Clara's voice was so soft and almost melodic.

"I see the paintings, the marble table and ... that's all."

"Aiden, tell me what were you wearing that day?"

"I had a dark grey jacket, a white shirt and dark blue trousers."

"What about Robert, what was he wearing?"

"Similar, but his jacket and trousers were brown and he was wearing a hat."

"You remember very well. Now, tell me again what was in the room that day?"

"The four paintings and the table ... with candles on it."

"Aiden, tell me, were the candles lit?"

"Yes, they were ... not all of them ... no, they were ... and then they were no longer."

"Aiden, tell me, did you blow out the candles?"

"I did not."

"Did Robert?"

"I don't know."

"Aiden, what did Robert tell you before you left?"

"He said I could go and that he still had something to do there."

"Aiden, tell me, what did you hear when you left?"

"I heard ... something turning ... like a mechanism."

"Aiden, tell me, how did it sound?"

"Irregular–itsoundedlikeitwasturningindifferentdirections."

"Aiden, well done, you are going to open your eyes and be back with us," Clara ended.

As soon as Aiden opened his eyes, he was fully conscious. I could not believe what I had just witnessed. Clara's ability was amazing and so scary at the same time. Aiden was completely under her control until she released him. Naturally, we all looked at each other and all our eyes turned to the marble table with the candles. Robert must had done something to the table and put out some of candles in the process, which then revealed the secret door. I noticed that the optimal view of all the paintings, was from the middle of the room – it was the perfect angle to see every little detail. Luca was studying the table.

"So, do we think the turning mechanism comes from the table?" asked Luca.

"I think so," said Aiden while unsuccessfully trying to turn it.

"Hold on, maybe there is some kind of clutch system," suggested Luca.

"How do you mean?"

"You know, like when you change gears in the car, some kind of latch that allows a mechanical movement basically!" he explained easily.

Luca was trying to gently push and pull the table, until finally he understood the system. He pushed down on the table and it sank about twenty centimetres into the stone platform supporting it. From then, we only had to figure out which way to turn it. We tried first to rotate it in the order of the story, from the first to the fourth painting, but nothing happened.

Luca was carefully scrutinizing the mechanism while we were turning the table and said:

"Hold on, if there is a combination to find, it should work like a normal lock and we should be able to hear the clicking sound of the dials, as they move into their correct position. We have to find the sequence – it has to be something related to the paintings."

We looked at the canvases trying to identify something they all shared. They all had two things in common: Lucius and the events were happening at night. Luca grabbed the table with one hand on each side and proceeded to twist slowly the marble until he heard a 'click'. Only Kindreds were able to hear such an audibly subtle sound and even then, it required our full attention. Luca examined the table to find some sort of mark. He moved the candles around and saw a faded line in the middle of it. It seemed to be aiming at Lucius on the second painting, so Luca twisted the table again until the line pointed at Lucius on the third canvas, but there was no sound. He tried the fourth one, but again, no click. Lucius' position was not the solution, so we studied the paintings again.

"What about the moon?" suggested Aiden after a couple of minutes.

"What about it?" replied Luca uncertain of what he meant.

"Each painting is happening at night, but in each of them there is a different moon. Try the order of the moon phases in the northern hemisphere, as the scenes are taking place in the Carpathians Mountains."

Luca aimed again at the second painting that we knew was right from our first try. It had a waxing crescent moon. Then, he turned the table to the full moon on the first picture, which produced a successful click. We realised Aiden was right – the phases of the moons on the paintings did define the sequence of the lock combination. Luca kept repeating the same process and aimed at the next moon, the waning gibbous, displayed on the fourth canvas. He then moved round to the last remaining painting that showed a third quarter moon. Every time, we heard a dull click, and after the fourth click, the whole wall holding the second picture moved back. No wonder we couldn't find a door. We were in awe, but remained focused and quickly went inside the vault.

We entered the small dark room using the flash-lights on our phones and were disappointed to find it completely empty. The wall closed shut behind us, but it did not prevent us from investigating the place thoroughly and we each took a stone wall to study. I felt something a bit odd, like a crack. I looked closely and tried to wiggle the stone, which loosened a bit of dust onto my hand. It confirmed what I thought and I showed my finding to the others.

Luca took out his folding pocket knife and gave it to Aiden, who immediately went along the crack with the blade. He managed to clean all around the stone and then pulled it. It did not resist long and revealed a secret cavity that held a large leather covered book and a wooden box. Aiden pulled the book out and wiped the dust off it with the palm of his hand. We were all gathered around him, curious to discover its contents. He slowly opened it and delicately turned a few pages: they contained handwritten names with dates and other numbers. I noticed some of the identities were neatly crossed out. Aiden, Luca and Clara recognised most of the names, including Kyle's and even found their own. The book was a census – a list of all the Kindreds that had ever existed: it detailed their original names and the new ones when applicable; their dates of death; their age at the time of passing and Makers' names. The crossed-out names belonged to Kindreds who had chosen to leave the world forever.

Finally, Robert's note was making sense! With such a directory, we could easily identify the next Elders in line. Aiden picked up the wooden box and opened it: it contained a feather quill dip pen, a small vial of black ink and an old wooden ruler. The three of them looked at each other full of emotion and Clara proceeded to cross out the names of their late comrades. They also found what we had come for: the names of the next five Elders to fill the seats of Ordinem.

"I think we should destroy the pages with the names of the next Elders,' said Aiden.

"Why?" asked Luca

"We still don't know what Kyle's plan is, maybe he will be after this book too. We cannot afford for him to know who the next members of Ordinem are!"

"Good thinking!" agreed Luca.

"Can you do your thing and remember the names? The best thing would be to destroy a few pages so he doesn't go after the next generations of Elders either. We cannot take any risks."

"What is the point of having such a gift if not to use it?" answered Luca.

I asked Clara what they were talking about and she told me about one of Luca's abilities: his photographic memory. His head was probably the safest place to store the information, unless he became an enemy of Clara's; luckily, it was the complete opposite. Luca delicately ripped out a couple of pages which revealed some of the future generations of Elders. Then, the three of them exchanged another one of their collaborative looks.

"Now, we just have one more thing to do," said Clara mysteriously.

"What is it?" I asked. Clara handed the quill pen to Aiden and he looked at them with a smile. He turned the pages to the last one and wrote:

Louise Bailey – Saturday 6th October, 2018 / 31 – Aiden Wood

I understood it was a symbol of their acceptance. I thanked them, truly moved by the gesture. Aiden softly blew the fresh inked letters dry before he closed the book and replaced it in the secret cavity, along with the wooden box. We made sure to replace the stone properly and threw some dust to cover the crack. The way out was much easier: we simply had to pull a handle near the wall. Once we got back in the main room, we made sure everything was as when we first came in and Luca set the table back to its initial position. We double-checked one last time that everything looked normal and left The Chapel. When we emerged above ground it was still daylight, but I had no idea of the time.

"I am going to learn the names by heart," Luca said.

"Thanks, how about we rest for a bit? We can meet tonight for the burials," Clara offered.

"Yes, sounds good," agreed Aiden.

We walked silently back to the castle, protected by the dense forest. The day had been difficult and long – we were exhausted. We went to our separate rooms on the first floor, except Aiden, who came with me. He led me to a large yellow en-suite bedroom. At the sight of the bed, I sighed with relief and went straight to lay down on it.

"So, how are you finding your first days with us?" he said sarcastically. I looked at him, taken aback. I was definitely not expecting a joke now and burst out laughing.

"Peachy!" I responded equally sarcastic.

"How do you feel about making another exception today regarding our sleeping arrangements?" asked Aiden. I felt he was overwhelmed and imagined he didn't want to stay alone after what we had been through.

"Of course, I can behave myself."

Aiden went to shower while I checked my phone. I had received a text from Naomi: "*Seeing Ian tonight for dinner, not sure what to wear. Help!*" Sometimes, I think, it's nicer to show curves and let the imagination do the rest, so I replied: "*Go for the tight black dress you got couple of weeks ago, perfect for you! X*". I hadn't had a second to think about Naomi today, but now that I did, I really missed her.

Shortly after, Aiden came out of the bathroom and the thought of a shower appealed very much to me, so I took his place. Once the hot water was running on my skin, I realised how much had happened since my last shower, from awesome to awful. I stayed in the shower for a while – I felt very dirty and unable to get rid of the smell of smoke in my hair. When I finished and returned to the room, Aiden was asleep in the bed. He had not slept for a long time and after the recent events, he was drained. I quietly got under the cover, not too close to him as I didn't want to wake him up. Soon after, I fell deeply asleep.

At 10pm, Aiden's alarm rang; we got up slowly and went to meet Clara and Luca in the living room. Although we had only slept a little less than six hours, I felt rested. We stocked up on drinks and blood and ran to the burial place Clara and Luca had chosen earlier on. We had also taken a few lanterns. The run there refreshed my mind and triggered the feeling of alertness. We arrived in a small clearing; the two cases were on the side with two shovels. Aiden offered to dig by himself as the task at hand was easy for one Kindred. We then carefully and respectfully emptied the contents of the cases into the hole and Luca covered it up with the fresh soil that had just been dug up. Clara and I arranged a couple of dead tree trunks so we could sit around the improvised grave. We poured glasses of whisky and drank them straight down in memory of the eight late Council members and the two guards. We assumed that although he had been taken, Robert was still alive. If Kyle wanted him dead, he would have killed him with the others – I wondered what his agenda was.

I was looking at Aiden, Luca and Clara sharing memories. Clara was so intriguing: I recalled the couple of amazing stunts she had pulled off today and was fascinated by her. I had already noticed she was the wisest one of the trio and the boys were very attentive of her opinions. I asked Clara if she would come for a walk with me, which she accepted enthusiastically.

"How are you doing love? Your first few days were ... overwhelming!"

"One way to say it! I am just trying to keep up!"

"You are doing pretty well for a five-day old!"

"I am so sorry for your loss!"

"Thanks. To be honest, this is still so surreal!"

"Fair enough. Talking about surreal ... what you did with the Customs officials, at the airport, was incredible!" I said admirably.

"Ah yes, sorry we didn't warn you – it must have been horrible for you!"

"My heart stopped a couple of times!" I confirmed.

"We are so used to it!"

"Your ability is amazing and frightening at the same time! Scary to think you can get inside anyone's head so easily!"

"Well, it was not always that easy and it required a long period of intense training. Like you said, it can also be frightening as I could damage somebody's brain. You and the others are able to hypnotise one person at a time and alter the way they've experienced things, whereas I have further possibilities. I can convince them in the present as I tell them that something is happening. It doesn't matter what they see or hear or smell, what will count is what I say or describe at that moment. I can work on several people at the same time and most importantly I can get into the mind of a Kindred which is quite unusual."

"So, are you also the reason why nobody checked or even noticed the cases back in Malta airport?"

"Yes, we had no time, so the best thing to do was to make them ignore the cases, as if they weren't there."

"That is brilliant! You are amazing!"

"Thanks Louise." We exchanged a friendly smile before I resumed my questioning.

"Only Makers and pupils can share something from their minds, right?"

"Some of them yes, but a strong bond is required though. Even then, this isn't hypnosis, but rather a connection. But for me, I can access any Kindred's mind if they let me."

"And if they don't?"

"I think I could still do it, although it will be harder. I have never had to do it against anyone's will! Some of us are so old, they need a little help to remember some parts of their past."

"So, the rest of us can use hypnosis on Humans, but not on our kind?"

"To hypnotise our kind is a nasty process. For it to work, you would need the mind you want to control to be very very weak and unable to fight."

"Do you mean like if they were starving?"

"Yes, the blood is our weakness – without it we can lose control in every aspect, so craving it is no good! That's why learning how to manage our diet is critical, you will get there soon!"

"Yeah, Aiden is on top of it for now!"

"He will always be on top of everything! That's Aiden! I am glad he found you!"

"I am glad I found him too, and also you guys by the way!"

"Welcome to our family!"

"You guys are very close – how long have you known each other?"

"A long time, we are about the same age and we met at the early stage of our new lives, we got on really well and bonded straight away!"

"It is more than that, you work together like you have been colleagues all your life!"

"Well, that is true in a way: we ran many operations for Robert!"

"Like his secret service?"

"I suppose so!"

"I am very curious to ask you something, but I don't mean to appear intrusive..."

"Go on."

"Who were you before you died?"

"I was a confidence trickster, but unfortunately I got a fatal illness. Maybe it was karma. But I got a second chance and I took it!"

"That makes sense, con artists can be very good at mind games!" I joked.

Aiden and Luca called us and we headed back. They were waiting for us to return before eating and had reached a certain level of hunger. After we had eaten, Luca stood up and announced he had memorised the names on the pages of the census and was going to burn them. He warned us that in case something unfortunate happened to him, he had taken pictures of the pages and saved them on a USB stick that he had hidden in the woods. He gave us the coordinates and we learnt them by heart, before we watched the old pages being devoured by the flames of Luca's lighter.

"We need to discuss what we'll do next," said Aiden pensively.

"Aren't we going to Cambodia to Chhay?" asked Luca.

"Yes, we are. I thought we could plan our search for the Elders over there and travel as soon as we locate them."

"Yes, so did I!" confirmed Luca with a smile.

"When are we leaving?" inquired Clara.

"How do you feel about early morning?" asked Aiden.

"The earlier the better!" responded Clara. I nodded in agreement with them.

"OK, if everybody agrees, that's great. We can travel during the day and arrive in Cambodia in the evening. With the time difference and time of travel, we should leave around 5am to arrive there at 7pm."

"Sounds good, finally a solid nine hours of sleep during the flight!" agreed Luca.

"Don't forget there is an extra six and a half hours drive to get to Chhay from the airport too," reminded Aiden.

After a few texts and phone calls, our trip was arranged. We had to leave the house at 3.30am, which was only in a couple of hours. We reviewed our plan, buried the two empty metal cases so we did not leave any traces and finally tidied the shovels back in the garden shed. Soon after, we were driving back to the airstrip and at 5.15am our jet took off. We ate again on board and all of us were asleep a short moment after.

Chapter XXVI

Chhay had arranged for someone to pick us up from the airport. The driver took us to a local style van; we hopped in and he started the long drive. Aiden had asked the driver in Khmer, the local language, if he could take the passenger seat, which he had gladly agreed to. He didn't expect to be spoken to in his mother-tongue and enjoyed the easy way of communicating.

I plugged my headphones into my mobile and put some music on. I had received a few emails from my ex-colleagues and I was quite looking forward to reading them. They were probably recounting what happened after I had resigned. They all congratulated me on making such a wise choice and informed me that my speech had inspired everyone from the old team to look for new jobs. A couple of them had already dropped their resignation letters on Eleanor's desk. Apparently, after I left, the woman spent the rest of the day in her office, with the door closed. Her assistant told some of my friends she was furious that I had humiliated her in front of her employees. It was one of the best things I have ever done!

Throughout the journey, I looked outside the window. Although it was pitch black, my newly acquired night vision enabled me to distinguish the small towns we passed through. After 10pm, there were almost no lights, so you could tell everybody was asleep. The further we drove, the more remote and mountainous the area was, and the villages became rarer.

Luca was reading an engineering book while Aiden chatted away with the friendly driver. Clara invited me to watch a film on her laptop. A while later, the driver stopped along a dirt road in the middle of nowhere. Aiden explained that the house was further away up the mountain, only accessible from a narrow trail in the jungle. We took our bags and started the night walk to reach our final destination. After ten minutes, we stopped in a clearing displaying a remarkable wooden structure: after four steps, there was a platform and tall thick vertical beams holding the dried grass roof; the space was all open for the most part. We walked up to a man who was waiting for us in front of the small set of stairs – I guessed that he was Chhay. He was about 5'5, with black short hair and he appeared to be in his late thirties. He was lean and looked strong. Aiden greeted him with a hug, speaking in Khmer; Clara and Luca followed before we were introduced.

"Nice to meet you Louise!"

"You too Chhay!" I responded enthusiastically.

"Please, let's all come up!" he said while climbing up the stairs.

It was perfectly cosy: there was a lounge area with built-in sofas on both sides, as well as large cushions and a couple of tables in the middle of the room. At the back, on the left, was a closed room exposing the first wall of the structure; on the right side, was a bare open kitchen area with a counter. The back and right sides of the kitchen were also protected by wooden walls. Only the lounge area was open to the outside. There were no windows to protect it from the rain, but Chhay had arranged some blinds made from tarpaulins to loosen in such event. He also had set up an outdoor lounge by the kitchen with a little staircase for access. I was amazed to find such an arrangement in the middle of the jungle. Chhay invited us to sit there while he brought back some beers. Then, we told him what had happened to the Ordinem members, including Robert.

"I cannot believe this! Are you sure?" he asked shocked.

"Considering we had to watch the whole thing on video and clean the place out, yes we are sure!" replied Luca.

"*Somtoh bong*[7], it's just that ... it's ..."

"I know, it's sick!" said Luca disgustedly.

"I was just talking to Robert two days ago, about Louise actually!"

"Yes, we were with him then. We agreed you would be the best trainer for Louise," explained Aiden.

"I will do my best, but it doesn't mean it will be easy!" Chhay said, looking at me.

"I don't expect it to be, but I am OK with that!" I replied honestly.

"I like your motivation! First rule is: you sleep alone! There is a choice though: either you can settle in the shed in the back or we all sleep here but no fooling about, I need you to be hundred per cent focused and I won't accept any distractions."

"Sure, I only have one question, how safe is it to sleep here during day time?"

"I had the house built in a specific location, the mountains cover us from the sunlight and you will see tomorrow, we are surrounded by tall trees that completely shield the house. The tarpaulin shades are not even necessary, their sole purpose is to protect us from the heavy rain."

"To be honest love, we won't be here all the time so choose whatever suits you! If it helps, we have all slept here many times!" Clara reassured me.

"OK then, I would rather sleep here," I confessed.

"So, it's sorted then! Tomorrow we will start at 6 after sunset with an evaluation. I would like to assess your skills – Robert told me he suspected you to be very strong and mentioned your previous experience in fighting. After the assessment, I should be able to define a suitable training program!" explained Chhay.

"Sounds good to me!" I agreed.

7   Sorry brother

"If you don't mind me asking, Louise, how did you end up in this mess being only a few days old?" asked Chhay.

"You can tell him the truth," encouraged Aiden.

"Well, Kyle is the reason I died – he made it happen."

"But why specifically you?"

"Louise and I used to be a couple until Ordinem found out from Kyle. Eventually, I had to comply and remove myself from Louise's life. I think one of the reasons is that Kyle wanted to punish me or something!" explained Aiden.

"What! I know this isn't allowed, but in any case, it's not his place to intervene! He's completely lost it! We can't have a psychotic Kindred on the loose!"

"Agreed!" said Aiden and Luca at the same time.

"That is why we need to find the next Elders to re-form Ordinem, very fast!" stated Aiden.

"Do you know who they are?"

"Yes, we have their names from Robert – he had time to leave us enough clues. If we act fast, we can have it sorted in less than a week!" responded Luca.

"Actually, what about Robert?" asked Chhay.

"If Kyle took him, Robert is still alive and it means he needs him for something. We will look for him after we find the Elders, who can then prepare the election of the Younger members. It's one more reason to work as efficiently as we can," detailed Aiden.

"You're right, count me in to help you find Robert!"

"Oh! And one more thing: Kyle has some kind of army, a dozen of people from what we could see!" added Luca.

"What the hell? Who are they?"

"Good question *bong*[8]!" replied Luca.

"You know... I don't know what Kyle's agenda is, but there is something odd here, I mean I doubt his actions are thoughtless! Maybe he was planning to take down Ordinem all along, despite what happened to me!" I suggested.

8   Brother

"We are definitely missing some parts of the puzzle here, but I believe Kyle is not expecting us to have the right keys to rebuild Ordinem so fast!" said Clara.

"That's definitely a plus! What do you think Kyle's motive is though? Why is he doing all of this? He does not fit Aiden's description of the way we should behave!" I insisted.

"No, he doesn't and I don't think any of us have experienced a Kindred going rogue! I have been thinking about what happened – seeing Ordinem removed like that was … tough and even if we managed to rebuild it, how do we deal with what happened?" asked Clara sadly.

"We will figure it out *Clarita*, but for sure, we will get justice!" answered Luca.

"I hope you are right; I fear this could be the beginning of much trouble!" she added.

"Robert is Kyle's Maker too, right?" asked Chhay suddenly.

"Yes indeed!" responded Aiden.

"Do you know why he made him?" continued our host.

"If I remember well, he needed the skills of a talented book-keeper to start a new business venture. He found out about Kyle who was described to him as a hard-working man and skilled at banking, but there were rumours that he was suffering a bad case of pneumonia. Robert turned him before his sickness got too bad, but officially, he died of natural causes of course."

"What was their relationship like? I thought they got on fine," wondered Chhay.

"Pretty good actually, Kyle was always happy with the change to his life and stood by Robert for a long time."

"What has changed then?" I asked confused.

"The last election. Kyle presented himself to the Elders for the Youngers election shortlist, but he did not make it to the final selection. He thought that the last trio of Youngers who were elected, were to put it in his own words 'useless morons with no vision'."

"How does the Youngers election work exactly?" I inquired curiously.

"The Elders select six candidates who are then voted for by us. Every young Kindred of at least a hundred years old can present their profiles, like a job interview. The Elders can also call people they are particularly interested in. The Youngers members are elected every twenty years and can try to renew their mandate individually if they wish."

"So, basically he is angry because he lost?" I summarised.

"He is a narcissist! He thinks he can do better than everyone!" said Clara suddenly.

"To be honest Aiden, I think he also didn't appreciate that they approached you and I and offered us a position on the final list," added Luca.

"He definitely has an issue with you Aiden and you too Luca!" agreed Clara.

"But we declined, I was not ready and I am still not!" Aiden defended himself.

"Which is precisely why he dislikes your success. You didn't want the job and you got it, but he wanted it and didn't get it!" simplified Luca.

"Do you know why they denied him the chance to be on the shortlist?" I asked.

"Because of his lack of social skills and field experience. The job of the Youngers is to be close to the community and know what is going on, such as trends and how we can evolve alongside Human society. They have to be very much aware of what is happening in our world as well as the Humans', whereas the Elders are wiser and more traditional. They did say Kyle had more of an Elder profile than a Younger one, but he took it as a lame excuse!" Aiden explained.

"Aiden and Luca, on the other hand are very sociable, they know everybody!" added Clara.

"What about you Clara, are women not accepted as equal members of Ordinem?" I wondered.

"Of course they are, love! There is no concept of gender discrimination in our society, actually there is no concept of any sort of xenophobia really and you can have relationships with any Kindred you want! The colour of skin is equally un-important to us. It is probably the number one thing that I don't miss about the Human society. As for my future with Ordinem, I am afraid I will never be offered any sort of higher position because of my mind control ability. I guess they worry I could use this skill to serve my own agenda," explained Clara.

"I see, it makes sense. When was the last election?" I asked.

"Seventeen years ago and since then, Kyle has been distant with Robert: he stopped accompanying him on business and visited him a bit less. I guess Kyle expected Robert to do more for him, but even if Robert is one of the top Elders, he can't make decisions alone. Kyle is still attached to him, he is his Maker after all, but, that day something broke and was never repaired," Aiden said.

"What about your relationship with Kyle before that?" I questioned Aiden, keen to find out more.

"Alright, we got on fine but we never had the same am-bition: he was always interested in Robert's affairs, whereas I was more concerned about life in its general sense. Robert has always trusted me and valued my honest opinion and free mind. Clara, Luca and I often ended up handling assignments for him, but we never cared for the politics."

"Do you think this could have bothered Kyle?" asked Chhay.

"I don't think so, Kyle is more of a thinker, he does not like running operations and logistics so no, I don't believe he felt left behind. He actually more enjoyed ordering people around on Robert's behalf," stated Aiden.

"So, Kyle attacked Louise because of this election feud?" simplified Chhay.

"My personal take on that is that he found out about Aid-en and Louise and informed on them to Ordinem. I guess he then judged their ruling not to be severe enough and decided to punish Aiden himself, despite the fact that he had already obeyed Ordinem and disappeared from Louise's life," said Luca.

"You're right. Maybe, for him, it was the final straw... But I think the trigger was the last election, I believe he has been waiting for an opportunity to take his revenge on Aiden, like a childish 'you steal from me then I steal from you' tantrum. I guess the fact that Robert is both their Maker didn't help. He probably thought he took your side, which he did not," added Clara.

"But I did not steal anything from him!"

"Rationally, you absolutely didn't do anything wrong, but in his narcissistic mind, they – including Robert – chose you over him, so it became your fault. He did not go after Luca, at least not yet, although he got the same offer as you. It's personal," argued Clara.

"You're right! And it doesn't help that you stayed with us when he was courting you!" Luca said to Clara.

"What? Kyle was into you?" I asked Clara, surprised.

"A very long time ago, he fancied me but I didn't reciprocate. He is good looking, however something always put me off and until now, I wasn't sure what."

"Well, the guy is obviously the type to hold a grudge, so let's consider everything!" said Luca.

"So, what are we going to do with him?" asked Chhay.

"That's the Ordinem's decision, that's why we need to find its new Elders as soon as possible. Then, we can find Robert and deal with Kyle accordingly," answered Aiden.

"I keep wondering what he needs Robert for?" said Clara.

"His insurance and protection at the same time, his hostage basically!" replied Luca.

"I think there is more to it. Robert is a key member of Ordinem, the most respected amongst all the Elders; he built the community we are now and knows everything about our kind.

If Kyle destroyed our leaders—" Clara started when Aiden suddenly interrupted:

"Could it be a coup?"

Chapter XXVII

We all looked at each other and realised Aiden was completely right – it was very likely to be a coup. Robert must have understood too and guided us to find the new Elders especially to prevent such a thing. If we found them in time, Kyle would not be able to set his plan in motion. However, we could not figure out why he took Robert; he would never give Kyle any information, so obviously we were missing something. At least, we had a considerable head start: Kyle still had no idea that we had all the keys we needed to re-form Ordinem. It was our biggest advantage, so we had to keep this quest quiet and most importantly, we had to act fast.

It was almost morning and after eating, we all went to sleep. I had to make my bed away from the others, under the scrutiny of Chhay. I fell asleep quickly, satiated and calm. When I woke up, the sun was about to set and the sky had darkened. Chhay and Clara were already up. She showed me the way to the bathroom: it was basic with a toilet; a large plastic bucket full of water with a plastic bowl scoop and a sink under a simple mirror. Every now and then, Chhay pumped water from the nearby stream to refill the bucket, which was used for showering and flushing the toilet. After washing, I came back to the main area; Aiden and Luca were now awake. I went to my improvised bed and tidied the duvet and pillows. Aiden walked up to me, looking cute, as he had just woken up:

"Hey, how are you?" he greeted.

"Hi, I am good and you?"

"Fine, did you sleep well?"

"Yes! And you?"

"Yes! How do you feel about your skills assessment today?"

"I am looking forward to it! I am curious too."

"Me too, to be honest. Louise, I know we have not been so close those past few days, but I wanted to say that I miss you," he confided.

"I miss you too!" I responded with a big smile.

Chhay gave me a small glass of blood to drink and told me we would be leaving in thirty minutes. I drank and used the little free time to send a text to Naomi, asking her how was her date with Ian. She would find it extremely strange if I didn't ask! Anyway, I wanted to ring her later and hear her voice.

Chhay called and instructed me to follow him to the test location. Aiden, Clara and Luca were not ready and followed a few minutes later. Chhay took me up a steep mountain jungle track at a rapid pace. Half way up, he accelerated and I had no other choice than to speed up. An hour later, we reached the top. Aiden, Clara and Luca were already there.

"How did you guys make it here before us?" I asked panting slightly.

"We took the shortcut!" responded Luca clearly amused.

"There's a shortcut?" I said surprised.

"There is no shortcut with training!" replied Chhay calmly.

There was nothing around, except for a few solar lights that were illuminating a small space, where the mountain slopes fell steeply away – a bad fall could seriously hurt! Chhay gestured at the middle of the area and I went to start there, while the others backed off to the edge of the patch. I didn't like having an audience, but I had to ignore them and avoid any distractions. He picked some items out of his bag: a few focus pads and a couple of sticks. He asked me if I knew the traditional boxing punch numbers, which I did, so he told me the combinations he wanted me to do. Next, he asked to see my kicks. He then demanded a mixed sequence of punches and kicks. So far, it was easy, but I knew it was only the warm-up. Then, he took two medium sticks that he assembled into one long cane. Chhay wanted me to avoid all of his strikes completely without being touched by the baton, falling or hitting him back. He started slow and increased his speed to a proper attack intensity. Avoiding the cane became more and more difficult and I got hit quite a few times in different places, which annoyed me. Although he didn't really hurt me, every time he hit me I wanted to retaliate, but I couldn't as it was part of the exercise. By the end of it, I could feel a ball of anger and frustration forming in my gut, very similar to what I had experienced before I ended up in Karuna's shop ten days ago.

Chhay was relentless and complicated the exercise by blind-folding me, so now I had to avoid the stick by relying on my other senses. He advised me to ignore everything around me, in order to focus solely on the sound and smell of the cane and himself. He gave me a minute to focus and made the first strike that I avoided successfully. I could hear the pace of his movements increasing, but he never went as fast as he previously had. He wanted to see how good I was at using my senses to avoid the danger. The exercise was difficult and even if I avoided many of his strikes, I still got hit several times.

He had been evaluating me for quite a while, when Chhay told me to remove my blindfold and get in a fighting position. He placed himself in front of me and we bowed each other. I instinctively positioned myself in the boxing style I had learnt when I was younger. Chhay had a completely different style, similar to karate. He threw together an overwhelming combination of punches and kicks that I managed to mainly protect myself from. Finally, I could retaliate, but he fended off most of my strikes. We carried on like this for a while – both our defences were strong and we moved fast, until Chhay sent me to the ground with a high kick, jumped at me and blocked me with a choking position. There was no way I was going to tap out, so I fought back looking for ways out. The ball of anger in my stomach was growing. His grip was tight, but I found a way to free one of my knees and counter-block him; however, he escaped my hold. This locking, chocking, counter-blocking and escaping went on for a long time. Ground fighting like wrestling was exhausting. It took so much strength and effort, especially with a super strong experienced Kindred. Eventually, Chhay found a way to have me completely locked and choked. I did not want to give up, even though he kept tightening his grip. The ball of anger kept rising. He told me to tap out, but I wouldn't. I felt fine and wanted to fight my way out of it. I kept trying and he kept increasing his grip. I could hear that Aiden was worried and whispering for me to tap out, but I still didn't – I was sure I could find a way out. Suddenly everything went black, I was out cold. When I opened my eyes, I saw four blurry shapes above me.

"Louise, are you OK?" asked Aiden still worried.

"Yes ... what happened?" I said, clueless.

"You were stubborn and did not tap out!" replied Chhay calmly.

"Why would I? I was fine!" I responded sitting down.

"Apparently you weren't, since you passed out!" continued Chhay.

"Did I?" I asked, puzzled.

"Did you not feel your struggle?" inquired Chhay.

"No! I was still trying to work out how I could escape your lock!" I explained.

"If I may Chhay, Louise is not a stubborn kind of person, I mean she wouldn't not tap out to make a point!" Aiden defended.

"Yay that's me! Not a sore loser!"

"Interesting, so you did not feel anything?" double-checked Chhay.

"No, except for this weird ball of anger or energy in my stomach."

"OK – I know very well what you're talking about, let me think about it! Let's go back to the house. That's enough for today," concluded Chhay.

We took the shortcut and descended the mountain much faster than Chhay and I had gone up. As soon as we arrived back, I went to the bathroom. When I undressed, I saw a few bruises and marks already appearing on my body – that was fast! – however, I could not feel any pain nor tiredness from the intense evaluation. Clara knocked at the door to let me know we were going to chill that evening. It was a good idea, I think we all really needed a break from the stressful last couple of days. I supposed it also meant that they would be leaving tomorrow and wanted to regroup before they initiated their quest to find the Elders. When I joined them, Chhay was still getting ready, while Aiden, Clara and Luca were settling down in the outdoor lounge area. There were some drinks as well as a cooler that contained our dinner. Out of nowhere, music came out of a portable speaker; I looked up and realised it was Chhay setting up a playlist.

"I hope you like 90's hip-hop love, Chhay is crazy about it since his last life in the US!" warned Clara.

"No worries, we'll get on just fine!"

"You were amazing today!" Clara complimented.

"Yes, except for passing out without even realising it!" I joked.

"She is right, you did pretty well. I didn't know you could fight like this!" added Luca.

"I trained a lot when I was younger!"

"I still kicked your butt!" teased Chhay.

"Enjoy! The student might beat the master some day!" I replied equally amused.

Aiden was sitting on the sofa looking at us. He finally came up to me and pulled me to one side; he gently touched my collar bone and said:

"That is a nasty bruise!"

"I'll be OK!"

"Does it hurt?" he said brushing my blemished skin with his fingertips.

"Not at all. Neither do the others!" I said feeling aroused and trying to act normal.

"Do you have a lot of bruises?"

"I think five or six more."

"And it does not hurt at all?"

"Nope, is it supposed to?"

"Well, yes, we recover very fast, yet we still hurt for a bit depending on the extent of the damage!"

"I really am fine! Don't worry! I am going to ring Naomi and I will be back with you soon," I ended softly.

I broke away from the group and walked a little further away. Naomi answered her phone almost right away – I could tell she was waiting for my call. She recounted her evening with Ian and confessed what she feared: the more time she spent with him, the more she liked him. I encouraged her to enjoy this new relationship and reminded her that they already knew each other very well. She asked me if I had heard back from the fictitious man I had met on my equally fictitious trip to the countryside. I pretended that we had texted a few times and were planning to meet up when I was back in London. She inquired about making a quick visit one weekend, but I stopped her, using a substantial amount of work as an excuse. We chatted a bit longer about her work and gossiped about our friends as well as the London scene – I missed the city!

After ending the call, I returned to my companions, who were talking about the next stages of the plan. They agreed on a route that would be the most time efficient. Aiden and Luca were going to travel west – to the Netherlands, Czech Republic and Croatia – while Clara was going to head to Hong-Kong. They were still trying to locate the last Elder, so they decided they would all meet up later wherever the future leader was.

As I expected, they confirmed their departure the following day, except for Clara who was going to leave later. As soon as the details were all sorted, we resumed trying to figure out Kyle's plan.

"Guys, I know there are so many things to talk and think about, but can we address Kyle's army for a minute?" demanded Clara.

"Sure, it is definitely a matter of high importance, we have to figure out who these guys are!" confirmed Aiden

"That's a scary thing!" let out Chhay.

"What do we think?" Luca continued.

"He cannot hypnotise and keep under control that many people at the same time, so I guess he is either turning them or hiring them," Clara deducted.

"Those two options are both disastrous. Whether he hired or made them, he puts us all at risk of being exposed and exterminated. He endangered our well-being and above all, he dishonoured all of the Ordinem legacy. Of course, should he be the Maker of his army, we can expect a grisly battle and serious collateral damage. The last thing we need is a group of untrained and dangerous Kindreds going on a killing spree," summarised Aiden. There was a long silence, Aiden's reflections were scary.

"What would he gain from exposing our world? I mean surely he would also be hunted down along with the rest of us," I said logically, hoping to be right.

"If he is staging a coup to take over Ordinem, he would want to avoid exposure at all cost," said Luca.

"Technically yes, but while we don't have the full picture, we should still consider it and be prepared," Aiden advised wisely.

"Yes, we should definitely be prepared for the worst!" Luca agreed.

Then, Aiden leaned towards Chhay and asked him something discreetly. I knew I could listen if I wanted to, but I remembered Aiden telling me he respected my privacy, so I thought the least I could do was to reciprocate. Next, he got up and asked me if I wanted to go on a walk with him, which I gladly accepted. I understood he had asked my new official trainer if it was alright. Since they were leaving the following day and the real training was going to start tomorrow too, Chhay was kind enough to let us have a private goodbye. We walked back to the top of the mountain where I had undertaken my test a short while ago.

"How are you doing Aiden?"

"Honestly, I don't know. But being here with you now makes me feel better."

"It's been a rough couple of days, I am sorry."

"I am the one who should be sorry for dragging you into this mess."

"You didn't do that – Kyle and only Kyle, did. If it wasn't for you, I wouldn't be here."

"If it wasn't for me, you would not have died in the first place."

"Aiden, I accepted my fate, why don't you?"

"Because I worry I am failing you. Everything I told you about us and our world seems so far away. Instead, we are racing against the clock to rebuild Ordinem and find Robert. People have died horribly and I am going to leave you alone to train. Not really what I pictured for us."

"Listen, I am OK with that. I really think it is best for me to train here alone with Chhay, even though I will definitely miss you all. I want to be ready when it comes to finding Robert and fight."

"Sometimes I forget how strong you are."

"So are you. Don't worry, I don't regret turning."

"Really?"

"Yes!"

"I love you Louise. I can't wait for this to be over!" he said devotedly.

"I love you too, we'll get there!"

It was the first time since we had found our way to each other that we shared our mutual love. I needed to hear that, we both did. I could feel his desire for me and he could feel mine for him. Aiden slowly bit his bottom lip, I have always loved when he did that and found it so sensual. Then, unexpectedly, he took me in a warm and tight embrace. His passion got me truly aroused which resulted in me tightening my grip around him. He probably felt my excitement and gently parted his strong body from mine.

"I am sorry, I shouldn't have. I just wanted to be close to you for a bit."

"Don't worry, it was worth it. Let's go get some ice!" I joked. He laughed and we headed back to the house.

When we reached Clara, Chhay and Luca, they were chatting and laughing. It was nice to hear something other than sorrow. Soon after, the first lights of dawn appeared and it was time for us to sleep. Once in my bed, I replayed our amorous embrace, barely able to control my thoughts. It took a lot of effort to steer my mind away from Aiden, but eventually I managed to visualise today's training assessment and reviewed all my movements, as well as Chhay's.

Chapter XXVIII

The noise of people moving around woke me up, although I did not even realise I had fallen asleep. Aiden and Luca were gathering their stuff together, while Chhay was organising the last details of their journey to Phnom Penh airport. They were travelling during the day, so he had to make sure the transportation was 'daylight proof'.

It was going to be my first time without Aiden since I turned. Although I agreed it was best to train alone with Chhay, it still reassured me that Clara was going to stick around a bit longer. A part of me thought she had delayed her trip to ease me into the isolation, so I would not lose everyone at once. When they were ready, Aiden took me aside:

"Are you ready to start your apprenticeship?"

"Yes, more than ever!" I responded enthusiastically.

"Clara will be here for at least a couple of days. I know you have just met Chhay, but you've seen, he is really a nice guy. He will take good care of you. I also know you must still have tons of questions and I am sorry we haven't had a chance to address those. But don't worry, Chhay is here to guide you. You can ask him anything."

"I will and I am sure I'll be fine."

"Chhay is taking your training seriously and he likes to be efficient, so expect long hours of work to achieve the results."

"I can't wait to start! I cannot stress enough how much I am looking forward to being completely in control!" I said, recalling the emotion I felt last night.

"Me too!" he said with a provocative smile.

"You are going to Amsterdam first, aren't you?" I inquired.

"That's right."

"And you already know the Elder you are going to meet, right?"

"Yes. It's fine, the older Kindreds know that duty may call at any given time! By the way, Chhay recommended that I don't contact you while I am away, so I will keep him updated and he will pass it on."

"Fair enough."

"Regarding your feeding schedule, Chhay will take over and teach you how to adjust it to your needs."

"That's great, I would like to be independent with my feeding. I don't want to be a liability to you for ever, or anyone else for that matter!"

"Don't worry, you will get there soon!"

"Aiden! Luca! The van has arrived, he is waiting for you on the road," informed Chhay.

"We must go now, we have to go through the jungle quickly to stay protected from the sun and literally jump in the van!" explained Aiden.

"Chhay, are you sure they followed the instructions with the windows and covers, not like last time?" teased Luca.

"Yes *bong*[9], I explained you are undertaking medical treatment and are extremely photosensitive, so they won't take any risks!"

"*Vale! Awkun chiran bong*[10]! We'll see you in a week or so! Aiden, let's go!" said Luca.

Aiden nodded, wished me good-luck with the training and said goodbye along with Luca. I watched them disappear into the thick jungle. The clock had just struck 4pm and Chhay

9 Brother

10 Alright! Thank you very much brother!

advised me to go back to sleep and rest before training at 6.30pm. He added that we would continue working on it all night, which convinced me to comply with his suggestion.

A couple of hours later, I ate and followed him to a different place. It was only five minutes walk from the house, but it was a proper training pitch. We began the first day of what was going to be an arduous week. Chhay started with an exercise he had devised overnight.

"I thought of something, but it sounds very brutal," he started.

"OK, go on."

"I believe you may have a higher tolerance to pain than most of the other Kindreds, which is why you didn't feel yourself passing out and I would like to assess the extent of it."

"Sounds like you are going to do painful stuff to me!"

"Well, it is up to you, the exercise here is not to hold onto pain, but to let me know as soon as you feel it."

"OK then, let's do this!"

"I will not hold off, I will keep going further until you tell me to stop, you get it?"

"Yes."

We began our fighting session. It was nothing like yesterday – Chhay was stronger and faster. It made sense, as if we wanted to know when I felt pain, I had to be hit first. The fact that I knew how to handle myself when threatened, only made the challenge more difficult for him. Little did I know that he had planned for this, and that day I discovered several higher levels of his strength. Shortly after we started the combat, he increased his speed and power, which made it impossible for me to fend off all of his attacks. I got hit hard quite a few times, but I could keep going. Chhay backed off for ten seconds, then circled around me while I got back in position. The next time Chhay launched at me, his power and speed had doubled. I fell on the ground and as soon as my defences were down, he kicked me many times. I could feel each of Chhay's strikes; he was incredibly strong, yet his power was perfectly balanced.

Only then did I start feeling pain and told him to stop. He immediately retreated, which allowed me to sit up.

"Louise, are you OK?" demanded Chhay.

"I guess so, a bit dazed though!"

"Did you only feel the pain when you asked me to stop?"

"Yes. It's odd, I could feel every hit and their intensity but it didn't hurt that much, well, at least not until I told you. How did I do?"

"Not bad. Your tolerance is definitely higher, but not infinite. To give you an idea, I was not at my maximum strength. You could still be knocked out, but it would take more power or people than usual. Now, I am curious to see if your limits are the same depending on your emotional state."

He helped me up and we moved on to a Qi-Qong session – which is very similar to Tai Chi – to practice working on my energy levels and learn how to feel them. After an hour of slow controlled movements, we continued with meditation. It was hard to empty my mind completely, but I concentrated hard and the efforts paid off. Chhay did all the exercises with me so that I could copy him.

Next, he sent me on a hunt through the jungle: he had hidden a bag somewhere in the vegetation and I was to retrieve it. The only clue he gave me, was that I should follow the smell of lemongrass. He hinted at the direction to take and then left. I stood in the jungle, trying to identify the scent of the lemongrass, but smelt nothing. Luckily, this was not my first time and I thought of Aiden's footprints that had led me to him when we had played hide and seek. Unfortunately, I couldn't detect anything on the ground and then I remembered the trick of going up into the trees. I tilted my head back and looked to see if any of the branches had been disturbed by someone climbing and moving around up there. I was happy to see some clues to follow. Chhay must have climbed and jumped from tree to tree, so I copied him. I kept advancing cautiously until I noticed the branches ahead were intact – unlike the ones under me – he probably had climbed down, so I did the same. Once I was on the ground, it was easy to track his footprints and soon after I identified a faint scent of lemongrass – I was near. It took me a little while to determine which direction to take next, as the smell was all around me. I focused entirely on my olfactory sense and finally distinguished where it was coming from. I walked carefully in its direction in case I missed a turn or a hiding spot for the bag. Finally, I found an old yellow satchel simply nailed to a tree trunk, above a patch of lemongrass.

I took the liberty of picking some leaves to make tea as I used to love it, but I had no idea if I still would. As I was bending down, I heard a noise – something was moving very close by. I slowly straightened up and analysed the environment. I could definitely hear something in motion but could not see it yet. I waited patiently behind the tree trunk; it was getting closer. Then, I saw a dog roaming. He looked very similar to a Vietnamese Phu-Quoc Ridgeback: his fur was light brown, almost golden, but gradually darkening at the tip of his muzzle, ears and tail. When he spotted me, he stopped and stayed still. Curious, I softly took a small step towards him, he growled and then hid behind a bush. I noticed he was very skinny and looked quite weak – he was probably looking for food and water.

Unable to help him at the moment, I took the yellow bag partly filled with lemongrass and headed back to Chhay. He asked how I had found the bag and congratulated me. We had been training for almost six hours, but Chhay wanted to finish with another session of Qi-Qong, so I did as instructed. He explained the first step in controlling my energy was to find it and feel it flowing inside me, which was the purpose of Qi-Qong.

I could not stop thinking about the dog, so after the session, I asked Chhay if he had by any chance some food suitable for a starving dog. He told me to check in the kitchen as sometimes, people who took care of the place when he was away, would leave things behind. I checked and found a few packs of dried noodles. I cooked them, rinsed them with cold water and put them in a plastic bowl. I took another identical recipient and washed out an empty bottle before filling it to carry some water. I left quickly, hoping he would still be there.

When I arrived back at the tree, I picked up his scent, so he was still nearby. Then, I saw him a few metres away, still very weak and barely holding up. He caught my scent too and looked at me; I moved one step forward and it startled him. I decided that it was close enough to get his attention and set up the bowl of food and the other one of water on the ground. I then backed off a few metres away from him. It took a minute before he started moving towards the food. Even then he took wary steps, regularly stopping, sniffing and checking I had not moved towards him. I was trying not to look at him, as I knew eye contact could be taken as provocation in dog language. About twenty minutes later, he had finally reached the first bowl; he took his first mouthful and straight away looked around to check all was well. The second mouthful was identical, but after that, he put his head down and he finished the food rapidly. He also drank all the water, the poor thing was starved and dehydrated.

I had placed the water bowl a little bit away from the food, but closer to me. Slowly and warily, he came towards me; it took him a few minutes to get to me. When he was a metre away, he stretched his neck to the maximum so he could study my scent. I wondered if we still smelt like Humans. I remained still and he came closer. I kept avoiding eye contact with him and let him smell me as much as he needed. Then, I gently patted him on his shoulders and under his neck, which he allowed. Soon after, I could see a change of behaviour – he understood I was here to help him. We stayed there for a while; he let me pet him more and he seemed to really like it. I waited until he was completely relaxed and trusting before I got up. I told him I would bring him more food tomorrow. I knew he didn't understand my words, but I hoped he understood my intention. I was a bit upset to leave him there, but I knew if I stayed, I would be here until sunrise.

As I started to make my way back, I noticed the dog was shadowing me, but I didn't mind – I was secretly hoping he would stay with me forever. When I arrived at Chhay's place, the dog was still with me, but he stopped when he noticed another person. He moved cautiously and smelt every inch of the place. We ignored him, as it was important not to force anything and to let him come to us at his own pace.

"What are you doing Louise?" asked Chhay.

"Me? Nothing," I replied, unsure of how he would react to the dog.

"Oh really? Because it looks like you got us a dog!" he said lightly.

"Sorry, but I couldn't let him starve to death – look at him he is so cute! A bit skinny yes, but he will get better once I take care of him!"

"Fair enough! To be honest, I don't mind having him around, but you will have to care for him on top of your training. If he turns out to be a distraction, he will go! Alright?"

"Yes! Thanks, it won't affect my training or motivation in any shape or form! Do you know where I can get some more food for him?"

"At night it will be tricky in such a remote area. How about I get someone to do some shopping and deliver it at sunset along with the block of ice?"

"Oh yes please!"

"No ready-made dog food though, you will have to cook for him."

"OK, so rice, long green beans, carrots and chicken or beef meat and some liver."

"How do you know that?"

"Not my first time!"

Chhay was getting a heavy rectangular block of ice delivered every few days that he would place in a big cooler to hold the stock of blood. It was very common in Cambodia to see such a cooling system; it was actually more common than fridges, which were rather a city luxury. The cooler would also enable me to preserve fresh meat for the dog.

I was exhausted, I had been training almost all night and then taken care of the dog and now sunrise was only an hour away. I just had enough time to eat and have a wash. When I came out from the bathroom, the dog was lying in front of the door, waiting for me. I went to sit in the cushion area on the floor and settled down with him next to Clara, who got the chance to meet him properly. After petting him for a bit, Clara's attention turned back to me:

"Love, I was wondering, how do you know to fight?" she asked.

"I learnt when I was younger," I said shortly.

"I know that already. You don't want to tell me?" she insisted.

"It's just not a happy story,"

"But it's yours," she comforted.

"OK. I don't know if Aiden told you, my parents died when I was eight. My grandparents took me in and were always so caring, but I was heartbroken and remained an uncommunicative kid for quite a while. One day, after school I saw an outdoor class of Muay Thai training in the park and it really captivated me. I went there every day and as soon as I was in my bedroom, I would copy the lesson I had watched. I loved it – every kick or punch felt like a release to me. Once, the instructor who had already noticed me, called me over to help him organise some of his gear. He tried to talk to me but I didn't say much, I guess he could feel I was broken and he was moved. From that day, he took me under his wing. My grandparents were not exactly thrilled with their ten year old granddaughter taking up boxing classes, but they had to admit it was a beneficial hobby when I started to speak to people again."

"A sad story with a happy ending! So, you've been practising since a very long time!"

"Well, for a good ten years, it was my salvation! Then, I got into other stuff, as adults do! But I have kept going on a martial arts retreat every year, of Muay Thai of course, but also, I took a particular liking to Viet Vo Dao. And, I regularly go to the boxing gym to let off steam."

"You must have kicked a lot of arses!" she said admirably.

"I didn't need boxing class for that! As a kid, I hated bullies and was always trying to defend the underdogs. Plus, you know, as experienced fighters, we are not supposed to fight outside of the ring. Although, I admit, I did end up defending myself a few times!"

"Are your grandparents still around?"

"Nope, they passed a few years back."

"So, all your siblings are gone too?"

"I have Naomi!"

"Is she your sister?"

"No, well kind of – I was an only child, but we have been best friends since we were fifteen and have stayed together since then."

"Is she the person I have seen you calling and texting?"

"Yes, but she has no idea what is truly going on though."

"How did you handle this?"

"I lied to her and I pretended I had to be in Spain for a month, for a job."

"You must hate that!"

"I do, it does not feel right but for some peculiar reason, the lies come out of my mouth super easily, I don't even think twice."

"You have no choice Louise, I understand this is tough, but it is the only way to keep a relationship with her."

"I know, maybe that's why it is so easy to make up lies."

We talked a bit more and then went to sleep. The following evening, I freaked out when I woke up and couldn't see the dog, until I got up and spotted him with Chhay.

"I see you are getting to know each other!" I teased Chhay.

"He's cool! He came to me when I woke up and has been following me around since then. He kept checking on you though, see if you were awake, which was cute, I can't deny!"

The dog immediately came to me, wagging his tail, licking my hands and asking for attention. I could not tell his age exactly, but he was still young and I guessed about one and a half years old. I needed to find a name for him, but it had to be right and so would probably take me a couple of days to see what fitted him best.

A man driving a local motorbike arrived through the narrow trail, carrying a huge block of ice and a bag of groceries. Chhay had emptied the cooler before he took it outside, so the guy could place the ice in it. He then handed over the shopping bag; Chhay gave him some money and he left. I ran to him and took the food for the dog. I still had forty-five minutes before we started our session, so I had time to cook his rice, vegetables and meat and I could feed him afterwards. Clara appeared from the bathroom and the dog greeted her with confidence – he was setting in.

Chapter XXIX

For the second day of training, Chhay had planned the same Qi-Qong session as a warm up, except the location was different again. This time, we walked for twenty minutes to a hidden waterfall filling a pool that fed a little stream passing through the lush jungle vegetation. The dog went in the water, which was good considering he could definitely use a wash. At first, Chhay and I practised on the rocks next to the water. Later, he asked me to get in the water to practice one of his own sequences of movements. He had developed his own style that had many influences, such as Tai-Chi-Chuan, Yoga and even Kung-Fu. I loved his choreography: there was a progression of moves from slow and gentle to fast and powerful. He told me he had figured out this routine at the beginning of his Kindred life, when he was struggling to control his strength.

He advised me to focus solely on my inner energy flowing through my whole body. Once I felt it, he instructed me to increase this energy to its maximum, then expel it to the water in harmony with the motions of the choreography. The Kung-Fu like cycle was very fast, precise and required a lot of power. The last strike was meant to allow the energy to be released into the water. Then, we started a chain of slow movements, gradually increasing the speed and intensity. These enabled us to draw the energy from the water, back into our bodies. It took a few tries for me to completely memorise the sequence.

Once I had, I was able to feel this energy travelling through me and to discharge it into the water, as well as drawing it back. However, I was not yet capable of increasing or decreasing its force. Still, the exercise was quite soothing and for the first time, I sensed I could be in control of myself.

When we finished the waterfall session, I told Chhay I liked the work-out he had created and found it rather amazing to control the flow of energy. He explained that I needed to know that I was able to control myself and the energy running through me, in order to progress.

Next, Chhay wanted to work on my climbing and jumping skills. We moved to a denser part of the jungle that had tall trees. First, he demonstrated how to climb efficiently, using as little strength as possible. On the ground, he stood back three metres and ran straight towards the trunk, which allowed him to easily push off from his legs and jump at least four metres high. He caught two different branches on each side of the trunk and pushed hard with his legs, which propelled him a few metres higher. He repeated the same actions again until he reached the top of the tree. To descend, he jumped straight down, caught a branch half way and executed a perfect three hundred sixty degrees swing, before letting go of the branch to continue his fall and epically land on the ground, like a super-hero. He looked like a professional trapeze artist. I was speechless, I didn't expect something so technical!

"Your turn now."

"Seriously? I can't do that, I mean the high jumps and swingy thing!" I responded, confused by his high expectations of me.

"You can, just do it exactly like me. The impetus at the beginning is the key, the bigger it is, the more powerful you will be."

He went over the technical aspect of the climb once more. I was to use the momentum from the impetus of the run, to jump from the lower part of tree as high as I could and catch two branches on opposite sides of the tree; then push with my legs on the trunk with all my power in order to thrust myself upwards. As for the descent, he advised me to locate the right branch to catch prior to jumping down, about half way down the tree in this case. He specified that the descent was all about breaking it down into sections and using the help of whatever was on the way, such as branches or something else to catch hold of. The longer the descent, the more supports we had to catch in order to facilitate the leap. Regarding the trapeze trick, he used it to balance himself and simply because he liked it!

After his clarifications, I agreed to try. He allowed me to take a longer running distance for greater impetus: I went five metres back and started sprinting towards the tree, but I missed the take off and smashed into the tree trunk. The momentum was indeed powerful. I got back on my feet, more annoyed than hurt and restarted the process. This time, I managed to jump, but not very high and quickly lost the benefit of the momentum. I ended up climbing most of the tree until I reached the top. I remembered Aiden, when we were playing hide and seek in the woods at his house, but I shook the memory off and went back to the current matter at hand. I looked for a stable branch to hold onto during my descent and flew down, feet first. I successfully caught it, but I lost my grip as I tried to replicate Chhay's swing and crashed to the ground. I was hurt and told Chhay, since he was also monitoring my pain level. I got up and tried again. It took me at least ten attempts to master the descent, which was indeed great fun, once I stopped crashing! The way up was harder, it required much more power, but by the twentieth try I finally overcame the challenge. Chhay was very pleased and praised my tenacious attitude. He told me to redo the exercise a couple more times to make sure it wasn't a fluke. Luckily it wasn't, and I was amazed to see how much easier it got every time I repeated the exercise.

We walked back to the training area close to the house, followed by the dog who had been shadowing us patiently.

When we arrived, Chhay gave me a twenty minute break to recover. He then showed me a thick cement wall and casually told me to break through it. It was about my height and one meter wide. I looked at him doubtfully, thinking he was joking at first, but his serious posture and face confirmed his instructions. I took position in front of the wall and waited for some kind of guidance from him. He told me to focus on my inner energy. I punched the wall once – nothing happened – a second time, still no cracks. It seemed impossible for me to succeed and my hand was hurting from the shocks. Chhay advised me to focus on something that made me sad or angry and try again. I thought of my parents before I hit the wall a third time, but in vain. Then I imagined Kyle's face, but even that did not help much, except for a little chip on the cemented plaster that partly revealed the red bricks behind. I told Chhay my hand hurt: it was bleeding and felt broken. Clara, who had just joined us, saw my frustration. She first whispered a few words with my trainer, then came up to me:

"Love, would you like me to help you?"

"How can you do that?" I asked, confused.

"I can help you find your strength."

"OK then, let's try it your way." I understood she was suggesting that I let her get inside my head.

"I should warn you though, it may be an unpleasant experience."

"How do you mean?"

"It might be emotionally difficult."

"I don't see how I'm going to break this wall, so if you can help, I am up for it." Clara was in front of me and placed her palms on my temples. She asked me to relax and not to resist. She removed her hands, stood beside me and took over the instructions.

"Louise, the only way to help her is to break the wall!" she said energetically.

"Who are you talking about?"

"Louise, tell me, can you hear her screaming?"

"Yes!" I was under her control.

"Louise, tell me, do you recognise her voice?"

"I am not sure … it sounds like it's coming from underground!"

"Louise, tell me, what is behind the wall?"

"Somebody is buried alive in that room … the oxygen levels are low."

"Louise, tell me, do you know who is buried?"

"Oh no! It's Naomi!"

As soon as I visualised Naomi, locked alive in a coffin, suffocating, I became enraged and fuelled with energy. I kept hitting the wall, one punch after the other. The wall started to crack a little, yet it was not breaking. The images of Naomi became clearer: she was so scared, crying, begging for help and struggling to breathe. I felt like my heart was going to explode; I could no longer take these images and in a burst of rage, I punched the wall one more time. It collapsed completely in a dozen of pieces. I jumped on the other side and dug frantically with my bare hands until Clara's voice stopped me.

"It's alright Louise, you made it, you broke the wall and Naomi is safe."

I immediately stopped digging and stood up. It took me a minute to come back to reality. Only then, I understood the purpose of the exercise: Chhay was trying to understand how my strength worked and what triggered it. My hands were in shreds and I wasn't sure whether to be upset or happy. Clara didn't say anything. She let me regain my calmness and then apologised for showing me one of my biggest fears. As a Human, Naomi was all I had; however as a Kindred, I was still not sure how she would fit in my life, but I knew I was not ready to lose her.

Chhay was happy that I passed the test and instantly moved on to a final meditation. The dog was still with us – he had stayed for the whole session, even if sometimes he went for a stroll and came back afterwards. I was exhausted, the climbing and jumping exercise had drained me and finding the strength to destroy the wall finished me off, let alone the mind invasion. After I had showered, I noticed my hands had already started healing. Clara walked up to me – it seemed she was feeling a bit guilty and wanted to check if I was fine with her. We sat down with the dog and Chhay joined us with food for everybody.

"You did well today Louise!" started Chhay.

"Did I?"

"Yes, it's only your second day and you're making big progress!"

"Am I only strong when I am angry?" I asked, slightly confused.

"I believe it's a bit more complicated than that. There is a trigger, but it isn't rage or anger."

"So, what is it then?"

"Who did you think was behind the wall? Naomi wasn't it?"

"Yes, the only person left who is like family."

"Are you used to taking care of her?"

"We take care of each other."

"Again, Louise, I am so sorry we had to go there," said Clara, still on a guilt-trip.

"It's fine, I understand. It's just that I haven't really come to term with what is going to happen to my relationship with Naomi, you touched a very sensitive nerve."

"But that was the point, I wanted to see what triggered you! I was almost sure it was not anger or rage," continued Chhay.

"So, is it love then?" I deduced.

"No, I think it's protectiveness."

"Is it?"

"Louise, we only met a few days ago and I have already witnessed you trying to protect us, like for example when you took it upon yourself to clean up the charred corpses of the members of Ordinem and even offered to do it alone. Luca told me," added Clara.

"I can be a bit of a mamma bear with the people I love, I can't deny!"

"Who you're becoming, is based on who you were," continued Chhay as he suddenly stabbed my leg with a small knife. I screamed with pain.

"What the hell Chhay?" said Clara, taken aback.

"Sorry, sorry, I just wanted to see if Louise would feel this!" he said apologetically.

"I did! And it hurts!" I responded while I applied pressure on the fresh wound.

"OK, so we now know that your state of mind defines how much you feel the pain."

"Great!" I said sarcastically.

"Seriously, I know it was a bit harsh, like I said I'm sorry for that. But you see you felt that although it was much less than the pain I inflicted on you yesterday and today. Right now, you're relaxed and at peace and you feel the pain as much as any of us would. But when you are under a certain stress, your body response is completely different."

"Like adrenalin?" I asked.

"Yes, but in your case, I would rather say like someone with the mindset of a fighter."

I was exhausted and just wanted to sleep, so I went to my bed. The dog followed and hopped onto it with me. He then settled by my feet – he was so cute.

It was 5.45am when I heard Chhay's phone rang. I thought it was very likely to be Aiden after landing in Amsterdam, so I focused my hearing and spied on their conversation. Aiden and Luca had arrived safely in Amsterdam, but had not yet met the new Elder, as she was not home. They were now in a restaurant across the road, waiting for her to get back, hoping it would be before morning. Chhay summarised our day of training and told him that he had started to figure out what triggered my strength. He also informed him that we now owned a dog, which Aiden was happy about. The call ended as the Elder they were waiting for had just arrived home.

"Chhay, may I ask you something?"

"Yes, but me first! Were you listening?"

"Yes, sorry," I said, guiltily.

"You heard everything?"

"Yes."

"Good, we'll keep working on your senses!"

"You're not mad?"

"I think you did it because you expected Aiden to call! Didn't you?"

"Exactly, I won't do it again."

"Normally I would tell you not to do that, but in this instance you are learning, so let's use every resource we have around us as part of your training!" Chhay was really a nice person. "Anyway, what was your question?"

"It may sound silly, but how did Aiden and Luca get everyone's addresses so fast? Do you know where everybody lives?"

"Aiden and Luca have a huge network and they know everybody. But even without that, everyone's main address is registered, we just have to check with our administration."

"I see, thanks."

"No problem, you can ask me anything about us, you know – that's also part of the training."

"I will definitely take you up on that offer, when I'm rested," I said, falling asleep.

Chapter XXX

Aiden

Luca and I ran through the thick jungle to the awaiting van. It was exactly where we expected it to be. When the driver saw us, he opened the sliding side door and we jumped in. It did not have proper tinted windows, but the organisers had improvised with decent dark window film everywhere, which was good enough. We settled in the back of the van while the driver shifted into first gear. I did not feel at ease leaving Louise behind, although I knew she was in good hands. Plus, we had to get going. Luca noticed I was more pensive than usual and said:

"Don't worry bro, she will be OK!"

"I know, she is a tough cookie!"

"Yes, definitely."

"But sometimes even tough people can fall," I said realistically.

"I can't think of a better person than Chhay to help her! Remember how hard it was for him and how much he had to work to eventually control himself!"

"You're right, Chhay is unquestionably the best person to train Louise."

"I have no doubt we'll already see good progress when we get back."

Eight hours later, at midnight, we were boarding our jet to Amsterdam and arrived there twelve hours later. We landed at 6am local time and just had enough time to check ourselves into a hotel. At this time of year, the sunrise was not expected much before 8am. We went to a hotel that belonged to one of our hospitality companies. We had some pieds-à-terre in most places around the world, which made our travels easier. We were staying near the Elder's home, in the affluent and cultural *MuseumKwartier* area.

Luca and I planned to go to the Elder's house around 8pm and depending on what time we were going to finish, we would travel to our next destination immediately. We agreed not to divulge the whole traumatic story of the destruction of Ordinem until we had all the Elders in one room. For now, they just needed to know that there was an emergency that required their full attention. We decided that we would tell them to plan to be away for an unknown period, leaving in a few days. After we had visited them all, our strategy was to call them with a specific meeting location, date and time, where we could finally recount the whole story as well as show the horrendous images of the video surveillance.

Luckily, it was not the first time that Luca and I visited other Kindreds on Robert's behalf. We knew how to handle the task of locating them and importing information. After the second meeting with all the Elders, we would be able to set a plan to destroy Kyle, release Robert and protect our people from whatever Kyle was up to. I still could not believe what he had done! Louise's murder was bad enough, but now he had gone completely insane. There would not be any recovery from this and a long grieving process was to be expected. Sombre and troublesome times were upon us. On top of that, I could not help thinking about Louise, who had been dragged into this – not really what I imagined for us.

Luca and I discussed more about the Elder we were about to encounter: her name was Channeh and she was almost a thousand years old. Like most of the older Kindreds, she was a good friend of Robert and I had met her quite a few times. She was very knowledgeable and conversing with her was always interesting.

Once we had reviewed our course of action, we ate and then Luca retired to his own room to catch up on some rest. Before I went to bed, I read a chapter of my book about genetic mutations – biology being one of my favourite topics. I was trying to understand what happened to Lucius The First and how a chain of unrelated events had allowed such a change in the nature of his genome.

I then settled down in bed, but as soon as my head touched the pillow, many images of Louise travelled through my mind. I was very impressed with the way she was holding on and I had no doubt she could be part of my daily life. Sometimes, I felt guilty and selfish for bringing her into our world. Maybe she would have been better off without me, although I knew she never aspired to have what the Human society considered to be 'a normal life'. It was never my intention to turn her, at least not like that. I had thought of it before, when she found out who I really was, but it had to come from her. Well, in the end, it did not come from any of us, but from Kyle. I found her quite amazing in the way she reacted to her Human death and how she took it upon herself to fully understand my world. She was always a very good listener and observer, but her feisty nature could have impacted negatively and rushed her to dark conclusions.

I remembered the first time I met her at the botanical gardens, when she was wandering about. I felt her nostalgia being triggered by the beauty of the plants she was admiring. I couldn't resist talking to her, even if I knew it couldn't go any further. I should not have done so though, because as soon as we looked at each other and exchanged our first words, I knew she would be significant in my life. She had this strength in her – she had made sure to build a strong shell to protect herself and I could tell she had been broken a few times in her past. However, she also had this hidden sensitivity that transpired through her connection with nature.

Later, I realised her heart was full of love and warmth, but she usually did not let strangers in easily, except for me, as we both fell in love rather fast. I should not have pursued her – I have ruined her life. I did try, but not hard enough. When she came to my house in the country, I should have stayed hidden and not engaged with her. Actually, I should have disappeared! I would have if I was not madly in love with her. I had had romantic interests before, but nothing like Louise. When I had to erase her memory, I thought I would never recover from it and thought of disappearing somewhere far away until she died. I tried to keep my distance from her, but I couldn't resist: I had to keep an eye on her and make sure she was safe, although she did not need my help for that – well, except for that night... I have to admit, retrospectively, it was probably more for my own need and sanity than her protection. I wondered what she was doing now, probably sleeping considering the time over there. I wanted to call her, but I was not supposed too. I was tired and could not help drifting off.

My alarm rang at 5pm. I put some music on straight away as I often did when I was by myself. A couple of hours later, I met with Luca and we headed to Channeh's place. The walk there was lovely, the scenery quite beautiful with the typical red brick buildings and their many windows. She lived near the *Vondelpark*, on a very pretty street.

When we arrived in front of her house, we noticed there were no lights on inside. We still tried the intercom but there was no answer, so we agreed to settle in one of the restaurant-bars nearby where we could see her arriving. We found a good place to watch Channeh's home from and Luca ordered drinks.

Three and a half hours later, there was still no sign of Channeh so I decided to call Chhay. We spoke for a bit: Louise was fatigued after the last training session, but she was doing fine and they had advanced well. In addition, he told me she had found a dog in the jungle and that consequently, he was now part of the family. I really looked forward to meeting him, as like Louise, I was very fond of animals in general and always liked to have a pet near me. Since we did not need horses for transportation anymore, a dog seemed a very good choice!

Suddenly, Luca grabbed my arm and told me Channeh was entering her home, so I had to cut short my phone call. We left enough cash on the table to cover a fair tip and headed towards Channeh's.

Once we had introduced ourselves via the intercom, Channeh let us in. We climbed the stairs to meet her on the second floor. She owned the whole house, but it was split in two spacious apartments. The lower floor one was often rented short-term or used by other Kindreds. She invited us in and led us to her vast living-room. At this moment, I missed Louise's demeanour whenever she entered one of these impressive homes for the first time and how she scrutinised the features of the place. She would have been amazed by the incredible wooden floor and its Herringbone pattern. Then, her attention would have travelled to the sliding door on the side, revealing a dining room and a modern open kitchen. Finally, she would have studied the antiques pieces of furniture.

My attention came back to the matter at hand when Channeh offered us something to drink. We accepted and settled in comfortable armchairs.

"Channeh, thank you for inviting us in out of the blue!" I started.

"No problem, you are welcome. When did you get here?" she replied.

"Around 8pm."

"Oh dear, I hope the wait was not too boring! I was busy attending a private event to launch an exhibition by a new artist!"

"You were always quite an art philanthropist!"

"So, tell me, to what do I owe the pleasure of your visit? I doubt you just came to say hello."

"Well, I will be straightforward with you Channeh, although there is not much information that we can share at the moment. What I can tell you though, is that we need you to be available very shortly for a meeting, where the matter at hand will be disclosed."

"Very mysterious, is Robert aware of this?"

"Of course, we are acting on his behalf, but I am afraid he is out of reach at the moment."

"Aiden, there have been some rumours..."

"What rumours?" I asked surprised.

"Did something happen to Ordinem? It seems the place is in lockdown and nobody has heard from any of its members! I mean, it doesn't take a genius to infer that something odd is going on."

"Ordinem had to be ... moved, until further notice. We will be able to discuss it all with you at our next meeting. I apologise for being obscure, but I am afraid I am only respecting our orders."

"Am I the next replacement?"

"I am not sure, we only had the instruction to come see you and deliver a message," I lied.

"Obviously there has been some kind of security breach, otherwise they would not have gone into hiding," insisted Channeh.

"I have no idea. The only thing I was told is that we are dealing with a unique situation that requires our complete discretion."

"It is all very secretive."

"Yes, I know and I apologise for being so vague."

"Do not worry Aiden, I know how it works. Secrecy has served us well so far. Would you like to go on the terrace outside?"

"Sure, that would be lovely!" I accepted. Channeh took a bottle of whisky and led us to the roof terrace with a lovely view of the neighbourhood. She had arranged a few comfortable outdoor armchairs around a fire pit.

"So, you two have no idea what is going on?"

"Pretty much. But as I said, there will be a meeting very soon: Luca or I will call you with a place and time to meet. Only then, will we all be informed."

"How long before you get in touch?"

"A few days, perhaps a week."

"And when you call, how long will I have to get there?"

"The minimum you need, according to the place of travel of course. Unfortunately, I am not able to tell you for how long at present time, so you should plan to be away for some time." "I see, alright, minimum information for maximum confidentiality. I will organise myself and be ready to travel in due course."

"Yes, thank you. Talking about confidentiality, you can imagine we rely on your discretion about today's encounter as well as the next one."

"Of course, discretion is my forte."

We kept chatting for a little while, until Luca got a phone call. We had planned to fly out after our meeting with Channeh, but we didn't expect such a delay and had to put our next flight on standby. Of course, Luca had already texted as soon as we entered Channeh's place to say it was likely we would fly out tonight. The call was asking us to confirm. I nodded in agreement.

"Well, Channeh, thank you for having us, I am afraid we have to leave now. We have further affairs to attend to."

"Of course! Don't let me keep you!" she said, getting up.

She walked us to the door and we said our goodbyes. We went back to the nearby hotel to check out. Luca and I were quite satisfied with our story and how it had been received by Channeh – she was our guinea pig. We phoned Clara and told her how to present the situation for her upcoming meeting to make sure our stories would match. We also warned her about the rumours that were circulating. An hour later, we had reached the airport and were soon traveling to Prague to meet with the second Elder on our list, Viktor.

Chapter XXXI

When I opened my eyes, the first thing I saw, was the dog standing by my side, looking at me and wagging his tail. We began our new ritual of morning petting until the sunlight faded enough for us to go play outside. An hour later, I gave him food and had mine too.

The third day of training started as usual at 6.30pm and went on all night. Now that Chhay had figured out what triggered my strength, part of my training was aimed at controlling the energy inside me and to decrease or increase it whenever I needed to, despite my environment. We started with a peaceful forty-five minute Qi-Qong session.

Then, Chhay took me to the jungle, where we practised climbing and jumping again. I was pleased to succeed at the first try. He smiled and led me to another place with taller trees to challenge my new skill. I climbed up fine and managed an almost perfect descent. This time, the height of the trees did not allow me to descend by only catching one branch – I had to do it twice. The first catch went perfectly, but the second one was messy, which resulted in a bad landing. I hit the ground hard and rolled over, but I was fine. I got up and before Chhay had a chance to say it, I tried again. The second time was a complete success, I was ecstatic and loved the sensation of almost flying.

Chhay made me repeat the exercise for an hour, until it was time to move on to the next one. He instructed me to go and retrieve the same yellow satchel that had led me to the dog, but this time I had to use my ears. He advised to follow the sounds made by termites in their nest. Just the thought of it gave me chills. Even as a Human, I really disliked the sound of insects swarming and the local termites were huge!

Chhay explained that I had to try to dissociate each sound as if I was peeling off layers of noise one by one, until I found what I was looking for. He warned me that I would probably struggle to isolate sounds at the beginning, however that should not keep me from trying. I went into the jungle focusing solely on my hearing. As Chhay predicted, I could perceive every sound in my environment: the animals and insects; the vegetation swaying in the light breeze; the vehicles on the nearby road and even the dog breathing. Chhay had kept him to be sure I completed the challenge by myself.

The more I focused, the more I could hear from further away. It was amazing. I concentrated on every single sound and tried to separate them. I came up with an imaginary system: every time a sound was not relevant to my quest, I put it away in a fictional box so it would not bother me. Eventually, I identified the rustling sound of the termites moving and chewing on a dead tree. Then, I began to track the sound and the more I advanced, the louder it became, until I finally saw the satchel nailed to the tree. I snatched the bag and ran back to Chhay.

He asked how I had managed to find my way and I told him about my imaginary system. He found it quite inventive. Then, we hiked to the waterfall where we worked on his fast and slow movement routine to release and draw back my energy levels. This was my favourite exercise, feeling the energy moving through my body was incredible, even if I had not mastered the art yet. Finally, we ended the day with the usual meditation session. By the time we had finished, I was hungry. When we arrived at the house, I washed myself fast and was ready to feed. However, when Chhay arrived with my dinner, he had planned something different:

"Alright Louise, for tonight's dinner, I thought we could shake things up!"

"How so? I am starving!"

"So, the sooner we start, the sooner you'll eat. I'm going to put a cup of blood in front of you. You have two choices: one, you can drink it now, or two, you can wait twenty minutes with it in front of you and you will get an extra cup of blood as a reward for your patience."

"Are we seriously doing the Marshmallow experiment?"

"Ah great, you are familiar with it!"

"Yes, it's for kids!"

"Yes, and in this context, you are one!"

"I am so hungry, I'm not sure I can hold!"

"Try, divert your mind from the urge."

"I'll do my best."

These were the longest twenty minutes of my life – it was unbearable! However, I could clearly see the point of the arduous test, so I went to my 'happy place' in my mind. I thought of Naomi: I wondered how she was doing and when would be the next time I would see her. Suddenly, Chhay exclaimed "times up!" which brought me back to reality. Before he let me drink the two cups, he asked me to do it at a slow pace, as I had learnt with Aiden. The first couple of sips were tough, just like the first time I fed at Aiden's mansion, but I resisted the urge to drain the cups fast. Five minutes later, I was done and delightfully satiated.

It was morning and the sun was about to rise. I went to find Clara, who I had not seen all night. She was staying out of our way and did not want to distract Chhay or I. She told me she was going to go to Hong-Kong that afternoon, to meet one of the next Elders. She knew her very well, as the lady in question was no less than her Maker. Clara was going to Ho-Chi-Minh airport, which was actually closer to us, to get a commercial night flight. I hugged her, wished her good-luck and went to bed – I was beat.

The next day, Chhay woke me up one hour earlier and gave me five minutes to be ready. He made me skip breakfast and took me outside. This was the last thing I expected, particularly since it was quite early in the afternoon and still bright. He wanted to teach me how to move in the daylight and protect myself from the sun. I followed his exact steps from the house to the jungle. Every time my skin was in direct contact with the sun, it burnt like hell. I could definitely see a catastrophic spontaneous combustion scenario here! When we were in the shade, my skin tickled and it was uncomfortable, but bearable. However, it annoyingly itched whenever we approached rays of sunshine. Chhay explained that our skin was reacting to the UV light, the higher the level, the itchier our skin was and, in direct sunlight, we were destined to burn to death. He added that since we could feel the intensity of sunlight, we could then determine how and where to move. It was the first time I had used my new sense of touch to learn how to 'feel' the air around me.

Chhay gave me enough time to get used to these new sensations and then instructed me to take the lead back home. So far, I had been following him, but now it was my turn to feel the safest way. I moved carefully, avoiding the rays of sunshine piercing through the leaves. The ticklish feeling was very weird, similar to the healing of a wound, while the itching was very unpleasant and highly uncomfortable. Then, Chhay stopped me and said we would practice Qi-Qong in this specific location, which hinted that the next exercise would probably occur in the jungle. We started the familiar exercise and I could feel my inner energy flowing inside me in perfect rhythm with the movements. As I expected, we then practised climbing and jumping again. This time, there was no crash and it seemed my brain and body had registered how to adapt to the stunt.

Later, we came back to the waterfall and I started to get in the water as per usual, but Chhay stopped me:

"No, no. You don't need to go in the water for our next drill."

"OK, what should I do?"

"I want you to track something."

"The yellow bag again?"

"No. Before she left, Clara hid one of her jumpers somewhere in the jungle. I'd like you to bring it back please."

"Alright," I had left the house with Chhay so fast that afternoon that I didn't get the chance to say goodbye to her.

"It's the same process as yesterday's search. You have to identify and separate all the smells, just like you did with the sounds."

"But I am not sure what Clara's scent is like."

"Of course you do! As soon as you smell something, you catch the scent, it takes one time only! Remember last night, when you hugged her goodnight, remember how she smells, relive the moment and you'll find her jumper."

I nodded and walked back into the jungle. When I was a few metres away, I tried to recall Clara's scent, following Chhay's instructions. Her fragrance was well balanced and hard to describe, but it was slightly dominated by the scent of mint. Once that was mapped in my brain, I proceeded with the rest of the smells around me. I focused on all of them and applied the layer principle as I had done yesterday with my hearing exercise, except this time I was relying on my nose to fetch the information. It took me some time to single out Clara's perfume, but when I did, I could easily track her jumper.

Again, I wondered if we had the same body scent as in our previous life and when I returned, I asked Chhay. He explained that our Kindred physiology and chemistry were different than our Human ones, and therefore our original scent was altered, although some similarities remained.

Chhay was happy I had succeeded in the task and even more since he expected me to take much longer to find the jumper. I asked him if my profession as a wine connoisseur, which required quite an expert nose, could have facilitated the task. He concurred and reminded me that even if my sense of smell was already well developed, I was a very young Kindred and all my senses were going to sharpen over the years, with more experience.

We then moved on to his water workout, but today, it felt different: I was much more in control and could, for the first time, build up and decrease the energy throughout my body – it was intense. We had been working so hard for the past few days, that we were really thrilled to see the results. Finally, we concluded the day with the regular meditation.

As we were on our way back to the house, my gums began to be painful again – I had forgotten how horrible this was. I informed Chhay and quickly went to shower so we could proceed with dinner. I was so hungry that I was ready within five minutes. When I arrived in the lounge, my dinner was already on the table and Chhay was feeding the dog.

"We're going to do something new today," said Chhay as I was about to take my cup.

"Really? Again? I am starving!"

"I know, this is exactly what we need." He invited me to sit at the table and positioned himself in front of me. "I'm going to be pacing your feeding tonight, meaning that you drink one sip when I tell you."

"One sip? This is torture!" I was not happy with his proposal.

"Trust me, two sips would be much harder!"

Reluctantly, I nodded to show him I was ready to start. I took my first sip and put the cup down straight away. It was really hard to control – I wanted to drain the cup dry. After one long minute, Chhay allowed the second sip, so I took a bigger one and swallowed it slowly. He saw that and made me wait five minutes for the next one. I felt like a kid being punished. Then, thirty seconds later, he let me have the next sip. The fact that he was constantly changing the length of the wait in-between the sips was horrible and very unsettling. He kept the gaps in my feeding so random that again I went into my mental happy place, trying to push the urge away.

"That's right Louise, you get it – you can put your urge on hold. Tell yourself, now is not the time, but in two minutes it will be."

Chhay counted on the first part of the exercise to force me to control my urges. Then, he taught me how to trick my mind on a long-term basis. He explained that whenever I felt an urge coming, I should not dismiss it, but instead mentally postpone it. I was then to increase the delay, until my mind would simply move on to something else. We started with two minutes but by the end of the exercise, I could easily tell my mind to hold on for thirty minutes. When I finally drank the last sip, I was exhausted. I was about to go to bed when Aiden called Chhay. This time I didn't listen and waited for Chhay to update me. A couple of minutes later, he hung up.

"Did you listen?"

"No, I didn't."

"So, let me tell you what they've been up to. It's been quite a smooth trip so far, even though they had to wait for Channeh in Amsterdam. In the end, they managed to fly out to Prague before morning. They checked into a hotel when they arrived and met with the second Elder, Viktor, in the evening. He is well-acquainted with Aiden, so they spent quite some time with him and played poker almost all night! They couldn't travel anyway – the jet needed maintenance. They slept all day and flew out early this evening to get to Pula airport in Croatia around 8pm. Luca knows Tahir the third Elder well, so he called him to find out what time they could visit and he invited them to meet at midnight. Which is about now allowing for the time difference. And of course, I kept them updated on our work here."

"Very detailed! Thank you, Chhay."

"I always like a good story and details are important!" he joked.

Following his previous call, I had managed not to be obsessed with Aiden. The time-consuming training helped, as well as my new dog friend; but now, simply talking about him reminded me of all the desire I had for him. I still had no idea how to handle this sexual frustration – I knew it was only a matter of time before Aiden's return and I had had enough of staying away from him.

"What's on your mind Louise? You seemed bothered."

"Don't worry, I am fine," I said lightly, avoiding an uncomfortable chat.

"I didn't picture you as shy, what's going on?"

"It is rather private." I blushed.

"Does it concern your new self?"

"Yes!"

"So, by all means, you should tell me, I'm sure I can help you."

"Even if it's related to ... physical stuff?"

"What do you mean?"

"Erm, I mean ... sex. Sorry, this is quite embarrassing."

"Oh, I see. No, it's not, sex is part of our life too! We're not a very prudish species. In fact, we can be very sexually active."

"Of course, but opening up about my intimacy is a bit different."

"Fair enough, so tell me – what is the issue?"

"I ... I ... think I ..." I could not let the words out.

"It's OK Louise, you can tell me."

"It's Aiden, I want to be close to him, but we can't! It's killing me!"

"It's normal, we all went through the same phase. As a new Kindred, you have so much to learn and deal with that we tend to avoid excessive emotion that could be disorientating and affect you negatively. That's one of the reasons training is required."

"How long is this going to last? And how will I know when I am ready?"

"I don't know, but not for ever, you've been progressing well so we can be optimistic. I tell you what, tomorrow we'll try something I used to do when I was in your situation."

"What was it like for you?"

"It was tough, I involuntarily injured a few people as I didn't know my own strength. It took me a while to figure out a routine to keep me out of trouble. That's why I am helping you."

"Where was your Maker?"

"Dead! He helped me at the beginning, but I think he turned me as his last hope and motivation to stay alive. Of course, I wasn't enough and soon after he killed himself. I was still dangerously inexperienced, but luckily Robert took me in."

"Robert! Of course!"

"There's a reason why he's the most respected Elder! He helped a lot of us personally and he did so much for our community, we wouldn't have got this far without him."

"I wish I knew him better."

"I'm sure you will!"

Chapter XXXII

The following afternoon, Chhay woke me up early again and like yesterday, took me out in the daylight. This time, he instructed me to take the lead from the start. I navigated well, paying attention to the sensations on my skin. Once the sun had set, we began with the Qi-Qong practice, then I had to track him in the jungle. Although it was a long search, it was a lot of fun as he kept moving around and I kept missing and chasing him. I did find him in the end, using all my senses. I was looking forward to trying Chhay's exercise to control my sexual drive and was wondering when we would start working on it.

We headed to the waterfall, got into the water and Chhay instructed me to do everything as usual to reach perfect calmness. A moment later, I could feel my spirit completely at ease and my inner energy was growing, decreasing and flowing fluently. I was aware that Chhay was monitoring my behaviour and would soon give me a command. I heard his voice, telling me to imagine Aiden being in front of me and to keep the energy flowing steadily. Just the sound of his name troubled my inner peace and I felt warmer. Chhay said that until I returned to my serene self, the exercise would not stop. He added that in order to move on to the next level, I needed to succeed at this one. I focused, I was determined to pass the first stage and not to let the seductive images of Aiden impact on the success of the energy release and withdrawal. Fifteen minutes later, I managed to regain a tranquil state. Chhay noticed and pushed further. He asked me to visualise Aiden and myself kissing, which I did. I could feel his lips on mine and I started to feel really hot. I kept nurturing the lustful energy inside my stomach, unable to weaken it.

"Louise, don't keep it in, release the energy!" Chhay's voice felt really far away, I was in such a bubble of lust.

He kept repeating the same thing, getting louder and louder. Eventually, I got used to the feeling and managed to minimise it until it was finally under control. Soon after, I could flow the energy through my body again. He asked me to restart the exercise, which I did and this time it was easier to control since I knew what to expect.

"OK, well done Louise, you can come out of the water!"

"Are you sure?"

"Yes! You've been at it for more than two hours!"

"No way! I didn't realise, it felt like an hour tops!"

"Let's go meditate." I came out of the water and we settled on the large rocks around the pool in order to proceed with our meditation practice. Then, he sent me back into the water.

"Louise, instead of nurturing the energy and releasing it, I want you to keep it out of you."

"How do I do that?"

"You don't let it build up, let it out as soon as you feel it while thinking about Aiden like we did earlier."

"I should only do the slow movements then?"

"Yes, let's start like this." I complied and focused only on the calm motions. I was concentrating hard on the task and let the energy out as soon as I felt it.

"OK, now you're going to add faster motions, the five moves in-between the slow and the quick ones." Again, I applied my-self and managed to remain as cool as a cucumber, although it required more effort. Then, Chhay told me I could try to go further with my thoughts, challenging my chance of succeeding the exercise. It took everything out of me and by the end of the session I was exhausted.

"Well done, OK, half hour meditation and we'll do it again."

"I'm not sure I can, I am drained."

"Meditation is for recouping that energy! I know I'm pushing you Louise, but it's for your own good!"

"Fair enough." I had to power through, as I knew it would all be worth it in the end.

The meditation barely restored my stamina, but I went back to the water as instructed. I focused really hard, until I attained a complete state of serenity even having provocative thoughts. I didn't realise that Chhay had left the pool; I had caught a glimpse of him checking his phone, but I had no idea where he went after that. I pushed myself and continued, undistracted. A while later – I could never tell how long the water work out was – Chhay came back and watched me for a couple of minutes.

"OK, Louise that's enough for now. Finish with a thirty minutes meditation and that will be fine for today."

He meditated with me and the dog lay next to us until we got up and walked back to the house. As we got closer, I sensed something was different in the air and seconds later, a slight scent of bergamot teased my olfactory nerves. I asked Chhay if Aiden was here and he said with a smile that I should see for myself.

When we arrived at the house, Luca and Aiden were seated on the outdoor sofa and I strode happily towards them. The dog was wary of the two new guests and stood a little way off. However, when he saw our embraces, he came closer and started sniffing Aiden, then Luca. They gave him as much time as he needed and petted him as soon as he let them. He seemed to be particularly keen on Aiden. I had expected the guys to get here later, considering the long drive from Phnom Penh. Apparently, they had arrived a couple of hours ago, after renting powerful motorbikes to shorten the journey. Chhay added with a friendly wink, that he had told Aiden and Luca not to disturb me while I was still training. I smiled at him, appreciating his discretion.

"According to Chhay, you have been progressing pretty well!" Luca praised me.

"Yes! I feel much better thanks, but tell us, how was the meeting in Croatia?"

"Very smooth actually, it helped that Luca and Tahir are well acquainted," said Aiden.

"It was nice to see him!" added Luca.

"What about the others?"

"You know, we didn't tell them much, except that they will be expected at a certain time and place very soon," replied Luca.

"Was that enough for them?" I inquired surprised.

"Yes, we know when not to ask questions. Also, they all know that they will be fully informed at the next meeting. Of course, they all guessed something was going on, apparently there have already been some rumours," explained Luca.

"What kind of rumours?" asked Chhay.

"In Amsterdam, Channeh told us that it had been noticed that Ordinem was in complete lockdown and that the members had been out of reach," detailed Luca.

"What did you tell them?" continued Chhay.

"That we were going through a unique situation that required extra caution. We pretended the Ordinem members had been moved to a new confidential location. We used the good old 'messenger only' card," said Aiden.

"They're all on standby waiting on the information about the next meeting," summarised Luca.

"And what about the last Elder, have you found him yet?" I asked.

"Almost," replied Aiden.

We were interrupted by the ringing of Luca's phone. It was Clara, he picked up immediately and put her on speaker phone:

"Hey *Clarita*! You are on speaker – everybody is here, how are you?"

"Hi guys! I am good! I was hoping you would be back already!"

"Something wrong?" Luca worried.

"Not at all, I just wanted to let you know that my mission is done. I spoke with Jarena as soon as I arrived last night, she is waiting on our updates."

"That's great! Are you staying with her?" Luca asked.

"Yes I am. Also, I got confirmation that Erling is in Taiwan and is financing a charity ball the day after tomorrow in one of Taipei most luxurious hotels!"

"Sorry for interrupting, but who is Erling?" I asked.

"The last Elder to visit. That would be cool, wouldn't it? His events are always great!" Luca said, looking at Aiden for approval.

"Yes, most definitely, we could all use a bit of fun before the Elders meeting! Are we sure he will be there Clara?" checked Aiden.

"Yes, he invited Jarena but she couldn't make it, so she gave me her invitation."

"Great! So, we will stay here during the day and travel to the airport later this evening. We should arrive in the middle of the night in Taipei," Aiden worked out.

"Fine, I will get there before you, so I will arrange hotel rooms for us and I will let you know where."

"Thanks, alright, we will see you tomorrow," Aiden concluded.

"Bye *Clarita*," Luca ended warmly. He then turned to my trainer and said, "Are you coming Chhay?"

"I don't think so! I don't fancy wearing a tux! And anyway, someone needs to look after the dog!" he said calmly while petting the animal.

"Oh, please Chhay, if anyone has to mind the dog, it's me, don't miss out on my account," I said, guiltily.

"To be honest Louise, I would rather stay here with the dog. By the way, can we please find him a name?"

"Yes, I know! Are you sure you want to stay?"

"Yes, I think you should go to the event, not me! You deserve a bit of fun after all your hard work. But we're not finished yet. I expect you to be back as soon as you have contacted Erling."

"Yes! Thanks!" I said ecstatically.

"Great, I was hoping you would be in a generous mood!" joked Aiden.

"Aiden told me that you guys identified what triggers Louise's strength," said Luca.

"Yes, it seems that Louise's power or strength is linked to her protective nature. I think there's a bit more to it, but that's the big picture."

"How did you figure it out?" Aiden asked.

"We tapped into her darkest fears," Chhay replied honestly.

"Like what?" asked Aiden, as his face filled with concern.

"Clara helped me to see what I needed to get there."

"Are you OK?" Aiden inquired seriously.

"Yes, it was kind of messed up, but it had to be done! We now understand what triggers me, and therefore training has been more efficient! Don't worry, I'm OK," I reassured him.

The sun was about to rise, so we all got ready to go to sleep. Aiden was discreetly observing my routine with the dog and was obviously amused. Once I was in bed texting Naomi, he came and sat by me. He asked softly while pointing at the dog:

"Has he replaced me?"

"Aha! No, you silly! But I love him already!"

"He is lovely! What shall we call him?"

"I don't know, I keep finding names but nothing really suits him!"

"I know what you mean, but it will come naturally I am sure! By the way, I brought some things for him," he said as he handed over a small paper bag. I opened it and found some de-worming pills as well as ticks and fleas prevention treatments.

"Thanks! It's very thoughtful of you! You're the best!" I couldn't believe it, although it was just like him to be so prepared.

"You're welcome!"

"So, how do you feel after meeting most of the Elders?"

"Strange, I am really not looking forward to meeting all of them. I mean, the truth is so horrendous, I cannot imagine their reactions to those awful images."

"Are you worried about that?"

"Yes, it is horrific to think you are replacing someone who was burnt alive."

"What do you think will be their course of action?"

"Honestly, I don't know. I heard tales of a couple of Kindreds going rogue, but it was ages ago. We have not encountered this ourselves."

"At least they will be familiar with the situation then."

"In Kyle's case, going rogue is an understatement!"

"I couldn't agree more! And how are Luca and Clara doing?"

"Holding up, we are always stronger together! Clara is very good in critical situations: she keeps a clear head and is generally the wiser one."

"I noticed."

"And Luca is a thinker and a doer. He is very talented at thinking outside the box and he is very technically minded."

"I gathered that much too!"

"We are so used to working together – it's a smooth process. I am so glad we are with them!"

"Yes, frankly I am quite impressed to see how efficient you guys are. I am curious about one thing though: what is Luca and Clara's relationship?"

"Ah! Good question! It's a mix of love and friendship."

"I knew it! And you?"

"What about me?"

"Were you and Clara ever a thing?"

"No, never, she was always interested in Luca not me. After so many years, she is like a sister to me. I mean, don't get me wrong – I am aware Clara is beautiful, but I never fancied her like that!"

"Yes, I can definitively see their bond. She is quite something! What time will we be leaving this evening?"

"Well, the aircraft is waiting at Phnom Penh airport, so we'll have to leave the house by 6pm at the latest."

"Good, so we'll have time to take care of the dog before we go."

"Yes, you will have to show me what you two have been up to."

"We will! I have to say, I'm happy to be able to come with you to Taipei."

"Me too. I was ready to negotiate hard with Chhay, but there was no need! He is being fair I guess – he told me you have been really dedicated to your training and that it was paying off!"

"We both want to get results! You know something? I could smell you when we arrived to the house!"

"Of course you could! That's great! May I ask you something?"

"Sure."

"When Clara got into your mind, did you see Naomi being hurt?"

"Yes, she was buried alive, screaming and gasping for air!"

"That's horrible! I am sorry you had to endure that!"

"Clara felt really bad for going there! She asked me if I wanted help and I let her. I was very frustrated and needed another push. Don't get me wrong, the images of Naomi haunted me for a bit, but I could destroy a wall and that was amazing!" We chatted for a few more minutes before I was taken over by exhaustion. I think I passed out while we were still talking.

Chapter XXXIII

The evening arrived so quickly that I thought I had only slept for a couple of hours. Aiden joined the dog and I and we began our afternoon routine. Luca and Chhay then accompanied us on our jungle walk. It was great to be altogether and the dog seemed to connect pretty well with the guys.

When we returned to the house, we packed our stuff, got ready and ate. Then, we started on our way to the airport. I hopped on the tiny rear seat of Luca's bike. I recalled how I felt when I was close to Aiden and did not want to take an unnecessary risk, especially while riding.

Before our plane took off, Clara texted Aiden with the location and room numbers of the hotel. This flight was only going to be three and a half hours, which was time enough to watch a long film. As I looked through the selection, my mind drifted away and recalled Kyle's acts. I wondered why the woman who was supposed to kill me, did not just simply break my neck, it would only have taken a second. Maybe her real assignment was to turn me. I abandoned the film list to think further. I also remembered the directory we found in Romania, containing all the identities of the Kindreds that had ever existed. Then, I visualised all the crossed-out names – quite a few had passed away. I wondered how many of us were still around.

"Louise, what's on your mind?" asked Aiden.

"A couple of things. I was thinking about all the crossed-out names in the book we found in The Chapel. Many Kindreds have gone already."

"You know, being eternal is not a blessing forever. It is fun for a while, until it becomes a curse. I cannot imagine what it is like to have lived through so many centuries; have witnessed so much progress and evolution as well as many deaths and cruelty. We do know that after each period of war, there is an increase in the number of deaths on our side. The bigger the war, the more losses we suffer. We think it is either a result of guilt or a consequence of having watched horrific events repeating themselves over the years."

"It makes sense."

"I still feel like we were born yesterday!" said Luca, lightening the tone.

"Yes, me too! But we are young! Almost 150 years is not that old."

"I am in my tenth life and I love it!" Luca said enthusiastically.

"How many of us are left?" I asked curiously.

"I don't know exactly, five hundred more or less, I think," answered Aiden.

"Yes, something like that!" confirmed Luca.

"And how many of you were there before, say three hundred years ago?"

"Not that many more. Remember, when one of us wants to cease living, we have to find our replacement. This is a general rule, although, it has been overlooked in some exceptional instances."

"Now, you have one more, yay me!" I joked.

"Actually, there has not been a new Kindred for a while, well, except for you now! Shall we have a drink then?" offered Luca while getting a bottle of rum and glasses.

"Definitely!" I accepted the glass that Luca gave me and we toasted each other before I continued, "I was also thinking about something else."

"Well, don't keep us waiting!" invited Luca.

"I am still trying to get my head around the fact that if Kyle really wanted to kill me for real, I would be dead, right?"

"He tried and failed!" responded Aiden.

"Don't you think it's a bit odd that the woman would take the time to have a snack in the middle of the street? I think if she wanted to end me then and there, she would have done so in a second, just by breaking my neck or something!" Luca and Aiden looked at each other, forced to admit we had been missing something.

"You are making a good point," accepted Aiden.

"But why?" questioned Luca.

"That is the missing piece ... for now," I said.

"But then, why would Kyle take the risk to tease me just before it happened? I mean, right then I understood something was wrong with him."

"That night, I was out of cash and stopped the taxi before my house. I walked the remaining bit, but I got in a fight with two vile men. If she was watching me when I left the club and waiting for me at my place, then she would have got her timing wrong by ten minutes or so."

"Or, Kyle's narcissism got the better of him and his intention was not actually to tip Aiden off," simplified Luca.

"I believe he put a lot of thought into his plan. He is very organised and as we all know he is also very determined. So I doubt he couldn't resist bragging to Aiden, even at the risk of compromising his plan."

"It's not so much what he said but rather how he said it, his smirk and the look in his eyes did not promise anything good," specified Aiden.

"What if this was only a decoy? I mean, Kyle probably knew you were still watching over me. He had to get your attention, so his assassin could attack me in the meantime." They were both looking at me and listening attentively. I continued with my theory, "Aiden, you told me you were at the club that night and even Naomi saw you. What made you leave?"

"I received a text from Robert, asking me to check out a warehouse for him. It was nearby and I knew you were OK, as you had just got in the taxi. I didn't have much choice since officially I was not supposed to be near you! When I got there, Kyle was too, which surprised me a bit, but he told me Robert had sent him too – Damn! You right, he tricked me! How could I miss that?!"

"Aiden, it's not like we had a lot of free time to actually go over everything! Don't forget, at this point, there was no reason to be suspicious."

"To be fair, our mistake was to assume he tried to kill you. At no point did we consider he wanted to turn you! But why? What does he want with you?" said Luca.

"I'm not sure, but maybe it's just a trick to undermine Aiden. The man is cruel and I'm not sure if his plan was to hold up Aiden long enough so he would arrive too late, yet soon enough to realise what had happened, using the different scents that would have been left from my blood, myself and the assailant. Or, he wasn't planning for you to find out so soon and didn't expect you would work out his sick game."

"In both cases, he wanted you, Louise!" summarised Luca.

"The only reason I can see is to shake Aiden up. But maybe it was also to keep Aiden busy with my transition and training while Kyle attacked Ordinem. We should definitely consider everything!"

"You are right, we need to understand Kyle's plan if we want to defeat him. So far, we have managed to keep our advantage, let's hope he has not plotted another surprise," added Aiden.

This eye-opening conversation left us deep in thought for the rest of the flight. We landed at 4am and went directly to the hotel Clara had arranged for us. I was happy to see her – we had grown quite fond of each other. She was waiting for us in the lobby when we entered the impressive building and led us up to our floor. She had booked an elegant suite, so we would have a place to hang out and three superior bedrooms.

"If you don't mind, boys, we will need the suite before tomorrow's event. A private stylist will be coming in with a selection of evening dresses for Louise and I."

"I am happy for you to have the room," said Aiden.

"Me too, but what about clothes for us?" teased Luca.

"I thought you two would like to go to your 'secret' tailor!"

"You thought right *Clarita*, I already called them for an appointment!" said Luca.

We all went up to the suite, which was on the eleventh floor and offered an amazing view of Taipei City and a glimpse of the mountains of Yang Ming. Our other luxurious rooms were on the same floor but further down the corridor. We sat in the living room and had drinks and food while we filled Clara in on our latest reflections about Kyle. She agreed with our speculations.

Then, Clara recounted her meeting with her Maker, Jarena. It had gone well and she had not asked many questions. Apparently, Jarena was very military minded. Obviously, she realised something unconventional had occurred, but she did not try to squeeze Clara for more information. Either Clara played her messenger role to perfection or that simply, Jarena knew how to respect the protocol. Clara also relayed the information that Jarena was going to be away on a business trip in Berlin for the next few days, but would nonetheless remain available to travel to the meeting at any given time.

Just before we went to our rooms, Luca sent Chhay a text and a minute later he replied with a picture of the dog lying on my bed with a text saying: "*I think he misses Louise!*". It warmed my heart to see him and I felt a bit guilty for leaving him, even though I knew he was in safe hands with Chhay. Later, when I was in bed, I called Naomi – it was 10pm in London, a decent time for us to talk. She made me laugh and seemed very happy with Ian. Talking to her eased me into sleep.

Chapter XXXIV

Clara and I had agreed to meet up in her suite at 5.30pm while Aiden and Luca visited their tailor. When I entered the suite, I was in awe! Clara had gone full on! We had an extensive selection of evening dresses; many pairs of shoes; clutch bags; handbags; fancy coats and capes; jewellery for every body part; delicate scarves and shawls. Plus, she had set up a dressing table to do our make-up and hair. I could not believe my eyes.

"So, what do you think love?" she asked proudly.

"Well, it's outstanding! You spoil me!"

"I wasn't sure what you like, so I went for almost everything!"

"I love fashion, I just don't like spending time shopping though!"

"How do you do it then?"

"I shop fast and I know what I like! For me the perfect piece is the one you don't expect to find! And I have a bit of a weakness for shoes and trainers!"

"Me too for the shoes! I think you will love the selection we have here!" she said leading me over to them.

"But how did you know my size?" I asked surprised.

"I simply asked Aiden! And for your figure, I kind of guessed."

"Well, thank you very much! I am already enjoying this!"

We looked at the dresses and soon I had my eyes set on a long sleeved black dress. It had a v-shaped neckline in a typical wrap around dress style. I decided to try it on. Once I tied the

chic knot on the side of the dress, it displayed a fitted bod-
ice, highlighting my waist and hips, while the skirt part was
more relaxed with a front opening revealing one of my legs as
I moved. The shoulders were well tailored and decorated by
golden embroidery. The back of the floor length dress was as
fitted as the front, allowing the fabric to follow the curves of
my lower back. It was very elegant as well as seductive. Clara
loved it and agreed it was 'the' one.

Clara also found the perfect attire for her – a long dark
green dress, made of lace and embroidery. It was sleeveless and
fitted her perfectly. The straight, loose skirt was covered by the
embroidered lace. She looked absolutely stunning. We added
a black cape for wearing there and back. Then, we picked our
shoes: Clara went for classic black high heeled sandals, while
I chose bolder yellow satin high heels, decorated with crystal.
We also chose two different clutch bags: one black, covered
with sparkling crystals for me and a dark green one with a large
gold metal catch for Clara.

Finally, we moved on to our makeup and hair. Make up was
easy and fast as we were not wearing much of it. For our hair,
Clara made a large side braid, whereas I simply kept mine loose.

By 6.30pm, we were entirely ready and we still had an hour
and a half before Erling's charity event. We helped ourselves to
the mini-bar, put some music on and settled down on the sofas. We chatted about her trip to Hong-Kong and she opened
up about her relationship with her Maker, who had been really
important in Clara's life. A long time ago, Jarena was hoping to mould her into the perfect Younger Ordinem member,
as Jarena herself had been centuries ago. Unfortunately, her
expectations weren't met when Clara's gift for mind control
became more evident and an obstacle to any kind of political
engagement. Jarena had always been very involved with the
Kindred community and she had sat on the Ordinem board
for a few centuries before she got too old to occupy a Younger's position. Since then, she has been patiently waiting for

her turn at the Elders table and secretly hoping it would be possible for Clara to also join the leaders one day.

"We don't have the same sense of duty," said Clara, "I mean, I would rather take care of what needs to be done, whereas she is a thinker; follows the rules; makes them; loves them, actually! Aiden, Luca and I are really good at this, but she doesn't see it I guess."

"Maybe she does, but she sounds a bit strict."

"It depends, she is a nice person and means well. You'll see when you'll meet her."

At 7.15pm, Aiden called to say they were running late and didn't have the time to come back to the hotel, so they were going to meet us at the venue. They had rented a car to be more independent. Since we were ready and expected a bit of traffic on the way to the charity ball, we decided to leave and asked the hotel reception to arrange a taxi for us.

We arrived on time and found our way into the event quite easily. Clara showed our invitation card and informed the person at the entrance in charge of the guest list that both our companions were running slightly late due to traffic. She left their names, so the boys would be able to get in. The venue was splendid: the room was large with a high ceiling; there were several bars and a little further on there were dining tables where people could sit if they wanted. At the end of the room, there was a stage with an impressive grand piano where a band was playing modern jazz music. There were waiting staff everywhere, offering canapés and champagne to the guests on silver trays. The bars were serving cocktails, wines, spirits and liquors as well as soft drinks. Clara and I made our way to the closest counter and ordered two Old Fashioned cocktails. We were just taking the first sip of our drinks when Aiden and Luca entered the room. They looked dashing in their tuxedos! Aiden was absolutely dreamy, looking so fit and elegant in his marine blue tux. I could not take my eyes off him. Clara took one of my hands and brought me back to reality.

"You ladies look lovely!" complimented Luca.

"You are gorgeous, Louise!" Aiden whispered in my ear, which gave me insane goosebumps, luckily, I was wearing long-sleeves.

"Thanks, you guys look sensational too!" I said, getting a grip of myself.

They joined us for drinks and we looked around for Erling. When he saw him, Aiden told us and casually walked to the stage, patiently waited for the band to finish the song and spoke with the lead singer. Seconds later, they shook hands in a very friendly manner and the musicians left the stage to him. Aiden moved to the piano, sat down and started playing. At the first notes, a few heads lifted to see who was playing such a lovely melody, including Erling, who recognised the pianist immediately and smiled. Aiden continued playing effortlessly for a few minutes. When he finished, he stopped, got up, thanked the band who had returned to the stage and walked back towards us. All the guests gave him a round of applause. It only took a couple of minutes for Erling to appear in front of us.

"Aiden, what a remarkable entrance!" Erling said while offering a forearm handshake.

"You've always liked that piece!" Aiden's natural charisma was a real diplomatic asset.

"Indeed! Luca and Clara, it is lovely to see you too. And," he paused, "pardon me dear, I don't know who you are."

"My name is Louise, nice to meet you sir!" I responded politely.

"And you, Louise. So, what brings all of you here? I don't recall sending you an invitation – I hope you are not here to tell me how rude it was of me!"

"Of course not! But we would love to have a word with you in private," Aiden responded.

"I see, serious business."

"We are sorry for gate-crashing your event and it will only take ten minutes of your time. I am happy to wait until after the party if you prefer?" offered Aiden respectfully.

"No, no Aiden, don't worry, I imagine if you are here, the matter is rather urgent."

"Yes and also because your parties are always lovely!" Aiden joked cordially.

"Thank you, young man! Follow me – we'll go somewhere more private."

Clara offered to stay with me while Aiden and Luca talked with Erling. We had one more drink before the three of them returned. The host invited us to stay as long as we wanted and confirmed he would be available at any time, before he returned to mingle with his guests.

Now that we had met the last Elder on our list, we had to decide on the next safe meeting location. Luca and Aiden both had Moscow in mind and Clara agreed with them. The Russian capital was a strategic choice geographically, as everyone was going to travel last-minute from different parts of the world. We decided to sleep on it though – we could not risk making a mistake, with the next five Elders all in the same place at the same time.

"How did Erling react to your private meeting?" I wondered.

"Like the others and he has also heard rumours, but he understood the utmost confidentiality of the matter and will probably travel with us as soon as we confirm the location of our next meeting," responded Aiden.

"I am surprised none of them asked more questions."

"We did say that we had no idea what was going on. Plus, they are very old, so they know the rules better than anyone else. Many of them have helped to conceive those rules at some point in their lives."

"I see what you mean, it makes sense – they wouldn't challenge their own rules!" I smiled. "By the way, what did you tell the band?"

"Nothing special, I only asked them if it would be alright for me to play a song!"

"So no mind manipulation here?"

"No, we really don't use it that much at normal times!"

Clara was in a festive mood and asked Luca to dance with her. I noticed Aiden had his eyes fixed on me. It was satisfying to know we were longing for each other equally. I tried to ignore him but I couldn't. I wanted to be close to him, but I wasn't sure I was a hundred per cent ready. Aiden ended the dilemma when he extended his left hand, asking me to dance. I hesitated for a second; the venue was full of guests, so there was no room for mistakes. At the same time, I knew the training had changed me: I was much more in control and experienced at managing my emotions and feelings. Plus, I was not being taken by surprise.

I accepted his unspoken invitation and he led me near to Clara and Luca. He then drew me closer to him; I slowly wrapped my arms around his neck and he placed his hands just under my waist line. Finally, his eyes locked onto mine and he started leading the dance. It felt so good being in his arms. A million butterflies whirled in my stomach, but I managed not to get overwhelmed, which was a good start. After a few seconds of peaceful slow-dancing, I rested my head on his chest, breathing in his distinctive woody bergamot scent and for a moment I forgot where I was – only Aiden and I mattered. It was intense, everything around us disappeared and we were only left with each other. I tightened my hold on him and he did the same to me. At the end of the song, Aiden stopped.

"That was great!" he said contentedly.

"That's it? We could dance more?" I offered, slightly disappointed that our romantic interlude ended so prematurely.

"I have another idea!" he said mysteriously. He exchanged a few words with Clara and Luca, they nodded and then he took my hand to follow him. I just had time to wave goodbye to our friends and went with Aiden. They were waving back, smiling, while we made our way outside the venue.

"Aiden, what are we doing?" I asked confused at the sudden change.

"You'll see, I would like to take you somewhere."

"Alright, you like to keep the suspense level up, don't you?"

"Don't worry, it's not far!" he said while handing his car receipt to the valet and removing his bow-tie.

A few minutes later, we were driving to Aiden's mysterious surprise location. I was so happy to finally be alone with him and was curious to know what he had in mind, especially now that I could handle being close to him. He drove for half an hour, through the main roads of the city centre, then he took an exit and continued through smaller streets. At some point, he parked in what seemed to be the middle of nowhere and invited me to get out of the car. For practicality, I removed my high heels and we followed a narrow footpath down-hill, edged with grass and bushes. It led us to a tiny secluded pebbled beach.

"How do you fancy a swim?" asked Aiden, facing the water.

"Well, I did not expect that, but now that we are here, how could I possibly say no?" I teased.

He started removing his shoes, his perfectly fitted jacket off, then his impeccable white shirt, ending with his trousers. I enjoyed watching him revealing his lean and fit body and proceeded to undress too. I lost the dress in a second, simply by untying the bow holding the dress together. Aiden was looking at me in the same way I was at him – we could only see each other. Wearing just our underwear, we walked into the water, holding hands. The still water was chilly, but it did not affect either of us. The view was amazing: the sky was clear; the stars were showing off while the moon was lighting the way for us. When the water reached my chest, we stopped. Then, Aiden came close to me and said:

"I heard Chhay taught you an interesting workout in the water, would you show me?"

"You mean his own routine of movement?" I asked, taken aback.

"Yes, the one where you move your inner energy in and out. He told me you got pretty good at it. But only show me the slow part, I don't want to make you do a full session!"

"OK, I wasn't expecting that! But why not! How about I show you first and then we do it together?" I offered.

"Fine by me."

I began the slow routine while I looked at Aiden, devouring him with my eyes. I felt a shiver down my spine and a little burst of lustful energy in my stomach that I easily controlled by focusing on the movements. I made sure not to let it grow and to release it into the water as soon as it formed, as Chhay had taught me. When I finished the choreography, Aiden moved towards me and stood next to me. I repeated the movements and he copied perfectly, almost like he was familiar with them. He came closer and stopped right in front of me. Our arms touched above our heads and we lowered them together, until they met underwater. At this point, several rushes of passionate energy hit me, but I kept focusing by moving even slower than before and managed to keep myself under control, still in harmony with Aiden.

When I was calm, he slowly brought my arms around his neck and he lifted my legs up around his hips. Once more, it seemed like time had paused – nothing mattered, except us two. He unconsciously bit his lower lip, which turned me on even more. We moved closer and kissed. I wanted him so much; I had been longing for him since I had followed him to the mansion. Soon, we were consummating our love for the first time since I became a Kindred. It was incredible: our connection was so acute that every touch; kiss; or move was pleasurable. I remembered that intimacy with Aiden had always been amazing and sort of otherworldly, but this time it felt slightly different – perhaps because of the long wait, as well as my new state.

A while later, we came out of the water still feeling ecstatic. We put our clothes back on and headed back to the car. We were still damp from the sea water, but we didn't care until the residues of salt started to make our skin itch. Aiden drove fast to the hotel; we couldn't wait to shower and feel the relief of a salt free skin.

That night and part of the next day, I rediscovered Aiden in a different way, with my new enhanced senses. We were so infatuated, we could not get enough of each other.

Chapter XXXV

I was deeply asleep, when a loud knocking on the door woke me up. It took me a minute to realise it came from my hotel bedroom door. I got up and looked around for some kind of attire to cover my naked body. The room was a complete mess: our clothes were all over the place and many items had fallen on the floor. The night had been intense, both physically and emotionally. Aiden was still asleep, but not for much longer considering the knocks on the door were getting louder. I wrapped myself in one of the bed sheets and opened the door, Clara and Luca were in front of me. As soon as they saw my face and my draped figure, they could not contain their amusement:

"Afternoon! I guess we now know where Aiden is!" joked Luca.

"Hey!" I greeted softly.

"Speaking of the devil!" added Clara as Aiden joined us.

"Hi guys! Sorry, we seem to have lost track of time," said Aiden drowsily.

"Yes, it looks like it!" responded Luca, looking around the disorderly bedroom.

"Our flight is scheduled for 6pm, in less than three hours basically," Clara informed us.

"Do we still all agree on the location of the next meeting?" asked Aiden.

"Yes, I think Moscow is ideal!" confirmed Luca while Clara nodded in agreement too.

"OK then, we'll meet you in forty-five minutes in the lobby. Luca, do you mind confirming with Erling that he will be flying with us? If so, we'll pick him up on our way to the airport as we agreed yesterday. Also, we have to inform the other Elders on the next location," said Aiden, always able to get himself organised.

"Yes, that sounds good! Clara and I can take care of all of that, can't we *Clarita*?"

"Yes, definitely!"

"That would be great, thanks guys."

"No worries, see you then!" ended Luca.

Aiden closed the door and turned to me with a suggestive smile. He lifted me up and carried me to the bed where he released me.

Soon after, we were in the car, on the way to pick up Erling. It made sense for him to travel with us since they were going straight to the meeting location after dropping me off at Ho-Chi-Minh airport. Chhay would be waiting for me there and taking us back to Mondulkiri.

Aiden was driving and entertaining the Elder, while Luca, Clara and I were sitting in the back. Now and then, Aiden and I would exchange a look through the rear-view mirror. Clara and Luca told me all about their evening and the after-party they went to. Then, she grabbed my arm in a friendly manner and whispered in my ear:

"And you, how was your evening?"

"Satisfying!"

"I can imagine!"

"Seriously, before last night, it felt like we were a couple of dogs that could not be left alone, but now that this tension has been released, I feel much better!"

"I understand! Intimacy can be truly overwhelming for a new Kindred, especially with all these new developed senses, it was wise to wait as long as you could!"

"I suspect Aiden was planning this and I am glad he did!"

"It is possible – it hasn't been easy for him too. Surely, he wouldn't miss the opportunity if it presented itself."

There was a bit of traffic, but we managed to be at the airport on time and our plane took off as planned. Half way through the flight, Aiden and I sat away from the rest of the group, as we knew that we would soon be separated again for a couple of days. I was not a big fan of public displays of affection, however, simply holding hands and being close was enough to awake our desire for more.

"Aiden, when did you plan this little trip to the beach in Taipei?" I asked to distract us.

"Erm... I guess I am busted!" he replied laughing.

"Yes, you are! So, tell me, did you plan it all?"

"Well, when you put it like that, it does not sound great!"

"It was great!"

"So, when we came back to Chhay's house from our trip to Europe, you were in the middle of your workout. Chhay explained the technique of the exercise and did not want me to interrupt. To be honest, I knew most of the movements already, as I had seen Chhay training many times in the past."

"How did you know it would work?"

"I didn't, but I thought it was worth a try. Chhay told me you were mostly in control and it was all about not letting the energy build up, which, as you know, was the whole point of only focusing on the slow movements. I supposed that in our case, the more we waited, the harder it would get. I knew you would feel safe and in control moving in the water. Basically, once you saw you were in control, you knew how to be your new self: no fear, no build-up and control – everything we needed!"

"I love how your brain works! Good call!" I praised him.

"I still have plenty of ideas for later when we return from the meeting!"

"Me too!" I agreed before I changed the subject, "But, what do you think will happen once Ordinem is reunited?"

"We will find Robert and Kyle no matter what. And I am sure the new Elders will provide us with all the resources we need to do so. Plus, we could definitely use their guidance."

"So, after the meeting, the hunt will start."

"Yes, hopefully we will find them soon."

"Please, take me with you – I want to help."

"Trust me, there is nothing I want more than being together. Let's see how the meeting goes."

The landing was near and my heart was heavy; I did not want to leave Aiden, especially after the intimacy we had shared. I just wished we could hide ourselves away for days, but I was fully aware our newly recovered relationship was currently not a priority. Soon, the aircraft's enormous tyres bounced onto the tarmac, breaking my spirit at the same time, as it was only a matter of minutes before I had to leave them. Luca and Clara hugged me before I exited the plane, Erling shook my hand and Aiden accompanied me out, down the staircase. He took me in his arms and we held each other tight for a minute.

"I will see you soon, text me when you get to the house. Chhay is waiting for you on the other side of Customs."

"I will and please do the same once you reached your destination."

He nodded and watched me walk away. I turned around and we exchanged a final wave, before he disappeared inside the jet. Exactly as Aiden had predicted, Chhay was waiting for me after Customs. He surprised me by coming with the dog, who jumped up at me excitedly, whining and licking me. I was so happy to see him; it lifted my mood and I forgot Aiden for a second.

We went to the car and were soon on our way. The plane had stopped at Ho-Chi-Minh airport, as it was easier to drop me off and take off again straight away. The airport was bigger and turned out to be closer than Phnom Penh's was to Mondulkiri; however, it was usually easier to arrive straight in Cambodia rather than crossing another border by road.

The dog was with me on the passenger seat – I had missed him. Chhay told me that nothing special had happened during the last couple of days and that the dog had been following him everywhere and sleeping on my bed. He then asked how the trip to Taipei was. I told him mostly about the charity event and mentioned that I could be physically close to Aiden now without any issues. He smiled and said that when it came to training, hard work usually paid off. I thanked him for helping me finding my new self.

For the rest of the journey, we tried to find a name for the dog. Chhay warned me that if I didn't, he would simply call him *Tchkaï* like many locals did, which meant "dog" in Khmer. The border crossing was not difficult: Chhay handled it all and I just handed over my passport.

When we finally arrived at his place, we decided to have a short relaxing training session together. The water exercise was easier than it had ever been so far. After the session, I had just enough time to go for a long walk in the jungle with the dog. Soon after, we were all in bed.

Just before I fell asleep, I got a text from Aiden, telling me they had arrived in Moscow. Thinking of him made me feel nostalgia for my connection with Naomi. It was strange not to share with her how my relationship with Aiden was flourishing and most importantly how much I felt for him. We were used to confiding in each other and over the years it almost became a necessity. I wished I could simply call her and tell her everything, but I knew it could only be a fantasy. Aiden and I had to agree on some new way to disclose our relationship to her. Considering how preoccupied we had all been with Kyle's drama, it had been impossible to resume the conversation about Naomi and I. However, I promised myself I would, as soon as the moment presented itself.

Chapter XXXVI

Aiden

When I got back into the jet, I felt heavy-hearted – I did not like leaving Louise alone once more. I knew she was fine, but I simply wanted to be with her. At least, we had finally found our way back to each other. But for now, we had to remain focused; we were so close to reaching our goal: Ordinem was about to be re-formed and a proper mission order to find Robert was going to be issued.

"Are you OK?" Luca asked discreetly.

"Yes, I am just looking forward to having everything figured out," I said honestly.

"You and me both!" he agreed.

We could not talk much about the matter since Erling was with us, so it was the perfect time to relax and read, or watch a film. I opened my biology book to keep my mind distracted from Louise. The rest of the flight was quiet – everybody was in their own world. We arrived in Moscow at 2.30am local time and our meeting was scheduled for 4am in a city centre flat. We rented this one through one of Luca's Human contacts. We could not take the risk of being located by Kyle so close to completion.

We were the first to arrive; Erling and Luca stayed in the main room setting up the meeting area, while Clara and I went back downstairs to greet our important guests. By 4.02am, everybody was seated and it was obvious they were all anxious to know what the purpose of the meeting was. I decided I would not talk much – I would rather let the gruesome images of Robert's surveillance cameras speak for themselves. Luca had set up the TV to show the recording and once he was ready, I started my introduction:

"Thank you all for coming and making yourselves available at such short notice. You can imagine the matter is urgent. I shall not waste your time, so I will be direct. A month ago, Robert asked Luca privately to install a surveillance system on the premises of Ordinem, as he was under the impression things were being moved. Nobody else knew about it. About a week ago, we received an email from Robert titled '*under attack*' with only one word in the content of the message: '*see*'. From that email, Luca understood he could indeed see what was happening over there, so we accessed the cameras online and here is what we witnessed. Please be aware the content of the images is very shocking."

Luca played the video and they all had their eyes fixed on the screen, waiting to discover the mysterious truth. We could not watch it again – I think we would be haunted by those images for a very long time, especially since we had to clean up the results. I will probably never forget all the charred bodies – the sight or the smell.

While the video played, their facial expressions moved from puzzled to horrified, as well as sad and angry. At the end of it, the air in the room was heavy. Nobody spoke – they were all trying to make sense of what they had just watched. Just like us, they all recognised Kyle and were shocked to find out that he had orchestrated the massacre. I decided to intervene:

"I am sorry you had to see these horrendous scenes. We could not possibly tell you about this during our first visit.

We asked you here today because you are the next five Elders in line to form the new Ordinem. As you have seen, Robert was taken – we think he is still alive and has a part to play in whatever Kyle's plan is. We found the note that Robert left behind – the one you can see him writing during the assault. It had the specific instructions to rebuild Ordinem and this is what we are doing. I imagine you will have to take charge from here. Obviously, we cannot go back to Malta, so we will have to choose another place to host the new Ordinem. For now, we have cleared the site completely and put it in lock down. Nobody could possibly know or guess what happened there. I will leave you for a few minutes to process all of this."

I walked out, followed by Luca and Clara. The Elders were still in shock and it took a few minutes for them to find their composure. Eventually, we heard them starting to confer amongst themselves. We came back in, ready to discuss the next steps. Jarena was the most experienced with Ordinem, so naturally she took the lead in the conversation.

"First, I would like to say on behalf of us all, thank you for keeping this under control and clearing out Ordinem premises. I can't imagine what it was like to be there in person. Although the circumstances are ghastly, we are honoured to become the new representatives of Ordinem. We are also anxious to know what you did with our beloved comrades' bodies."

"We gathered their remains and travelled with them to Romania where we buried them. They are not too far from The Chapel," I answered.

"Good thinking! What about the rest?"

"We took everything – we emptied all the offices and hid all the documents in Romania also, near The Chapel but in a different place."

"We will need to retrieve all the documents. You see, normally, when a new Elder arrives at Ordinem, they are accompanied either by the other members, or their soon to be predecessor. None of us knows exactly how the Elders actually operate."

"We will have to figure it out. A new style might benefit us actually... and help us be less predictable," I reckoned.

"Jarena, I thought you started an apprenticeship for an upcoming Elder position, didn't you?" asked Viktor.

"I wouldn't call it an 'apprenticeship' as such – we didn't have the chance to complete it, as Charles was still introducing me to all aspects of the job. But yes, at least we have a tiny insight to work with. Aiden, did you find our names when you went to The Chapel?"

"Yes indeed."

"How did you know about it?"

"Robert left us some clues on the note – the one he hid under the carpet – that led us to you."

"Did you open the vault?"

"Yes, we did!"

"How?! Only the Elders of Ordinem know the procedure, not even the Youngers do. Charles told me we had a census book hidden in the Chapel and that the access would be shown to me, once I had officially taken my seat."

"It required patience and dedication, but we eventually found our way in. However, we had to detach some pages to protect your identities and the ones who follow. The names are safely stored in my head and on a hidden USB stick," said Luca.

"You are impressive – we should have you three as our Youngers," Jarena stated, looking at Clara.

"To be honest Jarena, I don't think we are good Ordinem material for now. However, I do believe we are the best suited to operate out in the field, in order to bring Robert back and put an end to Kyle's villainy. Clara, Luca and I are used to handling complex assignment and we know how to investigate discreetly."

"Fair enough! I must say, you are making a very good point," she conceded, "I personally think we should hold off the Youngers election anyway, until this mess is sorted out.

Of course, we will have to discuss this issue further amongst ourselves." The other Elders seemed comfortable with her idea.

"We have heard of two Kindreds who went rogue in the past. What happened back then?" I asked.

"This happened a very long time ago, when Ordinem was nothing like it is now and they were still trying to figure out how to fit in the world. It happened on two occasions – some time at the end of the first century and the beginning of the second. In both cases, it was blood lust – they lost control and fed on people. On the first occasion everyone was killed at a tavern; and on the second one, a Kindred went back to his family and murdered them all. Neither of the attacks was planned, but rather the accountable Kindreds were overpowered by their urges. Borna and Mislav hunted them down and executed them. After these two events, they understood that regular feeding was a priority. Their losses were not in vain," explained Channeh.

"OK, nothing like Kyle then," said Luca.

"Definitely not, it was not deliberate as opposed to Kyle," agreed Channeh.

"On the positive side, Kyle has no idea we are rebuilding Ordinem. How could he? I mean, to his knowledge, nobody is aware of his actions. Since Ordinem very rarely welcomed other people, we can pretend for a while. We think he is trying to stage some kind of coup. We need to act fast. So far, we have always been a few steps ahead of him, especially now that we have gathered you all. Realistically, if it had not been for Robert's last-minute instruction to focus on Ordinem, we would have most likely gone after him," I continued.

"Plus, he has no idea you had the information in the first place to find us," added Tahir.

"Yes, I think that's why Kyle took Robert. He must play an important part in his plan. From Kyle's point of view, Robert is the only remaining Elder with the necessary knowledge to form a new Ordinem," I stated.

"But Robert will never give in," said Channeh, obviously worried about her good friend while the other Elders nodded their agreement.

"Robert is also the only one who can present Kyle as a fit figure of authority," Viktor added.

"Which he is not, as Robert knows very well now. I just don't see how Robert could give him his support after what Kyle has done," continued Channeh.

"Of course, Kyle is a deluded maniac, but he must have some kind of leverage to make Robert comply with his wishes," I spoke.

"What kind of leverage?" Jarena asked worriedly.

"I have no idea, it could be anything, including threatening to reveal our existence to the rest of the world," I guessed.

"Robert would never let this happen!" defended Jarena, followed by the others.

"Precisely, Kyle knows how precious our anonymity is, especially to Robert who is one of the founders of our modern world," supported Luca.

"Hmm, isn't it an obvious empty threat though?" asked Tahir.

"Kyle has literally nothing to lose – Robert is his only way to Ordinem now. He knows we will be coming for him, as long as he is not protected by Ordinem or Robert. And that has to be worse than being hunted down by inexperienced Humans. But I am just guessing here, we have to be prepared for anything," I reflected.

"I think it would be wise indeed not to underestimate Kyle. His actions have proved he is ready to take every risk," summarised Jarena.

"Something else is rather worrying – we have been wondering whether he turned people to make his army or if he hired Human hit-men," I continued.

"Both are extremely endangering for our kind. However, I would rather deal with an army of hit-men than one of Kindreds. Plus, we have no way of knowing if the latter can control themselves. We cannot take the risk of such exposure. We need to end this now," said Erling.

"One more reason to start looking for him. Are we able to locate him?" I asked

"We'll try to tap into his mobile phone signal, but I would not get my hopes up on this one. It would be rather silly of him to still have his phone on," Jarena said.

"Also, he would expect that. Kyle has been very close to Robert for years and has always been keen on Ordinem operations," I reminded them.

"We can ask our administration to narrow down our search," continued Jarena.

"I'm sorry, but if you allow me, we need to remain cautious here. We don't know who Kyle has enrolled and for now you can't act as the new legitimate Elders of Ordinem. We need to keep our advantage. This operation needs to remain extremely discreet," said Luca.

"Actually, I am wondering how did Kyle pull this whole thing off? He must have had some kind of inside informant. He obviously knew when the meeting was taking place," observed Tahir.

"Well, we studied the events on the video thoroughly and it seems that the assistant was the mole. He is the one who distracted Robert away from the meeting and chained the doors of his office. Which is strange, as Robert could have destroyed them so easily," I wondered.

"And the assistant was beheaded later in the video, so we are not sure whether he really knew what he was doing and the consequences of his actions, or not," added Luca.

"We think Robert understood what was happening and that he couldn't get out of it. There was no reason for him to destroy his doors. He could see the number of assassins on his surveillance software on his computer. It made much more sense to leave as many clues behind as possible instead," stated Clara.

Forced to admit the unique nature of the situation, the Elders started exchanging ideas amongst themselves. To be fair, they had just found out the truth, whereas we had had a full week to process everything and work out Kyle's agenda. As we were more familiar with the matter at hand, rather than delay any further, we decided to make them a proposition:

"If I may suggest, we do have an idea. We cannot find Kyle immediately, however, we should be able to trace his previous movements. Perhaps this will lead us to his current location," Luca offered.

"That is brilliant, you might be able to gather enough intelligence to work out what he has been up to," reacted Erling.

"Plus, we should have all our blood banks on a tight watch – Kyle has to feed, like any of us. I doubt he will go through the front door and will most likely stage a robbery for supply," reflected Jarena.

"He will definitely need a regular blood supply," I concurred while everybody in the room nodded. "Also, I can imagine he expects us to figure out Robert is missing at some point. I mean, I do interact with him every week or so."

"Yes, I don't doubt his plan is time sensitive," said Jarena.

"Moreover, there are a couple of reliable people we would like to assist us in our investigation. One of them has just been reborn. She was fatally attacked by one of Kyle's assassins, but I intervened. Robert is aware of the situation and that is why he called on an emergency meeting in the first place. He wanted to sort out the issue with Ordinem. At first, we believed he wanted to murder her, but we then realised he was actually attempting to turn her."

"How come you were conveniently there when she was attacked?" asked Jarena.

"To be honest, I wanted to turn her – I had had my eyes on her for a long time. I had already mentioned my wish to Robert, but fate decided otherwise and rushed me to act before

I had a complete green light. For that, I sincerely apologise," I confessed.

"What about the other person?" inquired Jarena.

"I believe you all know Chhay."

"Yes, fine," agreed Jarena.

"Am I the only one curious to know why Kyle attacked Aiden's interest?" asked Viktor.

"We think, she has a part to play in his agenda, but we are not entirely sure how yet. We also believe he used her as a way to get to me," I continued.

"She should not be left alone," said Jarena.

"She is safe with Chhay now and is more than able to defend herself," I responded.

"Very well, although I feel some rules may have not been totally respected here, we will grant you the benefit of the doubt. You have done so much to protect us all – we will overlook this issue for now. However, we expect explanations once order is restored," stated Jarena.

"I would like to add something," started Clara confidently, gazing at Jarena, "Louise, the person we are talking about, has been standing by our side from the beginning of her new life and has proved her loyalty more than once. She removed the remains of Ordinem members with her bare hands, just so we could give them a decent burial that she refused to be rushed. She helped us to find you and is now training to learn to manage her new self. She is a fighter, literally and metaphorically. I thought you might want to hear what type of person she was from somebody other than her Maker."

"Thank you Clara, we will keep this in mind, although I have no doubt Louise is fit to be part of our world. I and I guess everybody here, trust Aiden's judgement as well as yours," accepted Jarena and the other Elders nodded in agreement.

"Thank you Jarena. Another thing we need to discuss is a safe place for you, the next Elders, to stay. Of course, nobody can know Ordinem is reunited," I continued.

"We need to get off the grid," said Tahir, understanding the problem.

"Yes, but nobody should notice your disappearance either. It might show our hand to Kyle," said Luca.

"Right, how about we all go back to our own places and carry on with our regular occupations? We can communicate over burner phones and through weekly meetings, always on the same day, but the location will change every time. Obviously, we should never travel together. The phones should only be used to notify the time and place of the next meeting and in case of emergency," suggested Jarena.

"Sounds like a good start to me," said Luca.

"As for the search for Robert, we should start looking into Kyle's usual haunts and see when he was last seen. Do you agree?" I checked and they all nodded their assent.

"In the meantime, we will try to locate him in a way that won't raise suspicions. We might have to find a way through the tools of the Human world," mused Jarena.

"Actually, he would never suspect that," confirmed Luca.

"Alright, so we should go back to London then and start the search there. It's the last time I saw him, the night he had Louise killed," I suggested.

"Yes, I think it is a good place to start. Moreover, it would be helpful if everyone here could think of their Human contacts and how we could exploit them," stated Jarena.

"Yes, we will look into it," Tahir agreed.

"Us too. In addition, considering how confidential the situation is, I think it may be easier to have one Ordinem member to coordinate with," I recommended.

"That's a good idea," said Jarena looking around for a volunteer.

"Shouldn't it be you Jarena, since you are the most experienced with Ordinem?" asked Clara.

"I am also your Maker, so let's put this to a fair vote," she suggested with a smile. They complied and soon after, they had elected Jarena as their representative. It was not surprising, as she was much appreciated; she was known to be very fair; serious and trustworthy – and right now, she knew Ordinem better than anyone else in the room.

"If I may, something has been on my mind: our beloved ex-leaders were almost all Makers, what shall we do about their pupils? Won't they wonder where their Makers are?" inquired Clara thoughtfully.

"In such circumstances, I am afraid we cannot tell them the truth. At least for now and as long as Kyle is free. I think everybody here will agree," Jarena looked at the other Elders who all concurred with her.

We went over our plan once again and agreed we would bring the cases of documents still hidden in Romania, to our next meeting. Then, we departed separately. I was glad the meeting was over, it had taken a lot out of me, but it felt good to be surrounded by allies. Clara, Luca and I went quickly back to the airport and we managed to take off just before sunrise. I had time to call Louise to let her know we were flying back to Cambodia. I was really looking forward to seeing her and telling her our next course of action.

Then, my mind drifted away, remembering the night we had in Taipei. The moment I saw her in that black dress, my heart stopped – it fitted all of her curves perfectly. But my favourite moment was watching her undress at the beach – the way the dress slowly slid from her shoulders was incredibly sensual, and I wanted her for ever. Of course, what happened next and the rest of the night was even better! I could not wait to be with her again – she was very free and moved flawlessly; she could be untamed or gentle; whatever we wanted, we did. I was lost in my pleasurable thoughts when Luca interrupted me.

"Aiden, when are we going back to London?"

"Soon I guess, tomorrow or the day after. Finding Robert is now the new priority."

"Chhay is coming, isn't he?"

"I think so, but let's check with him first."

"OK, shall we take a place together like old times?"

"I think Louise and I would like that!"

"I'll try to find a place with plenty of space and privacy!" Luca joked.

I could not wait to tell Louise that we were going to head back to London. I wanted to surprise her and arrange a meeting with Naomi. She would be very excited! We still had a four to five hour motorbike ride from Phnom Penh, so I slept for the rest of the flight.

Chapter XXXVII

At some point during the day, my phone rang and woke me, it was Aiden. They had finished their meeting and were now on their way back to Moscow airport. I wished him a good flight and told him I was really looking forward to having him back. I returned to sleep for a few more hours until it was time to get up, take care of the dog and start training again.

Today, Chhay wanted to start with a feeding exercise: he had hidden four small cups of blood in the jungle and I was to find them all before I could feed. It was torture to be hooked on the blood scent but not being able to have it. Plus, he made me carry the cups as I found them, so I was being constantly tempted. It took me two hours to find them all and by that time I was famished. Resisting the craving to drink the blood was tough, but my will to postpone the urges was stronger, and despite the primordial need, I remained in control of myself. After I fed, we moved on to a quick meditation session to restore my mind after such a challenging exercise.

Later, on the way to the waterfall, Chhay told me that we would work on my strength and how to use it efficiently and in a timely manner. He said it was a similar process to the energy flow exercise he designed, only much more difficult. Once we arrived, we started our Qi-Qong session on the rocks by the waterfall.

After half an hour, I noticed the air was different than usual – there were unknown scents that I could not recognise. As I registered that, the dog suddenly stood to attention, ears and tail up. We looked around, but there was nothing to be seen, until out of nowhere, a massive spear was thrown at Chhay who miraculously stopped it with his right hand.

Everything happened extremely fast: we both got up, looking for our assailants when a second spear hit Chhay who ended up pinned to a tree. Suddenly, several attackers appeared: they headed for Chhay and two of them proceeded to shock him with stun gun batons while three others tied him to the tree with barbed wire.

The scene was horrific, Chhay had no chance to fight back and I couldn't help him as two other men hit me on the head and threw me to one side. The dog tried to intervene, but they stunned him too and he passed out. The sight of my two distressed friends made me furious, I wanted to kill all the intruders. I felt a ball of energy building up inside me and had no intention of taking it down, so I let it nurture itself.

My two attackers launched at me again, but I swiftly got up and knocked one of them down with a high kick, while I caught the other by the neck and broke it. Chhay was unable to move, almost unconscious. I started to run towards him, but his assailants stopped me. They all fought me at the same time, but I kept kicking, punching, locking and breaking bones – nothing was going to stop me! Eventually I had most of them down, until another three jumped on me out of nowhere and diverted me, allowing some of the others to recover and resume their attack. They battered me with all their strength, but at no point did they try to kill me, which made me even more relentless. I had to defeat them to get to Chhay and the dog, so I kept fighting fiercely. I started to get a clear advantage over the thugs, until a sudden clapping sound made them back off. Slowly, a tall man came out of the shadow of the jungle.

"Well done, quite impressive young lady! I expected a struggle from Chhay but not you! You can never be too prepared!" he said viciously, still clapping his hands in a sarcastic way.

"What do you want?" I demanded angrily.

"I would like you to come with me, please," he responded confidently.

"Why should I?"

"Do you know who I am?" he asked, full of arrogance.

"I'm not sure. What do you want?" I lied in order to keep all my cards close to my chest.

"I can't believe the Almighty Aiden did not tell you about me!"

"Are you that Kyle guy?"

"That's better. Yes, I am that charming guy! And it is lovely to finally meet you in person, Louise."

"Are you the one who ordered my death?" I played dumb trying to get some intel.

"I never ordered anyone to kill you, well at least not for good! You were supposed to be turned and brought back to me. Now that I have found you again, everything is falling back into place."

"Well, you can't make me come with you!"

"Hmm, physically speaking, you may be right; however, I do have a very good incentive that you might be interested in. As I said, 'you can never be too prepared'. It took me a while to find you. And now that I have you, I have no intention of letting you go!"

"What do you want from me?"

"You shall find out, in due course!"

"I'm not coming with you! I don't know you!"

"Don't be so hasty darling, don't you want to know what your incentive is?"

From the moment I saw Kyle, I knew who he was but decided to pretend I didn't. He had no idea we had already watched the destruction of Ordinem and Robert kidnap, as well as how far we were in gathering the new Elders together.

We had to keep it this way. To his knowledge, we had never met, so I couldn't know his face. I had a big advantage. Plus, he had no idea who I was and where I stood – he just wanted me to hurt and weaken Aiden.

Kyle had also confirmed that his real intention was to make me a Kindred and that I definitely had a part to play in his plan at some point. He had obviously underestimated me on the physical level, but he had no idea how much I could take mentally. Life had challenged me quite early on and dramatically toughened me up. Following him was the only way in to understand and prevent his plan. But he could not think for one second that I came willingly, I had to push his limits.

"I don't see how you could possibly force me to follow you."

"Well, why don't you take a look at this?"

He handed to me a small tablet – it was a compilation of video clips of Naomi, showing every part of her life: going to or leaving work; having dinner with Ian or friends; even in her house while she slept. I did not expect him to know about her, which threw me off my game for a minute. At least, now, I knew how far to go and then and there, I swore to myself to kill him. It was one thing to be fighting amongst Kindreds, but bringing in a defenceless innocent, was taking the conflict to a whole new level.

Quietly, I looked at Chhay who was badly hurt. He could not move and let out a faint grunt. I felt a storm of anger and hatred towards Kyle: he needed to be terminated for Robert's sake; Ordinem; Naomi and all of us. Since Kyle had a specific interest in me, I should use it against him. I would play his game, but with my own rules.

"If you touch her, I'll kill you!" I threatened.

"Feisty, aren't we? Exciting! Even if you kill me, she will still be dead! Nobody wins. However, should you come with me now, your friend will remain safe and sound. Now that's what I call a win-win situation."

"How can I be sure you are trustworthy?" I confronted him.

"Truthfully, I have no interest in your friend, the only thing I want is for you to join me. What do you know, you might enjoy my company more than you ever thought you would!"

"I doubt that, but since you leave me no choice, fine, I'll come."

"Lovely! I knew we could find some kind of common ground! Oh, one more thing, as you brilliantly stated earlier, we do not know each other and therefore I would be a fool to let you walk freely without using some kind of restraint," he said while gesturing at his minions to come forward.

I recognised the woman who had assaulted me back in London and changed the course of my life forever. She grabbed my arms and zip-tied my wrists while another one of Kyle's lackeys put heavy metal shackles on my ankles. I looked like a convicted prisoner. I did not move. He had no idea how much I wanted him to take me to his world so I could destroy him. I hated him so much that I would do anything, even if it meant compromising myself. Kyle's men regrouped and before we left, he went over to Chhay, smirking like the sadist that he was.

"Chhay, my man, my sincere apology for barging into your place like this. What can I say – collateral damage, I guess. I must say I am rather disappointed that Aiden is not here, I was so looking forward to seeing him. Anyway, since you are here, I might as well use you. I need you to deliver a message to Aiden. You see, I knew he would hide his precious Louise somewhere. It took me some time to search, but eventually I thought of you and your remote training place. You know it was not easy for me to come here, I hate this tropical climate! I want Aiden to know, what it is like to be so close to your goal and see it being taken by someone else. Plus, of course, since I have her, he better not try anything that would jeopardise her well-being."

Chhay was unable to move, as the barbed wire held him tight against the tree where the spear had propelled him and he was attached from head to toe. His face was bleeding from the penetrating wire. Kyle put one of his fingers in the spear wound, pressing the inner flesh and Chhay groaned with pain.

"Ah! There you are, just checking you heard me! I dislike very much having to repeat myself," he said sadistically, "Oh, I just realised, if Aiden fails to return before the sun rises, don't worry about the message. I guess your ashes will speak louder than my words! Alright, our work here is done, let's go back home lovely people!"

I took a long last look at Chhay and the dog, who was still out, but breathing. I had broken the necks of three opponents, who were still lying on the ground – their comrades picked them up and carried them back with us. They woke up a couple of hours later in the van we were travelling in, which definitely confirmed that Kyle's thugs were Kindreds too.

I had no idea where we were going, but we weren't taking any of the routes I had seen so far. Kyle was probably trying to cover his tracks so Aiden could not follow us. Aiden... I knew I would not see him for a while, but it was a sacrifice I was ready to make in order to annihilate Kyle. Aiden and I would have eternity to catch up. My heart ached thinking of him, Luca and Clara, arriving at the house, finding Chhay in such a state and that I had been abducted. For now, I decided to remain quiet and give Kyle the silent treatment until I figured out how I was going to play him. One thing I knew for sure: I would not let him terrorise me.

Chapter XXXVIII

Aiden

When we arrived at the airport, we collected our bikes and rode to Mondulkiri. I was impatient to see Louise, which resulted in a faster, shorter ride. When we arrived, it was 1.30am and I expected to find her training with Chhay at the back of the house or at the waterfall. The main house was empty and very quiet, barely lit from the solar lamps. We put down our bags and walked towards the training area behind the house. There was a peculiar scent, one that had not been here before; maybe it had been raining, or some animals were close by. It was hard to identify, as there were plenty of different smells, which confused us. But the more we walked, the more intense the scent became, until we realised it was the smell of Kindred blood. The idea that something had happened to Louise and Chhay was unbearable. We ran to the training pit but there was nothing – no Louise, Chhay or even the dog. We then sprinted to the waterfall and found Chhay covered in blood, half alive, tied to a tree with barbed wire and with a spear through his shoulder. Luca arrived with cutting pliers to detach the wire that had perforated his skin. We then removed the spear in one swift motion. Chhay's injury was quite bad, but now that we freed him, his wounds could start healing.

"I'm so sorry Aiden," Chhay murmured.

"Where is Louise?" I asked anxious.

"He took her," he said weakly.

"Kyle?" Inside, I was boiling with anger.

"I'm so sorry." Chhay was devastated.

"It is not your fault," I said walking away, wanting to scream my frustration.

Clara came and took me in her arms. She was also very worried, since she and Louise had become good friends. Luca carried Chhay back to the house so we could clean him up and feed him to hurry the recovery. Clara stayed with him while Luca and I took our motorbikes, trying to track Kyle. I took the way to Phnom Penh, while Luca went towards the Vietnam border. The whole time I was riding, Louise's face was in my mind. I worried she had been hurt, considering the state of Chhay. Although she was strong, there is only so much one person can take. I could not believe he managed to snatch her away from me, so close to our goal.

I could not find anything, not a recent tyre print, not any scent that would indicate I was going in the right direction. After an hour of riding around, there was still no sign of Kyle or Louise. I decided to drive back, hoping Luca's search had been more fruitful. When I reached the house, Luca had just arrived and looked as disappointed and upset as I was. While we were away, Clara had cared for Chhay so well that by the time we returned, he was able to talk properly.

"Aiden, I'm so sorry I failed you! If anything happens to her, I'll never forgive myself!" mourned Chhay.

"Stop! The only person responsible here, is Kyle," I said.

"What happened?" Clara asked calmly.

"I don't know, it went all so fast and they were ready for me. In less than a minute, I went from sitting down with Louise to being nailed and wired to a tree, half conscious."

"OK, try to relax, you're still in shock," said Clara.

Chhay took a minute to regroup, then recalled what had just occurred. "We were practising Qi-Qong, when suddenly we sensed something unusual. The dog got up and straight after they threw a spear at me. I caught it, but they threw a second one that pinned me to the tree. Then, everything happened extremely fast – there were five guys on me, shocking me with stun guns and tying me up with barbed wire all at the same time while a couple of other guys attacked Louise."

"Did they hurt her?" I asked hastily.

"No, they stood no chance against her. I think they expected me to put up a fight, but not her. They focused their main effort on me. But as soon as I couldn't move, they all jumped on her."

"I am going to kill him!" Luca shouted out, full of rage.

"Louise fought hard and they could not get her to back down," continued Chhay.

"Sounds like her." At this point, I needed anything to hold onto and ease my anxiety.

"What? She won the fight?" interrogated Luca.

"Yes!"

"How did they take her then?" I inquired, fearing the worst.

"Blackmail, he showed her someone on a screen and she said she would kill him if he touched her."

"Naomi!" I understood.

"He knows more than we thought," admitted Luca.

"No, he knows nothing, but thinks he knows it all," said Chhay angrily, wincing.

"What do you mean?" Luca asked.

"He expected Aiden to be here and gave me a message to deliver. He thinks we were hiding Louise here and wants Aiden to know what it's like to be so close to your goal and lose it to someone else. Also, I believe he is not aware that we know what he did to Ordinem and Robert."

"He is completely mad!" complained Luca.

"He is using Louise against me. He thinks it's his leverage for me to stay away, or I think that is the choice he will give me when we find him," I guessed.

"When did this all happen?" inquired Clara.

"Some time around 10pm I think," answered Chhay.

"When we arrived in Phnom Penh... so, you stayed like that for almost four hours, that's horrible," she said apologetically.

"At least, you came in time, Kyle said that if Aiden didn't make it before sunrise, my ashes would be the message."

"He is a sadist! I am sorry Chhay, we are here now," reassured Clara while patting his back. Luca was outraged, he was pacing up and down, trying to contain his frustration.

"He said something else, but it could very well be a trap. He mentioned that he hated this climate, would that help to find him?"

"Kyle was never a big fan of hot and humid climates, that's true – it's good to remind me. He will definitely be more likely to be located in a more temperate climate," I confirmed.

"Also, his men are definitely Kindreds too. Their scents and strength gave them away."

"That's bad!" exclaimed Luca.

"Yes, it is. Plus, we can now be sure that Kyle wanted to turn Louise and not kill her," reminded Clara.

"Yes, he said he wants her by his side, but for what? I don't know," Chhay confirmed.

"The silver lining is that Louise is alive and will be for a while," said Luca looking at me meaningfully.

"I think so too," I accepted.

"Some parts of the attack are still blurry, but Louise played him and pretended not to know him."

"She kept our advantage. Smart Louise!" I said proudly.

"By the way, where is the dog?" Clara asked suddenly.

"Have you not seen him? They shocked him too when he tried to defend me! He passed out somewhere near me. We have to find him – he belongs to Louise! I've already let her down – I have to find him!" he said, getting up painfully.

We all went with him – Luca physically supporting him, while Clara and I were walking ahead calling the dog. We did not find him for a while, but eventually we were able to track his smell. I guessed he was hiding somewhere, probably traumatised. We traced him sheltering behind the waterfall where Louise usually trained, probably waiting for her to appear. It was sad to watch. We called him, but it took him a few minutes to catch our scent and understand we were here to help him. He came, limping, with a couple of hairless burns on his leg and rib cage. It broke my heart to see him like that and I could not imagine what Louise felt when she saw Chhay and the dog being stunned. I picked him up in my arms, took him back to the house and put him on Louise's bed.

A feeling of frustration and raw anger overtook me, so I ran hard through the jungle in order to let it out. I reached the top of the mountain where Louise had been practising with Chhay the day after we arrived. Just recalling this moment made me angrier. I screamed as loud as I could and fell on my knees. I could not believe I had lost Louise again.

Luca found me, he knew how much I was hurting. He did not say much, except that they would do everything in their power to find Louise and Robert as well as to destroy Kyle. At least I was not alone. We walked back to the house and started organising our way back to London. Chhay confirmed he wanted to come with us, which was great as we were going to need all the help we could get. We agreed it was safe to assume that Robert and Louise would soon meet again, as they would probably be held together or at least near each other.

We organised a van to pick us up in the afternoon, so we could fly to London in the evening. We called Jarena and reported Kyle's latest attack. As we were finishing packing, we heard a phone ringing – it was Louise's. She had left it on the table near her bed. Clara picked it up and showed me the screen – it was Naomi. We all looked at each other, not knowing what to do. I had not thought about Naomi, but they chatted every two days or so. If I wanted to cover up Louise's disappearance, we would have to pretend to be her. Clara realised the same thing, nodded and took the phone with her to text Naomi, as Louise would have done.

That night, on the plane to London, Chhay still was recovering while we were trying to regain some strength for the battle to come.

I swore to myself I would find Louise and Robert and destroy Kyle at any cost.

TO BE CONTINUED…

Afterword

Please stay tuned for updates on the Ordinem Legacy book series. In the second book, we will find out what happens next to Louise. We will follow Aiden, Luca, Clara and the Elders in their quest to find and stop Kyle. Will they succeed in saving Robert and Louise from his evil grasp?

Website: www.ordinemlegacy.com

Facebook: @ordinemlegacybooks

Instagram: @maddie_caser_ // @ordinemlegacybooks

Twitter: @MaddieCaser

Listen to Louise's, Aiden's and Chhay's playlists!
Spotify @Maddie C